The Seekers

The Seekers

A Novel in Three Parts

By
Jean Carwardine

Front Cover Illustration by Danielle Carwardine

authorHOUSE®

AuthorHouse™ UK Ltd.
1663 Liberty Drive
Bloomington, IN 47403 USA
www.authorhouse.co.uk
Phone: 0800.197.4150

Published by AuthorHouse   02/05/2014

ISBN: 978-1-4918-9054-7 (sc)
ISBN: 978-1-4918-9151-3 (e)

To my loyal readers: Barbara, Janet, Sherry, and especially Rosanna.

Front Cover Illustration by Danielle Carwardine

PART I

Marjorie's story
Spreading her wings

Baltimore, 1967

Chapter I

A house for rent! Marjorie felt a stab of excitement as she read the ad on the bulletin board at the University House Office. She copied down the details, noticing the Charles Street address. The street name meant nothing to Marjorie, who was a newcomer to Baltimore, but it sounded distinguished. Images of spacious, elegantly furnished rooms floated through her mind. She had to see this house!

But Jennifer would most certainly object. Dear, earthbound Jennifer, her college friend and partner in this house hunting endeavor. Jennifer would hang back, dithering, unwilling to take the risk. Jennifer would still be dabbling her toes in the stream, musing the consequences of crossing it, while Marjorie was already submerged in the icy waters, chilled to the bone and enjoying every minute of it.

It was time for Marjorie to exercise her persuasive powers. She flew back to the rooming house where they were staying, ran upstairs and flung open the door of their tiny room. Jennifer was sprawled one of the beds, reading and chewing an old apple core. She was wearing a faded cotton bathrobe and her honey-brown hair was pulled back into a skimpy pony tail.

"Whew! It's hot," she said, by way of greeting. "Where've you been, Marge?" She sat up and laid apple and novel on the bedside table.

"To the Housing Office! Look what I found!" Smiling triumphantly, Marjorie handed her friend the details of the house.

Jennifer scanned the paper, and then looked up, frowning.

"A house! Marjorie, all we need is a small apartment. How could we possibly afford to rent a house?"

Marjorie eagerly marshaled her arguments. "Jennifer, can you say, in all honesty, that we've seen a single decent apartment since we started our search?"

"No, but we've only been looking for a couple of days."

Marjorie sat on the other single bed and faced her friend. "Look, Jennifer, this may be the opportunity of a lifetime. Instead of renting

1

one of those cramped little hovels, we could be living in style! With elegant rooms, space to study, possibilities for entertaining."

Jennifer wrinkled her nose in an expression that was all too familiar to Marjorie. "Marjorie, graduate students are as poor as church mice. It's well known. They, we, live in garrets or cold water flats. I repeat, we couldn't possibly afford a house."

"If we shared with say, two or three other students, the rent wouldn't be a problem."

Jennifer sighed, as if weary of the argument. "How are we going to find other students? We don't know anyone here."

Sensing Jennifer's sigh as a sign of weakening, Marjorie pressed home her case. "Of course not. Not yet. But we could easily advertise. There must be other students who'd jump at the opportunity of sharing a house. Anyway, we could at least see the place. It would be a little adventure. There'd be no obligation to commit ourselves."

"I think that would be a waste of time," said Jennifer.

But over the next few days they saw nothing they could agree on, and Marjorie brought up the house whenever she found an opening. Finally Jennifer gave in, and at the beginning of the next week the two girls walked in the breathless autumn heat to the area where the house was located. Marjorie, having scanned a city map, had determined that it wasn't far from the University where they were enrolled as Master of Arts in Teaching students.

"Look at the lovely row houses!" said Marjorie, "These must have been built in the last century."

"A real old ladies' neighborhood," said Jennifer.

They stood on the steps of number thirty-four, Marjorie fanning herself with the city map. They waited for several minutes before the door opened. The woman who stood just inside the doorway was small and stooped. Her face, wrinkled like a crumpled piece of paper, was that of a very old person, possibly someone in her eighties. She clutched an embroidered shawl around her shoulders in spite of the heat.

"Yes?" She peered out into the bright sunlight. It was as though she hadn't been expecting anyone.

"We spoke on the phone. We're here to see about the house. About renting the house."

"Ah, yes, you'd better come in." And as they crossed into the dim hallway, "I'm Miss Mayberry, Miss Carla Mayberry."

The two girls followed Miss Mayberry into the living room.

"I'm Marjorie Dunnock, and this is my friend Jennifer Hill. We're M.A.T. students. Future teachers of America!"

"Graduate students?" Miss Mayberry appeared confused for a minute. "Oh, you're answering the advertisement I had put up at the University. I had hoped you'd seen the one in the <u>Sun</u>." She scrutinized Marjorie's face, the corners of her lips turned down. "Graduate students!" she repeated. "I hope you don't make a lot of noise. This is a very quiet neighborhood, you know."

"I assure you, Miss Mayberry, we're very studious."

Marjorie looked around the living room. It had an odd, subterranean feeling; there was only one window, looking out on the street, and that was veiled in curtains. When Marjorie's eyes adapted to the dark, she realized that the house lived up to her expectations. Everything was a deep, rich color, maroon or purple; the chairs and sofas looked as if you could sink miles down into their upholstery; the legs of the two little coffee tables were intricately carved. Looking further back toward the dining room, she had the impression of a cave with infinite vaults. Marjorie could imagine Jennifer's nose wrinkling.

They passed into a formal dining room, which had a large oak table and an elaborate chandelier made up of what seemed like thousands of tear-drop crystals.

Miss Mayberry touched Marjorie's arm with her tiny pointed fingers, like a bird's claws. "I'm obliged to rent it out, you see. It's been too big for me since my sister died. How long ago was it?" she paused, musing. "I shall have to move to a smaller place. But how could I sell this house? There's the history of a lifetime here."

Jennifer, who had remained silent—skeptical, Marjorie knew—suddenly spoke up. "Miss Mayberry, she said, "These antiques look very valuable. Are you renting the place furnished?"

"I couldn't possibly move these heavy furnishings. Besides, they belong here. I can only hope and pray that whoever rents my house will respect my property."

3

Miss Mayberry was addressing Marjorie although Jennifer was asking the question. Marjorie was used to this. She expected people to be drawn to her because of her magnetic personality.

They went through the house to the kitchen. It was a pokey little room. The linoleum was scruffed up and heavily marked, and the stove and refrigerator were of another era. Marjorie moved to the sink and looked out. The back garden was small, parched, and overgrown with weeds. "Never mind," she told herself. She was eager to see the bedrooms. They went up the back staircase. A back staircase suggested intrigue to Marjorie, possibly intrigue of a sexual nature.

The bedroom at the back of the house above the kitchen had been the master bedroom. It had a four-poster bed draped with white curtains and an old fashioned vanity table. The window was westward facing, overlooking the garden. It would get the afternoon sun.

"This bedroom will be mine," thought Marjorie. She knew Jennifer wouldn't care enough to fight over it.

There was another, smaller bedroom on this floor at the front of the house. The bathroom, opposite the second bedroom, had a tub raised on feet and no shower; it was just acceptable.

"The third floor is the same," said Miss Mayberry, "Two bedrooms and a bathroom."

They went back downstairs. Miss Mayberry led them into the dining room, where they stood in the darkness, under the unlit chandelier.

Beside her, Marjorie could feel Jennifer shifting her weight from one foot to the other. "How could we possibly afford to live here?" she whispered.

Marjorie squeezed Jennifer's arm to shut her up. "What is the rent, if I may ask, Miss Mayberry?" she asked.

"It's two hundred dollars a month, plus utilities. There will also be a damage deposit, amounting to one month's rent."

"I don't think we could . . ." Jennifer began, but Marjorie interrupted her.

"Would you be willing to rent to more than two students? Possibly . . . four?"

"Oh, dear. I hadn't thought of that. Four students? I might do better renting to a young couple."

"Oh, Miss Mayberry," said Marjorie with her most radiant smile. "We do love the house so much. Would you consider renting to us?"

"I shall have to ask for references. From all of you."

"I'm sure we could provide excellent ones."

Miss Maryberry's little sharp fingers touched Marjorie's arm again, this time more like an eagle's talons, gripping it with surprising force.

"You're such a lovely young woman," she said. "You will look after it, won't you?"

Marjorie gently moved her arm away. She didn't wish to appear rude. "Of course. You have my word."

*   *   *

They moved in on a hot day at the beginning of September. Really, there was little to move, since everything—cutlery, crockery and cooking utensils—had been provided. Marjorie took the second floor master bedroom, as she had planned. Jennifer ended up by liking the house and accepted that the rent, divided by four, would be no less than that of a small apartment. She was also content to take the third floor room, especially as it had its own tiny balcony overlooking the garden, and she was a romantic about balconies.

Having arranged her clothes in the bureau and the closet, Marjorie went downstairs to examine what Miss Mayberry had provided in the way of china. She was disappointed to find that the dishes were ordinary plastic and rather chipped at that. The flat wear was stainless steel. Jennifer came clattering down the back staircase to look over her shoulder.

"It's just as well," she said. "One less thing to worry about. The antiques are enough to look after."

"Well," said Marjorie, sighing and sitting down at the rickety little kitchen table. "Now we have to find suitable roommates. We'll put an ad in the Housing Office, of course. We could word it like this: 'Room in charming row house, university district, for female graduate student. Use of kitchen. References required.'"

5

Jennifer agreed, and Marjorie phoned the ad in on a Thursday and they waited. Waited through Friday and through the weekend.

"What are we going to do if no one answers the ad?" said Jennifer on Monday morning. "Do you think there's any way we can get out of the lease?"

"It's still early," said Marjorie, soothingly. The last thing she wanted to do was to give up this house and start looking all over again. But she, too, was concerned. Time was passing; classes would begin in just over a week.

Finally, late that afternoon, the phone rang. The voice of the person calling had a deep, resonant sound, which made everything she said seem important. "I'm Madeleine O'Connor," she said. "I see you have a room for rent in a house on Charles Street."

She agreed to come and look at the room the next day. Not long after, another woman called and made an appointment to come just after Madeleine.

But by dinner time that night there were no more phone calls.

"Oh, well," said Jennifer, "We only need two to help pay the rent."

"Jennifer," said Marjorie. "We don't just need cash and a couple of bodies to fill the rooms. We want kindred souls, young women of taste, young women of spirit!"

"Let's hope that we can find young women with a brain or two!" said Jennifer.

The next day the two girls took places at the massive oak dining room table and waited for the doorbell to ring. It was always dark in that room, and Marjorie had turned on the big chandelier overhead. The many small voltage bulbs dappled the table with light.

Marjorie felt elated. She was setting out in life, without parental supervision, without dormitory rules. She glanced at Jennifer. Her friend didn't seem to share Marjorie's mood. Her little face seemed pinched, and she was twisting a crumpled tissue in her hands. It was so typical of Jennifer, Marjorie noted, to be worried for no reason.

She went back to the table and sat at the head, facing the entrance to the living room. She stroked the smooth surface and imagined a grand dinner. She would be like Mrs. Ramsey in To the Lighthouse, serving soup from a big tureen. "You could seat ten people here easily. Think of the dinner parties we can give here," she said rapturously, "the witty conversation over tinkling glasses filled with fine wine, the flirtations with charming men, the lovely dresses we'd wear, the jewelry."

"Most elegant," said Jennifer, "served on Miss Mayberry's shabby plastic plates."

"We'd substitute something. Jennifer, you can be annoying, with your mundane details."

Jennifer merely gave her one of her knowing looks, as if to say, "Someone has to keep us earthbound."

The doorbell rang, two clear notes. A remarkably young voice for such an old house, Marjorie thought. Jennifer, who had twisted her feet around the table legs, struggled to stand up.

"What are we going to say? What questions are we going to ask?" Jennifer hated to face a situation unprepared.

"Don't worry, m'dear," said Marjorie. "I have an infallible instinct about these things. I am an excellent judge of character."

Jennifer smirked. "What about your last two boyfriends?"

"Well, in affairs of the heart, I sometimes get carried away. But we're choosing female roommates, not lovers."

The two notes rang out again.

"Go ahead and usher her in," Marjorie said. She wanted to be sitting at the head of the table to interview this person, whoever she was. "Let's see what the fates have offered us."

Jennifer disappeared into the front part of the house, while Marjorie remained seated. There was a glass bowl that stood in the middle of the table. Marjorie picked it up and turned it round and round on the table so that it caught and refracted the light from the chandelier. All the colors of the rainbow. She wondered what treasures Miss Mayberry had taken from the house. Apart from the furniture and a few decorative items like this bowl, there was little of true elegance.

A harsh grating sound recalled her to the present. The front door. It would be the girl with the hollow voice. Her name was Margaret? Possibly Marian? She tried to picture her, but only conjured up someone tall with a big chest.

She heard footsteps on the wood floor and looked up to see, blocking out little Jennifer, the figure looming at the entrance to the dining room. This person was pallid and somehow waxy-looking, like an over-sized mannequin in a shop window. She was dressed in a shapeless greenish-brown garment, buttoned up to the neck. A thick ropelike brown braid fell to the base of her neck.

To Marjorie, for whom appearances were supremely important, this person was completely unsuitable. How could anyone get herself up to look so unattractive? But Marjorie stood up to greet the apparition hovering in the doorway. "You must be Margaret . . . ?"

"Madeleine O'Connor," said the applicant, smiling unpleasantly with her lips pressed together. "I thought our appointment was for two o'clock."

"Surely we didn't keep you waiting. Jennifer went straight to the door when we heard the bell."

"I rang twice."

"Sorry." Yes, it had rung twice. But surely this lumpish person hadn't had to wait long. Marjorie felt they had made a bad beginning. Already.

"May I see your references?" Madeleine approached the table uncertainly and took out several papers from her large purse. Marjorie took them and pretended to peruse them. Then she looked up at the sexless creature, now hovering over her.

"Well, I'm Marjorie Dunnock and that," she gestured over Madeleine's head, "is my friend Jennifer Hill. Won't you sit down?"

Madeleine gave Marjorie a questioning look and lowered her thickly-clad backside onto one of the chairs. She was leaning forward so as little as possible of her body touched the piece of furniture in question. Marjorie looked straight into the girl's face. She had a coarse, lumpy complexion but regular features, luminous hazel eyes. It was as though her face was in neutral, neither smiling nor frowning. She must have practiced this expression in front of the mirror to perfect it.

"Well, just a few questions to see how we'll get on. What are you studying?"

"I'm completing a double Master's degree in political science and religious studies."

Religious studies! Religious studies didn't fit in with Marjorie's notion of young women of spirit.

"Do you have other interests?" she asked. "For example, are you fond of the cinema or the theatre?"

Madeleine smiled again, just with the corners of her mouth. "I hardly have time to amuse myself. I have a double major and a job."

Jennifer had been standing in the doorway, shifting from one foot to the other. She suddenly spoke up. "Would you be able to commit yourself for the academic year? We have a contract that runs till June, and . . ."

Madeleine swiveled in her seat to face Jennifer. "I do need to see the room first. And there's been no mention of the rent."

Jennifer smiled in embarrassment. "The rent is two hundred dollars a month. Your share, of course, fifty dollars. Plus utilities."

Madeleine made no comment at this.

"Do you have any questions?"

"Well, do you have a policy about quiet hours? I may study some in the library, but I'd like to be sure I could study in my room, or even here, in this room, if I wanted to."

Jennifer and Marjorie exchanged a glance. They hadn't thought about quiet hours.

"Of course," Marjorie said with absolute assurance. "Quiet hours, evenings after seven o'clock and weekends, er, after ten."

"Hum," said Madeleine, "that might work for me. We'd have to discuss weekends and some afternoons. If you play loud music or have the television on, that would be unacceptable."

"These things are negotiable," said Jennifer quickly.

"And meals? Do you plan to have communal meals? I do have dietary requirements."

"No, no," said Jennifer, possibly, Marjorie thought, appalled at the thought of having to meet Madeleine's dietary requirements. "We cook separately."

"There would have to be a schedule for kitchen use."

Marjorie was beginning to lose patience. "Go ahead and show her the rooms, Jennifer." Then to Madeleine: "There's a room on the second floor and one on the third. They're the same except that you have to walk up more stairs to get to the third. That is, if you are still interested."

Madeleine paused, seemingly for effect. Then she said, in a gallows tone, "I'll see the rooms."

Jennifer led Madeleine upstairs while Marjorie sat waiting for the other girl to arrive. She thought uncomfortably of Madeleine. The girl was a misfit, someone who had given up on her appearance, possibly a dedicated scholar. The thought of sharing this house with her was repulsive. She wished she and Jennifer could afford the house without renting out rooms. It wouldn't work with other tenants. She was sure of it.

The doorbell rang again and Marjorie went slowly to answer it. She had lost her enthusiasm.

"Hello, I'm Marjorie Dunnock."

"I'm Denise Spaulding." The girl standing on the doorstep looked older, twenty-three or twenty-four. She was short and stocky, not fat, but solid, as if well rooted into the ground. Her dark hair was cropped short, and she had a broad, rosy face and round cheeks. She was wearing a short, loose-fitting dress in various shades of turquoise over black tights. A large, brassy pendant hung from a leather strand around her neck. Comical face masks dangled from her ears. Her look, whatever it was intended to be, didn't quite come off. Marjorie wondered if it was an effort at artiness or if the girl was simply amusing herself. She led her back into the dining room.

`Without waiting to be asked, Denise Spaulding sat down and looked around the room appraisingly.

"You have references?"

"For what they're worth." She handed Marjorie several papers that she pretended, again, to scrutinize.

"They're mainly to reassure the landlady." Marjorie paused a few seconds. "I also need to ask you a few questions. Just to see if we'll all be compatible."

"Go ahead," said Denise smiling calmly.

"I assume you're a student. What are you studying?"

"I'm getting an M.F.A. at The Institute of Fine Arts. I'm just starting out. What about you?"

"My friend Jennifer and I are students in the M.A.T. program at the University."

"Oh, teachers." The smile faded from Denise's face.

"But we're both interested in the arts," Marjorie added quickly. Having an art student might add a certain panache to the household.

"The arts with a capital A," said Denise. "I'm more into art with a small A."

Marjorie wasn't quite sure how to take this. It sounded as if Denise was calling her a snob. Uncomfortable, she changed the subject. "Would you agree to follow house rules, concerning quiet hours and the use of the kitchen?"

Denise sighed. "Rules. For the past couple of years, I've been living in a rented room, working to get money for my education. I was hoping for a little freedom. But quiet hours, no, I have no objection to quiet hours. I'm not an especially noisy person." She got up and walked around the room.

"It's a lovely house, don't you think?" said Marjorie.

"It's period, all right. It's a bit like the Old Curiosity Shop. You couldn't boogie in here."

"I hope you weren't planning to boogie! I wouldn't mind, but the girl Jennifer is showing around might take exception."

Denise laughed. "I gather this other person is difficult? Don't worry, Marjorie. I can get along with just about anyone. If you met my family, you'd understand. May I see the room?"

"Of course. But let's wait until Jennifer comes back down with Madeleine."

Denise continued her little tour of the dining room, moving slowly, studying the pictures hanging on the wall, which Marjorie had never especially noticed. To her, these pictures all looked similar—dark, rather ugly landscapes and buildings. But Denise was studying them as if each was a masterpiece.

As she surreptitiously stole glances at Denise, Marjorie shuffled through the two sets of references. She noticed that both Denise and Madeleine had B.A.'s from small colleges. Both were honors students.

The staircase creaked. The others were coming downstairs.

Marjorie looked up as Madeleine, followed by Jennifer, reappeared.

"Jennifer and Madeleine, this is Denise. She's also interested in becoming a part of our household." Denise faced the others.

The three muttered their hello's. Marjorie caught Jennifer's eye inquiringly; she wondered how Madeleine had reacted to the room. Jennifer merely frowned.

"Madeleine prefers the room on the second floor, Denise. I'll show you the one on the third. It's the same, really."

"Could I see the kitchen, too, Jennifer?"

"Of course. We'll go up by the back staircase." The two went back toward the kitchen.

Marjorie turned to Madeleine. "Well, what did you think of the room?"

"The room is all right," Madeleine was speaking a little too slowly. She didn't seem convinced. "But there's something else I need to get straight before I could even think of renting here."

"Yes?"

"Will men be allowed?"

Marjorie couldn't believe that even this girl in her sack-like dress, could be asking such a question. "Allowed to what?"

"You know. Allowed within the premises."

Marjorie knew she had to be polite to Madeleine. But she was having serious doubts. "This isn't a walled nunnery. I don't see why we shouldn't have male visitors."

Madeleine was smiling her controlled smile but her voice seemed to be cracking under the weight of unexpressed rage. "So you're planning to have male visitors. Out of the question. I could never rent a room under such circumstances."

"Well, we'd be discreet about it. Of course. In fact, if one of us invited a male friend in, I doubt that you'd even know about it."

"There absolutely must be a rule that no man can spend the night under this roof." Madeleine was clenching her fists as if to ward off the men about to enter the house.

Marjorie hated to give in on this point, but it now appeared necessary. "All right," she said, sighing, "But I'll have to get the others to agree."

"My requirements aren't unreasonable," said Madeleine. "All I need is a clean single room, a kitchen where I can prepare a simple meal, peace and quiet to study. I have my spiritual needs, which I will not hope to impose on anyone else."

"That's quite all right with me, Madeleine. But from time to time, there may be parties, and, yes, male visitors. Because we're students, it doesn't mean an end to our social life." She leaned forward and looked Madeleine in the eye. "Do you think you could accept that?"

"It's not what I had in mind. Not at all what I had in mind."

It looked as though Madeleine was unwilling to compromise. Sighing, Marjorie said, "So will you give me a call in a couple of days to let me know your decision? Do you have my number?"

"The other girl gave it to me. I will let you know of my decision."

"The other girl is called Jennifer, by the way."

Madeleine collected her large pouchy purse and was about to leave. Just then the staircase creaked again. Denise and Jennifer were coming down the front staircase.

As Denise entered the dining room, she was frowning, whether from the change from light to darkness or displeasure Marjorie couldn't tell.

"Well, you've seen the room and bathroom," said Jennifer to Denise. "They're quite nice, don't you think?"

Denise said, "Yes, but the room is dark. I was hoping I could work in it. I'm not sure how much studio space I'll get at the Institute." She paused. "And, well, the kitchen seems small for four people."

Things were not going well. First Madeleine and now Denise, "Do you think you'll take the room?"

"I'll think it over."

Jennifer gave her friend a despairing look. Marjorie said, "Well, don't think it over for too long. We want to make a final decision by weekend."

"Of course," said Denise. "I'll probably call you in the next couple of days. Maybe tomorrow."

"Let me show you to the door," said Jennifer.

"No, that's okay." Denise was also picking up her purse. "We'll find our way."

The two seemed an oddly mismatched couple; Madeleine was tall and thin in her strange, greenish garment, while Denise was stocky, close to the ground and brightly attired, like some tropical bird. When they had left, Marjorie turned to Jennifer in despair. "Jennifer, this isn't going to work."

Jennifer came to the table and sat beside her friend. "Why? Denise sounded fairly positive."

"But I don't think Madeleine will take the room. She can't bear the idea of male visitors. Wants to stay, apparently, in a nunnery where all the inmates take vows of chastity. Besides . . . I don't think she and Denise will get along."

"Why not? Denise seemed quite easy-going to me."

"But the two have completely different requirements. Madeleine wants all kinds of rules. Denise doesn't want any. And I'm not sure I like either of them. Madeleine is weird! And Denise is like no art student I've ever seen. She's far too solid. And she has no sense of style."

"Do art students have to be impeccably dressed, ethereal creatures?"

"No, of course not. But Jennifer, I hated her jewelry!" Marjorie put her face in her hands. She was close to tears.

Jennifer didn't respond.

Marjorie raised her head and said, "I suppose you're going to say you told me so."

"As a matter of fact, I did tell you so. If you had listened to me, we would have a nice modern apartment without worries about money or roommates."

"How could I have foreseen, with such a large pool of students, that we'd only have two applicants?"

"Marjorie, that's not the question. The question is, what do we do now to get ourselves out of this mess? It's a bit late but we could start advertising again."

"If they both turn us down, we'll have to. Oh, Jennifer, I'm beginning to wonder if this whole thing has been a terrible mistake."

Jennifer patted Marjorie's hand. "We'll work something out. Don't worry. If worst comes to worst, we'll advertise in the <u>Sun.</u> We might even get the nice young couple Miss Mayberry wanted!"

The two girls suffered agonies of uncertainty through Tuesday and Wednesday. But Madeleine's reluctance was possibly feigned. She called on Thursday, saying she'd move in on the weekend, provided that Marjorie would keep her promise about male visitors. Denise called to accept later the same day. It wasn't what Marjorie had hoped for, but they were set for the academic year.

That evening Marjorie and Jennifer uncorked a bottle of wine to celebrate.

"It's rather a Pyrrhic victory," said Marjorie, as she poured the wine into two of Miss Mayberry's plastic wine glasses. "I had had such hopes of sharing the house with women who were kindred spirits. Instead . . . It seems that we're stuck with these two. Can you imagine having to put up with these women—the one in sackcloth and the one with clangy jewelry—until next June?"

"Don't worry so much, Marge. We probably won't have much to do with them anyway. And we still have each other."

Marjorie sighed again. She was very fond of Jennifer; the two had been close since their sophomore year of college. But Jennifer was so young and so cautious. Marjorie needed to expand her horizons, make friends who were sophisticated and worldly. She needed to leave the nest for the great world. She needed to spread her wings and fly.

*   *   *

It was two o'clock on a stifling September day, Sullivan Hall, room 257, History of Education. The first day of classes. Marjorie was sitting at the back of the lecture hall. She and Jennifer, who were both enrolled in the course, had planned to sit together, but the crush of students coming in had separated them.

It was so difficult, at this distance, to pay attention to the lecturer. Marjorie was trying to take notes. But her mind kept straying. She was watching the young man in the seat directly in front of hers. She couldn't see his face, but his head was bent toward his notes in an attitude that suggested seriousness. She recognized him by his full head of white hair, prematurely white, of course. She had seen him taking coffee at the Campus Corners that morning. He seemed more mature than the other men in the class, mature in bearing and quite attractive. She resolved to seek him out him after class and start up a conversation.

The men in the classes she had attended so far, Philosophy of Education and Teaching English in High School, hadn't looked different from the overgrown boys in college. They had a cowed look, as if frightened by life and by the rigors of academia. So far, this white-haired man was the only one she would consider going out with.

She knew she should be concentrating on the lecture, not scanning the room for possible dates. But after all, she did have her social life to consider. She glanced at her watch: 2:52. Thank God, about five more minutes. Then she'd have to cross campus and find Quigley Hall, where her only non-education course, "The School of Donne," was scheduled to take place. She was looking forward to meeting a different type of student in it.

The professor was writing the assignment on the board, always a favorable sign that the bell was about to ring. "Read and summarize chapters one through three of <u>Founders of the Educational Tradition.</u> Be ready to discuss." Marjorie marked this down in her notebook, put the notebook in her highly professional-looking briefcase, and got up. She was in luck. The white-haired man was going out directly in front of her.

She bumped into him as he went through the classroom door.

"Excuse me. How clumsy of me!" she said.

He turned and smiled a very white-toothed smile. "Not at all. It was my fault. My name is Thomas Bradley. I think I saw you at Campus Corners this morning."

She walked along beside him. He seemed a little too conventional, a little too nice, but he was a possibility.

"My name is Marjorie Dunnock. I'm a student in the M. A.T. program. Are you also in the program?"

"No, I'm going all the way! I'm doing a Ph.D. in education. Part time. My school has put me on partial release time to study."

Marjorie couldn't think of anything to say to this. She couldn't imagine anything more boring than getting a Ph.D. in education.

They had gone downstairs now, about to leave the building.

"Well, I'd better hurry," he said. "I have a meeting back at school. My wife is picking me up. I'm very lucky. She runs me everywhere."

"So he is married!" thought Marjorie. "I should have known! And has an adoring wife who runs him everywhere. Too bad, but . . ."

She smiled a polite good-bye and looked around for Jennifer. The two had agreed to walk across campus together to find Quigley Hall, where they both had graduate classes, required in one's major subject by the M. A.T. curriculum. Marjorie was in English lit, Jennifer's in French.

Looking around, Marjorie saw no sign of her friend. She assumed that Jennifer, in her concern for being prompt, had left without waiting for her. She couldn't blame her; ten minutes was a short time to cross campus and find an unfamiliar classroom.

The sprinkler system was on in a last ditch effort to revive the parched lawn. It was now even hotter than it had been that morning, and Marjorie, hurrying and taking little detours to avoid the sprinklers, was sweating. She had put on a navy blue fall suit, which, with her elegant briefcase, gave her a sophisticated look. But now her hair was beginning to curl out of control and her forehead was damp with sweat.

She heard a voice calling and looked over her shoulder. One of the girls in her education courses was hurrying to catch up with her.

"Hi," she said. "I'm Susan Strathmore. I think you're in a couple of my courses. Are you by any chance taking 'The School of Donne?' The instructor is Dr. Frazier."

"Yes, I am in that course. I'm Marjorie, Marjorie Dunnock. Do you know where we should be going?"

"Of course. Didn't you look Quigley Hall up on the map?"

With Susan's guidance, the two girls arrived at the classroom just as the Dr. Frazier was beginning his lecture. He interrupted himself and stared at them as if they had hideous but interesting deformities.

"I believe it is written in the syllabus," he said nasally, "that this class begins at three o'clock."

Marjorie and Susan murmured apologies and took places at the big conference table that accommodated the entire class. Except for Susan and Marjorie they were all men! Seven of them. But the members of the little group were exchanging glances and those glances weren't friendly. Marjorie felt as if she had invaded a private party.

The lecturer, a sandy-haired, elfin man in his forties, was talking about tropes. He read a poem called "Aire and Angels" and commented on the logical form. "Thesis, antithesis, precarious synthesis," he said. Marjorie had no idea what he was talking about, but the other students, with the exception of Susan, were nodding their heads like a Greek chorus. Marjorie normally coped with academic classes easily. So far she felt lost here, and at the small conference table, she was sure it showed. Trying not to make any noise, she took out a pen, a notebook and the course text. She wrote down some notes. She had been in class since early that morning—from nine to eleven and then from one to three—and she was probably just tired, which was why she couldn't concentrate.

"Notice," continued the professor, "the use of paradox in line six."

Marjorie had found the poem in the text. Line six read, "Some lovely glorious nothing I did see." The meaning escaped her.

"Highly characteristic of Donne, especially in the love poems," said one of the male students, without raising his hand.

"A point well taken," said the professor, "as you will see in many other examples, including, his famous, 'The Anniversary,' which, as you remember, we studied in detail last spring."

Marjorie wondered what "we" he was referring to. Not one that included her and Susan. She liked to participate in class discussions, but as Dr. Frazier continued to find examples of paradox, personification, and antithesis, she found she had nothing to say. She kept her head down, pretending to take notes, but actually sketching. Dr. Frazier spent the balance of the period on this poem, ending up with an analysis of the rhyme scheme. A couple of the men contributed erudite remarks.

Afterwards, two or three of the men in the class gathered around Dr. Frazier, asking questions. Marjorie went directly out. Susan was standing in the corridor, looking confused.

"I'm not sure what I'm supposed to be doing now," she said. She consulted the schedule in her hand. "Oh, thank God. I'm finished for the day!"

"What did you make of that lecture?" asked Marjorie.

"I don't know. I guess I'm not very good at the academic stuff."

"Well, I hope it will get better. I hadn't read that poem. Do you think somehow we missed an assignment?"

"That's not possible, Marjorie. This is the first day of class!"

The other students were filing out now, paying no attention to the two girls.

"You know, Susan, I think we've stumbled into a men's club."

"I'm afraid you're right. I wonder if I've made a big mistake in choosing this course." Susan picked up her book bag. Her shoulders drooped as though under a great weight. "Wow, I'm tired. I need a pick-me-up. Marjorie, do you have time for a cup of coffee? The Campus Commons is just across the Diag."

"Maybe some other time. I was supposed to meet my friend after class."

Susan nodded and took off in the direction of the café. Marjorie felt terribly alone. It was close to five o'clock—the seminar lasted almost two hours—and it seemed as though it was growing dark. Where could Jennifer possibly be? Twice in one day she had stood her up. Jennifer, her best friend! She waited a few more minutes, feeling exhausted, and then walked slowly back toward the house. She hoped that somehow Jennifer was still on campus and would catch up with her before she got home.

She found the house in partial darkness. But there was a light on at the back, probably in the kitchen area. Hoping to find Jennifer there, she put her briefcase on one of the chairs and went back toward the kitchen. But it wasn't Jennifer she found there; it was Denise. She was heating a can of soup on the stove.

Denise turned away from her soup with a smile. "Hi, Marge. What's up? You look done in."

"I am." Marjorie sank into one of the metal chairs by the kitchen table. "Have you by any chance seen Jennifer?"

"I was going to tell you. She came in about a half hour ago. She wanted you to know. She didn't wait because the professor let the class out early. She and Madeleine have gone to the library."

Marjorie sighed deeply. She had hoped to talk her day over with Jennifer. "But Denise. The library? On the first day of classes?"

"I don't know. She said something about having a lot of work to do." Denise turned the burner off under the soup. "Hey, you look like you could use a drink. Do you know Nick's? It's a friendly student bar about two blocks from here. Get your purse and we'll go there together."

Marjorie felt a sudden spurt of energy, the kind that hit her after her first cup of morning coffee. "You know, that's the first good idea I've heard all day. Just let me run upstairs and freshen up and I'm yours!"

Twenty minutes later they were sitting in a booth at Nick's, which was crowded, noisy, and smoke-filled. Denise was sipping a double whiskey and Marjorie a glass of Chardonnay.

"But Marjorie," Denise was saying, "I don't understand. Why did you take an esoteric course like that? Wouldn't something like an intro to poetry be better for an English teacher?"

"No, it had to be a graduate level course. And, well, I always liked Donne when we read some of his anthologized poems in college." She had to lean in over the table to make herself heard.

"Well, it sounds like a bummer to me." Denise's voice carried better over the ambient noise. "All that weird terminology. If you can't enjoy a poem without analyzing it for hours, it doesn't seem worth reading."

"Sometimes poetry does take some analysis. But Denise, those guys in there. It was as if they were bonded. And as if other M.A.T. student and I were intruders."

"Well, I haven't had much to do with the academic world. But I did work my way through college. And that's where I first ran into narrow, ignorant snobbishness. That's what you're dealing with. Academic snobbery."

"You'd think the professor would rise above it."

"Oh, it's just the opposite." Denise took a deep drink of her whiskey. "The profs are maintaining the system. Hate to say it, Marge, but you're fighting the odds in that course. MAT isn't PhD. And the prof, whatever his name is, is very much aware of that."

"All the more reason to do really well." Marjorie finished off her Chardonnay.

A young man with a blonde crew cut and a strong jaw was leaning over the table. "Excuse me, ladies," he said. "My friend and I would like to join you. If that's okay."

Denise and Marjorie exchanged a quick, almost imperceptible glance.

"Thanks," said Marjorie. "But we were just about to leave."

Denise nodded. "It's been a long day, buddy," she said. "See you some other time."

The two went out into the lamp-lit street. Marjorie was feeling light-headed from the wine on an empty stomach. But for the first time since she donned her stylish suit that morning, she felt happy. Denise had real potential as a drinking partner.

"Denise, let's do this again. It has really given me a lift."

"Sure, Marge. I'm always good for a drink and a laugh."

*   *   *

Classes were well underway now, with the trees shedding their leaves and the burden of term papers weighing on Marjorie and her fellow students. Marjorie was working in the library. She was in the reading room, sitting at one of the big desks and compiling notes for her History of Education term paper, "The Influence of Benjamin Plumb on Progressive Education." She was bored to the point of numbness and thought, finally, she'd go home, heat up some left-over chicken, and have an early night. She closed her source books and began organizing her notes. Suddenly she became aware of a presence.

She looked up and her eyes met those of a young man. She wasn't sure, but she thought he must have just arrived, seen her, and chosen to sit across from her. He wasn't exactly good-looking— he had a pointed nose and his face was too narrow—a glint in his eyes suggested mischief. Marjorie's curiosity was aroused.

"Hi, I'm Leroy Patterson," he whispered, and she noticed that his teeth, too, were pointed. "Looks like you're doing some pretty serious studying."

She tossed her head to make her hair move, sensuously, she hoped.

"Oh, it's just a boring term paper for Ed. Hist.," she said. "I've just about had enough. I'm going home now."

"Would you like to stop for a coffee? The Student Union's still open, I think."

They walked across the campus in the semi-darkness. It was still warm and humid, though the evenings were drawing in, and

Marjorie took off the light jacket she had taken to the library as a precaution. "You're a student, too, I suppose?"

"Yeah, mechanical engineering."

That was a conversation stopper for Marjorie, who didn't know what a mechanical engineer did and wasn't interested enough to ask. They continued walking in silence to the Student Union, which was quite busy.

"What do you want to drink?" asked Leroy, as Marjorie sat at one of the empty tables.

"Coffee, I guess. Anything to perk me up." Marjorie still felt half-asleep from her long stint in the library.

Leroy returned from the cafeteria line with two coffees and a piece of pie, which he proceeded to devour as if he hadn't eaten for days. It apparently hadn't occurred to him that Marjorie would want something to eat.

She watched him spearing neat slices of pie into his mouth. Do I really want to go out with this guy? she thought. His manners leave a lot to be desired and he has no conversation. Then, his head bent down over the plate, Leroy looked up at her like a little boy who had been naughty. He smiled a knowing smile. Marjorie's heart melted. Let's give this a try, she thought.

He walked her home. To fill the silence, she told him about her course work and her interests. "I love English lit, especially poetry. I've always wanted to teach it," she said.

"That's cool. I like engines."

As they walked down Charles Street, Leroy slowed down to look at the cars parked along the curb. "You live in a ritzy area," he said. "Look at these Cadillacs. At the Mercedes." He whistled appreciatively.

"I'm only renting a room in a house. That is, my roommates and I are renting."

"Oh, you have roommates." They were almost at the house. "Well, I'd better be . . ."

They stopped at the doorstep. "Thanks for the coffee," said Marjorie.

"Um, I'd like your phone number. Maybe we could go out some time."

Leroy called the next day, inviting her to go out to a movie. "You suggest one," he said.

They went to see <u>Breathless</u> at an arty cinema near the campus.

"Well," Marjorie said, as they came out of the theatre into the wet street. "What did you think?"

"Dunno," said Leroy. "I couldn't make out why anyone did anything. And the camera work seemed pretty rough to me."

"I loved it," said Marjorie, still under the spell of the film. She was disappointed that Leroy hadn't liked it, but at least he was honest. Some of the men Marjorie dated in college tried to impress her by giving long speeches on films they didn't understand.

"Hey, come and have coffee or something with me. At my place," he said, smiling the wicked, small boy smile that Marjorie found irresistible.

They walked through the autumn rain to his flat. It was still in the university district but to the west of campus. The neighborhood had seen better days. Many of the old buildings looked derelict and some had "For sale" signs. Marjorie dreaded seeing the inside of Leroy's flat. She imagined something sordid, with dirty coffee cups everywhere and cockroaches lurking in the cupboards.

They went into one of the decrepit buildings and climbed a flight of stairs. "Here goes," said Leroy under his breath, and turned the key in the door.

It was a studio apartment, hide-a-bed in the sitting room and kitchenette in one corner. It was immaculate. There were almost no possessions anywhere, not a paper on the coffee table, not a dish in the sink, not even a picture on the walls. The only sign that anyone lived there was the little pile of books on the table where Leroy obviously did his studying. It made Marjorie think of a monk's cell.

"You keep everything ship-shape," said Marjorie. "It's really . . . tidy."

"I hate clutter," said Leroy. "You should see my parents' house." He shrugged vigorously, shaking off the clutter from his parents' house.

Marjorie sat at one of the chairs by the work table while Leroy busied himself in the kitchenette. He prepared two mugs of instant coffee and neatly spread peanut butter on a plate of Ritz crackers. Marjorie was touched to see him prepare this little snack for her.

Hoping he would open up, she asked him where he came from and what his parents did. His responses were terse; he kept stealing furtive glances at her. When she had finished her coffee, she got up and stretched.

"Thanks, Leroy, that was lovely," she said. "But it's late and I'd better be on my way."

He got up from the hide-a-bed where he had been sitting and came toward her.

"You're so beautiful," he said, plunging his hand into her thick hair and pulling it. "Stay with me tonight, baby, stay with me. You won't regret it."

"Let go," said Marjorie, half-laughing. "I spent hours getting my hair to stay up."

"It's better down," said Leroy, simultaneously ruining her hairdo and kissing her passionately.

Marjorie ended up staying the night. To her surprise, Leroy was an accomplished lover. And he was obviously smitten with her. For the first couple of weeks, they met regularly at Leroy's flat, mainly to make love. Marjorie was at first reluctant to invite Leroy to the house. She could hardly make love while Madeleine slept virginally in the room across the hall, and she was concerned that her housemates wouldn't see the attractive side of Leroy.

But one day as she was leaving for a morning class, Denise stopped her on the doorstep. "Marge," she said, "I'm having a boyfriend over for dinner Friday night. I thought I'd ask if it's okay with you if I sort of commandeer the kitchen late Friday afternoon. Jen and Maddie both said they'd make other arrangements."

Marjorie was annoyed at being consulted last. But she had a sudden idea. "Denise, how would you like to do a joint dinner? I have a friend I'd like to invite. We could share the cooking."

*   *   *

Marjorie was in the kitchen, kneading her French bread one last time prior to putting it into the oven. She loved the feeling of the dough, elastic in her hands; she loved pounding it roughly. She shaped and scored the dough, making fine crosses along the top. As she put it in the oven, she heard a shuffling in the hall, and Madeleine appeared for the second time. She hovered in the doorway, a tall, craggy figure in her shapeless green dress. She had come in earlier, but found it impossible to cook lunch with Marjorie's bread-making spread all over the kitchen.

"Aren't you done yet?" she asked, irritably. "It seems like a terrible effort just to make bread. You could just go out and buy a loaf at the corner store."

"Wait till you smell it baking. There's nothing more delicious than the aroma of home-baked bread!" Marjorie gathered up the bowls and spoons and whacked them into the sink.

"In the meantime, do you think I might have a corner of the kitchen to make lunch?"

"It's all yours," said Marjorie, leaving the dirty dishes in the sink. She was aware, too, that she hadn't wiped off the work surfaces. But she was angry with Madeleine. "Go to the corner store and buy a loaf of Wonderbread." As if the horrible bread you could buy in the store had the slightest resemblance home-baked bread. As if her cooking skills had no value!

Besides, she and Denise had a lot to do before seven o'clock. She drifted into the dining room.

Jennifer was sitting at the big oak table, twirling an apple by its stem and looking despondent.

"Hi, Jen," said Marjorie. "Have you seen Denise?"

"Not today." As Marjorie was about to run upstairs to search for her fellow cook, Jennifer stood up. "Marjorie," she said somberly, "could we talk?"

"Sorry, Jennifer. You know I'm having a dinner party tonight. Every moment is precious."

"But Marjorie, I never seem to <u>see</u> you anymore. You're always off with some boy or studying at the library. What's happened to our friendship?"

In fact Marjorie had seen relatively little of Jennifer since they had failed to make connections that first day of class. Jennifer had apologized but she felt slighted and had begun seeking Denise's companionship. It wasn't that she wanted to cut Jennifer out. But not now, Jennifer, not now!

"We'll talk some other time. Really."

"Well, in that case I'd better have dinner out," said Jennifer. She looked quite woebegone. Instead of feeling sorry for her, Marjorie felt manipulated. She ran upstairs to look for Denise. The two almost collided on the landing.

"Denise," she said. "Where have you been? We need to work out tonight's menu."

"That shouldn't be a problem," said Denise. She was wearing a paint-speckled smock and carrying a box in which she kept her paints. "I was just going down to add some finishing touches to 'Red No. 7.'"

Marjorie followed Denise back down to the dining room, settled at the big oak table and took out pencil and notepad. Denise, oblivious of what Marjorie considered the urgency of the situation, was contemplating "Red no. 7." The painting rested on an easel against the sideboard. It was, indeed, quite red with great splurges of purple. The sideboard was now decorated with little splatters of paint.

"Denise," said Marjorie, "Can you stop painting for just a minute? We need to get things organized if we're going to eat tonight." She felt annoyed that Denise could be so casual about the whole thing. She felt like interposing herself between Denise and her painting, which she considered to be fit for the trash can, anyway.

"We have a lot to do, you know," she added. "We have to plan a meal, do the shopping, cook, set up the dining room table, and serve. And tidy up the living room, which is an absolute mess."

Denise had opened her box of paints and was adding splashes of yellow to "Red no. 7."

"I don't know about Leroy," she said, "But I don't think Rufus much cares about tidiness. I don't think he'd notice if the room was hit by a hurricane."

"But he does want to eat, I assume."

Denise stopped painting and looked directly at Marjorie. "Listen," she said, "We buy four steaks, grill them rarissimo, and get a couple of bottles of cheap wine. And put some records on, of course."

Marjorie shuddered. "Don't you think your menu is a bit primitive, Denise? Like hyenas tearing meat off a carcass?"

Denise, unfazed, had gone back to her painting. "Possibly," she said. "But it's what men like."

"Well, if that's the case, we should exert a civilizing influence on them. I was thinking of an elegant repast of chicken breasts a la crème, a bit of salad, a sorbet. And French bread. I have a wonderful recipe for French bread, which, by the way, is baking in the oven at this moment."

"Elegance is for ladies," said Denise. "Elegance serves to impress. We're feeding a couple of men who are principally concerned with filling their bellies. If you are dead set on making some fancy dish, go ahead, but it's not worth the trouble."

Marjorie was deflated. She had, in fact, intended to impress, and she suspected that Denise might have a point.

"I don't think Leroy is such a philistine," she said plaintively, knowing this was probably untrue.

Denise was still absorbed in painting. She made another stroke and stood back to admire her work.

"Do you think I've improved the general effect?" She was speaking more to herself than to Marjorie.

"No," said Marjorie nastily. "I think you should have left well enough alone. It looks like a cluster of road kill." She was beginning to think better of the whole idea of collaborating with Denise, whose concept of a dinner party was so different from hers. "Look," she added, "Maybe we should forget about working together and entertain our boyfriends separately."

"No, no," said Denise. "Let's go ahead. It might turn out to be quite a laugh. Tell you what, I'll do the shopping if you straighten up the living room and set the table. We can do the cooking together."

"That's quite all right with me, Denise."

She went back to her painting, while Marjorie rather dolefully composed a shopping list. Suddenly Jennifer came in from the rear of the house. She was holding a smoldering pan, full of blackened ashes.

"I don't know what this was intended to be," she said. "But I smelled something burning and got this out of the oven."

"My bread!" Marjorie struck her head in despair. "All that effort gone to waste! The only decent part of the meal, and it's ruined!"

*   *   *

Late that afternoon Marjorie was putting the final touches on the table. She had done her best, but Miss Mayberry's plastic ware looked odd on the big oak table, even after Marjorie had spread her mother's Cyprian lace tablecloth over it. She put candles in the center and was contemplating the final effect when Denise came in through the kitchen.

"Well?" she said. "How do you think it looks?"

"Do you want my true opinion?" Then, seeing that Marjorie was upset, she said, "Oh, Marjorie, don't take the whole thing so seriously. Nobody's going to notice the table setting." Denise was wearing a loose-fitting smock over jeans. Marjorie had spent a long time on her hair and make-up and put on a simple black cocktail dress and little heels.

The two girls looked at each other critically. "We're not going to the Ritz, you know," Denise said, grinning. Marjorie, not to be deterred, went back up to her room and put on some tiny diamond earrings. As she came down the back staircase, she heard the doorbell ring.

"It's only 6:20," she said to Denise. "Do you think one of the guys got the time wrong?" The invitation had been for seven.

She went to the door to find Leroy standing on the doorstep in the rain, wet to the bone.

"Come in, come in," she said, irritated at having to cope with Leroy before she had made the final preparations. She was also annoyed to see Denise's horrible painting prominently displayed in the middle of the room.

Leroy came into the living room, shedding rain onto the Persian carpet. He looked different. Marjorie had always considered him attractive, if not exactly good looking. But looking at him now, she was shocked. With his little pointed ears and pointed nose he looked like a rat. His hair was slicked back against his head. A water rat. He looked around the room as if he was casing the house for a burglary.

She turned to find Denise standing behind her at the entrance to the dining room. "Denise, this is my friend, Leroy. Leroy, my roommate, Denise."

"Let me take your coat," said Denise, and he handed her the rumpled garment.

"Nice place," said Leroy, sitting on one of the Louis XV chairs by the radiator. "Reminds me of my grandparents'."

Denise came back from the front hall, where she had hung Leroy's coat. Her smile looked forced.

"So, Leroy, where are you from?" She asked perching on the couch next to the dining room. For someone so plump and earthbound, she looked as if she was ready, at any minute, to fly away.

"Passaic, New Jersey."

"Been here long?"

"Two years."

"Leroy is a student in Mechanical Engineering," Marjorie added, hoping this would move the conversation on. There was a silence. Marjorie noticed a gentle gurgling coming from Leroy's part of the room. At first she thought it was the water in the radiator. Then, noting it was a lower tone, she realized it was Leroy's stomach. "My God," she thought. "I wonder his if he's eaten at all today."

"What are you interested in? I mean, apart from your major?" Denise was making an effort to bring Leroy out of himself.

"Engines. I love engines."

"We enjoy the movies, don't we, Leroy? A couple of weeks ago we saw <u>Breathless.</u>"

"I hate foreign movies."

Denise leaned forward in her chair. "All foreign movies? There're so many different types."

"I don't like reading subtitles. Go to the pictures, it's to see pictures. And in that one, <u>Out of Breath </u>or whatever it was called, the camerawork was awful."

"I think they used a hand-held camera for a reason," said Denise. "To lend greater immediacy to the action."

"To me it just lent amateurishness." Leroy smiled as if he had scored a major point against Art. That ended that topic of conversation. Marjorie was beginning to feel embarrassed.

"Would you like a drink, Leroy?" she asked. "We have both red and a white wine, whichever you prefer."

"I don't drink wine," said Leroy. "Do you have any beer?"

"I'll get some," said Denise, hastily. "And the Chardonnay for you, Marjorie?" She disappeared toward the kitchen, leaving Marjorie and Leroy to stare at each other in silence.

"Are we going to eat pretty soon?" Leroy asked finally. "I'm starved."

"So I hear. Sorry, Leroy, there's someone else coming and we can't start without him." To fill the silence, which seemed heavier and heavier, Marjorie began to babble. She babbled on about her "School of Donne" course, about the new outfit she was thinking of buying, about the next door neighbor's six cats, about her roommates' strange eating habits.

Leroy stared at her with his opaque rats' eyes. Denise, whatever she was doing, remained in the kitchen.

Eventually the doorbell rang. Marjorie glanced at her watch. It was just after seven. "Excuse me, Leroy," Marjorie said, "I'd better get the door."

The young man standing on the doorstep was very attractive, tall, strong-jawed, with a gorgeous physique. "You must be Rufus," said Marjorie.

"Where is Denise?" he asked. He brushed past her and went on back into the kitchen. He barely nodded to Leroy in passing.

"That's the other guest?" said Leroy. "The one we've been waiting for for the past two hours?"

"Well, it hasn't been two hours," said Marjorie. "I expect Denise will introduce him when she comes back."

"What about my beer?"

To Marjorie's relief, Denise and Rufus came back almost immediately. Denise was carrying a plate of crackers and cheese, and Rufus had a bottle of Chianti in hand. There apparently was no beer, or Denise might have forgotten it. Marjorie hated Chianti, which she found harsh and scratchy, but she was determined not to say anything negative. She could feel arrows of hostility coming from all directions. She was doing all she could to avoid them.

"Rufus," said Denise, "this is my housemate, Marjorie Dunnock and this is . . ."

"Leroy Patterson." Leroy offered Rufus his hand without getting up.

Denise was passing around glasses of Chianti. Leroy took his but put it down immediately on the little end table. Marjorie picked up the plate of crackers and passed it to Rufus.

"Rufus," she said. "Are you a student here too?"

"Arts academy with Denise, here. Specializing in sculpture. I am enamored of form." He took a cracker and bit it vengefully.

"You're not as keen on painting?" asked Marjorie, tentatively.

"I like the dimensionality of sculpture," Rufus said, putting down his cracker. "I can appreciate two-dimensional art, but I don't enjoy creating it."

"Rufus and I have had this conversation before," said Denise. "I maintain that painting is not two-dimensional and that it's the job, or one of the jobs, of the painter to make the observer see that." She had taken a seat beside Rufus near the entrance to the dining room. She drank down the contents of her wine glass. "You'll have to excuse me," she said. "Kitchen duty calls."

She got up and headed for the kitchen.

"I'd better help her," said Marjorie. She got up, leaving Leroy and Rufus staring at each other. Let them figure out what to say to each other, she thought.

"Oh, good," said Denise, as she arrived in the kitchen. "I need your advice. We have a problem here. I've put the potatoes in to bake," here she opened the oven and prodded one with a fork, "and they're almost done. But we can't have the broiler on while the oven is on, so how're we going to cook the steaks?" She stepped back from the oven, gasping from the heat.

"Fry 'em," said Marjorie, for whom the niceties of cooking no longer mattered.

"Yeah, I suppose. They're not as good that way, but . . . Marjorie, do you know how long it takes to fry steak?" Denise had already turned on one of the stovetop burners and was getting out a frying pan.

"Twenty minutes, maybe?"

"Oh, I don't think that long. The potatoes will be done long before that."

"Well, let's sort of compromise. After ten minutes stick a fork into the steak and see how much blood comes up."

"That's my girl!" For some reason, this response pleased Denise. "I tell you what, you go back into the living room and ply the guys with wine, while I finish up."

"Denise, Leroy doesn't drink wine. Don't we have any beer?"

"Nope. Get him a coke."

Marjorie went reluctantly back into the living room. The two men were in exactly the same position as when she had left, except that Leroy had the plate of crackers on his lap and was finishing them off.

Marjorie offered Leroy a bottle of coke, which he gulped down.

She filled Rufus's wine glass. Taking a deep breath, she embarked again on the vast, hopeless sea of conversation. "What kinds of things do you sculpt?" She asked. "I mean what's your subject matter?"

"Heads, bodies. Mostly human." Rufus drank a sip of his wine and looked at Marjorie as if seeing her for the first time. "I didn't catch your name. You are?"

Before Marjorie had a chance to reply, Denise appeared, red-faced, at the door to the dining room.

"Dinner is served."

All four of them took their places at the vast dining table. Marjorie sat at the end toward the living room and Denise at the end toward the kitchen. The two men sat on either side of the table. It was wrong, all wrong. Marjorie should have been at the head of the table, serving a delicious soup from a decorative tureen. This table, which had long been the center of Marjorie's fantasies, now seemed sadly under-populated.

Denise had put the plates on the table. Marjorie stared at hers, which supported an underdone steak, a baked potato and a pile of yellowish string beans, which had doubtless come out of a can. She felt disinclined to eat.

"Where did you get this wine?" asked Rufus, disapprovingly.

"Is there something wrong with it?" Denise looked up from the business of dismantling her steak.

"It's not drinkable, Denise. Your friend here," he nodded in Marjorie's direction, "has been forced to drink white wine."

"I just don't like red wine," said Marjorie.

"Nobody drinks white wine with steak," said Rufus, ignoring her. "Not in public."

"Is this a public place? I thought we were a private little party," said Marjorie.

"Don't be a prick, Rufus. You know I hate snobbishness about wine. Besides, you're embarrassing Marjorie."

"All you have to do," continued Rufus, as if no one else had spoken, "is to go to the little wine merchant on Fifth Street. I'll take you there some time. He has an excellent selection of French wines."

Leroy, who had kept his head down until then, suddenly said. "Isn't there any gravy? I can't eat meat without gravy. Especially raw meat." He was pushing the untouched piece of meat around his plate.

"Sorry, Leroy," said Denise. "No gravy."

Leroy made the salt rain down on his dinner and ate a large piece of potato. Rufus cut and speared his meat with surgical precision and introduced it into his mouth. "Gravy," he pronounced. "Huh. You don't ruin a good piece of meat with gravy."

Marjorie struggled to get down a bit of potato. It was the only decent part of the meal. At least she didn't feel hungry. She felt like burying her face in her hands and weeping. She suddenly remembered that she had made a big salad earlier that afternoon. It was still sitting in the refrigerator. It wasn't too late to bring it to the table. But the effort of getting up from the table and going the length of the dining room back to the kitchen to retrieve the salad bowl seemed monumental. She continued to play with her food.

"Have you used the big new studio at the Institute?" asked Denise. "It's a great space. Everyone is working on different projects there. Everything from painting to sculpture to graphics. You'd love it, Rufus."

"I don't do art communally. Inspiration involves solitude." Rufus cut the last piece of meat on his plate and put down his knife and fork. He was ready for something else, something delicious.

"I've got ice cream for dessert," said Denise.

"I'm done, man," said Leroy. He got up and left the table. Marjorie was half tempted to go and bring him back like a disobedient child, but by now her energy was drained. She had given up on the evening. She helped Denise clear the table. Denise brought in the ice cream carton and served into Miss Mayberry's melamine dishes.

At least we could have had a sorbet, thought Marjorie. It would have been a little less ordinary. But she said nothing.

"I think it's great to do art communally," said Denise, spooning up a great mouthful of ice cream. "You get inspired from watching other people work."

"That depends, my dear Denise on your talent, your originality. Small talents need the support of others."

"And big egos are independent?" Denise said. Her face had grown red.

"Normally the two, talent and ego, are linked."

"Bullshit, Rufus. Bullshit, bullshit, bullshit." Denise got up, leaving her ice cream to melt in its melamine dish, and went into the living room. She stood in front of her painting. Rufus and Marjorie followed her. They found Leroy sprawled in front of the television, watching wrestling.

Denise ignored Leroy. "This, my dear Rufus," she said, indicating the painting, "is talent. It came exploding from my brushes after Dr. Wilcox gave that lecture on Abstract Expressionism. Impressive, you have to admit."

Rufus looked at the painting inscrutably. Leroy turned up the volume of the T.V. After a moment, Rufus said, "Sorry, Denise. Abstract Expressionism is out. Painting is out. Art is a now happening. Your painting has no tactility."

"How can you say that, Rufus?" Denise was shouting now. "Look at the edging and the sunbursts of yellow. It is the essence of tactility."

Marjorie had nothing to add to this conversation and so she said, "Does anyone want coffee? I'm making some Ethiopian blend."

Leroy was staring at the image on the set. "No coffee," he said. "One more round and I'm gonna leave, babe."

Rufus and Denise were arguing about the painting and paid no attention to Marjorie. So she headed back to the kitchen and started making coffee for herself.

Suddenly Madeleine appeared at the kitchen door in her bathrobe and slippers, sleepy-eyed and waxy yellow.

"What in heaven's name is going on here?" she asked. "I thought you were having two in for dinner. It sounds more like twenty."

In fact the noise level had risen considerably. Rufus and Denise were both shouting and Leroy had turned up the volume of the T.V. to compete with them.

"I'm sorry, Maddie. I think things have gotten a bit out of control."

"Well, you'd better bring them under control. And if you don't, I will."

Marjorie, horrified at the idea of Madeleine confronting the party in her flannel nightgown, was spurred to action. Standing at the entrance to the living room, she shouted in her most stentorian voice, "Silence! Everyone!" She felt as if she was confronting an audience of thousands.

Startled, Denise and Rufus fell silent. Leroy, shamefaced, turned off the television.

"I was just about to split anyway," he said and sidled out without a word of thanks or a "good night."

"I was going to leave myself." Rufus kissed Denise tenderly. Marjorie stared in disbelief. They had been fighting all night and now Rufus was kissing Denise.

"I'll see you tomorrow, right?" He turned to Marjorie, "Thanks, err, Maggie." He left. The party was over.

The two women faced each other. Marjorie felt suddenly exhausted, as if she could fall, weeping, to Denise's feet. Denise looked at her in contempt.

"You've got to ditch that boyfriend," she said. "He's an utter creep."

"Well, I wasn't too impressed with yours, either." Marjorie, even at her most defeated, was not to be put down. "He's wildly egotistical and his manners are disgusting."

Denise, ignoring her, was determined to drive her point home. "You're selling yourself short, Marjorie. He's stupid, insensitive, ignorant. And he's not even good-looking."

In bed that night Marjorie, who had thought she would go out like a light from sheer exhaustion, was unable to sleep. She was hounded by humiliating images from the dinner party. The words, "You're selling yourself short, Marjorie," kept coming back like the theme in a symphony. Eventually she got up, took four aspirins and resolved to break up with Leroy. It was still early in the term. She would aspire for better.

*   *   *

A week later, Marjorie was about to meet Leroy in the campus cafe at four o'clock. She rehearsed her lines, as she crossed campus. She wanted to keep it short and sweet. She arrived twenty minutes late, wearing an understated trench coat, her hair pulled back from her face, make-up applied only around her eyes.

Leroy wasn't there. Marjorie, furious, went to the pay phone outside the cafe and dialed his number. No one answered. "The bastard!" she kept saying to herself, working herself into a rage. "He's stood me up!" She thought of going straight to Leroy's apartment but she realized that if he wasn't answering the phone, he probably wasn't answering the door either.

She went back into the cafe and ordered a coffee. She sat down, trying to regain her composure. Suddenly she realized that someone was standing opposite her.

"Leroy?" she almost said, and then looked up.

The person she saw was vaguely familiar; she had seen him around campus before. He was slightly older and quite good-looking, clean-cut, with light brown hair.

"Excuse me for bothering you," he said. "I've seen you quite a bit on campus and I assume you're a student like me. Is there anything wrong? You do look upset."

"Oh, not really," said Marjorie, pushing her tangled hair back from her face. "I've just been stood up, that's all."

"It happens to the best of us, but that doesn't stop it hurting. My name is Clive Barnes. Do you mind if I join you?"

Clive sat down and moved his coffee cup to the table. He explained that he was a graduate student too, majoring in modern history. "It's a step I've taken that I probably will spend the rest of my life trying to justify. I just happen to love history."

"I know what you mean. I love English lit, but there's little you can do but teach it."

"Born into the wrong century, both of us. But as a compensation, do you think you might like to go out with me some time? We could discuss our passions and our disappointing careers."

"You know, Clive, that's about the best suggestion I've heard for a very long time."

*   *   *

Marjorie began seeing Clive right away, relieved to have found a civilized replacement for the unsavory Leroy. It was a relief to be going out with someone who shared so many of her interests, who was easy to talk to. But seeing Clive made it necessary to finish with Leroy, and she resolved to do so as soon as she could. One rainy afternoon she went to his apartment and found him sprawled on the hide-a-bed, watching cartoons on television. He showed no remorse as he greeted her. She didn't really care, but she had expected a warmer reception.

"You stood me up," she said.

"I waited ten minutes. That's my limit for women like you."

"For women like you! What do you mean by that remark?"

Leroy merely smirked and took a swig of beer.

Marjorie went to the television and turned it off.

"Look at me, you little weasel," she said. "Your behavior the other night was inexcusable. We're finished."

"That's what you think," said Leroy, jumping up with extraordinary alacrity and grabbing her by the hair. Marjorie fought him off with a sharp kick to the groin.

"Here's what I think," she said, twisting away from him and squeezing through the half-open door. She clattered downstairs and out onto the street. As she walked along, the cold air calmed her rage and panic. She realized that Leroy probably would have raped her if she had stayed a moment longer. She was horrified to think that she had been out with this man, had slept with him! She remembered Denise's words, "You're selling yourself short, Marjorie." That had to be the biggest understatement Denise had ever made.

*   *   *

Now the evenings seemed to come too early; it was starting to get dark by five o'clock. After classes were over and they had come home to study, the girls drew the velvet curtains in the living room. Marjorie had been seeing Clive for several weeks now and one evening she prepared a special dinner for him. They had finished and were sitting in the living room, at the end near the dining room. They were having coffee. Marjorie had gone so far as to buy a china demi-tasse service for the occasion. The little cups had a delicate blue flower motif that she loved. She had turned on only one of the tasseled lamps, so the light was subdued. A vase full of white lilies that Clive had brought was sitting on the coffee table.

"White flowers," Marjorie had said. "How lovely!"

"For me they represent purity," Clive answered.

Marjorie wasn't in the mood for purity. She had put on her navy blue cocktail dress with her mother's pearls. She felt elegant and sexy. Her dinner had been a success. Clive had loved her chicken a la crème and asked for seconds. The evening was going well.

"How did you find this wonderful house?" asked Clive. "I knew from the address that it would be special, but I wasn't prepared for the atmosphere. It's very much old Baltimore."

"I fell in love with it myself immediately," said Marjorie. "It was only a question of finding roommates to share it."

"But there's only one clashing note. What is that painting by the sideboard?" Denise was working on a new painting, "Valiant Women."

"That's Denise's latest contribution to the décor of the house. Denise is one of my roommates. Don't you like her painting?"

"Well, I can see that art students have to copy, but why not copy the Old Masters? Why this dreadful Cubism?" The women's faces had, in fact, been reduced to a series of triangles.

Marjorie laughed. "Well, I agree, but I suppose Denise identifies more with twentieth century art."

"Just a question of personal taste, Marjorie. I've always been attracted to old things, antiques, classical music, the Old Masters. Things that stand, have stood, the test of time."

Marjorie gazed at Clive fondly. He had dark, deep-set eyes, a finely etched mouth. He was conservatively dressed, as usual, in a suit jacket and navy blue tie with gray squiggles. Very attractive, she thought, perhaps not ruggedly masculine, but very attractive. She continued to gaze into his eyes, feeling more and more drawn to him. She leaned forward. Their faces were almost touching.

The front door let out a high-pitched squeak.

"Oh, hell," said Marjorie under her breath. "It's Jennifer."

"Another one of your roommates?"

Marjorie nodded as Jennifer appeared at the entryway. She was glassy-eyed from studying. She was wearing a baggy sweater and a loose-fitting pleated skirt and carrying an armful of books.

"I hope I'm not disturbing something."

The moment of seduction had passed; Marjorie could only hope that Jennifer wouldn't stay long.

"No, Jennifer, come in and meet Clive. I think I mentioned I was inviting him for dinner."

Jennifer crossed the living room as though she was walking across a stream on slippery rocks. Clive got up and stretched his hand out to her.

"Why don't you join us, Jen?" she asked. "Do you want some coffee?"

"No, it's too late at night for me. I'd climb the walls if I drank coffee now." She turned toward Clive. "Are you a student here, too, Clive?"

"Yes, I was just explaining to Marjorie that I love old things. Perhaps that's why I'm an historian."

Jennifer brightened. "Really! My favorite course here is Medieval French literature."

"I don't go back that far. I've always felt the Middle Ages were, well, barbaric. The Church dictating. The peasants suffering. Filth and squalor."

"Oh," said Jennifer, apparently taken aback. Marjorie wished she would show a little spunk and defend the Middle Ages. But she just stood there, looking deflated in her baggy clothes. She hadn't even sat down.

"Clive, you mustn't denigrate the Middle Ages!" said Marjorie, "The age of chivalry, knights in shining armor, courtly love." She laid an affectionate hand on Clive's shoulder.

"My dear Marjorie. Forgive me for saying this, but such ideas are largely an invention of Romanticism."

"Yes, but not entirely," said Jennifer, now drawn into the conversation. "Think of the poetry of the troubadours!" She was about to say something else when the door squealed again and Denise burst in.

"It's awfully dark in here, Jennifer," she said in a loud voice. "Can't I turn on some lights?" Then she noticed Clive and Marjorie. "Oh, I'm sorry. Marjorie, I'd actually forgotten you were entertaining." She walked across the room and shook Clive's hand. "Denise Spaulding."

"Clive Barnes."

"Denise is our artist in residence," said Marjorie. "She did that painting." She gestured toward the women's triangular faces.

"Ah, you must be a student at the Institute of Arts."

"Yes, for my sins. You like Contemporary Art, Clive?"

Clive crossed the room and inspected the painting. "Well, I prefer the Old Masters, as I was just telling Marjorie. True mastery of art. Well, well. Very colorful, your work." He took his place on the couch beside Marjorie, but with a distance between them.

Denise was enraged. "Contemporary artists also have a mastery of art. We just aren't bound by old fashioned strictures and rules."

"Of course," said Clive, soothingly. "I meant no such slur. And it's the duty of each generation to free itself from the preceding generation by creating something new."

"Well, the Old Masters aren't exactly the preceding generation," said Denise. "More likely the Abstract Expressionists. But I do take your point. And if you'll excuse me, I ought to leave you two in peace."

"I'll join you, Denise," said Jennifer. The two disappeared through the dining room to the back staircase.

"Denise tends to be a bit blunt," said Marjorie. "I hope she didn't offend you."

"Not at all, not at all. She must defend her art. I'm in awe of artists. Such courage in expressing their ideas. And the other one, is it Jennifer, appears to be very studious. So I've met two of your roommates. What about the third?"

"That's Madeleine. She has probably gone to bed."

"Well, so, four of you." Clive frowned. He looked as though something was bothering him. "Marjorie, it's been a lovely evening and a delicious dinner. But I think it's time for me to go, too."

"Oh, Clive, it's still early."

"No, really, it's time for me to be on my way."

Marjorie followed him to the front door. She hesitated for a second before opening it for him. Then, impulsively, she pulled his face down to hers and kissed him. He pulled away gently and traced her lips with one finger.

"Not now, Marjorie. We mustn't rush things."

*   *   *

That evening, so carefully planned, had been a let-down, though of course a full-blown seduction in the Charles Street house was not a possibility. At first Marjorie was worried that something about the dinner or the way she was dressed had put Clive off but decided he simply wanted to take things slowly. He continued to invite her out to arty films, concerts, local museums. It was like being courted by a gentleman from another era, and Marjorie appreciated being treated like a lady. Clive was almost the exact opposite of Leroy, which was wonderful. But Marjorie secretly missed the rough-and-tumble of her relationship with Leroy.

One evening when they were going out to dinner, Clive arrived at the house looking even more serious than usual. He stood on the threshold to living room, immobile, looking at the floor. Marjorie, who always dressed with special care for their dates and was used to his flattering glances, realized that something was wrong.

"I have to talk to you, Marjorie," he said, his delicate brown eyebrows drawn together.

"What is it, Clive? Has something happened?"

He handed her a piece of paper. She sat down on the loveseat to read it. At first she couldn't make any sense of it. It was written in a childish scrawl, with lots of smudges and crossings-out. It read like a series of obscene threats with references to her affair with Leroy.

Finishing it, Marjorie felt sick. She realized that it had come from Leroy and was intended to cheapen her in Clive's eyes.

"Clive, none of this is true. I swear. None of it." She scanned his face to see his reaction.

"Do you know who could have written this?" Clive was looking at her gravely.

"Oh, my God, Clive, it's . . . a former boyfriend. I met him at the beginning of term and made the terrible mistake of getting involved with him. What he says here, if you can even make any sense of it, is, I repeat, simply not true."

"What concerns me more than your error in judgment is the question of your personal safety. I can only imagine this man's motives. But what he has written is the product of a twisted mind." Clive coughed delicately. "Marjorie, I have a friend with a black belt in judo. If you have . . . this person's address, it might be an idea for me to send Steve over to him, just to make sure."

Marjorie looked at him in disbelief. "You wouldn't have your friend beat Leroy up?"

"No, no, no, no. It's simply a question of showing him that you're protected. You can't underestimate the seriousness of this threat."

"No, really, Clive, I think the best thing is to ignore Leroy. Eventually, when he sees you and I are serious, he'll go away."

Clive shook his head. Throughout dinner he appeared preoccupied. Marjorie tried to laugh the incident off, but she ended up by feeling worried too, wondering if Leroy might have a screw loose. She remembered how he lived in seeming isolation, and some of the odd things he did, sometimes pinching her painfully, sometimes pulling her hair. If he was in fact deranged, he might attack her or Clive. The thought of Leroy's letter hung in her mind like the sultriness before a storm; something was going to happen, but impossible to predict exactly when it would happen or how serious the consequences would be.

*   *   *

For some time Jennifer had been asking Marjorie if they could have a private talk. Marjorie hadn't been deliberately avoiding her friend, but with the demands of classes and Clive's courtship, time had simply evaporated. One afternoon in early November the two finally managed to sit down together. It was early afternoon and they had made sandwiches, which they took into the dining room and ate at the big oak table.

Marjorie looked at Jennifer with some concern. Although they were taking several courses together, she hadn't paid much attention to her friend's appearance. Now she noticed that Jennifer wasn't looking well; she had lost weight so the skin seemed tightly pulled over her cheekbones and there were black marks under her eyes. She touched her arm lightly.

"Are you all right, Jennifer?" she said, "You seem . . ."

Just then doorbell sang its two clear notes. Marjorie put down the sandwich she was eating and went to answer it. On the doorstep was a motley group of people, tall and short, all dressed in black with great colorful splurges of makeup on their faces.

"Hello?" Marjorie wondered briefly if they could be Hallowe'en trick-or-treaters mistaken about their dates—it was a couple of weeks too early. They certainly weren't the sort of people she expected to turn up at their house.

"We're here to party," said the tallest, a well-built black man. "We are the members of Denise's art party!" Marjorie gazed at him in astonishment. His voice was deep and mellifluous. Could Denise conceivably have a black boyfriend? In Baltimore? It seemed highly unlikely. She looked more closely at the little group and saw there were only five people there, two women and three men. "Well, you'd better come in," she said.

The little group traipsed through the living room, dragging behind them what appeared to be great rectangles of gray plastic. Suddenly Denise clattered down the front staircase. She was wearing overalls—overalls, to a party?—and had a radiant smile on her face.

"Hello, people!" she shouted. "I see you've brought the stuff. Far out!" She turned to Marjorie. "Marjorie, these are my friends, Moses," indicating the black man, "Patricia, Morgan, Hubert, Joella. They've come for a party. We're going to do some sculpting."

A group of apparent hippies about to do some sculpting in her house! Marjorie was speechless.

Jennifer appeared by the entrance to the dining room. She stared at the little group in surprise.

"But Denise, where?" she asked, "and what is that gray stuff?"

"Oh, don't worry. It probably will make a mess, but we'll take it out to the back yard. It's polyurethane. We got it at one of those places where they make prostheses. Artificial limbs and stuff. We got it for free! C'mon, people. Let's get sculpting!"

The five followed Denise through the dining room into the kitchen and out the back door.

Jennifer turned to Marjorie, touching her head with the fingers of her right hand. "What on earth was that about?"

"Well, it looks as though we're being invaded by Art Institute people. I seem to remember Denise saying something about an art party. She and her friends apparently meet every week to create some artifact. But . . . I didn't quite expect this!"

"Well, I suppose it's innocent enough. Providing they don't make too much of a mess." Jennifer went back into the dining room at sat at the table. Marjorie followed her.

A booming voice sounded from the kitchen. "Knives, knives. We've got to have some knives." They could hear the clinking of flatware as someone rummaged through the kitchen drawers.

"God, knives!" said Marjorie. "As long as they don't start attacking each other!" She picked up the partially eaten sandwich she had left on her plate and put it down again. "I've completely forgotten what we were talking about," she added. They had been having a serious conversation, trying to catch up on each other's concerns.

"Well, it was about classes, I guess. I was telling you that I'm having doubts about teaching. I love my Medieval French course and I'm leaning more and more in the direction of graduate studies. In fact, the professor . . ."

"You're not! Surely you don't want to wall yourself up in the ivory tower!" To Marjorie, becoming a scholar was tantamount to entering a nunnery.

"But you see, Marjorie, I can't see myself in front of a group of rowdy high school students. I just don't have the personality . . ."

There was a noise in the kitchen. Two of the people in Denise's party had come back in and were arguing. Curious, Marjorie and

Jennifer got up and went to the door to the kitchen. There were Denise and a small woman wearing a black wig. They continued their discussion without paying attention to Marjorie and Jennifer.

"Boudicca," Denise was saying, "The Celtic woman warrior!"

"Nobody's heard of her, Denise. What about Joan of Arc?"

"But Boudicca has so much going for her! She's Celtic, to begin with. She's an underdog, defeating the Romans. She's perfect! With Boudicca, we're sure to win!"

Jennifer looked at Marjorie helplessly. "How can we have a reasonable conversation with all this going on?"

"Well, we can't, Jennifer. Let's just watch and see what happens. And hope they'll finish and leave soon."

Denise and the small girl went back down the steps into the yard. The yard was now quite barren, with the grass completely dead and only a few bushes near the house showing wisps of green. The group had divided in two, with the men at the back near the perimeter fence and the women on the other side near the house. Hundreds of slivers of plastic were flying through the air as the sculptors worked their knives.

"We're making Boudicca!" shouted Denise. "And the men are making Nero! It's a contest to see who'll finish first and who will make the most life-like figure!"

"Musica!" called out one of the men, who had scraggly shoulder-length hair. "We gotta have de musica! Denise, where's your record player?"

"It's in my room. You bring it down. I'll get some records and see if I can scare up an extension cord."

Marjorie looked at Jennifer and shook her head. "Jennifer, I'm afraid this is going to get out of hand."

"Well, it's Saturday afternoon," said Jennifer. "I don't see what harm it can do."

"The harm it can do, Jennifer, is that it just might get us evicted!"

Pretty soon the record player was set up and rock music was blaring out as the sculpting continued with the knives glistening in the afternoon sun. Marjorie watched, unable to decide whether to intervene or let the party run its course. She saw a face emerging from the grey plastic in the men's corner.

"We'd better have a word with Denise," said Jennifer, raising her voice to make herself heard over the din. "I don't think the neighbors are going to like this. We don't want anyone complaining to the police."

"Right. I can't imagine what she thought she was doing!" Marjorie was about to go down the little steps into the back yard when she heard a noise on the back staircase. It was Madeleine. She was wearing her gray garment and her lips were tightly pressed together. She stood by the back door, looking out.

"I'd like to know what is going on here," she said.

"Denise is having a party with her friends," said Jennifer. "They're creating art forms."

"What they're creating," said Madeleine, who knew how to make her voice carry, "is an infernal racket. I can't read, I can't study, I can't meditate. This is unacceptable."

She marched down into the yard and grasped Denise by the shoulder. This could cause more trouble than the neighbors' complaints. Marjorie strained to hear what Madeleine was saying but the noise drowned out the sound of her voice. In seconds, Denise went to the record player and unplugged it. Everyone stopped sculpting and looked at Madeleine.

"We'll just finish here and be on our way," said Denise very loudly. She gave Madeleine a poisonous look. "We'll have to discuss this later, Madeleine."

Madeleine came back into the kitchen, where Jennifer and Marjorie were still standing. Her face was expressionless as it always was when she was angry.

"Marjorie Dunnock," she said. "You have broken your promise to me. We were to have quiet hours for study and no men on the premises. First we have male visitors and noise until the most ungodly hours of the night. And now we have this . . . this hippie fest with obscene music and knives being waved around. Who are these people? They look like devil worshippers to me! I cannot live under these conditions. I may be forced to leave."

"Madeleine, I am truly sorry," said Marjorie. This was half what she had expected; too much dissention in house, leading to a break-up before the lease had expired. She was furious with Denise, but tried to appear calm. "Look, Madeleine," she continued, "We'll have to work out something, some definite rules. As soon as these people leave, we'll have a meeting. I promise you."

"Well, I won't be able to talk until later. I'm having visitors soon. And I can tell you, they aren't going to be impressed with the atmosphere in this house." Madeleine spoke with emphasis, turned and went back upstairs, treading heavily on each step.

Jennifer and Marjorie were left staring at each other in the little kitchen. The sculpting party carried on in spite of Denise's promise. But it was quieter now, with only an occasional shout or a whoop of laughter.

"God, Marjorie, I wonder if we'll be able to reconcile these two," said Jennifer. "Do you think that Madeleine could just walk out on us?"

"I'm afraid that's exactly what might happen. I'm not sure how, but Denise and Madeleine will have to agree on some kind of compromise. Surely Denise must realize that she can't bring people like that to the house and give noisy parties in this neighborhood. And Madeleine has to give in on some points." Marjorie faltered. "Why did we have to get two such weird roommates?" she wailed.

Jennifer shrugged. "I wonder. I always said we were an unlikely quartet."

The doorbell rang again. "You don't think that's the neighbors complaining about the noise?"

"Oh, God, it could be. C'mon, Jennifer, let's face the music together." Marjorie took Jennifer by the hand and they went through to the front door. Standing on the doorstep were two men dressed in black carrying black briefcases. For a moment Marjorie thought they were reinforcements for Denise's party. But they were far too smooth and well-groomed for that. One was virtually bald despite his youth and had no eyebrows. The other had a broad, toothy smile.

"We are members of the Brothers of Light congregation," said the one with the teeth. "We have come to see sister Madeleine."

The two men came in. They looked like members of the Seventh Day Adventist Church that sometimes came to proselytize on Sunday mornings. Jennifer looked at Marjorie in alarm.

"I think she's in her room. I'll go up and tell her you're here."

How typical of Jennifer to leave her to deal with these people! Marjorie sat down and gestured for the brothers to sit too. She had no idea what to say. They sat staring at her, smiling. From the back yard, an occasional yell could be heard. Marjorie cringed as she heard a stream of obscenities.

"Um, one of our housemates is having a little party. They're doing a bit of sculpture," she said, realizing how lame this excuse must seem.

"Graven images," said the man with the teeth, continuing to smile.

"Um, is Madeleine considering joining your, um, group?" She stared at the toothy-faced man, wondering what on earth she could say to appear respectable and what on earth Madeleine had to do with them. Leaders of a religious group! Doubtless some sort of cult.

"We are here to assess her spiritual potential," said the man without eyebrows. "We choose those who join us." He looked at her with the same lack of expression Marjorie had often seen on Madeleine's face when she was angry.

Just then Moses appeared at the dining room door. He had taken off his tee shirt and his face was glistening with sweat, despite the cool of the afternoon. He stood there in his majesty, beaming down at the two seated men.

"You must excuse me, gentlemen," he said. Then turning to Marjorie, "We are lacking the inspirational elixir, dear lady. Could you possibly fill this lacuna?"

"You mean beer? Excuse me," Marjorie said to the Brothers and escorted Moses into the kitchen, happy to escape the Brothers of Light. The kitchen was also a mess now, with empty beer cans everywhere and ashtrays full of burnt out stubs. Joelle was sitting under the rickety table, her knees pulled up to her chest, partly conscious. There was no more beer in the fridge or in the cupboard.

"Moses, you know, you're going to have to pack up and leave very soon. Some of us need to study, and we're out of beer, anyway. And, I have to say, someone will have to clean up this mess. It's disgusting!"

"I hear you, my charming lady, I hear you. It seems the gentlemen in the living room are not connoisseurs of the fine arts!"

"You're absolutely right, Moses. They represent the establishment, or their version of it."

Denise came up from the yard, carrying Boudicca. Boudicca's head was almost finished. It was massive, with a large hooked nose. But the rest of her was a barely shaped rectangle of polyurethane.

"Well, we didn't finish, but we had a damned good time. Didn't we, Joelle?" Denise kicked Joelle and she stirred fitfully. "Marjorie, thanks for being patient. My friends are just going to take the sculptures to Morgan's garage. I'll be cleaning up in back here. If you want to talk, come and call me in. Is that okay?"

"Well, you'd better clean up the kitchen too! I can't imagine what you thought you were doing!"

The other members of the party came back into the kitchen, carrying Nero in two parts and the knives they had used for sculpting. "C'mon, Joelle," Denise pulled Joelle out from the kitchen table, and she stumbled to her feet. Moses and the two other men went out first, followed by Patricia and Joelle, still half-asleep. Marjorie followed behind, her curiosity overpowering her dread of the scene in the living room.

The Brothers of Light were sitting exactly as they had been a few minute before. Madeleine was sitting opposite them. Jennifer had come back down and was standing behind Madeleine's chair, in the shadows. Neither the two Brothers nor Madeleine registered any expression as Denise's party trooped through with their bits of polyurethane.

As Moses reached the door, he turned and cast a brilliant glance over the seated group. He bowed solemnly. "Many thanks, my dear ladies. Thanks to you for fostering our artistic endeavors!" He swept out first, followed by the other members of the party. A sweetish odor of cannabis lingered in the air as they left.

"I think it's time for us to go too," said the toothy Brother. "Thank you for your time, Sister Madeleine. We will be in touch." He turned to Marjorie and inclined his head. "Good-bye, Miss. May the Lord be with you. May He shield you from temptation."

The two men got up in a single movement and went to the door. When they had left, Marjorie turned to Madeleine. "I'm sorry, Madeleine. I'm afraid we've ruined your chances of being accepted by that congregation or whatever it is."

Madeleine fixed Marjorie with a glassy stare. "You seem to wish that was the case."

"No, Madeleine. It's whatever you want for yourself." It was a hypocritical thing to say, but Marjorie felt the need of keeping up a modicum of politeness.

"Well, if that is true, you'll be pleased to hear I've been accepted. The Brothers feel that living here will be a excellent test of my faith."

"That's wonderful, Madeleine," said Jennifer, coming forward from her hiding place.

"Well, as I say, if that's what you want." Marjorie sighed. "You said we need to set down some ground rules, and I agree a hundred per cent. Denise is in back, cleaning up. Shall I ask her to come in?"

"Marjorie, I need some peace and quiet. I'm going up to my room to meditate."

"What about the rules? I thought you said you needed rules." Here was an excellent opportunity to talk things out, and Madeleine was going to her room to meditate.

"What the Brothers said has changed everything." Madeleine gazed at Marjorie with a curious light in her eyes. Then she turned and disappeared through the kitchen door. Marjorie and Jennifer stared after her.

"I don't understand," said Jennifer.

"I suppose we'll have to wait for another opportunity."

Just then, Denise came in from the yard, holding an enormous pile of polyurethane scraps in the dust pan. She stood in the door between the dining room and living room.

"Well, I suppose that will have to do for the moment. I'll finish up tomorrow. It's still an awful mess. Maybe I should use the vacuum cleaner on the extension cord." She put the dust pan down and scrapings of polyurethane flew around the room.

"Don't you dare!" said Jennifer. "You'll clog the mechanism and we won't be able to use it again. I'll help, if you like."

"Maybe tomorrow." Denise rubbed her hands together. "Where's Madeleine? I thought we were going to have a little talk."

"Madeleine seems to have had a change of heart," said Marjorie. "I guess she's decided to put up with us for the time being. She went to her room. But I wanted to say . . ."

"That's too bad," said Denise, interrupting her. "I was hoping to have it out with her. I've just about had enough of her snotty attitude. Well, if that's the case, I'd better be going. I promised to meet Moses and Morgan to make plans for our next party."

"Which won't take place here," said Marjorie emphatically.

"No, we'll look for a place with better karma." Denise was crossing the living room on her way out. "Oh, by the way, Marge. That horrible little pipsqueak of a boyfriend of yours was hovering in the bushes while we were doing the carving."

"Not Leroy?" Marjorie had been so sure she was rid of him.

"That was the one. Don't worry. He took one look at Moses and ran for his life. I saw him disappearing down the alleyway. Well, I'm off. See you." With that, Denise went out the front door.

"Who's Leroy?" asked Jennifer.

"Oh, that's right. You never met him. He's just someone I never want to see again. But it looks as though he's still hanging around."

"What about that talk we were having, Marjorie?"

"Oh, Jennifer, I couldn't just now. I feel totally discombobulated." That was an understatement. It was as though the house was falling apart, if in fact, it had ever functioned as a unit. It wasn't enough that Marjorie had one roommate that was a hippie with drug-sodden friends, another that was a religious fanatic about to join a cult, and a third who was spineless and afraid to assert herself. Now it seemed that Leroy was spying on her! Marjorie's heart literally felt as if it was sinking. She looked at Jennifer who had one of her pitiful expressions on her face. "I'm so sorry, Jen. I have too many other problems to contend with."

*   *   *

It took the three of them three afternoons to clean up the mess in the back yard. Only a couple of Miss Mayberry's scraggly rosebushes had been damaged. Marjorie was worried that Leroy might come back. But probably Moses had frightened him away for good. As fall tilted into winter, there was no sign of him, and courses ran along without much incident. Madeleine was spending more and more time in her room, studying and meditating. As for Denise, she never seemed to be around anymore. Marjorie wondered if she had moved in with Moses. It seemed a shame the housemates saw so little of each other, but at least for the moment there was no conflict.

Marjorie was satisfied with her education courses, but the "School of Donne" eluded her. She had done poorly on the mid-term, making only a "B," which had never happened to her in a lit course before. On Wednesday and Friday afternoons, when the course met, she entered the classroom with the sense of entering alien territory. She was used to participating in class and being acknowledged for her intelligent comments. But when she raised her hand to make a contribution in her Donne class, Dr. Frazier either ignored her or received her comment with a stony stare. She sometimes even imagined that the other students, the male Ph.D. students, were exchanging disparaging glances at her expense. Donne's poetry, apart from the few frequently anthologized pieces that Marjorie was familiar with, remained prickly and unapproachable.

At some point in the semester each of Dr. Frazier's students was required to do a presentation on a subject to be developed into a term paper. Marjorie, eager to show her willingness to work, volunteered to be the first presenter. She read and re-read the love poems and buried herself in Donne criticism. She eventually set out to prove that despite the frequent Petrarchan elements, Donne's love poetry was essentially earthy and sensuous.

This thesis, once formed, seemed clear and easy to prove. Marjorie scanned the poetry, finding numerous supporting examples. In a relatively short time she was able to put together what she considered quite a creditable presentation. She typed it out and made note cards, sure that she would finally gain Dr. Frazier's favor.

On a grey day just at the beginning of November, she ran through her notes one last time. She was already relishing the image of Dr. Frazier, highly impressed by her talk, conceding that a mere M.A.T. student could be the intellectual equal of the other graduate students. She dressed carefully, putting on a rather somber dark grey skirted suit, little platform heels, and plain silver earrings.

She arrived in class and took her place at the big conference table. Looking around, she felt her confidence flagging. All Frazier's minions were lined up on the other side of the table, smirking.

"We will have the pleasure of hearing Miss Dunnock speak today," said Frazier. He gave a barely perceptible emphasis to the work "pleasure." He was standing at the head of the table, his eyes fixed on her. He motioned her to stand just in front of him, so she could feel his breath on the back of her neck.

She stood behind the lectern, arranging her notes in little piles.

"'Donne and the Petrarchan Tradition, an Ironic Relationship,'" She announced and began presenting her paper.

After a few minutes, she heard Dr. Frazier's voice just behind her ear. "Miss Dunnock, where are you going with this?"

Marjorie was furious at having been interrupted. She turned to face Dr. Frazier. He was looking at her ironically, one eyebrow cocked.

"Well, I don't think that's such a deep secret, considering my title."

Dr. Frazier tapped his pen lightly on his left hand. "I think, that being the case, that you should cut to the <u>irony</u>," he said. "Your plethora of historically weighted examples is obfuscating your theme."

Marjorie could feel her face burning. She fiddled with her note cards, which suddenly seemed to have no order. There was a silence, a very long silence, broken by the sounds of paper crumpling, a cough, a chair grating on the floor. She looked up and made eye contact with her classmates. Some looked uncomfortable, but most were pleased.

"I've lost," she thought. But she tried to deliver the conclusion of her paper with some measure of dignity, and sat back down.

Without comment, Frazier opened his book. "Let's turn to page · 47, 'Love's Wake,'" he said. "Here you will notice the use of logistical progression through the first two stanzas."

Leaving the classroom, Marjorie almost collided with Terrence Sneed, the ringleader of Frazier's minions. He smiled broadly and gave her a thumbs-down gesture. Marjorie was incensed. Terrence Sneed! That miserable sycophant, triumphing over her! Tall, thin almost to the point of emaciation, rubbery of limb, Terrence Sneed was Dr. Frazier's pet. He hung on his every word, laughed uproariously at a mere hint of a joke. Marjorie was certain he didn't have a single original idea. How dare he give a thumbs-down on her paper!

Dr. Frazier invited her to his office a week later to discuss her presentation. He had given her a B-, an absolute disgrace for Marjorie, and a failing grade in graduate school.

The paper, an outline of her talk, was lying on the outside corner of his desk when she arrived. He thumped it with his fist.

"Haven't you learned <u>anything</u> in this course?" he asked.

Marjorie was genuinely surprised he could ask such a question. She had never been in such limbo in a course before. "Why, have you taught us something?" was her immediate reaction. But she knew better than to be fresh. She held her tongue, not wanting to get into any worse trouble.

"Miss Dunnock," he continued, "You must learn to dispense with historical trappings and attack the poem itself. The poem itself," he repeated stroking his chin. "If it doesn't stand on its own, it doesn't stand. Do I make myself clear?"

"Yes," said Marjorie, who hadn't the slightest idea what he was talking about. Her mental faculties were paralyzed by rage and humiliation.

Later, over a glass of wine in the dining room, she and Clive performed a post mortem on her presentation and its consequences.

"It was a good paper," said Marjorie. "Dr. Frazier ripped it to shreds. No, it was worse than that. He merely dismissed it with a wave of his pencil."

"I'm sure it was good," said Clive calmly. "But sometimes in graduate school you have to make a study of the professor rather than the subject."

"You mean you have to figure out how to please him?"

"In a sense, I suppose. You find out his approach and copy it. In Soviet History, for example, Dr. Petrovitch espouses dialectical materialism. I no more believe in dialectal materialism than I believe . . . in Mormonism. But for Dr. Petrovitch I become a dialectal materialist. Doing that is a kind of discipline in itself."

"Well, Clive, it's not a discipline I can respect." She shook her head angrily. "Why should professors have the right to humiliate students who have made an honest effort? No, Clive, I'm not going to pander to Dr. Frazier or his minions."

"Marjorie," said Clive, taking a little sip of his wine, "I understand that Frazier has hurt your pride. But we're in a system here, like any social system, where those in power prevail. If you take a rebellious stance, believe me, you will be crushed."

Marjorie was grateful to Clive for listening to her. It was like having a lifeboat sent out on troubled waters. She also realized there was a certain truth in what Clive was saying. The only way she could assert herself was to master Frazier's vocabulary and approach. She resolved to pass the course and pass it honorably.

Dr. Frazier had scheduled an exam prior to the final. For the next two weeks, Marjorie immersed herself in tropes, irony, oxymoron until she could toss the terms around with great facility. She made a respectable A—on the exam. She was sure that the minus was a reminder she was not one of the pack.

*   *   *

"I cannot stress enough the importance of attending tonight's lecture," Dr. Frazier had said in Friday's class. "Dr. Charles Rayburn is a visiting professor of Renaissance literature on leave from Brown University. He will lecture tonight on Renaissance poetry. His insights will be invaluable to you in your analysis of Donne's poetry."

So on a chilly winter night, instead of meeting Clive for dinner, Marjorie put on her trench coat and trudged over to Langley Hall. Her expectations were low. She visualized a greying professorial type, droning on tonelessly from the podium about topics so boring it would be almost impossible to take notes. She slid into a seat just behind Frazier and Sneed and settled back, preparing herself to drowse gently in the overheated lecture hall. The important thing, she reminded herself, was that Frazier noticed she was there.

Gwendolyn Stapleton, the academic dean, preceded Dr. Rayburn to the podium and chanted his praises, his publications, his degrees, earned and honorary. Dr. Rayburn moved from Ms. Stapleton's side and took over the podium. Marjorie sat up straight. Dr. Rayburn, far from being middle-aged and professorial, was a youthful Mediterranean type with passionate dark eyes, an aquiline nose, and thick black hair. Marjorie was mesmerized from the moment she saw him. Without paying too much attention to the content of Dr. Rayburn's speech, she followed his every movement.

What she did notice in his introductory remarks was a single statement: "No man is an island, and no poem exists in isolation." Marjorie was pleased to learn that this scholar took an entirely different view of poetry from Frazier's. She would like to have seen Frazier's face, but from where she was sitting she only saw the back of his head.

Rayburn was talking about Spenser's poetry, which was Greek to Marjorie. But she was enjoying the way he moved on the platform, his rather exaggerated gestures, the way his expression would change suddenly as he made a point or quoted a line.

During the question period, Frazier and some of his students hounded Rayburn with questions. He answered quickly and smoothly, with a superior smile, as though he knew something they didn't know. At the end of the session, as he went back to the podium to gather his notes, his eyes very briefly met Marjorie's. It felt like an affirmation.

Frazier had invited Rayburn for a post-lecture drink and the students tagged along. They met at Nick's, which by that time was one of Marjorie's favorite haunts. The little group ordered drinks, wine for Marjorie, beer for Frazier and the four other students, whiskey for Rayburn. Marjorie was excited to be so close to this attractive and charismatic man. He was sitting directly opposite her. She didn't utter a word. She could hardly follow the conversation, which revolved around some historical question about the Faerie Queene.

She imagined—could it be true?—that he eyed her a couple of times in a certain way. She wished that she had taken more care with her hair and make-up. Who would have thought it necessary for an academic lecture?

Dr. Frazier suddenly got up. "Sorry to break up what has been a stimulating evening," he said, "But mundane reality, in the form of promises to the espoused, intervenes. I told Edith I would be back before ten. One must obey one's better half."

Dr. Frazier had a "better half!" And one whose wishes must be obeyed! Marjorie was astonished. It had never occurred to her that this man could have any sort of family life.

The group rose from the table as one.

"Does anyone who doesn't live on campus need a ride home?" Dr. Rayburn asked.

Two of Dr. Frazier's students answered yes. "I'm going toward Federal Hill Park."

"Could you take me too?" asked Marjorie, although Federal Hill Park was downtown, in the opposite direction from her house. She felt reckless, though; why not see where this might lead? It would be exciting just to ride in this man's car. She got in the passenger seat beside him; the two others climbed in the back.

Dr. Rayburn let the two other students out near their apartment. Then he turned to Marjorie. "Where is it you live?"

Marjorie had been hoping that he would invite her up to his apartment. She had to invent something quickly. "Why don't you let me out at Federal Hill Park? It's near my house." It wouldn't be easy to get back home from there, but she would find a way.

Leaning toward her, he touched her hand lightly. "We're neighbors, then," he said, smiling as if in delight. "Will you come up for a drink?"

Marjorie looked him straight in the eye and without saying a word nodded.

The apartment where Dr. Rayburn lived was extremely cluttered. When he switched on the light by the door, Marjorie had difficulty orienting herself. The living room seemed like a maze of objects rather than a place where you could sit comfortably. It had a number of glass-fronted cabinets full of odd figures, brass animals, dolls in various native costumes, plates painted in gaudy colors, framed photos from the 1920's. The walls were hung with colorful Indian tapestries and there were a number of African sculpted figures standing at odd intervals throughout the room. The lighting was dim, and it was difficult to move around without bumping into something. Marjorie, amused, wandered among the displays.

"It's like a museum," she said.

"I love collecting beautiful things," he said, giving her an appraising look. "Do you want a drink? Whiskey?"

"Do you have any wine?"

"Not on the hard stuff. Is white okay?"

He poured her some wine in an enormous goblet. It tasted strongly alcoholic to Marjorie, but not being sophisticated about drinks, she wasn't sure. He put a record on. The music was strange—very exotic, very rhythmic, with a whining sound.

"It's Turkish folk music. Do you like it?"

"I'm not sure."

Dr. Rayburn had poured himself a large whiskey. When he came close to her, she noticed that he was shorter than she realized, shorter than she was, in fact. He looked her up and down, and coming close, ran his fingers up and down her neck, making her shiver. He kissed, and then licked her fingers, looking slyly at her. He took her by the hand and led her down the corridor into a dimly lit bedroom with a canopied bed. Suddenly he looked uncertain, his shoulders sloping down, the light going out of his face.

"You're very young," he said. "Are you sure you want to do this?"

She was worried for a moment that he would be tentative like Clive. But once they got started he was far from that.

"You're so lovely," he kept murmuring.

Afterwards, she asked him where the bathroom was. "I've got to shower and get dressed."

"You're not leaving? Stay. Sleep over with me. I'll make you a fantastic breakfast in the morning."

Marjorie shook her head. The offer put her off. It was like payment for services rendered. And she never ate breakfast.

He drove her home, laughing when he realized that she lived on the other side of town.

"Little schemer!"

"You aren't annoyed?"

"No, I like a woman who shows spirit."

She was surprised when he asked her for her telephone number. She had thought it was truly a one-night stand.

It was still relatively early when she came in. Someone was banging around in the kitchen, probably Jennifer. She passed Denise putting the finishing touches on a painting in the living room. Denise greeted her with a nod, barely looking up from her work. The house was making its old house winter noises, creaks, sighs, gurgling of the radiators.

It was as if she had been away on a long trip, and returning, found nothing had changed.

*   *   *

Marjorie never expected to hear from Charles Rayburn again, but in fact he called her a couple of days later. They continued to see each other at odd intervals for the rest of the semester from mid-November till the end of classes in December. This presented some problems for Marjorie, who was still seeing Clive. Sometimes she would have a date with Clive and Charles would call at the last minute. "I'm dying to see you, Marjorie. Can you come right away?" Then she would cancel her date with Clive, which was sometimes embarrassing and difficult. She knew that Clive, sweet and tolerant as he was, was beginning to lose patience with her. But she could never pass up an opportunity to see Charles.

Their meetings were always at his apartment, which, she learned, was actually not his at all. It belonged to another faculty member, on sabbatical in Italy, who was renting it to him. So the beautiful things Charles had said he liked to collect weren't his at all. Marjorie still loved to wander from room to room, barefoot, examining this sculpture or that wood carving. She felt that she was in a jungle of artifacts.

Since Marjorie's meetings with Charles were irregular, she suspected he might be seeing another woman. But there was something about the spontaneity of their affair that precluded jealousy. It was fun, and she always enjoyed their encounters. They met at night, sometimes staying in the apartment, sometimes going out to Federal Hill Park to see the sun rise, sometimes eating at odd restaurants that stayed open all night, sometimes going to low dives, sometimes going to see one of Rayburn's arty friends, who wrote rather lewd songs and played the guitar.

*   *   *

Throughout this period, Marjorie saw her two lovers and at the same time managed to keep up with her class work. She had mastered Dr. Frazier's approach to poetry and was annoyed that she received little recognition for her effort. The minions, led by Terrence Sneed, still dominated the class. Thankfully, Leroy Patterson was now a thing of the past, at least as far as she knew.

Then, just before Christmas break, Sneed was scheduled to do his presentation, the last of the term. Marjorie knew, as he stood beside his place at the table, that his talk was going to be a re-hash of Frazier's approach. Just watching him deliver it made her squirm with loathing.

But when he launched into his introduction, Marjorie's ears pricked up. Was it possible? What Sneed was saying was a repetition of one of Dr. Frazier's monographs. She knew because, anticipating exams, she had just read it. She looked sharply at Frazier; his face showed no emotion except one of approval. She looked around the class; none of her fellow students were reacting. Stunned, she waited for Frazier's reaction at the end of the lengthy talk.

"Well done, Mr. Sneed," he chirped. "Solid work. I'm proud of you."

Marjorie couldn't believe her ears. Most of the other students' work was derivative, but this had been lifted, verbatim. Terrence Sneed had plagiarized, apparently with Dr. Frazier's collusion. She was disgusted. But at the same time, here was an opportunity to get revenge on these bastards.

At the end of the class Terrence collected the outlines he had passed out. Marjorie pretended to put hers under the pile, but in fact held on to it. Evidence.

As she walked out of the classroom and crossed the campus, Marjorie pondered the best way of using this opportunity. She could go behind Sneed's back and present the monograph together with the outline of the paper to the Ethics Committee. They might suspend Sneed or even expel him; that would be a satisfactory outcome. But Marjorie needed to confront Sneed in person; she had to see his face; she had to hold her triumph over him. Then he'd know who can turn thumbs-down on a perfectly good paper.

The following week after class Marjorie waited in the hallway for Terrence to detach himself from Dr. Frazier. As he emerged from the classroom, she laid a gentle hand on his forearm.

"Let's go into this empty classroom," she said. "I have something I need to talk to you about."

She led him into the classroom across the hall, and stood so that the light from the windows fell directly on his face. She wanted to savor his expression.

"Well?" he said, "What's up? I have an important seminar in ten minutes."

Marjorie paused for several seconds, relishing her moment of triumph. "Your presentation was plagiarized," she said. "And I have proof of it." In fact she had brought a copy of the monograph whose introduction matched Terrence's outline, word for word.

Terrence looked at her with a smile spreading over his narrow face. "Is that all? Let me ask you, Marjorie Dunnock, who do you think could give a flying fuck?"

"I'll take it to the student Ethics Committee. I'm sure they will be interested."

"I don't see Dr. Frazier pressing charges."

"No? Then there's collusion and he's involved." It was disconcerting that Sneed stood there smiling, unmoved. He should be writhing at her feet, begging for mercy.

Terrence Sneed's smile continued to spread, making deep creases around his mouth. "I wouldn't get on my high horse if I were you. Your own ethics have a distinctly rancid smell, if I'm not mistaken."

Marjorie straightened up to her full height. "I don't know what you mean. My conduct has been perfectly ethical."

"Has it? I have it on good authority that you're one of the women lining up to jump into Charles Rayburn's bed."

"That's my business!" Had she been so careless that everyone knew about her affair with Rayburn? Still. it was hardly a matter for the Ethics Committee. "That's consensual. Besides, I'm not even his student."

"Well, quite apart from the ethics of it, there's the question of your reputation on campus. I don't think I'd be too happy to be labeled number one whore, if I were you. And I don't think your boyfriend would be too happy about it either."

Marjorie hesitated for a second. "You're making empty threats, Sneed. How do you even know I have a boyfriend!"

"Miss Dunnock," Sneed was laughing now, a gurgling laugh. "There aren't many secrets on this campus. You've been seeing Clive Barnes for the last six weeks."

"If I get the slightest hint that you've told Clive about Rayburn, I'm going to expose you, Terrence Sneed, and your lover-boy professor!" The last remark slipped out. She hadn't intended to mention her suspicions about Sneed's sexuality, but she had lost control.

She ran downstairs and out onto the campus, out of breath, simultaneously chilled and sweating. She was furious at having let this opportunity slip; in her eagerness to confront Sneed, she had lost the chance to go behind his back to the Ethics Committee. She walked swiftly toward the house. Her thoughts rattled around in her mind like the objects in a badly packed suitcase. She couldn't focus on one idea. How did Sneed know she was seeing Clive? He was spying on her, collecting evidence to get her! But that didn't make sense. But he did know, he knew Clive's name! The humiliation of a creep like that knowing about her private affairs!

She walked more slowly, collecting her thoughts. She had lost. Marjorie Dunnock, who had always been a winner, had lost. And she had lost to this creeping, fawning Uriah Heep of a man! A person who could only get ahead by sucking up to his superiors.

And her affair with Charles Rayburn, which had always been an innocent bit of fun, a fairy-land escape from the drag of graduate school, this affair now was tainted. She saw herself, disheveled and slovenly, lining up with a group of similar women to jump into Charles Rayburn's bed. Horrible! And what if Clive found out? What if he already knew? New thoughts, debasing, humiliating, even frightening, kept popping into her head.

It was late afternoon when she got home. She went up the steps to the house and finding the front door locked, unlocked it. If the door was locked, that usually meant that no one was home. No sign of any of her housemates downstairs. Good! She didn't want to see any one of them, and most especially not Jennifer. Jennifer, innocent Jennifer, who looked up to her. Jennifer, she knew, would never two-time anyone as she had two-timed Clive.

She climbed the stairs to her room, threw her books and papers on the bed, kicked off her shoes and lay down. She felt exhausted.

Totally done in. It was as if all the defeats of the semester had come down on her head. She fell into a fitful sleep.

It was in the middle of the night, two or three o'clock, that she woke to a terrible sense that something was wrong. Then she remembered her confrontation with Terrence Sneed, her failure. She couldn't believe it had happened, couldn't believe that this could mean and might very well mean the end of her relationship with Clive. Sneed would tell on her, and Clive wouldn't tolerate that kind of infidelity. Everything had gone wrong that semester. Tatters of memory haunted her—Leroy Patterson dripping rain in the living room, Denise's noisy sculpting party while the Brothers of Light sat smirking, herself standing in front of a sniggering classroom as she delivered the presentation she had thought was so good. How could so many horrible and humiliating events happen in the course of four short months?

Three o'clock in the morning and there was no hope of sleep. She was too upset, too enraged. Tomorrow was the last day of classes before exam week; she had to be alert to her professors' instructions. She had to calm down, to get herself to sleep. Suddenly she remembered that Jennifer sometimes took over-the-counter sleeping pills. She scaled the steps to the third floor, went into the bathroom, and looked into the medicine cabinet. Sure enough, on the top shelf was a bottle of Sominex. She read the label: "Take one or two tablets with the evening meal."

"Four won't kill me, but four should do the job," She thought, swallowing the pills with a glass of tap water, went downstairs in the sleeping house, and got into bed. It took her what seemed like hours to calm down sufficiently to go to sleep, but when she did, she slept like a rock.

Marjorie had no intention of cutting classes on the last day before exams, but when she woke late the next morning, she had already missed one—her history of education course. And besides having a kind of hang-over from the pills, she had a sore throat and a stuffy head. She was coming down with a cold. She tried to rouse herself and go downstairs, but the strength and the will power simply weren't there. Sleep infolded her.

She awoke, unaware of the time or even the day, to a persistent banging on her door. She sat up; who could dare to intrude on her privacy? She didn't allow anyone to come into her room without being invited.

The door opened a crack, and Marjorie could discern a small head peeping in.

"Jennifer!"

"Marjorie, I'm sorry to disturb you." Jennifer came in and stood just inside the door. "I was worried about you. You just disappeared into your bedroom. For two days! Are you sick?"

"Oh, Jennifer, you might as well come all the way in." Marjorie got out of bed and put on the bathrobe that was hanging on the bedpost. "I've got this lousy cold." She pulled a crumpled tissue from her pocket and blew her nose. "What day is this anyway?"

Jennifer was just standing there, looking distressed. Marjorie didn't have her contacts in and saw her friend as a blur, but she could tell from the way she pulled her shoulders together that she had been studying too much. "Oh, Marjorie," she said, "have you lost track of time? It's Sunday afternoon, the day before finals. Don't you have any exams tomorrow?"

"Oh, my God. Exams. Tomorrow. How could I lose an entire day? How can I put off taking exams?"

Jennifer looked at her in alarm. Her face, blurred by Marjorie's near-sightedness, seemed spectral, absolutely white. "I don't know, Marjorie. Maybe you could go to Administration tomorrow and explain that you're sick. Or could I go for you?"

The mention of exams brought Marjorie to wakefulness, but she had no idea what to do. How could she contact her professors to explain? She imagined Frazier, looking at her skeptically, one eyebrow cocked. He would say something like, "Sick for exams, how very convenient."

"I've got somehow to deal with this," Marjorie said, half to herself. "I've got to get dressed, get something to eat . . ." She began walking across the room, from the bed to the closet, but she felt an enormous weakness engulf her. She sank into the little chair by the dressing table and looked at Jennifer. "What does it matter? How can I study for exams in this state? I hardly know what day of the week it is. I've missed the last session of every one of my classes, the instructions about exams, when and where to take them and even the important points to study. I'm in a mess. What in God's name am I going to do?"

"There must be some way of letting your professors know," said Jennifer, "of taking the exams later."

Marjorie felt helpless. It all seemed so hopelessly complicated. She couldn't put together the steps of going to the infirmary and somehow having a message sent to her five professors. "It just seems so much easier to give up and fail."

Jennifer came over to Marjorie and put her hand on her arm. "Oh, Marjorie, you can't just give up now, at the very end."

Marjorie looked up at her friend. At this distance, she could see her more clearly. She looked pinched and yellowed as though she were part of an old manuscript. One of the medieval manuscripts she was studying. "Jennifer, I sometimes wonder what I'm doing this for. I despise the hypocrisy of it all. I don't see the point of it."

"Marjorie," said Jennifer earnestly, "I didn't know you were so down on school. I thought you had a strong vocation for teaching."

"At the moment, Jennifer, I don't have a strong vocation for anything. I really never want to set foot in that university again."

"But what are you going to do?"

"Right now, the most important thing for me to do is to get something to eat. I'm going to get dressed, go to Nick's, and get a sandwich and a glass of wine. I might even see what I can pick up in the way of male companionship."

"Marjorie," said Jennifer, "please think about what you're doing."

"I am thinking about it," said Marjorie, "and it seems a very good idea. Now if you'll excuse me . . ." She went to the closet and began looking for something to wear. The thought of food and drink revived her. She turned to give Jennifer an admonitory look, but her friend had already left.

"Clothes—what's clean? Does it really matter?" In the depths of the closet, she found a low-cut silk blouse and a black skirt. She was feeling better and better. "Heels." She seldom wore heels because of her height, but she loved what they did for her legs. She put on a pair of stiletto heels and teetered back to the mirror.

"God, I look awful," she said. Her nose was red, her eyes were puffy, and she had a cold sore on her upper lip. "A little make-up will do the trick." She made up her face, going heavy around the eyes and twisted her hair into a chignon. Then she slinked down the back staircase.

No voices in the kitchen. "Thank God for that." No voices in the dining room either. But as she went through the door, she saw the silhouette of a person sitting at the table, her back to her. She could hear her slurping soup. "Madeleine! What rotten luck!"

She thought of returning to the kitchen and going out the back door, but it was too late already. Madeleine had turned toward her and was staring at her, an expression of outrage on her face.

"Marjorie Dunnock! You look like a two-bit whore! What in the name of all that's decent do you think you're doing?"

Marjorie was shaken. Madeleine's outrage, her uncharacteristic use of vulgar language was like a douse of cold water in the face. Madeleine, the mother superior of the house, spoke with unshakable authority.

She felt, however, that she had to brazen it out. "I'm going to go out, get something to eat and drink, and pick up a good-looking man."

Madeleine's usually heavily-lidded eyes were wide open, her lips turned down at the corners. "Have you taken leave of your senses?"

"No, I know exactly what I'm doing."

Madeleine put down her soup spoon and stood up. "I've put up with a lot since I came to live in this house. I've put up with noise while I was trying to study, and smells and dirty dishes in the kitchen sink, and a bathroom strewn with cosmetics. But I came here to study and up until now I've managed to do that. But this . . . this is beyond anything. You promised me at the beginning that there would be no men in this house. You've broken that promise countless times. But what you're doing now . . . It's indecent."

"You're exaggerating, Madeleine." Marjorie attempted to sound in control.

"Have you thought of a thing called self control?"

"Huh?"

"Self control," repeated Madeleine. "This means that you don't simply give in to your impulses without concern for the consequences. Look at yourself."

Madeleine suddenly seized Marjorie's hand with her talon-like fingers and dragged her in front of the ornate full-length mirror in the corner of the room. Marjorie stared at the image in front of her with some degree of surprise. The effect wasn't at all what she was aiming for. She looked cheap, yes, but still worse, she looked down-and-out. Her runny eyes had smeared her make-up and her nose looked twice its normal size.

"Oh dear, I thought I looked glamorous. I'm a bit of a mess, aren't I?"

"You're disgusting." Madeleine turned her away from the mirror and pointed her toward the stairs. "Now, go up, change, get your books out and start studying."

Marjorie felt as though something was crumbling inside her. "Oh, Maddie," she said, on the point of tears. "What's the point? I've got this lousy cold and I missed the last couple of days of classes. I'll never pass now."

Madeleine let go of her and returned to her place at the table. "Well, your lousy cold doesn't seem to have prevented you from going out to pick up a man at the local bar." She looked critically at Marjorie. "Marjorie," she said, "I have studying of my own to do. I don't want to get involved in a discussion of this with you now. But why did are you giving up on your studies at this late date? How do you think your parents will feel if you fail without even trying? Aren't they the ones who are financing this?"

Marjorie was faltering. She took a place at the table, hiding her head in her hands. "I don't know. I don't know. I just don't think I can cope with it all."

"That's an excuse for not applying yourself, and you know it."

"It's . . . it's . . ." No one could have applied herself more completely than Marjorie, but she could think of no way of justifying herself to Madeleine, who hardly noticed her pathetic condition. "I suppose you're right. But what's the point of going through the motions of taking exams when I'm almost sure to fail?"

"If you don't, you'll be giving yourself an excuse to wallow in shame and self hatred. You're wasting your time and mine. Go on, get up and pull yourself together. It's what?—six o'clock. You have at least five hours before bedtime. Make good use of it."

*   *   *

Leaving Madeleine, Marjorie went back up to her room. Madeleine was unnecessarily harsh, but there was something bracing about her uncompromising manner. Marjorie's head had finally cleared. She thought for the first time of practical realities. She could still pass. She knew that. And in the end, wouldn't that be the best revenge on Frazier and his minions, on the whole cursed University? To pass. To pass with honors. To be able to hold her head up high when she received that diploma from the Dean on graduation day.

She realized that she had no idea when or where her exams were scheduled; the exam schedules had been passed out on the last class meeting. She was pretty sure that administration posted an exam schedule for all graduate courses, but offices would be closed until the next morning. That meant that if one of her exams was taking place first period Monday morning, she wouldn't be able to show up in time for it, much less study for it or pass it. She took off her sleazy clothes and changed into a bathrobe. Then she went down the hall to the bathroom and threw cold water on her face, returned to her room and gathered up her course notes. She would allot two hours to each of the education courses and three to the Donne course. That way she could sleep for four hours and be at the Administration Building at eight o'clock. If she was lucky, her first exam would be no earlier than ten. If she was lucky, not a great deal of new material would have been presented in the final meetings of any of her classes.

Marjorie managed to study until almost midnight, but then fell asleep, her head on her notes. She hadn't yet glanced at her Donne notes. Waking at about six, she dressed and went down to the kitchen. There she made herself a super strong cup of coffee, which she swallowed as she sat at the little table, staring out the window. The house was asleep. Feeling an incongruous sense of adventure, as if she were meeting a lover, she ran through the chilly, damp early morning. She arrived, panting, in front of the Administration Building. Scanning the papers posted on the door, she found and copied the dates of her four exams. She was in luck. Her first exam wasn't until Wednesday.

*   *   *

A week later, Marjorie and Jennifer were alone in the house. Madeleine and Denise both left to go home, Madeleine to Smirthport, Pennsylvania and Denise to Cincinnati, where they would receive their grades by mail. But both Jennifer and Marjorie had to stay on to attend a ceremony marking the completion of the academic part of their studies. Both of them were worried. Marjorie had reason; Jennifer was constitutionally worried. They had finally had a couple of good talks and shared meals. But Marjorie, who had always considered Jennifer a younger sister, now thought of her as a daughter. She felt so much older. There was no way she could confide in her friend; the events of the semester had created a great gulf between them.

She spent the first few days sleeping, reading Romantic poetry and Victorian novels, and generally keeping to herself. She was trying to put the past behind her, trying to nourish her spirit and prepare for teaching. She was enjoying the emptiness of the house.

But she couldn't help thinking about Clive. He hadn't called since before exams, and it seemed more and more likely that Terrence Sneed had told him about her affair with Rayburn. Sneed had said he would do that if she went to the Ethics Committee, but he was just low enough to do it anyway for spite. As time went by, she became more and more concerned and finally she called Clive's apartment. His roommate Paul answered. Paul explained that Clive was out for the day but was still in Baltimore and would stay on between terms. "You could call later," he said, and there was something about his tone that made her even more worried. What if Clive had told him to make up some excuse if she asked for him?

Late that afternoon she worked up her courage to call again. She dialed the number and waited, actually trembling, feeling as though she was about to go on stage. The phone rang and rang. Clive answered on the seventh ring.

"Clive?" To Marjorie, the sound of her own voice sounded strange, small and far away.

Clive didn't need to ask who was calling. He answered abruptly, without pausing. "I don't want to speak to you, Marjorie," he said. "I don't want to see you, smell you or touch you. As far as I'm concerned, you're dead."

Marjorie hung up the phone, went back into the living room and sank down into the couch. She had known that Clive might be angry, but she didn't expect such uncompromising rejection. She felt breathless and sore in the middle of her stomach, as if someone had punched her, hard. That vicious rat of a Terrence Sneed had told Clive about Rayburn! She hadn't gone to the Ethics Committee and he had told Clive anyway! She should have reported him. Vicious, lying little rat!

And why hadn't Clive given her a chance to explain? Did he have to accept Sneed's accusations without questioning? Thinking of that, she turned her anger against her former boyfriend. To believe Sneed over her!

The thought crossed her mind that she could write Clive, trying to explain and set things right. But of course that wasn't possible. She had slept with Rayburn; there was no explanation that would excuse that in Clive's eyes. She remembered how he had reacted when he got that note from Leroy Patterson. He had said he was concerned for her safety, but there was more to it than that. He wouldn't accept infidelity; he was too upright, too moral.

Still, Clive had been more than a boyfriend. He had been a friend, a loyal companion, a mentor. And now, because of Terrence Sneed's spitefulness—there was no other word to describe it—she had lost her best friend. Clive, the most decent young man she had met! She missed his sweet attentiveness, his cool, reasoned approach to problems, his company. She held her head in her hands, expecting the tears to come. But her emotions were too mixed—rage, disappointment, grief—all in one poisonous cocktail. Terrence Sneed!. How she hated that creep! She thought of revenge, briefly, but she couldn't bear the thought of seeing his repulsive face again.

She went back to the kitchen, needing to talk to Jennifer. There was no way she could explain what had happened, but she needed her company, her support.

She found her housemate in a fit of cleaning. The oven door was open and Jennifer was kneeling in front of it, her arms covered up to the elbow in grease.

"What on earth are you doing, Jen?"

"Can't you see? I'm cleaning the oven. This place is a tip, Marjorie. We have to do something before it gets worse. What will Miss Mayberry say?"

Of all the things Jennifer could have been doing, this seemed the most unsuitable. "Cleaning the oven? What a filthy job! Can't we get someone in to do it for us?"

"Well, Madeleine and Denise aren't here to give the go-ahead. I thought I should make use of my spare time. Here, take a chisel and help me scrape off some of this muck."

Marjorie couldn't believe what she was hearing. "Jennifer, my world is falling apart, and all you can do is clean the oven!" She slumped into one of the kitchen chairs and put her head in her hands.

"Marjorie, what's happened? Is there anything I can do?" Jennifer sat down opposite her and placed one filthy hand on her shoulder.

"I've broken up with Clive."

"But why? Did you have a fight, Marjorie? He was such a nice man."

Marjorie looked at her friend and tried to think of some explanation, but it was too complicated. She didn't know where to begin.

"Let me make you a cup of coffee," said Jennifer. She plugged in the coffeemaker, poured water into the head and measured out grounds. Marjorie didn't want coffee; she didn't really want anything. But she knew the gesture was an expression of sympathy when words were of no use.

"Did this happen just now, Marjorie? Or was it when you took to your room just before exams?"

"I've just been on the phone to him, Jennifer. It's all over now."

Marjorie swallowed hard. Clive never wanted to see her again. His words came back to her like a series of slaps across her face. Hard slaps.

"Next semester," Jennifer was saying brightly, "things are bound to change. We'll meet new people, have different challenges." She got up and looked in the cupboard. "Hey, here are some pretty coffee cups. Shall we use them?"

It was the demi-tasse set Marjorie had bought for the first dinner she had cooked for Clive. The cups with the delicate blue flowers.

On that evening he had brought her the gift of white lilies. She saw him at the door, the flowers in one hand. She saw him sipping his coffee from the demi-tasse cup, looking at her affectionately. She took a deep breath and the tears came. The tears came from a place deep inside her chest and felt as though they would never stop coming.

*　　*　　*

Final grades were sent out two days later, the Friday before Christmas. Marjorie, who had retired to her room to avoid Jennifer's fit of housecleaning, was feeling marginally better. Thinking it over, she realized that Clive, while very much the gentleman, was perhaps wrong for her. She needed someone less rigid, more willing to compromise. She was still angry with him for listening to Sneed, for refusing to see her. She deserved better. She was desirable, well-educated, articulate. She had always attracted men. She would find someone else, someone equally attractive, who would love her and appreciate her good qualities. But Clive! His rejection, his harsh words still rankled.

She had also been worrying about her grades. She had pretty much winged it on the finals, and she was good enough at doing that to pass her education course exams. But it was just possible, knowing Dr. Frazier, that he would flunk her. And that would be the end. "Oh God, let me pass!" she thought. "Then I can put the entire rotten semester behind me and focus on teaching. That's what I'm here for, after all."

She went to get the mail that day at just after noon, knowing that the fatal envelopes would be in the box.

"Well," she said to herself, "The day of judgment has arrived!"

She took the two envelopes to Jennifer, who was in the kitchen, eating a peanut butter sandwich.

"Here's what we've been waiting for!"

"Our grades!" Jennifer put down her sandwich. "Open yours first, Marjorie. I don't think I can face mine just yet."

Marjorie opened the envelope and unfolded the paper inside. All A's in the education courses, except for an A—in Philosophy of Education. And in the School of Donne she got a B+! She breathed deeply. She could hold her head up now. She showed her results to Jennifer, unwilling to show her deep relief.

"That's really good, Marjorie, considering your absences and all."

"So, have a look at yours. How bad can they be?"

Reluctantly, Jennifer tore open her envelope. She made a strange noise. Marjorie wasn't sure whether she was laughing or crying.

"Well?"

"Identical to yours. Except that I got a B in language teaching methods and an A in late medieval French poetry. That just shows how much good studying does."

"Wait a minute. I studied hard that last night."

"I studied from the beginning of the semester."

"Well, that just proves that I'm more brilliant than you are. Now, cheer up and give me a bite of your sandwich. We'll go to Nick's together to celebrate."

The fog had lifted. Marjorie had made it after all! In spite of everything, every conceivable thing going wrong, she had managed to pass! She could hold up her head at the mini-graduation. She had passed the academic part of her training. The teaching apprenticeship would surely be easier. That, after all, was the real part of her training. Not the theory. She would do well. She had the makings of a wonderful teacher. She was sure to excel.

Chapter II

Marjorie returned from Christmas vacation late on a Saturday night; her apprenticeship was to begin on Monday morning. She loved early departures and late arrivals when she traveled; the cover of darkness added to her sense of adventure. She took a taxi from the train station and arrived at Charles Street just after ten o'clock on a chilly January night.

She stood outside the house. It was dark except for a light in the top bedroom window overlooking the street, Denise's room. She unlocked the door and ran up the two flights of stairs to the third floor. She could hear rock music, playing at a low volume, in Denise's room. No noise emerged from Jennifer's room. She tapped lightly on the door, then opened it.

Jennifer was in bed with a book in her lap. Her eyelids were heavy with sleep. She looked so small and cozy, wrapped in her flowered comforter, that Marjorie could have hugged her.

"Marjorie! I was beginning to wonder if you were coming back. We're supposed to start on Monday."

"I know. I wanted to take the fullest possible advantage of my vacation time. Mind if I come in?"

She set her bags on the floor and sat at the end of Jennifer's bed. In this room under the roof she could feel the wind rumbling. "Can we talk?" she asked.

"Of course. It's good to see you." Jennifer was sitting bolt upright now, her eyes fully open.

"Well, how was Christmas in the Midwest?"

"Very traditional. Ghastly. The cat ate too much turkey and was sick under the tree. My mother complained nonstop about the work of cooking Christmas dinner. My sister wanted to exchange all her presents. And my father wished he was back at work."

"That's nice." Marjorie had hardly heard what her housemate said. She was envious of Jennifer with her family Christmas. She thought of her own Christmas day: a catered dinner at a colleague of her father's with everyone immaculately dressed. "Did you have masses of lovely snow?" she asked, hopefully.

"Two feet of the stuff. We were worried that Daddy would have a heart attack shoveling the driveway."

"How enchanting! I wish I lived in the country. I spent most of my time shopping with mother. You know, Saks Fifth Avenue, Bergdorf Goodman."

"Christmas shopping? In Manhattan with all the lights and decorations? Now that would be enchanting." Jennifer got up, went to the closet, and got out a bathrobe, which she wrapped tightly around her body. "I'm freezing. Aren't you cold, Marge?"

"No, I've still got my winter coat on, as you see. Well, we bought some Christmas presents, but I mainly got clothes for myself."

"More clothes, Marjorie? You already have a closet-full! You hardly need any more!"

"'Reason not the need!' Actually, I do need more. I'm teaching now. I'm a teacher! It's a completely different persona. Let me show you . . ." Marjorie was on her knees, about to open one of her suitcases, but Jennifer interrupted her.

"I don't want to be rude, Marjorie. But if you're planning to stay much longer, I'm going to have to go downstairs and turn up the thermostat. I'm freezing!"

"Oh." Marjorie was disappointed by her friend's lack of interest in her new wardrobe. "Well, I did have this neat idea I needed to talk to you about." Marjorie had thought up her idea on the train and was more and more excited about it. She and Jennifer would give a reunion brunch for Denise and Madeleine. It would bring the four closer together and make for smoother relations.

"Yes?" Marjorie sensed that Jennifer was impatient to get back to bed.

"Let's give a reunion brunch tomorrow! It's Sunday, and everyone's likely to be here."

"You mean a reunion for us, for the house?"

Marjorie nodded. "To start off the new semester. To catch up on one another's lives."

"Well, it will be Sunday. Will we be able to get the ingredients for a meal?"

"Most of the ingredients are probably in the fridge. And I can pick up anything else at the corner store. I was thinking we'd have an omelet, fresh orange juice and French bread. Home-made French bread."

"French bread? Oh, Marjorie, you're not going to get up and make French bread in time for brunch?"

"Of course. We wouldn't eat until eleven. If I get up at six, there's plenty of time for the bread to rise and bake."

"You're totally out of your mind. Well, if you really want to, I'll help. But I'm not getting up at six!"

*　　*　　*

Marjorie and Jennifer were setting the table with a basket for the bread in the middle, a glass of fresh squeezed orange juice at each place beside a little pat of butter on one of Miss Mayberry's horrible plastic dishes. The coffee was perking in the kitchen and

Jennifer had whipped up the omelet, which she was ready to cook. The bread was still in the oven, giving off its wonderful aroma.

Madeleine was already awake when Marjorie tapped on her door to invite her. Now she was sitting at the place by the entrance to the living room, staring blankly at the kitchen door, her hands folded in her lap.

"But where's Denise?" asked Jennifer.

"I've tried to rouse her a couple of times," said Marjorie. "I even pounded on her door, but there was no response."

"Do you think I should try again?"

"No, let's get started. She can join us when she's ready."

Marjorie went to the kitchen to get the bread out of the oven and Jennifer started cooking the omelet. Marjorie and Madeleine were seated at the table and Jennifer was serving the omelet when they heard a noise on the front staircase.

"Hey, Denise," Jennifer shouted. "We've cooked brunch! Come and join us!"

Denise came back to the dining room. She had thrown her winter coat over a pair of paint-spattered overalls and was carrying a large bag. She seemed to be in a hurry.

"Hi, people," she said. "Marge, I didn't know you were back. I was heading out to the Institute studio, but I'll have a bite with you. Sure smells good."

She folded her coat, laid it and her bag on one of the empty chairs, and sat at the table, helping herself to omelet and bread.

"You're doing your art work at the Institute now?" said Jennifer.

"Yes, we've got a great space at the studio. I'm into collages." She reached over to the chair, grabbed her bag, and unpacked part of it. She took out old rags, odd bits of wood, cheap jewelery, a used handbag, part of a broken violin.

"Well, I hope you do use that space at the Institute," said Jennifer. "Last term you did considerable damage to the furniture. I don't know how we're going to get those paint spots off the antique sideboard."

"Surely they'd come with a touch of solvent," said Denise, beginning to wolf down her breakfast.

"You have to be careful about what you use on that wood. You could just ruin it."

"I'm not going to ruin Miss Mayberry's precious furniture, Jennifer. And in any case, I won't be working here this term. So, you have nothing to worry about." Turning to Marjorie, she said. "So you're back, after all! I hear you were about to give up the idea of graduate school just before exams."

The coffee in Marjorie's mouth turned to acid. She swallowed and composed herself. Pretending to take the remark lightly, she turned to Jennifer. "In the end I did quite well, didn't I, Jen?"

"I think you might give me a little credit for that, Marge," said Madeleine, who had finished her eggs and was cutting the crust off the bread. All that was left was tiny squares.

"Not to belittle your efforts, Madeleine, I think it's time to let bygones be bygones and welcome the new semester. Anyone for more bread?" Marjorie used this pretext to go into the kitchen. She was furious with Denise mentioning last semester's episode and annoyed with Madeleine for pursuing the subject. All she wanted to do was to forget about what had happened and start her apprenticeship on a wave of optimism. She took the second loaf from the oven. It was a good sign, she thought, that the bread had turned out perfectly.

She took it back on a tray to the dining room. Determined to change the tone of her little party, she looked around the table at her housemates, Jennifer opposite her and Madeleine and Denise on her right and left, respectively. They were eating in silence, each absorbed in her own thoughts.

With a big smile, Marjorie said, raising her glass of orange juice, "It's a time of new beginnings and I, for one, am in a celebratory mood." She took a sip and looked at each of the girls. "Happy New Year! Happy new semester! And lots of success to us all! We are so different and yet we share one thing: We are the exceptions, career women, looking to find our way in the world, independent, not marriage bound."

Madeleine put down her fork and laughed, a short bark. "Well, this may be news to you, Marjorie, but throughout the ages, people with a religious vocation have embraced celibacy. This is tradition. There's nothing exceptional about it."

"And you know, Marjorie," said Denise, a spoonful of omelet in her hand, "I wouldn't object to marriage, not on principle, not if the right guy came along."

"But you still put career first, don't you, Denise? Otherwise, you wouldn't be here."

"I'm here because I love to paint. I love art. Well, if marriage meant giving up those things, I guess I'd resign myself to spinsterhood."

"You see," said Marjorie triumphantly, still standing. "Whatever you may think, you're both exceptional women, women with a vocation. We're looking for something more than a conventional life, with marriage and children. We want more."

To Marjorie's surprise, Jennifer said in a loud, clear voice, "I couldn't agree more! A career and independence! That's what I've always wanted." She finished her orange juice and set down the glass. "And we're about to begin! By the way, Marjorie, have you got your teaching assignment yet?"

"Well, no. I didn't realize the paper had arrived. As you know, I've been busy all morning, preparing this feast!"

"Oh, go look in your mail. The notification tells the name of your school and the first day you have to attend."

Marjorie put down her coffee cup and moved quickly to the little table in the hall where old mail was stacked.

"Here it is. It has the official stamp of the university on it. Let's see." She ripped open the envelope. "Fielding School. Four courses in the English department. First day of attendance, January 12. It also gives a list of phone numbers for carpooling."

"Oh, Marjorie, we're assigned to the same school! It's an exclusive private school, with small classes and bright students! We'll probably be in the same carpool."

Jennifer was thrilled, Marjorie perhaps less so. Jennifer could be such a wet blanket! But then, she thought, it might be fun teaching in a private school, the city's elite, as Jennifer had put it. "You see, Jennifer, I was right to buy new clothes. We'll have to be careful to dress elegantly. Our students will be coming from wealthy families."

"I'm sure the clothes you wear will make all the difference to your teaching," said Madeleine, sarcastically.

"Of course they will. First impressions are vital," insisted Marjorie. She poured orange juice all around. "Let's have another toast. To Fielding School and new challenges!"

"And to new directions in art," said Denise, clinking her glass against Marjorie's.

Madeleine wasn't about to raise her glass to anyone or anything. "Let's just hope for a little more order in the house," she said. "And peace and quiet so we can study."

*   *   *

On Monday morning their carpool picked them up at the door.

"Hello, I'm Joyce Kettlehut. I teach ninth and tenth grade social studies."

The woman who stretched out her hand to them was about thirty-five and was pleasantly unattractive, with bald eyelids and a round face. Marjorie looked at her closely. There was something about her, possibly the lines of discontent around her mouth, that made Marjorie wonder if teaching at Fielding School was much fun, after all. But of course anything could have etched the lines on Joyce Kettlehut's face—health problems, an unhappy love life, a difficult family.

"Today all you have to do is meet the administration," Joyce said, as she drove them from the congested city streets out toward the suburbs. "Actual classes don't begin until Wednesday."

"Do you enjoy your work?" asked Marjorie. She was sitting beside Joyce in the passenger seat. The car smelled strongly of dog.

"It has its moments," Joyce replied, without expanding on the subject. She was leaning stiffly forward, keeping an eye on the traffic. Marjorie decided not to pursue the subject.

The Fielding School was located well outside the city center, on wide, beautifully manicured grounds that made Marjorie think of a country club. The buildings, mostly brick, seemed old and weather-beaten.

"I'll leave you in front of the Administration Building," said Joyce Kettlehut, pulling up in front of an ivy-covered building. "As you're both teaching Humanities, your supervisor will be Dr.

Rittershoff, first office on the right. I'll see you back here at noon. A half day, today. Good luck."

Something about Joyce's final wish sounded menacing, but Marjorie was determined not to be intimidated. They entered the building and found the office. Smiling confidently, Marjorie knocked on the office door. Jennifer was looking apprehensive. She had a cold and kept twisting a tissue in her hand.

"So," said the grim-faced woman who opened the door. "You are our two new apprentice teachers, Miss Dunnock and Miss Hill." She stretched out a bony hand to Marjorie, then to Jennifer. Dr. Rittershoff bore a striking resemblance to a vulture, with her large beak of a nose, her wattles, her scrawny neck. She had a faint German accent and spoke in a high, shrill voice. "I am Dr. Rittershoff, Dr. Gisela Rittershoff. Sit, sit, if you please." She sat down herself and took a sip from the paper cup on her desk. Marjorie wondered briefly what was in it.

"What I must first impress upon you," she said, speaking with emphasis, "is that the Fielding School is a student-centered institution. We foster each student's development. The focus is on the individual. Each student is encouraged to attain the very highest level of his abilities." She eyed them, first Jennifer, then Marjorie, critically. Jennifer was looking more and more distressed. Marjorie was afraid she might burst into tears.

"That means a great deal of the burden is on the teacher," she said.

"Indeed it does. My deepest belief is that there are no bad students, only bad teachers. If you respect your students and teach well, you should never have any discipline problems. If, as inexperienced teachers, you should allow a problem to occur, you must handle it yourselves, in class. No teacher at the Fielding School ever sends a student to the headmaster's office."

She went on at some length in a similar vein, occasionally taking a sip from her paper cup. After almost a half an hour, she looked at her watch. "I think you have a full faculty meeting next, during which you will be assigned your committee duties. Unfortunately I will be unable to attend. That's all I wanted to tell you today. But I will need one thing from you. At the end of each week, I will require your daily lesson plans. You can put them in my box, which you will find in the basement of this building."

"And will you discuss them with us afterwards?" asked Marjorie, who had realized there would be little support from this woman.

"Not unless you're having serious problems. I don't have time for such things. I have important administrative duties."

Such as drinking a pint of Bourbon on the job, thought Marjorie, but she smiled broadly, determined not to let Dr. Rittershoff have the upper hand.

The rest of the day was heavily imbued with similar propaganda. In the full faculty meeting, they got their committee responsibilities—Marjorie had curriculum development and Jennifer parent relations—and received a pep talk from the headmaster on the importance of contributing time and effort to the school. She half expected the faculty to rise and give the school cheer at the end of the talk, but there was only subdued applause.

Finally, the Latin teacher, a mousy individual by the name of Miss Boyce, gave them a little tour of the campus. She showed them the classrooms, the language lab, and the teachers' room ("Our little retreat. You can have lunch and make coffee here. It's also where you can catch up on the gossip.") The gymnasium was in a separate building and the playing fields were down the hill. "We're very well appointed, you see," said Miss Boyce said, smiling a smile that was marred by bad teeth. "We count ourselves lucky to teach here. I hope you'll both feel as we do." With that she guided them back to the administration building, where Joyce was waiting for them.

"So you've had your dose of school propaganda," she said, opening the door for the two girls to get in. They both settled in back, feeling tired and a bit disheartened. "Well, don't take it too seriously." Joyce started up the little car. "At the Fielding School, it's largely a question of arriving on time, attending meetings, however boring, doing requisite paperwork and not upsetting the apple cart. Be good little girls and all should go well."

Marjorie gritted her teeth. Being a good girl wasn't a goal she aspired to.

I suppose you know, our supervisor, Dr. Rittershoff?" asked Jennifer.

"Yes, of course. You poor things. I didn't want to put you off initially, but I'm afraid she's the most difficult of the supervisors."

"She's already given us a lecture on disciplining the students," said Jennifer. "She says we have to handle discipline problems in class. There are no bad students . . ."

"Only bad teachers," said Marjorie, completing the quote. "And you know what I say? I say that there are plenty of bad students. And I'll send students to the headmaster's office when I need to. It's my class."

"Of course you shouldn't let Dr. Rittershoff intimidate you," said Joyce. "But be careful, Marjorie. That woman has immense power in the school." She took a breath. "Okay, you have a day off to prepare. Then, on Wednesday, we start in earnest. I'll pick you up in front of the house at seven thirty, if that's all right."

Both girls agreed and they sat for some time in silence as Joyce drove them back into town. Finally, Marjorie could contain herself no longer. "Joyce," she said. "Dr. Rittershoff was drinking something the whole time we were in her office. And I don't think it was water."

Joyce laughed a tittering laugh. "Umm. You're very observant. Don't say anything, Marjorie, but Rittershoff has a drinking problem. It's well known. I'll tell you about it some time."

*   *   *

On that Wednesday, Marjorie, excited by the prospect of her new role as teacher, dressed carefully. She selected a burgundy wool dress with long sleeves and a ruche of white lace at the neck. She put on higher heels than usual to give herself the advantage of height. It was important to make the right impression—not to intimidate the students but to show her authority.

She scanned the piece of paper with her schedule of classes. She was teaching one section of English at each of the high school levels. The curriculum was similar to what she had had in high school: stress on grammar and sentence structure for the freshman, introduction to literature for the sophomores, American lit for the juniors and English lit for the seniors. She also had library supervision from ten till eleven.

That first day as she walked into that nine o'clock class, she felt a kind of sinking in her stomach. What would the students think of her? Would she be able to control them? She put on her most confident air to meet her students. Everything went swimmingly until last period, at two o'clock, when she had the tenth graders.

She sauntered into the classroom a couple of minutes late. She greeted the students, who were sprawled on their seats, already looking bored. Just as she turned away to write her name on the blackboard, she heard a shuffling and a suppressed giggling. She turned abruptly to confront the culprit. One of the girls in the second row was blushing and had her hand over her mouth.

"You!" snapped Marjorie. "In the second row, in the striped shirtwaist dress. Stand up!"

The girl in question, a rather small child wearing braces, stood, blushing. Silence settled over the class.

"What's your name?"

"Elsa, ma'am, Elsa Crabtree."

"My name is Miss Dunnock, not ma'am."

"Yes, Miss Dunnock."

"Now would you care to share with the class this very funny joke?"

"There was no joke, Miss Dunnock. I was just . . . a little bit nervous. I . . . I sometimes giggle for no reason."

Scattered laughter broke out over the class.

"All right, Elsa. There'll be no more giggling in my class. For any reason whatsoever, or for no reason at all. Is that understood?"

"Yes, ma'am."

"Yes, Miss Dunnock. Now sit down and pay attention."

The rest of the class went relatively well, except for a bit of whispering in the back row. Marjorie was quick to silence the culprits, two overgrown boys.

After class, Elsa Crabtree and one of her friends approached Marjorie's desk.

"Miss Dunnock," said Elsa. "It wasn't really me at the beginning of class. It was Hugh Parsons and Jack Peabody in the back row, making dirty jokes. They're the real troublemakers."

"Thank you, Elsa. I'll keep an eye on those two."

The next day Marjorie moved Hugh and Jack to the front row and put two of the well-behaved girls between them. The boys continued to misbehave, whispering and passing notes. She tried keeping them after school. She tried to embarrass them. She even practiced threatening expressions in front of the mirror. But they remained trouble-makers.

Apart from the mild discipline problems with the tenth graders, Marjorie's classes went well from the beginning. She liked dressing up for her students, dramatizing her little lectures, even terrorizing the few miscreants. She felt in her element. Writing weekly lessons plans was a time-consuming drag, but she wrote them and turned them in faithfully. She felt in no way bound to these plans and deviated from them when the spirit moved her. Dr. Rittershoff returned them without comment, which was either a good sign or a sign that she hadn't read them.

What Marjorie hated at Fielding was the biweekly committee meetings, which took place on Friday afternoons and felt like a bite out of her precious weekends. As luck would have it, her committee, the curriculum committee, had Dr. Rittershoff as it chairman. From the beginning in February until the last meeting in May, these meetings hardly changed. They consisted of lengthy debates between Rittershoff and an elderly science teacher, Mr. Wellfield, about the language requirement. Dr. Rittershoff opposed the language requirement on the grounds that some students were incapable of mastering a foreign language while Mr. Wellfield supported it as part of a well-rounded education. There were other topics, of course, but nothing ever was resolved and the debates went on fruitlessly.

On those Friday afternoons, Marjorie looked around the conference table at the faces of the committee members, all middle-aged or elderly, all marked by lines of serious concentration. Then she gazed out the window at the fields beyond the building, first etched in frost, then changing to green as the spring arrived. She felt a longing to be anywhere but where she was, wasting her youth in a stuffy classroom, listening to boring people discuss topics that she found irrelevant. Marjorie had begun to resent Dr. Rittershoff bitterly. She called her "Der Uebermensch" because of her frequent allusions to over-achieving students as the model Fielding School was striving for.

When she mentioned Rittershoff's new nickname to Jennifer, she said, "Der Uebermensch! I like that. But shouldn't it be Die Uebermensch?"

"No, decidedly not. It's Der Uebermensch."

Jennifer wasn't doing so well. She was having serious discipline problems but was afraid to send students to the headmaster's office after Dr. Rittershoff's lecture. She was intimidated by her students. She hated her teaching materials. Her beginning French class was too big and her third and fourth year classes had been combined so that she had several different levels during one period.

"Oh, Marjorie," she said one Friday afternoon when they had finished for the week. They had gotten into the habit of having a glass of wine together in the kitchen after Joyce delivered them back to Charles Street. "How am I going to survive this semester? Everything is going wrong that could. I hate teaching and I'm doing badly."

Marjorie looked critically at her friend. She looked shrunken, her baggy sweater and skirt hanging loosely around her body. She felt a familiar blend of pity and impatience with her.

"You know what I think, Jennifer?" she said. "I think you need to improve your image. You may think appearances aren't important, but they are, especially at a school like this. You'll never be able to control your classes if you go schlepping around in those nondescript clothes. You have to project confidence. And authority."

"But I don't feel confident. And I certainly don't feel like an authority."

"Jennifer, I have an idea. Let's go downtown and buy you a new wardrobe. I guarantee it will change your image. You'll feel like a new woman."

""But I can't <u>afford</u> a new wardrobe."

"Come <u>on</u>, Jennifer. We're making money in this so-called job. You can afford one or two new outfits."

The two went shopping, and at Marjorie's bidding, Jennifer bought some clothes that actually flattered her.

But in the days that followed, Marjorie was disappointed not to see the transformation she had expected in her friend. She did wear the new outfits once or twice but then apparently put them aside.

"What happened to that smart yellow suit we got?" Marjorie asked a few weeks later.

"Oh, that. It just wasn't me. I didn't feel comfortable wearing it. I gave it to my younger sister."

"Oh, Jennifer. You're absolutely hopeless. I give up. I give up completely. I don't even think you <u>want</u> to change."

*   *   *

Dr. Rittershoff observed the apprentice teachers twice during the semester, primarily in order to find fault with their teaching and make suggestions aimed at improving it. These visits were the most dreaded events of the term, comparable only to a very painful dental appointment.

As luck would have it, Jennifer was scheduled to be observed fairly early on, on the sixteenth of February, a Wednesday. Dr. Rittershoff had not told her which of the classes she was going to observe, which meant that if she chose the last period, Jennifer would spend the entire day in a state of terror.

On Monday evening, Marjorie tapped on Jennifer's bedroom door. Her housemate, after a curiously long delay, opened the door, looking pale and disheveled. She had books and papers strewn all over the floor.

"What on earth are you doing? Studying for an exam?"

Jennifer lowered herself onto a cushion on the floor. "I have to prepare for Friday," she said. "I have to prepare all four courses for Friday since I don't know which one she's coming to."

"I don't see the point of making elaborate preparations," Marjorie said, "seeing that the students know virtually nothing. And what about Der Uebermensch? Does she even know French?"

"Well, not as far as I know, but . . . ."

"Jennifer, the class is supposed to be conducted <u>in</u> French. What is Rittershoff going to observe? Not, surely, the content of the class."

"But there has to <u>be</u> a content."

"Follow the book, Jennifer. And for God's sake, relax. What Der Uebermensch is going to observe is how you handle the class, not what you teach them."

"I'm not sure I know how to handle a class."

"Wing it. Pretend you're Queen Jennifer. Shout 'off with his head,' 'off with her head.' Threaten them. But don't look scared. That's exactly what she'll be expecting. And she'll have you for it."

Jennifer's expression changed. She gave Marjorie her most thunderous look. "<u>Will</u> you stop giving me advice? And give me some peace, for God's sake. I'm trying to create an all-purpose lesson on pronouncing the French 'u'."

Marjorie shrugged. At least she had provoked a strong reaction from her friend. What she couldn't stand was Jennifer's spinelessness.

*   *   *

That Wednesday afternoon after school the two girls were to meet Joyce Kettlehut in the school parking lot. Marjorie was the first to finish class business. She had finally persuaded Jennifer to wear the taupe suit and some little heels for the observation, so she would at least look the part of teacher. Now as Marjorie watched Jennifer emerge from her post-observation interview with Dr. Rittershoff, she thought her friend looked wilted. "Oh, no," she said to herself. "It's gone badly. Just as I feared."

Jennifer merely greeted Marjorie with a nod and got into the back seat of Joyce's car.

There was a tense silence on the way home. Joyce, who knew Jennifer was going to be observed, was too discreet to ask her how it had gone.

The silence persisted as they got out of the car and mounted the steps to the house.

"Aren't you going to say anything, Jennifer?"

"I'd rather not talk about it."

"Come on, let's go and have a drink at Nick's. I can see that you need one."

It took three glasses of wine before Jennifer would open up.

"It went so badly, so badly," she said, finally. "I want to forget about it as soon as possible. What I really want is never, ever to face that class again."

"I think you should talk about it," said Marjorie. "Get it out. It's much worse to hold it back and brood over it. What did Der Uebermensch have to say?"

Jennifer looked at Marjorie with wounded eyes, like a dog that has misbehaved and been punished. "She said it was totally incoherent. She said I might as well have been talking gibberish. She told me that I had absolutely no hold over the class, that I had completely lost them."

Marjorie wished that Jennifer would scream or sob, but instead she just kept looking at her with those wounded eyes. It was hard to console someone who seemed so defeated, so hopeless.

"Well, you have another chance at the end of term. At least there's plenty of room for improvement."

"Oh, Marjorie, do you know what she said at the end of the meeting? She said that I should be thinking of an office job, preferably one that didn't involve dealing with the public."

Marjorie was outraged. Rittershoff had the right to be hard on Jennifer for teaching a poor lesson but she had no right to condemn her future. She was worse than an uebermensch; she was a vicious, hateful bitch. She leaned toward Jennifer and put her hand on her arm. "Jennifer," she said, "you didn't deserve that. And it isn't true!"

*   *   *

"Today, class, we're going to talk about a short story by Edgar Allan Poe, 'The Tell-tale Heart.'" Marjorie was standing in front of her tenth grade class, wearing her best gray suit and anticipating Dr. Rittershoff's arrival. She was slightly worried about the observation but determined not to be intimidated. In fact, she hadn't made any special preparations. "Let her observe the class as it is," she told herself.

What she had done was to choose a text by Edgar Allan Poe in hopes of arousing interest among the more recalcitrant boys, who tended to like morbid things.

"Before we discuss the significance of Poe as a writer," she was saying, "let's talk for a few minutes. What were your reactions to the story?"

At that moment the door opened with a whoosh, and Dr. Rittershoff appeared. She nodded, went to the back of the classroom and took one of the student's desks. A chill settled over the class as if Rittershoff had come in with a gust of cold wind. Marjorie repeated her question. No hand shot up. Dr. Rittershoff was already busily taking notes.

"Let's rephrase the question. What sort of person is the narrator? What do you think of him?" The class was silent, as if frozen. "Well, let's look at the text. Open your books to page 79. Elsa, would you read the first couple of paragraphs?"

Elsa got up and began to read. Her voice was so low that even Marjorie couldn't hear her.

"'True!—nervous—very, very dreadfully nervous I had been and am, but why will you say that I am mad?'"

"Elsa, would you read a bit more loudly? I don't think the class can hear." Marjorie was beginning to despair of getting a discussion going. She let Elsa finish the second paragraph. Then she consulted her notes and began to give a lecture on Poe's life and literary fortunes. She wrote the relevant facts on the board.

There was a stirring at the back of the classroom. Marjorie stopped dead in her tracks. She immediately identified the trouble-maker.

"Bob Knightly," she said. "Stand up! Would you care to explain to the class what you find so distracting?"

Bob Knightly stood, shifting from one foot to the other. "I . . . I . . . Miss Dunnock, may I be excused to go to the rest room?"

"Go on. It might be a good idea if you didn't come back before the end of the period."

Bob Knightly shuffled out. Marjorie finished her little lecture. The period, one of the longest Marjorie could remember in her short teaching career, still wasn't over. She talked briefly about Poe's poetry and gave a couple of recitations, of "The Raven" and "Annabel Lee." She had taken her suit jacket off and hung it on the back of her chair. She could feel the sweat staining the underarms of her silk blouse. She wrote the assignment on the board and excused the class. Five minutes early!

The students had left. Dr. Rittershoff stopped by Marjorie's desk as she left the classroom.

"I'll see you in my office in ten minutes. Don't keep me waiting."

Marjorie went to the teachers' room and tidied herself up before entering Dr. Rittershoff's office. Der Uebermensch was steely-eyed. A stack of papers was sitting in front of her. The situation recalled, alarmingly, Marjorie's meeting with Dr. Frazier last semester.

"Sit down, Miss Dunnock," she said. There wasn't a trace of a smile on her face. She made her wait a full minute, moving papers and sipping from her paper cup, before she spoke.

"Let's begin by the less serious mistakes," she said. She paused and looked Marjorie in the eye before continuing. "These are mere mistakes of fact. First, you spelled Poe's middle name incorrectly. It has two l's, not one. He was born in Boston, not Baltimore. His first collection was a collection of poems, not short stories. That's three errors of fact, Miss Dunnock," she said her voice rising. "Three. You always verify the content of your lecture before delivering them. NEVER convey incorrect information to students. That is a betrayal of our calling."

Marjorie couldn't believe her ears. She couldn't imagine how she had made three errors, however small, however insignificant.

"Let us proceed to more serious matters." Dr. Rittershoff paused to let her point sink in. "You failed to conduct a class discussion in a proper manner. You must never put answers in the students' mouths. If you do this, they will be silenced for good."

"But they had nothing to say. They had no ideas."

"In that case, you must rephrase the question in a way that makes them wish to respond."

"Such as?"

"Use your ingenuity, for heaven's sake. You're supposed to be skillful at handling students." She gave Marjorie a cold, hard look. "Then there is the question of the suitability of your material. Poe was a sensationalist, a scribbler. Stories such as 'The Tell-tale Heart' should not be read at the tenth grade level, if at all."

"The story was in our textbook."

"You should have omitted it. And don't answer me back. Finally I need to make you aware of the most serious mistake. Do you have any idea what you did?"

Marjorie shook her head. At this point, she wished the interview was over. She felt as though she were back in Dr. Frazier's office.

"You did something a good teacher never does. You completely humiliated a student."

Marjorie stared at Dr. Rittershoff in disbelief. Humiliation was a time-honored form of discipline among teachers and one that Dr. Rittershoff was using at that very moment. "But Bob Knightly was causing a disturbance. I had to nip it in the bud."

"Not the way you did it. You came across as a tyrant. That student may be alienated for the rest of the semester. That's more serious than anything else you did. It shows a failure of character."

Dr. Rittershoff made a mark on the top of her folder. ("A black mark on my record?" Marjorie wondered.)

She tidied up the papers in the folder. "Those are my comments for today. Do you have any questions?"

Marjorie had failed to answer Dr. Frazier. This time she wasn't going to take this type of criticism sitting down. She looked Dr Rittershoff straight in the face. "Yes. I do have a question. Do you have anything good to say about my teaching?"

"Miss Dunnock, you misunderstand the function of these observations. Their function is to bring to your attention your errors and weaknesses so that you can focus on trying to correct them. It is not to mollycoddle you. Is that clear?"

"It's a good thing I'm not Bob Knightly."

"Eh?"

"I refuse to allow myself to be humiliated, Dr. Rittershoff. I'm not going to be alienated for the rest of the semester. This, unfortunately, may not be true of all your apprentice teachers. They may already be lost, in fact." Marjorie was gathering her briefcase and purse. "I think you're quite finished with this little exercise?"

Before Dr. Rittershoff had a chance to answer, and she certainly would have answered, Marjorie had left the room. She knew she had defied authority and she knew she would pay for it in one way or other. But she didn't care. She had had her say.

*   *   *

Marjorie and Jennifer hadn't been seeing much of their housemates since winter term began. Fielding School activities kept them busy during the week and when Marjorie wasn't sleeping over the weekend, there was correcting and paperwork to do. The weekends were also busy for Denise and Madeleine, who both had jobs. Denise was working at a gallery in D.C. and Madeleine was doing outreach work for her church. Marjorie was vaguely aware that they seemed to have little contact—she noticed that Denise had moved her paintings out of the living room—but she was too absorbed in her schoolwork to be concerned.

She was surprised, one Thursday morning in early March, to find a note addressed to her on the kitchen table:

"Marjorie, please attend an urgent meeting Saturday, 8:00 P.M. Madeleine"

When Marjorie read the word "meeting," she realized it must be some form of house business. But what? If it came from Madeleine, it had to be unpleasant, something about cleaning or noise, and she didn't look forward to spending her Saturday evening arguing. The next morning, waiting for Joyce to pick them up, she asked Jennifer if she had had a similar note.

"Of course. It's obviously a meeting for the four of us."

"But why?"

Jennifer shrugged. "Maybe Miss Mayberry is coming to make an inspection."

"Or could she possibly be raising the rent?"

"I shouldn't think so. We're on a lease. And anyway, as we're the named renters, Miss Mayberry would have contacted us, not Madeleine."

Marjorie was mildly concerned but put the matter out of mind until late Saturday afternoon, when she was wondering how to spend the evening. Her social life hadn't picked up since the beginning of the term. At first she had been absorbed in her teaching, and the little band of admirers she had acquired in the senior class had to some extent made up for the lack of male attention. But now that her first observation was over and the pressure was off, it occurred to her that there was no boyfriend at hand or even on the horizon. She was just considering the possibility of seeking out Denise, wherever she was. She thought the two might go to a downtown bar as a change from Nick's. But she suddenly remembered the house meeting. "What a bore!" she thought. "We have so little time these days. The last thing I want to do on a Saturday night is to discuss house rules with Madeleine."

Nevertheless, at a few minutes past eight, she made herself a cup of instant coffee and went into the dining room. Madeleine and Jennifer were already sitting at the table. Jennifer was looking tired and long-suffering and Madeleine grim-faced and as waxy-yellow as ever.

Making an effort to be polite, Marjorie sat down, nodded to Jennifer and greeted Madeleine.

"Hi, Madeleine, is everything all right?"

"No, not really," said Madeleine sourly.

"Would you like to explain what this is about?" Marjorie sat down at the head of the table, balancing her coffee cup in her hand.

"I think we'd better wait for Denise. She's involved as much as I am." Madeleine closed her eyes and lifted her fingertips to her forehead in the attitude of someone with a headache or someone attempting to meditate. Jennifer was writing notes for one of her classes Monday. Marjorie sipped her tasteless coffee, feeling uncomfortable. She was worried. It looked as if this was something more serious than house rules.

After a few minutes, they heard Denise at the front door. She came in, looking uncharacteristically concerned. "Sorry to be late. Gallery business. But I know how important this is."

Madeleine lifted her hands from her face and opened her eyes. "Shall I tell them?"

"I think you should," said Denise. "You're the one who's had the most grief with this."

Marjorie felt a brief nervous stirring of her bowels.

Madeleine looked directly at her. "I've had a couple of encounters with a former boyfriend of yours, Marjorie Dunnock. Very unpleasant encounters."

"Don't tell me. Leroy Patterson."

"He's the one."

"What happened? What did he do?"

"The first time it was a phone call. An obscene phone call. I hung up pretty quickly. I wouldn't have known who it was except that he mentioned your name. And I knew it wasn't that other one. The pretty boy with the nice manners. It couldn't have been him."

Marjorie was concerned. She remembered Leroy's threats. "And the other time?"

"Times. Once I found him lurking in the bushes in the back yard. I told him I'd call the police, and he ran off. The last time, a couple of days ago, he was trying to break in through one of the ground floor windows."

"My God!" This was more serious than she had thought. "And did you call the police then?"

"I shouted at him and he ran off. By that time it wasn't necessary."

"Madeleine isn't the only one to be harassed," said Denise. "I've also answered a couple of his calls. This was about two weeks ago, before he started lurking around the house. He'd ask for you, Marjorie. Then when I said you weren't here, he'd launch into a stream of obscenities." Denise smiled. "I must admit I didn't hang up right away. Some of his expressions were quite unusual."

Marjorie sighed deeply. She was aware of Madeleine's disapproving stare. This wasn't only a worry; it was a real pain. She thought that Leroy had disappeared. "I suppose the first thing we have to do is to change our phone number."

"Get an unlisted number," added Jennifer, who looked shocked. "And then ask for police protection."

Denise shook her head. "Wouldn't work. Unless this character actually was caught prowling or attempting to break in again. The police won't protect you against something that might happen, but hasn't happened yet."

Madeleine suddenly stood up. "I'm not putting up with this, Marge. One more obscene phone call, one more sighting of this . . . degenerate boyfriend of yours and I'm leaving. I'm out of this house, contract or no contract."

Marjorie had a familiar sinking feeling. The threat to leave was a card Madeleine had played before; she didn't need to deal with both Leroy and Madeleine.

"Sit down, Madeleine," she said in as calm a voice as she could manage. "Don't make any hasty decisions. Let me think for a minute." She thought for a minute about Leroy. He was vindictive and brutal, but one look at Moses had made him turn tail.

"Listen," she said, suddenly inspired. "And don't act as if you're about to leave, Madeleine." Madeleine sat down reluctantly. "Leroy Patterson isn't such a challenge. He's stupid and he's nasty. But I'm pretty sure he's easily frightened. Here's my plan. I'll tempt him. I'll invite him here. And when he comes, we'll scare the pants off him so he never thinks of coming near here or calling again."

"But how?" said Jennifer.

"I haven't really thought this out. But it wouldn't take much. Just a little bit of vampire or witch make-up, pointed teeth like you buy in costume shops, weird noises. You get the picture."

"But suppose he came armed."

"You don't have to worry about that," said Denise, who was now getting into the spirit of Marjorie's plan. "I can deal with armed men. I have a black belt in karate."

"Really?" Marjorie was impressed.

"I needed one to survive in the area I grew up in."

"That's a big advantage. So it's a darkened living room, a recording of Hallowe'en music, and someone in costume to greet him at the door. Denise, you're up for it. What about you, Jen? If you have any doubts or scruples, say so now."

"I actually think it sounds like fun," said Jennifer.

"Good. You'll have to improvise costumes, you know."

"Sure. A torn sheet and plenty of white make-up would probably do for me." Jennifer was warming to the idea.

"I'd like to do something more elaborate, with a cloak and a pointed hat," said Denise.

"We might even make a witches' cauldron and think up some spells." Marjorie turned toward Madeleine, wondering how she would react to this piece of stagecraft. "You don't have to be involved at all, Madeleine."

"Oh, but I want to. I wouldn't miss it for anything in the world."

Marjorie was astonished and pleased. Unity in the house, for once! "A week from today, if he agrees to come. And we must show fortitude and determination. And no giggling."

*   *   *

Marjorie called Leroy that very evening to invite him over the following Saturday. She expected him to be hostile and possibly turn her down, but instead he was contrite, even humble.

"I just want to see you again, babe," he whined. "I've been missing you."

Marjorie's vanity was appeased but her resolve remained unbroken. "Come about eight," she said. "We'll go out for a drink somewhere."

The following Saturday night, the four young women met in the dining room at about seven thirty. They had put up cabalistic signs in the front windows, and Denise had borrowed drums from a friend, whose throbbing, punctuated by an occasional shriek— Jennifer had an earsplitting scream—would provide adequate background music.

Marjorie, Jennifer and Denise had made themselves up in fairly traditional witch style, with faces painted white, black circles around the eyes, and long, trailing dresses. Denise had added claw-like false fingernails. But Madeleine had gone all out. She had made her face a ghastly yellowish hue, painted her teeth orange, and strewn light gray yarn through her tousled hair to resemble cobwebs. She was wearing a tattered nightgown, dripping gray yarn, and her feet were bare, the large toenails painted black.

"My God, you do look a fright," said Denise. "What is that thing on your neck?" Denise pointed to an ugly mark that looked like a wound, extending from just under her chin to the side of her neck.

"Oh, that. It's a bacon rind I dipped in ketchup. I hope it stays on. I stuck it on with a piece of tape."

Marjorie was astonished. She didn't think Madeleine had it in her.

"I had planned to go to the door and invite Leroy in," she said. "But I've changed my mind. I think you should go to the door, Maddie. Will you do it?"

"With the utmost pleasure," Madeleine replied, in a voice that started as a screech and ended as a quaver.

The doorbell rang just before eight. The three girls followed Madeleine closely as she went to the door. Because the space was relatively narrow and because Madeleine filled it with her billowing gown, they couldn't see what was happening.

It was over very quickly.

Madeleine opened the door and her quavering voice was heard saying "Good evening." Then she turned away and shut the door.

"That's that," she said, pulling off the bits of cobwebby yarn. "He's gone. Judging by the expression on his face, I don't think he'll be back soon."

"Think of it. You're more intimidating than Moses!"

"Who's Moses?"

"He was one of the guys who came to do sculpting last term. Black, six feet four, weighing what?"

"A hundred and eighty pounds, all muscle," said Denise.

"Anyway, well done," said Marjorie. "Many thanks. Come on. Let's have a celebratory drink."

The four moved back into the dining room and sat under the twinkling light of the great chandelier. Marjorie uncorked a bottle of white wine that was sitting on the sideboard and filled four glasses. She was pleased with herself and delighted with her housemates.

"I know you don't drink, Madeleine," she said, "but maybe you'll make an exception for this occasion."

"No, I'll get myself a glass of water from the kitchen."

"Well, I hope she's right," said Jennifer as the three raised their glasses. "I hope he never comes back. Remember, Marjorie, you thought he was gone before."

"To the permanent disappearance of Leroy Patterson," said Marjorie. "From all of our lives."

Madeleine came back with her glass of water. She had started to remove her make-up and looked, if anything, more ghoulish.

"Don't you have any vices, Madeleine?" said Denise. "Wouldn't you like a chocolate as a reward for your good work? Or even a box of chocolates?"

"Having vices is a deliberate choice," said Madeleine quite seriously. "I've chosen not to have any."

"You don't know what you're missing!" said Denise.

"Leroy Patterson was vicious and didn't seem to realize it," said Marjorie.

"What a horrible man!" Jennifer had finished her first glass of wine and poured herself another. "Anyone else?" The two others nodded and had their glasses refilled. Jennifer looked searchingly at Marjorie. "That business with Leroy must have been terrible for you. Was that why you . . . disappeared at the end of the semester?"

"No, the Leroy business was much earlier," said Marjorie. "At the end of the semester, it was something else." She hesitated. For the first time since the nasty incident occurred, Marjorie wanted to talk about it. It might have been the wine or the sense of camaraderie in facing off against Leroy, but she felt reckless. She wanted to open up to her housemates.

"It actually involved a professor," she said finally. "A professor who did something quite nasty. And probably quite illegal."

"Wonderful," said Denise. "Give us the lurid details. I love lurid details."

Marjorie told the whole story of "The School of Donne," the class, the professor, Terrence Sneed's plagiarism and Dr. Frazier's collusion, but omitting details of her affair with Rayburn. She was surprised at the relief she felt unburdening herself of the whole sordid business. The three others listened attentively. Marjorie told the story quickly, feeling a growing rage as she remembered Sneed's face confronting her in the classroom.

"But why didn't you tell me what was happening?" asked Jennifer when Marjorie had finished. "Why did you keep it to yourself?"

"I wanted to tell you, Jen. But it was so complicated. And I guess my behavior wasn't always very admirable." She took a deep breath, unsure if she should continue. "You see," she said finally, "I was going with someone else while I was dating Clive." Marjorie took a quick look at Jennifer, but her expression was unchanged. "Sneed threatened to tell Clive I was two-timing him, so I backed down. As it happens, I shouldn't have backed down." Marjorie's throat suddenly felt dry. She took a sip of wine. "He told Clive anyway."

Jennifer let out a breath, "So that's why."

"I didn't break up with Clive, Jennifer. He broke up with me."

Madeleine, who had been restless for some time, stood up. "You deserved what you got," she said in disgust. "'Let him who is without sin cast the first stone.' I'm going to bed." She got up and left the room.

"I don't think she got the spirit of the biblical quote quite right," said Jennifer.

"Well, good Christian or not, Madeleine has never demonstrated a spirit of charity," said Denise. "Let's finish off the wine." They had already been through one bottle and were starting a second. "You know, Marjorie," she continued, pouring herself a glass. "There may still be some way of getting justice to prevail."

"By this time I'm sure it's too late. All this happened last semester." Having told the others about Terrence Sneed and Dr. Frazier, Marjorie no longer wanted to discuss the matter.

"It's just too bad you didn't tell us at the time," said Denise. "We might have been able to help."

"I don't know. The whole thing was such a mess. And I suppose I was a teensy bit embarrassed about carrying on that affair . . ."

Denise was intrigued. "Who was it, Marjorie? Was it anyone we know?"

"He's not at the University anymore. He was a visiting professor of Renaissance Literature last semester."

Denise laughed out loud. "Marjorie, you never cease to amaze me! That's quite a feather in your cap. A visiting professor, no less!"

Marjorie was quite surprised at Denise's reaction, and looking back, she wondered why she had been so secretive about her antics of the first semester. It might have helped, perhaps, if she had had some support. But no, she couldn't imagine confiding her secrets to anyone, even to Jennifer. And now she wanted to put the whole incident behind her. It seemed to have happened long ago, in a different life.

"Well, that's all over now," said Marjorie. She thought about Clive frequently, missing him, but she had hardly thought about Charles Rayburn since the end of the first term. "And I don't want to revive any of the sordid affair of plagiarism."

"Too bad," said Denise, draining the rest of her wine. "I like to see bastards get their just desserts!" Then leaning toward Marjorie she said, "But tell me honestly, did you really sleep with one of the professors? What was he like?"

By now the three had polished off the second bottle of wine and were quite tipsy.

"He was . . ." Marjorie started and then stopped herself. Why should she tell Denise the intimate details of her sex life? "I'll tell you some other time."

Denise sighed and got up. "Never mind. Anyone for a nightcap at Nick's?"

But the two others declined. Even on Sundays, the Fielding School stretched its sticky tentacles into their free time. Besides, they were both exhausted by the evening's endeavors.

*   *   *

Marjorie saw Denise the following Friday night. It was close to eleven o'clock and Marjorie had gone down to the kitchen to get a snack. Denise was frying bacon and eggs.

"So that's what I smelled," said Marjorie. "It's given me an appetite."

"Did you think any more about taking up that plagiarism case you told us about?" Denise asked, flipping her egg.

"Oh, that." Marjorie had stuck her head in the refrigerator and was trying to decide what she wanted. She found an old container of spaghetti and sniffed it tentatively. "I've decided to let it drop. It's old history now, really. And if I raised the issue now, it could backfire on me." She imagined Terrence Sneed bringing up details of her private life in front of a university committee.

"Too bad." Denise took a couple of slices of bread out of the toaster and sat down at the kitchen table to eat. "I hate to the bastards get away with their shit."

"At this point, the less I have to do with those people, the better." Marjorie put back the spaghetti and looked more deeply into the recesses of the refrigerator. She closed the refrigerator door and sat down opposite Denise. "I just want to put it all behind me. Do you know what I mean?"

"Not really. I like to see my enemies suffer. But it's your decision." Denise flipped her egg onto her plate and looked up at Marjorie. "By the way, aren't you eating anything?"

"The refrigerator smells sort of took away my appetite. Mind if I have a bite of your toast?"

"Oh, for God's sake, Marge." Denise batted away Marjorie's outstretched hand. "Don't be a parasite. Make your own."

Marjorie stretched lazily, wondering if she wanted to be bothered. Life seemed so busy and stressful now; making a piece of toast would be a gigantic effort.

"Oh Marjorie," Denise was tucking into her fried egg, which now looked slimy and repulsive to Marjorie. "I wanted to ask you something." She paused, her fork halfway to her mouth. "Would you be willing to pose for me? I'd like to do your portrait."

Marjorie, flattered, tried to appear indifferent. "Knowing your style, Denise, I'd be worried that you'd give me two noses. Or make me into a pure black canvas."

"No, I do representational, too, Marge. And quite well. You'll be surprised."

"Well . . . my time is pretty limited."

"Give me just a couple of hours three or four Sundays. Surely you can spare that."

"Umm . . ."

"Good. As you may have noticed, I'm not painting in the living room anymore. I have a wonderful space in our communal studio at the Institute. Meet me here Sunday at eleven (A.M., I mean) and I'll take you there."

"But why?"

"Why what?"

"Why do you want to paint my portrait?"

"I don't know. There's something in your expression I'd like to capture on canvas." Denise was sopping up the egg yolk with a piece of toast. "I can never explain why a subject grabs me. It just does."

"And one more thing. Why are you eating breakfast at eleven o'clock at night?"

"None of your business." Denise had finished and was running hot water over her plate. "Then it's agreed. We'll meet here on Sunday at eleven."

*   *   *

The studio where Denise now did her artwork turned out to be an astonishing place. When they arrived there the following Sunday morning, Marjorie discovered a repository of half-finished projects—sculptures, paintings, collages—stuff cluttered every corner of the giant room and even hung from the ceiling. As Marjorie came in the door, she almost collided with a partial staircase, painted vibrant orange, suspended at eye level. A gigantic plastic model of an eyeball bounced backwards and forwards across the floor. Three-dimensional figures of angels popped out of the walls. And easels were set up everywhere, showing every imaginable style of painting. At first Marjorie was startled, but as she looked around, she became enthralled. It was so different from the sterile world of school, so full of unexpected encounters, so spontaneous.

Denise began setting up an easel at one side of the room. She greeted Marjorie and had her sit on a broken-down easy chair, spread with a colorful shawl that had been damaged by moths. Marjorie sat gingerly, wondering if it could harbor fleas and even more worried about the stability of the chair itself.

"Wouldn't it be better if I stood?"

"I think you'll find it hard enough to keep a pose when you're comfortably seated." Denise was positioning her easel and getting out her paints. She looked at Marjorie critically. "You look as if you're about to fly away. Sit back. Now turn your head slightly to the left. That's it." Denise put her hand on Marjorie's chin and moved it. She was back at the easel in a flash, sketching furiously.

"Is this where you've been spending all your time recently?" Marjorie asked. "I hardly ever see you at the Charles Street house."

Denise said nothing for a few minutes. She was concentrating deeply on her sketch. "Marjorie," she said finally, "I'm going to have to ask you not to talk. It distracts me and it makes you change position."

The rest of the session passed in silence. A couple of students came in, a gangly young man in torn jeans and a filthy tee shirt with blonde curls cascading down his back and a radiantly beautiful young women in a paint-spattered smock. Both greeted Denise briefly and nodded at Marjorie. They looked at Denise's work, made encouraging gestures, and went on to do their own work in virtual silence. Marjorie was impressed by their level of seriousness.

The time dragged on. Marjorie's neck was sore, her bottom was beginning to go to sleep, and her arms and legs were numb. Eventually, just as she was on the verge of screaming, Denise called for a break. "Let's go to the Commons Room," she said. "They won't be serving on a Sunday, but at least at least we'll be able to stretch our legs. Cigarette?"

"No, I don't smoke, and I didn't think you did."

"Oh, just the occasional puff." Denise was lighting up as they walked down the corridor. The Commons Room was in the same building, on the same floor. It was open but empty except for a couple in deep conversation. As Denise said, no food was being served, but there was a lingering odor of French fry fat mingling with paint and old cigarette smoke. They took a table and sat down.

"To answer the question you put to me when we started, yes, I am spending quite a bit of time in the studio. But I also have a job, working in a local gallery."

"Ah, yes, I think you told me that at the beginning of the semester. Does it pay well?"

"It pays peanuts. But it's a question of contacts. Getting to know the art world and its patrons."

Marjorie only had a faint idea of what that meant. "It might lead somewhere?"

"Yes, and then the gallery owner . . ."

At this moment the lanky art student came in. Denise broke off in mid-sentence. "Oh, hi, Greg. This is my model, Marjorie."

"Hi, Marjorie." Greg sat down at a nearby table, his long legs folded like a grasshopper's. "What's up?" He extracted a joint from his jeans pocket and offered it to the girls who shook their heads. Greg then smoked his joint in silence, his back turned toward them.

"So Marjorie," said Denise, obviously wanting to change the subject, "What's new with you? School going well?"

"Classes are more or less okay, but it's all the meetings that get me down. Next week it's the P.T.A., and I've got to do a little talk for the parents of each of the classes. To bring them into the picture, I guess."

Denise inhaled smoke from her cigarette. "It's all a pain."

"Yes, it takes time and concentration and a lot of energy."

"You don't go out much, do you?"

Marjorie shook her head regretfully. This was a painful subject for her. "I try not to think about it. But it feels as if life is passing me by."

Greg twitched slightly and looked over his shoulder at Marjorie but then went back to his joint.

"Do you want me to fix you up with someone? There are some neat guys in the course."

Marjorie shook her head. "I'll just have to postpone living," she said. "It's only a few more months."

"The whole thing sounds like a drag to me. Maybe you should think of a career change."

Marjorie felt a surge of anger as though she had been attacked. "I love teaching, Denise. I wouldn't change it for anything."

Denise shrugged. "Well, if it's what you like . . . We'd better get back to the session. I'd like to make a little headway before I release you."

"May I see your sketch?"

"Nope. Not until it's finished. Or possibly when I've made real headway."

*   *   *

The night of the P.T.A. meeting, an evening in mid-March, it rained torrentially. Jennifer called Joyce Kettlehut to see if the meeting had been canceled. But no, Joyce said, it would take more than six inches of rain to make the Fielding School administration call off an all-important P.T.A. meeting.

So Joyce came around early to pick them up. It was rather earlier than necessary, 6:15 for a seven o'clock meeting. Marjorie, who was having an uncomfortable period and had bolted a peanut butter sandwich, felt decidedly queasy. She had prepared four little talks for the parents of her four groups, but they were similar, consisting of clichés off the top of her head about the importance of learning English grammar and the value of literature. She was afraid they wouldn't go down well and was hoping few parents would come.

It proved to be a long evening. She gave her little speech to small groups of the parents of the ninth, eleventh and twelfth graders and had very little reaction. Several parents came up to see her afterwards and shook her hand, saying their child enjoyed her class, but no one had much to say and she received no complaints.

Unfortunately, the tenth grade, her problem group, was last. It was only a little after eight, but she was exhausted. She stood behind the desk, sipping water from a paper cup and looking at the bulletin board on the Victorian novelists, which had been done by some of the loyal twelfth graders.

Little by little the parents came in. Evidently it was still raining, for they were stomping water from their shoes and shaking their raincoats. Two middle-aged couples came in together, followed by a single professional-looking woman. There was a silence, the five faces looking expectantly at her. Then she began, repeating more or less the same little speech she had made to the other groups. She was hoping her bearing and her perfect diction somehow compensated for the stupidity of what she was saying.

"I'm available now for questions about individual students," she said, and took a little gasping breath. To her surprise, she heard light applause from the back of the room. It was a man wearing a mackintosh, dripping rain, leaning against the far wall. She had only a minute to observe him because one of the couples was closing in on her.

"I'm Robert Knightly senior, and this is my wife Rita." said the man, a pink-faced rodent—like individual in a tight fitting suit. His wife was small and angry-looking with a rash across one cheek. "We object to your treatment of our son, Bob junior. And probably other students too. You have terrorized him to the point where he dreads going to school. We think you should change your attitude. We have cause for complaint to the administration."

"In the first place, you're exaggerating unreasonably," said Marjorie. She was having cramps now and was in no mood to be conciliatory. "I doubt that I could terrorize anyone and especially not a healthy young man like your son. In the second place, Bob Junior deserves to be disciplined. In fact, he requires discipline. I must discipline him, both for his own sake and for the sake of the class."

"But he's quite seriously . . ."

"How can I carry on a lecture with pupils like your son creating a constant ruckus?"

"But Bobbie's a good boy. In his other classes . . ."

"I would question that. His classroom behavior is totally unacceptable."

Mrs. Knightly face was crumpling up. She was about to cry.

"Come on, Rita," said her husband. "Obviously this is getting us nowhere. We'll have to take this up with the school administration."

"That is certainly your prerogative," said Marjorie, determined not to appear intimidated. She wondered what repercussions this might have. Was the other couple also there to complain? The two couples hustled out of the room, leaving Marjorie with only the professional-looking woman and the man in the wet mackintosh.

"Gilda Crabtree," said the woman, approaching and shaking Marjorie's hand. "I'm Elsa's mother and I personally want to congratulate you. I think you're doing a fine job."

Marjorie made a few quick comments on Elsa's progress—she had in fact improved greatly—and checked her watch. "I think our time is almost up. Thank you so much for coming." Mrs. Crabtree went out, leaving Marjorie alone with the man in the mackintosh.

"I know you're tired and probably want to go home," he said, "but I just wanted to second what Mrs. Crabtree said." His voice was gravelly, with a distinct New England accent. "I'm Franklin Forsythe, and I have to say you've done wonders with my daughter."

Marjorie searched her memory for a tenth grader with the surname of Forsythe. She always used first names in class.

"Helena."

Of course, Helena. A very quiet, retiring girl in the last row. With long, dark eyelashes and curly brown hair.

"Helena. A lovely girl. A pleasure to have in class." Marjorie was exaggerating. Helena was a neutral entity in class. She never spoke.

"Look, Miss Dunnock, can we speak for a minute? I realize it's late, but I have a proposition to make to you, one that could be mutually beneficial."

Marjorie was aching to go home, kick off her shoes, and pour herself a glass of wine. But there was something about this man's bearing that made her feel it was important to let him talk. Besides, her curiosity was aroused. What proposition could he be making? She sank down into the chair behind her desk. Franklin Forsythe, the mackintosh now slung over one arm, came to the front of the room. He was old, of course, in his early or even mid-forties, and quite distinguished-looking. He had a broad, intelligent forehead, rather curly graying hair and an expression of self-satisfaction. He looked as though he was used to getting his own way.

"What is it that you have in mind, Mr. Forsythe?"

"It's my son Richard. Ricky, we call him. He's several years younger than Helena, nine, in fact. He's having a bit of trouble with his spelling. His apostrophes especially seem to be an obstacle. Perhaps you could help out by tutoring him."

"I'm sorry. You must realize how busy we apprentice teachers are. I hardly have any free time." Marjorie quickly calculated that a nine-year-old who was still having trouble with his apostrophes would be pretty far behind.

"It would only be a couple of hours a week. My chauffeur would pick you up after school twice a week and take you back home, wherever you live."

"Well, I don't have much experience with kids that age. You might do better to hire an elementary school teacher."

"To be honest, Miss Dunnock, I'd prefer to hire someone I know at least by reputation. Someone who has a firm hand with young people. And I'd be willing to pay you twenty-five dollars an hour." Marjorie looked at him in astonishment. Five dollars would have been a princely sum. Twenty-five was staggering. "And another thing," Mr. Forsythe continued. "I'm a prominent lawyer. My firm is Forsythe, Forsythe and Pennington. Well known in Baltimore for twenty-five years. If you ever have a legal problem, I might be able to help you."

A legal problem. Marjorie scanned his face for signs of irony. "But why would a person my age have a legal problem?"

"You'd be surprised, Miss Dunnock. People have legal problems at any age. It's always beneficial to have a good lawyer on your side."

*   *   *

And so Marjorie accepted a job she was completely unsuited for.

The first day she was supposed to meet young Richard Forsythe, the chauffeur turned up outside the main entrance to the school. Liveried, no less. An elderly, courtly man, he escorted her to the limousine he was driving. Marjorie looked around to see if she was attracting attention, but Fielding School pupils took such indications of wealth in stride.

The chauffeur was discreetly silent as he drove toward the Forsythe's residence. It was located in a leafy suburb, set back from the road, with almost as much well-tended lawn as the Fielding School campus. When the chauffeur stopped the limousine at the back entrance, he turned to Marjorie. His face was kindly and deeply creased around the mouth and eyes.

"Working with young Master Forsythe?"

Marjorie nodded.

"Good luck."

Marjorie climbed the short flight of steps leading to the rear entrance of an imposing house. She was angry that as a professional she was being treated as a servant or tradesperson. There was no one at the door to receive her. She let herself in and looked around. She was in a sort of small reception room overlooking the back lawn.

As she entered the room and saw young Richard for the first time, she got a terrific shock. She had expected her new pupil to be quiet like his sister, or perhaps even slightly retarded. Instead she saw a young boy using the sofa as a trampoline, jumping up and down and sometimes landing on the floor to jump back onto the sofa again. While he did this, from his lips issued a stream of obscenities the likes of which Marjorie had never heard before.

Her first thought was, "I mustn't let him see how shocked I am!"

"Richard Forsythe," she said in her loudest voice. "Stop that immediately!"

The child paid absolutely no attention to her but continued to jump up and down, shouting all the time.

"All right," said Marjorie, "just keep on doing it." She sat down beside a small table that had been set up for tutoring. She figured the kid would have to wear himself out, not realizing that he had more energy than she had patience. After putting up with the row for a few minutes, she could stand it no longer. She lunged forward and seized Ricky by the feet, causing him to fall over. Then she seated him forcibly at the table. Fortunately, he was small for his age and relatively light. Ricky looked at Marjorie in astonishment. He evidently wasn't used to being manhandled by young women.

"My name is Miss Dunnock," she said sternly. "And I'm here to help you with your spelling."

"I hate spelling," proclaimed Richard Forsythe. "Ugh, ugh, ugh."

"I don't care what your personal feelings are." Marjorie took out the book one of the Fielding School Elementary teachers had loaned her, turned to page 1, and began an explanation of the apostrophes. It was futile. Richard only sat still for a few minutes, saying "ugh, ugh, ugh" repeatedly like a mechanical toy. Then he began to run in circles around the room.

Marjorie had no idea what to do. She was about to look for a member of the Forsythe staff and tell him or her to get the chauffeur to take her home. But suddenly Ricky stopped his circling and came to sit beside her at the table.

"What's your name?" he asked, looking at her for the first time.

"I'm Miss Dunnock, your tutor."

"Tutor, tudie, toilet," chanted Ricky. "You look like a horse. Horse face. That's what I'll call you. Miss Horseface Toilet." And he laughed in glee.

"And I'll call you Nightmare," said Marjorie. "Where's your mother?"

"Dunno, dunno, dunno." Ricky gave an exaggerated shrug. "Why do you care?"

"Because I'm going straight to see her. And tell her how badly you're behaving."

This apparently made an impression on Ricky, who must have at least been afraid of his mother. He settled down at that point and they were able to complete a page and a half of exercises before the chauffeur appeared to take Marjorie home.

"Would it be possible to speak to Mrs. Forsythe?" she said to the chauffeur as they made their way to the limousine.

The chauffeur gave her a complicit look. "I take it this is in regard to the comportment of young Richard."

"That child is impossible. Unteachable, I'd say."

"Quite so, Miss. You're not the first to make that observation. I'll get the message to Mrs. Forsythe. She may be able to see you after the next lesson."

*   *   *

Marjorie met Imogene Forsythe the following Thursday. This time a chamber maid met her at the front door and escorted her across the living room to an open space, furnished only by two white sofas facing each other with a coffee table between them. A massive oak staircase swept down into the middle of this area, which was brightly lit by a skylight some two stories above.

Marjorie sat down on one of the white sofas and waited. What was this woman like, she wondered. What kind of woman would attract Franklin Forsythe? What kind of woman would strike fear in the breast of young Richard?

Presently Mrs. Forsythe appeared, not using the grand staircase, as Marjorie had predicted, but from some room at the back. She was a small but very upright woman, with a pointed nose and an intense, hard stare. She looked at least ten years older than her husband.

She sat down stiffly. It seemed as though none of the joints in her body could move freely.

"Miss Dunnock," she intoned without introducing herself. Her voice was too deep for her small ribcage. "It seems my son is a challenge you have failed to meet."

Another intimidating woman! Marjorie resolved not to lose her composure. "I think your son has serious problems, Mrs. Forsythe," she said. "He needs professional help, but not from a teacher."

"Nonsense. Richard is merely an active child. Perhaps he needs to be taken in hand from time to time, but a competent teacher could surely manage him."

"He's not teachable. He can't sit still long enough to learn anything. He's totally uncontrollable."

"And so, Miss Dunnock," said Mrs. Forsythe, fixing her with her glassy stare. "You are giving up. My husband told me you were a professional. Professionals don't quit a job they have agreed to do."

So now this Mrs. Forsythe was insulting Marjorie. She sat up very straight. She had nothing to lose if she got fired from this job. She could afford to be brutally honest. "I can only repeat that your son isn't teachable," she said. "Until he gets some harsh discipline or some psychiatric help, I don't think the most gifted teacher in the world would get through to him."

"So you are going to quit? I must tell you that if you do, the Fielding School will have a negative report from us."

"The Fielding School knows my ability as a teacher. I have been observed and my work has been noted as satisfactory, if not superior," Marjorie lied, maintaining her exterior composure. "If I stay on it's out of consideration for your husband, who seems like a reasonable man."

Mrs. Forsythe showed her perfect little teeth in a semblance of a smile. Her lipstick was far too bright. "You will stay with us, then. I think you won't regret it." She rang a little bell for the maid to escort Marjorie to the door and left the room without saying good-bye.

*   *   *

"But I don't understand why you didn't quit on the spot," said Denise. It was the following Sunday afternoon, and they had taken a break from the painting session.

"Well, I don't fully understand myself. It isn't the money, though the money is fabulous. And Mrs. Forsythe's threat didn't really worry me. I suppose it must be the challenge," Marjorie concluded unconvincingly.

"What about the good-looking lawyer husband?" Denise gave Marjorie a penetrating look, her eyes narrowed. "Don't tell me he doesn't play a part in all this."

"Quite honestly, I'm not interested. He's too old, too established, too staid. Besides, I haven't even seen him since I started tutoring Ricky."

"But isn't that the carrot dangling in front of you? With a wife like that, Mr. Forsythe is surely in need of a little diversion."

"Denise, a wife like that would exact a terrible revenge." Marjorie thought of the cold, colorless eyes, the rigid back, the perfect little teeth behind the blood-red smile. "No, I wouldn't want to get involved with Franklin. The price would be far too high."

"Well, let's get back to the studio," said Denise. "I'm not sure how many hours of perfect light are left."

"So you can include all the worry wrinkles this is causing me."

"I won't spare you a single one."

*　　*　　*

Marjorie, without fully understanding why, was still tutoring Ricky at midterm in April. Of course she had devised strategies to deal with him, if not to control him. She had discovered a basketball hoop near the servants' entrance to the mansion. As a reward for concentrating—theoretically for a half hour, but in fact for far less—Marjorie would let Ricky shoot baskets with her. She wasn't especially athletic but her height gave her an advantage, and she was occasionally able to land a shot. Running around the court released some of Ricky's pent-up energy but did nothing to improve his manners. He called her "Horseshit face" and "Stinking toilet," and proclaimed her a rotten basketball player as well as a rotten tutor. He did turn out to have a photographic memory, until then only practiced on certain things like baseball scores going back to the 1930's. Marjorie was able to take advantage of this on the rare occasions when he concentrated. But something did stick, and Marjorie learned, not from Mrs. Forsythe or Ricky himself, but from the chauffeur, that he had actually passed a test.

"Congratulations, Miss," he said when he picked her up one afternoon. "You have achieved something that no one else has been able to do."

*　　*　　*

Suddenly it was spring break. Marjorie had been so busy that she hadn't seen the time go by. She and Jennifer had to make up and administer midterm exams. In Marjorie's case these elicited complaints because of their extreme difficulty.

"You're not in school to mess around and regurgitate facts," she told her senior students. "You have to start learning to think for yourselves, to analyze." This brought a groan from the boys and serious, worried looks from the girls.

Jennifer was now holding her head above water. She had gained status with her students by telling scabrous and mainly fictitious stories about her experiences in Paris. Her exams were thorough but scrupulously fair, which some students appreciated.

And now the two, having given exams, had to grade them, compute midterm grades and write individual reports on each of their students. Marjorie left Charles Street with a briefcase so heavy that it stretched the muscles of her arm. She was taking the train to spend a largely empty two weeks with her boring parents in Westchester County. She arrived home to a place that had never seemed much like home and settled in. Almost immediately, she was able to take over her father's study as he was usually working in the city. She spent most of her time grading exams and writing reports. In between times she gazed out the window, thinking of the house on Charles Street, the comings and goings of her housemates, Jennifer's struggles. Stressful as it was at times, she missed her life there. Her parents' house, with its sparse wooden furniture and neutral colors, seemed cold and empty.

Marjorie's mother occasionally came to the study with a cup of bouillon and a solicitous expression. "You're very quiet in there, dear," she would say. "Are you all right?" Marjorie's parents had always been very distant, very tall, very distinguished people, who paid the bills and worried about her morals. Marjorie had become resigned over the years to feeling little connection to them.

Most of Marjorie's high school friends had moved away and had full-time jobs. She went out once or twice with an old sweetheart, Simon Pollard, but things never took off. Simon was doing graduate work at Brooklyn College and dating an astonishing girl who ran marathons and was getting a Ph.D. in astrophysics. He couldn't stop talking about her achievements to Marjorie.

She got back to Charles Street on a rainy April evening. She was feeling mildly depressed but glad to have finished her grading and to escape the chill atmosphere of her parents' house. The lights were already on in the living room. Jennifer met her at the door, smiling a self-satisfied smile that to Marjorie shouted "boyfriend."

She went in, took off her mackintosh and laid her briefcase on the coffee table. There was something odd, subtly changed about the atmosphere in the house. She gazed at her friend. "Well, Jennifer, you look happy. What's up?"

"We have a guest!" Jennifer paused for dramatic effect. "Madeleine's brother Hank is visiting from Harrisburg."

This wasn't welcome news to Marjorie, who felt there were already too many conflicting interests in the house. "Oh, no. Not a relative of Madeleine's! Where is he sleeping? Is he planning to stay for long?"

"Don't worry, Marge. He's not at all like Madeleine. He's working out his future. He isn't sure what he's going to do with his life."

"That means he's probably going to stay indefinitely. Oh, well, I hope he contributes to the grocery bills."

"You must meet him, Marge. He's absolutely charming."

"I don't see how I could avoid meeting him if he's living here."

Although Hank proved to be unobtrusive to the point of virtual invisibility, there were always uncomfortable reminders of his presence. Marjorie tended to bump into him as she raced downstairs to get a cup of coffee before leaving for school or trip over his giant backpack on the living room floor. As for Hank himself, he struck Marjorie as being too young to be on his own; his eyes, magnified by very thick glasses, seemed permanently surprised by the newness of the world.

Madeleine never brought up the subject of her brother's visit to Marjorie, who found this annoying. But then, Marjorie didn't actually care enough to make an issue of the young man's presence; she was busy and she seldom even saw Madeleine. But something else bothered her. She sensed there was something going on between Hank and Jennifer. Sometimes when she and Jennifer came home from school, Hank would be there waiting. His face would light up when he saw Jennifer. The two would then fly up to Jennifer's room for a session of smooching and whatever else they dared to do. It seemed like an adolescent attraction, and it made Marjorie uncomfortable. Jennifer was chronologically at least four years older than Hank, though the two were emotionally the same age. "Could I be envious?" Marjorie asked herself, thinking of her own empty love life. No, no, certainly not. She felt she had passed that stage, lifetimes ago.

In any event, she was too busy to pay much attention to Jennifer's love life, or to her own for that matter. Now, in addition to school and curriculum committee meetings, she modeled for Denise on Sunday mornings and had tutoring sessions with Ricky Forsythe, which were more exhausting than an entire day of teaching. Modeling was the least stressful activity of the week, despite the physical discomfort. Marjorie liked to go to the Art Institute, where she could forget the worries of teaching. Besides, she had grown fond of Denise. Denise was somebody without pretense, somebody she always felt comfortable with.

Marjorie had taken to arriving a little early for modeling to have a look around the studio and see the work in progress. One morning in late April as she entered the studio she got tangled up in a mobile of garishly painted butterflies. She bent down to escape the colorful insects and found a pile of surrealistic paintings, which she rifled through. The paintings showed arms and legs growing out of the ground and sprouting leaves, mountains exploding into fire, dragons with human heads. As Marjorie was bending over to look more closely at these canvasses, Denise came in.

"Hi, Marge, sorry to be late. As usual." Marjorie stood up and turned to face Denise. Denise, red-faced, out of breath and perspiring. She was wearing an enormous, loose-fitting smock, smirched with paint smears, which made her seem even bigger than she was.

"What do you think of that stuff?" She asked. "Pretty bizarre, eh?"

"I sort of like them. It's like entering a different world. A dream world."

"Actually, these were done as exercises. To practice a style." Denise went to a cupboard at one side of the studio and began to get out her paints.

"As an exercise, that's a lot more fun than diagramming sentences. You know, Denise," she added, "when I come here, I feel as though I'm escaping the boring adult world of responsibility and entering a child's world, a world of fun and fantasy."

Denise, standing in front of her easel and mixing paints, looked at her solemnly with her wide-spaced grey eyes. "The creation of art is no child's play," she said. "It's a serious business!"

Marjorie looked at Denise closely, trying to tell if she was pulling her leg. "I'm sure it is. It's just that . . . when I look at this art, when I feel it, it takes me back to a time in my adolescence. A time when I retreated into my own fantasy world. I was pretty lonely as a teen-ager."

"Yeah? I didn't have much time for fantasy when I was a teen-ager. My father died when I was fourteen. My mother was depressed, and I had to take care of my little brother."

Marjorie was taken aback. She knew nothing of Denise's background. Or of her childhood. "I'm so sorry to hear that," she said.

"Well, shit happens. Actually, my dad's death helped me to be more self-reliant." Denise's eyes became soft and unfocussed. "I do miss him, though, you know."

Marjorie couldn't think of anything to say.

"Well, come on, we'd better get started," said Denise. Marjorie took her place on the shawl-covered easy chair, and Denise positioned her head.

Stepping back to the canvas, Denise lifted the cover she had put over it. She scanned her work. "I didn't realize! Marge, are you ready for this? I've almost finished the portrait. If you like, you can have a look at it."

"What, now?" Marjorie suddenly felt as nervous as if she were going into an exam.

"Yes. Ready?" Denise beckoned Marjorie to come to her side. "Still a few finishing touches, and then that's it. Well, what do you think?"

Marjorie gasped. She was looking at a woman, not a young girl as she imagined herself. This was someone with depth and experience, someone with strength and maturity. The eyes of the young woman looked straight ahead at the observer, but they were luminous, as though she had seen a vision.

"Is that me?" She was unable to match this face with the girlish innocent one she saw every morning in the bathroom mirror.

"That's you," said Denise.

*   *   *

It was that afternoon, feeling slightly disoriented by this new image of herself, when Marjorie returned to the house to find Jennifer in tears on the living room couch. She didn't even move when Marjorie came in, but continued to sob in a high keening moan which occasionally broke into hiccups. Marjorie sat down beside her and pulled her to a sitting position. She was as limp as a dead fish.

"Good God, Jennifer. What is the matter?"

Jennifer said nothing, but as Marjorie held her, her sobs tapered off slightly.

"It's Hank." Marjorie knew instinctively. Jennifer nodded. It took her a few minutes before she was able to speak and even then she was barely coherent.

"Hank's gone," she kept repeating. "Gone."

"But what happened? Did you have a fight?"

"No. It was so perfect. It was Madeleine. Madeleine." Jennifer began to sob again.

"Look," said Marjorie. "I'm going into the kitchen to get you a glass of water. While I'm gone, I want you to pull yourself together so you can explain what happened."

When Marjorie came back, Jennifer was sitting up, an enormous wad of kleenix in her hand. She looked a terrible wreck, her nose bright red and her eyes almost swollen shut. Taking the glass of water into her hand, she launched into her tale of woe. It turned out that she was more enraged than bereaved. "It was Madeleine," she hissed. "That sanctimonious bitch. That arrogant hypocrite. She marched right into my room. Hank and I were . . ."

"Making love?"

"No, no. We weren't even holding hands. We didn't . . . But she . . . She started shouting, hurling accusations at me." Jennifer paused to blow her nose. "She said I was corrupting her brother. She called me a whore."

Marjorie had to restrain herself from smiling. "And what did Hank say?"

"He didn't say anything. He left. Late this morning. He packed his backpack and left."

"He'll probably go trekking in the Himalayas," thought Marjorie, but she only said, "I'm not surprised. He probably was too embarrassed to look you in the face. His big sister was treating him like a witless child."

"That's all you can say? The only man who has ever loved me and that's all you can say?"

"Jennifer, use your head. If Hank really loves you, he won't lose touch. I wouldn't be surprised if you got a letter quite soon from some far-flung corner of the world."

"But suppose he doesn't really love me?"

"Then, alas my dear Jennifer, what have you lost?" Marjorie looked critically at her friend, trying not to show her exasperation. Jennifer looked an awful mess, and, even worse, she seemed to have lost all notion of self-respect. "You're going to have to pull yourself together," she said, aware that she was sounding like her mother. "We've got school tomorrow, and you can't go looking like . . ."

"I don't care. I don't care about school. My life is over."

"You're being silly, Jennifer, and you know it. Your life is definitely not over, and you have a job to do." Marjorie was beginning to lose patience. She couldn't take any of this seriously. "Try to get a grip on yourself. We'll talk later."

Marjorie left Jennifer, still in a heap on the living room couch and headed upstairs. "I have to change gears," she thought. "I have to get into classroom teacher mode. I'd better look at my lesson plans."

But she met Madeleine in the hallway. A grim faced—Madeleine, carrying a suitcase.

"I'm leaving, Marge," she said. "I've had enough of this household, if you can call it that."

"Madeleine, we've got to talk. Come into my bedroom." Marjorie hated to invite anyone into her bedroom, which was her private sanctuary. But for reasons she didn't fully understand, she felt that her pious housemate must not leave. She had to persuade Madeleine to stay on.

Madeleine followed Marjorie into the room but stood by the door. "I don't see that there's anything to discuss," she said. "I've had enough of the goings-on in this household. I have nothing in common with any of you, and frankly, your behavior disgusts me."

"Madeleine, sit down." Marjorie moved a pile of dirty underwear from the chair beside the dressing table, but Madeleine remained standing.

Marjorie sat down on the bed, thoughtfully stroking the bedspread. "I'm not quite sure why you're so angry," she said quietly. "I thought you were opposed to having men in the house. But I assume you invited Hank to stay here."

"Hank is my brother! As a relative, surely he's entitled to stay here! He's sleeping on the living room couch."

"Well, in the first place, you never consulted me about this." Marjorie stared at Madeleine coolly. She wasn't especially angry, but she wished she didn't have to deal with Madeleine at the moment. "And, well, if there was a romantic liaison between Hank and Jennifer, why does this offend you so?"

"Well, you weren't here to consult, as you well know. You were off enjoying a vacation at your parents' estate in some tony suburb of New York. And I have reason to be upset by Hank's shenanigans," said Madeleine, her jaw tight.

"Well, surely you didn't expect Hank to become a monk," said Marjorie, who had been genuinely puzzled by Madeleine's behavior.

"As a matter of fact, I did. He was about to join a monastery in New Mexico."

Marjorie stared at her housemate in disbelief. "You're kidding. Men don't join monasteries in 1968."

"Why is it," said Madeleine angrily, "that no one can believe in a religious vocation anymore? You supposedly have a vocation for teaching. Hank and I believe in offering our services to the glory of God."

Marjorie didn't know how to respond to this. All she could think of to say was, "Well, I'm truly sorry if Jennifer has led your brother astray. But," she added softly, "Hank is a free agent. He may have questioned his religious commitment even if he had never met Jennifer."

Madeleine picked up her suitcase and was about to leave.

"Wait a minute, Madeleine," said Marjorie. "I know you're angry. But surely you're only punishing yourself by leaving so late in the term. You'd have to find another place to stay and . . . how many weeks are left? Six? Stay on a finish out the time with us, Madeleine."

"If you're worried about money, Marge," Madeleine said with a gesture of impatience, "I'd pay the last two month's rent. You wouldn't be out of pocket."

"It has nothing to do with the money." Marjorie stood up and stretched her arms in front of her. "It has to do with . . . tolerance, I suppose. When we first rented this house, I had a vision of what life would be like here. I thought we'd all be friends, have fun together."

"Fun together." Madeleine's upper lip curled.

Marjorie ignored her. "It didn't turn out that way. We're all so different. We don't have much in common. There have been times, Madeleine, when I've felt utterly alone here."

"I always feel alone here."

"In spite of our differences couldn't you, in a spirit of Christian charity, forgive Jennifer? She's very young, not in years, but in development, my little friend. I think she's very scared of life. That's probably why she turned to Hank. He's younger than she is and not threatening."

Madeleine sank down into the chair by the dressing table. "Your friend has ruined my brother's life."

"Madeleine, don't you think you're exaggerating a little bit? Hank still can fulfill his religious vocation." Marjorie went and stood by the back window, looking out on the barren yard and the line of houses in the block behind them. "And is it even a question of that?" As Madeleine didn't respond but just looked at her without any expression, Marjorie continued. "I don't expect you to like Jennifer or any of the rest of us. All I want is for you to show some measure of respect for others' weaknesses. I don't think Jennifer fell in love to offend you. I think it happened because of her weakness and her loneliness."

Listening to herself, Marjorie felt sorry for Jennifer for the first time. She realized that she hadn't been very tolerant of her friend. She certainly hadn't been supportive.

She turned toward Madeleine, who was still sitting, eyeing her guardedly.

"What are you asking me to do? To tell Jennifer that I pardon her and want to be her friend?"

"Oh, don't be impossible, Madeleine. You know that would be absurd. All I ask is that you stay on, that you maintain a certain level of civility. To Jennifer. To all of us. You must realize that you haven't always been the easiest person to live with. You demand a lot of yourself, but you expect just as much from others. We can't all be perfect."

"Perfect! Huh!" Madeleine's lip curled in scorn, but her face had softened. "All right. I'll stay. But don't expect me to cozy up to Jennifer. Or any of the rest of you."

"Will you shake hands on that?" Marjorie took Madeleine's cold, reluctant hand. It was hardly a victory, but it was a compromise, which Madeleine had never offered before. The two left the room together, Madeleine clutching her battered suitcase, heading back toward her bedroom. Marjorie went up to Jennifer's room. She found her friend on the floor, her books and papers strewn around her. She seemed, if not happy, at least more in control.

"Madeleine has threatened to leave," said Marjorie. "In fact when I met her in the hallway she had her bag packed. But after some discussion, she agreed to stay on."

"Why on earth should you want her to stay on?" Jennifer stood up and confronted Marjorie angrily. "None of us like her. She's been a pain since the beginning."

"That's true," said Marjorie, "but your own behavior hasn't been angelic in this case. Didn't you know that Hank was about to join a monastery? That was very important to Madeleine."

"That is, if you'll pardon the expression, bullshit. Hank had questioned his so-called religious vocation for some time. Madeleine was being possessive and manipulative."

"Well, I'm not in a position to judge, Jennifer. Madeleine's staying, and all I'm asking is that you be polite to her."

"I'll stay out of her way. That's all I can promise."

Marjorie was too tired to reason any further with her friend. She understood how Jennifer felt about Madeleine, but she no longer wanted to deal with all this discord. She went down and sat at the little table in the kitchen, stretching her legs and wondering if she should have a glass of wine. It was true: She didn't like Madeleine any better than Jennifer did. So why was it so important that Madeleine stay on? Marjorie just felt that the four of them, the four that had started out together in this house several lifetimes ago, should finish the time together. She decided that she would have a glass of wine even though it was only three o'clock. She had lesson plans to do, but that could wait.

Thinking back over the day, she felt very old. It was as it was she, not Madeleine, who was the Mother Superior in a house of difficult young nuns. Here she was, siding with conventional morality against passion, acting as peacemaker when she thought of herself as someone who rushed into the fray. Mother Superior. She looked at bit like the Mother Superior in that painting Denise had finally finished. "But I don't want to be old!" she said to herself. "I want to be young and silly and enjoy myself. Do I really want to be a teacher?"

*   *   *

"What to wear? What to wear?" The eternal question. Marjorie stood in front of her closet, shifting her weight from one foot to the other. She was meeting Franklin Forsythe for lunch and she wanted to be appropriately dressed. Her impulse was to wear something frivolous, a frilly, low-cut blouse and a brightly colored skirt. But she had to give the right impression. So instead she chose a light, flowered dress with a high neck, feminine, but not especially sexy. She wondered if Forsythe was going to seduce her; she wondered if she would let him. She wondered why he had invited her; she wondered why she had accepted.

She took a bus downtown to the restaurant Forsythe had indicated. It was dark, cool, and relatively empty. Quite up-market, as Marjorie had expected. To her surprise, Franklin hadn't yet arrived when she came in. She had calculated the time so she would arrive just a couple of minutes late to show that she was conscientious but not obsessive.

Franklin Forsythe was about ten minutes late, looking slightly harried but impressive in his expensive suit.

"You must forgive me, Miss Dunnock," he said, taking a seat opposite her and nodding discreetly toward the waiter, who immediately came to his side. "Pressing business matters." He offered no further explanation but scanned the menu. "I'll have the Dover sole. And you, Miss Dunnock?"

"The grilled scampi."

"We'll have the white wine, then. Do you prefer a Chardonnay? Or a Riesling?"

"The Chardonnay, I think."

They made inconsequential conversation while waiting for the wine to arrive. Forsythe asked her where she was from, where and what she had studied, if she had any special hobbies or interests. "Why is he quizzing me?" Marjorie wondered. She watched his face, curiously, wondering where all this was leading. She felt from the beginning an absence of flirtation. This was serious business. Perhaps he, too, was afraid of Mrs. Forsythe.

They were well into their meal when Forsythe stopped eating and looked Marjorie full in the face. "You probably wonder why I've invited you here today." Marjorie nodded and took a sip of wine. "Well, it's partly to thank you for your work with Richard."

"Well, that's very kind of you, but I don't think I've done a great deal."

"Oh, but you have." Forsythe paused, slightly embarrassed. "I'm afraid that initially I rather understated the problem we were having with our son. He was about to be expelled from school."

Marjorie made a gesture of annoyance. "You hired me because I was young and naïve and wouldn't recognize a behavioral problem. Or would be afraid to kick up if I did."

Forsythe smiled impassively. "To some extent that is true. But it was also because my daughter spoke so highly of you. She said you could handle any situation in class. And . . ." he paused to continue eating, "it's not true that you were afraid to kick up. You did kick up. My wife told me that you complained early on, said we should get a professional to work with Rick. But nevertheless you persevered. And you won out in the end."

"I don't understand. In what sense did I win out?"

"Well, he's settled down. To the point where the school authorities say he can stay on."

"It may simply be that he's grown out of some of the disruptive behavior." Marjorie looked back on the last lessons. She hadn't seen a marked improvement.

"You give yourself far too little credit, Miss Dunnock. Young Richard adores you."

"Adores me?" Marjorie burst out laughing. "He calls me Horseshit Face."

Forsythe continued to eat impassively. "The psychology of a nine-year-old boy is sometimes difficult to fathom. But believe me 'Horseshit Face' is a mark of affection. Of esteem, even."

Marjorie shook her head and continued eating. The scampi were very good.

"Curiouser and curiouser," she thought.

Forsythe had finished eating. He laid down his fork. "Will you have dessert, Miss Dunnock? Or coffee?"

"Coffee, please." Marjorie looked at Forsythe expectantly. Was he going to pay her a bonus for work well done? He had already paid her handsomely. She still wasn't sure why he had invited her to lunch. It seemed a strange thing for a busy lawyer to do if he wasn't going to try to seduce her.

They talked for a few minutes about the Fielding School and young Richard's prospects of being accepted there. Marjorie tried to be circumspect, but she doubted he would pass entrance requirements. "Of course, he has time on his side," she said. "He could mature a lot before it's time to enter high school."

Forsythe frowned. "Perhaps you'd be willing to take him on this summer," he said. "A few lessons a week would help him improve his English."

Marjorie laughed. She couldn't imagine a worse way to spend her summer. "I'm afraid I won't even be here," she said. "I'm going back home for a rest."

The coffee arrived.

"I have something else in mind." Forsythe stirred his coffee carefully. He gave Marjorie a searching look. "Miss Dunnock," he said finally, "you are a remarkable young woman. I think your talents are wasted on teaching. Have you ever thought of going into law?"

"Never," said Marjorie, smiling. "And even if I had, I wouldn't want to start a new training program, now, at this stage of my life."

Forsythe laughed. "You could reasonably say that if you were my age. But you're still very young, not twenty-five, I suspect. You know there's something called on-the-job training. You'd like our team, Miss Dunnock. The work is fun, challenging, never boring. Think it over."

Marjorie left the restaurant, having refused Forsythe's offer of a drive home. She was slightly tipsy from the wine and needed time to clear her head and reflect. She couldn't believe it! She had gone in expecting a proposition and come out with a job offer. "Is it true that I'm no longer attractive?" she thought.

*   *   *

Term was almost over, to everyone's relief. Madeleine was taking exams; Denise was preparing her portfolio; Jennifer and Marjorie had almost finished their teaching assignment. On a warm day late in May, Jennifer and Marjorie were sitting on the bed in Marjorie's room, now fresh and tidy, the newly-washed curtains flapping in the open window. The girls were eating cookies and comparing notes on their final observations. Neither was especially happy about the results.

"I was so sure I'd get an excellent report," said Marjorie. "My final observation went like clockwork. I checked all my facts for the little lecture and I even rehearsed students to respond to the discussion questions, as Joyce suggested."

"So what did Rittershoff find to criticize?"

"Well," Marjorie took a cookie out of the packet, inspected it and put it down. "There was one incident with Roger Burden making a noise. Rittershoff capitalized on that. She said I came down too hard on discipline problems."

"That just goes to show."

"Goes to show what?"

"That Rittershoff is criticizing for the sake of it. She criticized me for the opposite reason. Said I was too soft, let too much go by."

Marjorie looked through the lace curtains at the small barren patch of land that made up their back yard. She felt exhausted, drained. She had worked so hard to have a perfect lesson when Dr. Rittershoff came to observe. And she got no credit for it.

"You see," she said slowly, "with me it's worse than a bad report on the observation. There've been complaints from parents."

Jennifer looked alarmed. "Why? What did you do that made the parents complain?"

"Nothing that teachers haven't done since time immemorial. I've insulted bad students, used sarcasm, raised my voice. It's not as if I ever beat a student up, for God's sake."

Jennifer chewed thoughtfully on a cookie. "You know, I think Fielding School parents tend to be overprotective. If a teacher shouts at their little darlings, it's almost a court case."

"There's something else." Marjorie paused. "I antagonized Dr. Rittershoff. After my first observation."

"Oh, Marjorie. She could end up by giving you a bad report."

"I know. I think I even knew at the time. But I couldn't help myself. I felt as though I couldn't let her remarks go by. Especially after the way she had treated you."

"Oh, Marjorie, I do appreciate that," Jennifer touched her arm gently. "But was it worth it? You don't get people like Rittershoff to change by challenging them."

"I did it for myself, Jennifer. I needed to say something . . . even if it made her think for a few minutes. But I begin to wonder . . ." Marjorie broke off her sentence and lapsed into thought.

"Wonder what, Marge?"

"If I'm really cut out to be a teacher. Uebermensch said, 'You'll have to learn to suppress certain aspects of your personality if you're going to succeed.'"

"But Marge," said Jennifer earnestly, "it's just those aspects of your personality that make you such a good teacher. In fact, I envy your enthusiasm, your self confidence. That's exactly what I lack."

"Would I really fit in, in a school system that requires conformity? I'm beginning to have my doubts."

Jennifer put her hand on her friend's arm. "We had this discussion about me, don't you remember? I was the one who was supposed to give up teaching. And I still might. But you, you wouldn't think of giving up teaching, would you? Not after all we've been through this semester?"

"It's just because we've been through so much that I'm thinking of giving it up. I feel as though I'd been groping my way through a long, dark tunnel. I don't want my life to be like that, Jennifer."

"But it will get easier. Everyone says that the first year's the hardest."

"I know that. But look at Joyce Kettlehut. How old is she? Thirty? Thirty-five, at the oldest? She's already worn away at the edges."

"What else would you do?"

"Ah, that is the proverbial question." And the thought came back to her, as it had many times in the past week, of Forsythe's offer.

"Marjorie," said Jennifer. "I didn't want to mention this, but I've applied to graduate school."

"You haven't!"

"I tried to tell you last semester when Denise was giving that party. You remember, when she and her friends made such a mess in the back yard? I was going to tell you then. Dr. Edelmann, my medieval lit professor, called me into his office to tell me I had promise as a scholar. He was impressed by one of my papers."

"Well, that's wonderful." Marjorie was actually horrified. Medieval literature! "But Jennifer, you don't want to go on being a graduate student and study old manuscripts and write theses. It's like becoming a nun."

"That's exactly what I want to do. If I get accepted somewhere."

Marjorie looked at her friend in dismay, wondering if the affair with Hank could have anything to do with this decision. "Well, it's your life, but I think that would be very sad."

She crumpled up the empty packet of cookies and smiled a radiant smile. "But why are we talking about miserable things? We ought to be celebrating. We're finished! Let's go to Nick's for a drink."

*   *   *

It was moving time, or almost moving time. After a council of war, the four girls had decided to bring in a team of cleaners to prepare the house for Miss Mayberry's inspection. Cleaning the house was the last thing any of them, with the possible exception of Jennifer, wanted to get involved with. For Marjorie and Jennifer, there were final exams to make up, administer and grade, final grades to submit, and their own job applications to deal with. Madeleine and Denise were equally preoccupied. Marjorie wasn't sure what they were up to, didn't have the time or inclination to find out.

It was the last day of school at Fielding, and the teachers had to meet each of their classes and hand out final grades. For Marjorie, the first hours had dragged slightly but gone reasonably well. She chatted with the students about their summer plans, made suggestions for reading and urged them to continue studying hard. Twelfth grade was final period. When Marjorie went back to the classroom at two o'clock she got a shock. The students had decorated the room with pink and white streamers and written, "We love you, Miss Dunnock" on the blackboard. They had pasted portraits of the Romantic poets on the walls, with snippets from their poetry scotch taped below. The girls were wearing extravagant Marjorie-style dresses with frills and paper flowers attached to the waists.

The girls swarmed around her, asking her what she thought of the decorations and telling her how much they had loved the class. They asked her where she'd be going in the fall. One of them presented her with a glass of punch and a slice of white cake. Marjorie would have been touched if the whole party hadn't been so cloyingly, nauseatingly sweet.

She took a bite of the cake, which was too heavily frosted. Over the girls' head she saw the faces of two of the more mature boys. They were exchanging sneering glances. When they realized she was glaring at them, they put on polite expressions.

"But they're right," she thought. "This entire demonstration is horrible. What have I been teaching these girls?" She took another bite of her slice of cake and could hardly swallow it. She looked at the remains of the cake, caved in on a plate in the middle of her desk. On top of this ruin were globs and curlicues of white frosting. It looked like a wedding cake, and it occurred to her that this was her wedding cake and the whole ghastly party symbolized her marriage to the teaching profession. Sneers and sickening admiration. Was this what she wanted, what she had spent her life preparing for?

She stuck it out and eventually made her way to some of the sneering boys, who were standing on the fringes. She offered them a couple of slices of cake, which they politely refused. "You'll probably be glad to get out of this place," she said. "I assume you're all planning to go to college in the fall?" The trio nodded, and little by little she drew them out, having them talk about their plans.

As the hour came to the close, she thanked the class, and they slowly filtered out, getting ready to get into their chauffeur-driven limousines and drive home. One of the sneering boys lingered. "Was there something you wanted to ask me, Bill?" said Marjorie, feeling his discomfort.

"I just wanted to say, Miss Dunnock, that we did like the class. But."

"I understand the but, Bill."

He shook her hand and went out. Marjorie stayed behind to take down the decorations, clean the blackboard, and get rid of the dirty cups and plates. She worked slowly, wondering what this vocation for teaching was really about. She had dressed well and strutted in front of her classes, trying to instill a love of literature in them. Had she been inspiring them or merely playing teacher? Had it been worth the lost Friday afternoons in committee meetings, the hours spent in creating lesson plans and correcting homework? She only knew that now what she wanted most was to lie on her bed in the bedroom in Charles Street feeling the breeze blow through the open windows and drowsing with a good novel in her hand. It upset her to realize that she didn't even care that no boyfriend was present. "What's the matter with me?" she wondered. "I must need a good, long vacation."

*   *   *

Ever since Fortythe had taken her out to lunch, Marjorie had been waking up with the same image in her mind: Franklin Forsythe, his trench coat flung over one arm, dripping from the storm. He was applauding her speech, on that rainy February evening that seemed so far away now. Applauding her speech! A rich, influential lawyer, and one with a horrible wife.

Now even after the lunch during which he called her a remarkable young woman, even after the job offer, she had heard nothing from him. She decided she had to see him again, possibly be less tentative, possibly be ready to make the first move. It would be a challenge. He was old, of course, far too old for her; he was married. And yet, Marjorie had to admit to herself, an attractive man. Even a desirable man.

She stirred in bed, wondering what an intimate relationship with him would be like—a rich, powerful man.

The alarm clock rang. It was seven o'clock, hot summer. It had been light for well over an hour. Her room was in chaos. "My God," she thought, coming out of her fantasy, "I've got to finish packing today. Miss Mayberry is coming this morning, the four of us are going out to lunch, and place will have to be cleared out by evening."

She felt queasy. "It's over," she thought. "The year is gone, we have our diplomas, we're about to start an adult life." She got up and put a few things in the open suitcase before going to shower. "It's over," she said to herself again and felt the tears forming in her eyes without understanding why.

On this stuffy, heavy summer day she was facing a number of good-byes—to Madeleine, the thorn in everyone's side, to Denise, whom she'd become quite fond of, to Jennifer, with whom she'd been through so much. And to this marvelous Charles Street house. The house, she thought, in a way, she would miss even more than the people. How could a house mean so much?

She got through much of her packing before Miss Mayberry arrived. Then she went downstairs and looked around the house. The cleaning company had done wonders, but there were still paint splatters on the Victorian sideboard in the dining room and on some of the furniture in what had been Denise's room.

Miss Mayberry arrived about two minutes early, just before ten o'clock. The other girls had left Marjorie to deal with her; they were still packing. The elderly lady greeted Marjorie frostily. She had noticed mud splatters on the front windows before she even came in.

As they moved from room to room, Miss Mayberry's hand fluttered in helpless distress. "Oh, my dear, my dear," she said. "Couldn't you do any better than this?"

Marjorie was furious. The cleaning company had been quite expensive, and Madeleine had balked at paying her share. She had been so sure Mrs. Mayberry would be pleased. But she knew better than to say, "You should have seen it last week!"

At the end of the tour, Mrs. Mayberry turned to Marjorie and snapped, "I shall have to keep your deposit money, you realize. What a foolish idea it was to rent out our darling house! Never again. I assure you, never again."

After this, Marjorie hardly felt in a celebratory mood. The girls had paid the cleaning company the money set aside for the deposit. Now they would all be out of pocket again. And Madeleine would doubtless refuse to pay.

Marjorie wandered through the house, feeling disconsolate. This house that she had loved so much, and they had never given the dinner party she had dreamed of. There had been, in the end, very few glamorous moments in the entire academic year. It had been mostly hard work and strife. She flicked on the chandelier that the cleaning crew had taken such pains with, removing all the little crystals and dipping them in a cleaning solution. The light made patterns through one of Mrs. Mayberry's cut-glass vases, the one that Marjorie had inspected that day so long ago when she and Jennifer had interviewed their housemates. "Mrs. Ramsey," she thought. "I thought of myself as Mrs. Ramsey, ladling out a wonderful soup to my guests." There weren't many guests, and in fact there wasn't much cooking of any sort. "And it's over now," she repeated sadly.

Now there was only the farewell lunch and the four would go their separate ways. Marjorie went up to her room to dress for the occasion. She decided to cheer herself by wearing something light and frivolous. She put on a summer dress with a ruffled v-neck that showed a hint of cleavage. Her mother's gold locket around the neck. Bright green shoes with buckles. No matter what she was feeling, this last lunch had to be a festive occasion. Besides, she might attract a few flattering male glances.

They had chosen to meet at a popular restaurant on the wharf. Marjorie, who could tolerate shellfish but not fish, had pushed for a French restaurant in town, but the others had voted her down; it was too expensive. Marjorie took a taxi to the wharf. "I've saved most of what Forsythe paid me," she thought. "Why not spend it?"

She gazed out the window, vaguely aware of the dismal cityscape, the lock-up garages, the run-down houses that no one seemed to care for, the abandoned businesses. She was worried about this luncheon, aware of the antagonism between Jennifer and Madeleine, aware that she hadn't made much effort to keep in contact with Denise since she had completed the portrait. She tried to remember the last time she had even seen Denise at the house. It must have been that time in the kitchen when Denise had been cooking bacon and eggs. Was Denise actually living there? Or had she moved in with one of her arty boyfriends? Marjorie couldn't even remember if there was any evidence—stacks of paintings, backpacks full of materials, partially-finished collages—that Denise had packed. Madeleine and Jennifer had their bags, stuffed and shut, near the front entrance. Where had Denise been these past weeks? What had she been up to? She wondered about the others' plans for the future. She was pretty sure that Jennifer would go on to graduate school, but what about Denise and Madeleine?

And she had her own announcement to make. About her future.

The taxi left her in front of the restaurant just after twelve. The place was crowded with customers, overflowing out into the street. Graduation ceremonies had occurred several days before, so there were new graduates in little groups and parents escorting their newly graduated offspring, as well as the usual suited businessmen. The line stretched from the entrance out into the street. Marjorie spotted Jennifer and Madeleine standing in line. To her relief they seemed to be speaking; at least they were keeping an appearance of civility. Jennifer was better dressed than usual in a pale blue dress with little gold flowers and a full, swirling skirt. She looked quite pretty. Madeleine had abandoned her usual greenish garment for a dark grey summer suit in a rather coarse material. Her thick braid was coiled on top of her head like a dormant snake, making her some four inches taller. It was extraordinary to see the two together, Jennifer so petite and dainty, with Madeleine's bulk towering over her.

She joined them, jumping a half-dozen places in the line. "Hello! Have you been waiting long?"

"Marjorie, how pretty you look!" Jennifer turned to greet her. "No, no, only a few minutes. The line has been growing steadily."

"I hope we won't have to wait all afternoon to be seated," said Madeleine. "I still have some packing to do."

"I thought you had finished," said Marjorie. "Didn't I see your bags in the hallway?"

"I still have to check my room to be sure that everything is in order. By the way, has Miss Mayberry been around?"

Marjorie wanted to avoid the subject of Miss Mayberry's visit, at least until they were settled in the restaurant. As they were moving rapidly toward the door, she thought she could safely change the subject. She merely nodded and said, brightly. "Apparently this is a very popular restaurant. The food must be pretty good."

"But where's Denise?" Jennifer looked at her watch. "I hope she is planning to come."

"Don't worry," said Marjorie, "She's tends to be late. I know she wouldn't miss this."

The three women stood quietly for a few minutes. Madeleine, preoccupied, didn't raise the subject of Miss Mayberry's visit again. Soon they were passing from the drippy heat of the city into the cool darkness of the restaurant. Like a genie shooting up from a bottle. a waiter greeted them. He looked to Marjorie like a young student working his way through college. He was wearing a formal suit with a white tie that seemed to be forcing the blood into his face.

"Could we have a table by the window? We're a party of four, actually," said Marjorie, "but could you seat us now?"

"So sorry, Madam," said the waiter with a bow, "All the window seats are taken. I can give you a nice booth in the main dining room."

"God, I don't remember anyone ever calling me Madam," said Marjorie, half to herself. "I must be getting old."

The waiter showed them to a booth in a darkened corner, more suited to an assignation than to a celebratory lunch. The seats recessed into a corner, forming a semi-circle, so Marjorie took the place between Madeleine and Jennifer as a buffer between them. The atmosphere was smoky and the smell of fish predominated. At one of the tables in the middle of the room was a noisy party of students, two boys and two girls, over-excited and quite drunk.

Every few minutes a whoop of laughter would erupt from the celebrants, followed by giggles and guffaws. Marjorie felt stifled.

The waiter presented them with poster-sized menus, which, if propped up on the table, rose above the level of their heads.

"I wonder whether we should order now or wait for Denise," Marjorie said, trying to lay the menu flat on the table without upsetting the glasses of freshly poured water.

The waiter, ever-solicitous, returned. He had to lean over the table to hear the orders above the din at the middle table. Jennifer ordered the crab, a specialty of the house; Madeleine chose the fish cakes. At last she was having something more solid than soup, thought Marjorie, noting at the same time that it was the cheapest item on the menu. She looked for something not too fishy. "I think I'll have a hamburger," she said. "It seems a bit philistine, but it's what I want."

"Yuck, and what about the wine?" said Jennifer in disgust. "I thought we were ordering white wine."

"What?" Marjorie could barely hear her friend for the ambient noise. "Don't be a snob, Jennifer. It's my lunch and I'm paying for it. You can order a glass of wine if you want."

Just as they finished ordering, Denise appeared. She looked resplendent, her broad face flushed, her jewelry catching the subdued light. She was wearing a gypsy outfit, a colorful tunic and pantaloons. Marjorie was no longer repelled by Denise's mode of dressing but found it rather endearing.

"Sorry, ladies, but things have become extremely hectic," said Denise, taking one of the outer seats. Marjorie was relieved to hear Denise's robust voice, which was clearly audible in spite of the noise level. The waiter reappeared. "I'll have the catch of the day," she said without consulting the menu. "And a bottle of Champagne." When the waiter had taken the order and left, she looked around the table triumphantly. "I have some exciting news." She paused, taking a breath. "I've won a prize for one of my paintings! It's going to be exhibited at a gallery in D.C.!"

"Congratulations, Denise!" said Jennifer.

"Congratulations," repeated Marjorie. "I didn't know you were entering any competitions. I've been in your studio every week for months and you never mentioned a word." She thought again, remorsefully, that she hadn't been in contact with Denise since she finished her portrait.

"Well, I entered my painting on the spur of the moment. I didn't expect to win."

The waiter arrived and uncorked the Champagne. He poured out four glasses. Madeleine pushed hers away. A whoop arose from the neighboring table. Someone had spilled a half bottle of red wine over one of the girls, who was wearing white.

"Excuse me," said Denise. "I've had enough of that row." She disappeared and when she returned, a senior looking waiter had followed her and was remonstrating with the people at the noisy table.

"Well, I hope that will take care of that." Denise rubbed her hands together and sat down.

"You are a seven-day wonder, Denise," said Marjorie, her spirits rising. "Who else could have stilled the barbarians with such ease and aplomb."

"I won't have my lunch spoiled by a bunch of rowdy children of the bourgeoisie." Denise raised her glass. "Here's to all of us," she said. "Here's to our differences. And here's to our careers!"

"And here's to the conclusion of an extraordinary year!" Marjorie said, raising her glass.

"A year that I sometimes thought would never end!" said Jennifer.

"I'm sorry to have been away so much. I would have liked to spend more time at the house, but I got involved with someone," said Denise. "For me, I have to say it's been a fabulous year!"

Madeleine was looking skeptical. "Yes, you were part of it, too, Maddie," Denise continued. "Remember the Hallowe'en costume you made to frighten Marge's jilted lover?"

"That pervert! Well, it did work," said Madeleine. "I must admit, I was rather proud of my costume."

Remembering the incident with Leroy, Marjorie finished her first glass of Champagne. She felt giddy and much happier. Denise filled the three glasses again.

"Denise," said Jennifer, "I've hardly spoken to you since February. What will you be doing next year? Have you got a job in the field of art?"

"No, nothing yet. But I'm hoping to find something in commercial art. I'm not sure what, but whatever I do, I'll never give up painting."

"Wonderful, Denise," said Jennifer. "And what about your exhibit? I mean the exhibit with the painting that won a prize? Will you invite us to the opening?"

"Well, I'm not sure when it will be. But of course I'll invite you, if you're still in the area."

The red-faced waiter brought the food and shuffled things around to fit the four enormous plates on the table. There was a silence as each girl prepared to attack her food. Marjorie attempted not to look at Denise's Catch of the Day, which lay on the plate, slit through to the spine, its dead eye staring upwards. Jennifer's ferocious-looking crustacean was only slightly more attractive and a greater challenge. Jennifer hesitated, staring at it, not sure whether to begin with the nutcracker or the slender little fork.

Marjorie couldn't help laughing. "It looks ready to eat you!" Turning to Denise, she said, "You should be able to get a job in the area. And what about you, Madeleine? We haven't heard about your plans for the future"

Madeleine took a bite of one of her fishcakes. "You remember the Brothers of Light? Well, they are sending me as a missionary to West Africa. In the service of the Lord. To Senegal."

Marjorie almost dropped her hamburger. "So you're really going to convert the heathens!"

"Don't be snide, Marjorie. I have a calling. You wouldn't even know what that means."

"No, I don't suppose I would," said Marjorie, quite unfazed. "Anyway, I admire your gumption. I wouldn't want to go to West Africa!"

"Well, I say bravo," said Denise. "That's wonderful, Madeleine. If that's what you want to do, go for it!" She raised her glass, and Marjorie and Jennifer followed suit, Jennifer laying down a partially-broken crab claw to do so.

"I don't go until next September," Madeleine added, removing a bone from her fish cake. "I'll be staying with my family in Pennsylvania over the summer."

There was an uncomfortable silence.

"And what about that wayward brother of yours?" Denise asked. Marjorie was shocked. Was it possible Denise didn't know about the business between Jennifer and Hank?

Madeleine's face turned a dark plum color. She speared a piece of lettuce on the salad side of her plate. Jennifer laid down her fork. Some object in her lap, possibly a stray piece of crab, had caught her attention.

Marjorie took it upon herself to change the subject. "Jennifer hasn't mentioned what her plans are," said Marjorie. She herself hadn't talked about the future with Jennifer since the time she had confided her doubts about teaching.

There was a brief silence and for a moment Marjorie was afraid Jennifer would burst into tears. Instead she took a sip of water. "I've been accepted for graduate studies at a small university outside Chicago. They've given me quite a good grant."

"You're entering the nunnery after all," said Marjorie, disappointed. She wasn't surprised, but she had hoped that Jennifer would give up the idea of graduate school.

"It's not like that, Marge. I've always wanted to continue my studies. And I think I'd be happier teaching older students."

"A real graduate student now! That's something to celebrate too!" Denise was on her fourth glass of Champagne and had barely touched her revolting fish. Her face was deeply flushed now. "What will you be studying?"

"French literature of the middle ages. It will be good-bye, Dr. Rittershoff." Jennifer sucked the last bit from a claw.

"Oh my God!" said Marjorie. "Well, let's hope it won't be hello, Dr. Frazier!"

Just then the red-faced waiter appeared. "Is everything all right here, ladies?" he asked, filling the water glasses. Marjorie looked around the table. Jennifer was well embarked on the conquest of her crab, and Madeleine, astonishingly, was almost finished. Denise had barely begun her dead-eyed fish, but she was hitting the Champagne pretty hard. It made Marjorie wonder. Denise was drinking far too much. Was there something going on that she hadn't told them about?

But she hadn't had a chance to spring her surprise. "Isn't anyone going to ask me where I'll be next year?" she asked.

"I know you were applying for jobs as an English teacher with the New York school system," said Jennifer. "But I never got a chance to ask. Did you have any job offers?"

"Several, in fact."

Jennifer raised her glass. "Isn't it wonderful to think we've all come out of this year with bright futures. And none of us has fallen into the marriage trap. We've all got promising careers!"

Marjorie took a large bite of her hamburger. "It looks as though I'll be the only exception," she said with her mouth full.

"Why, Marjorie," said Jennifer in surprise. "What do you mean? I thought you always cherished the idea of a career. You will accept one of those jobs in New York State, won't you?"

"Well, each of us had a little surprise to share at this lunch. My surprise is that I've accepted a job in Franklin Forsythe's law firm."

"Well, I'll be damned," said Denise. "You're actually giving up teaching?"

"For the moment, definitely. I'm not ready to dedicate my life to shaping young minds. I feel as if I've been in prison for the last five months. I don't know about you, Jen, but I haven't had any fun since Christmas."

Jennifer had put down her little crab fork and was staring at Marjorie. She looked stricken. "You can't do that, Marge. You're sacrificing a whole year's work. And the money your parents paid to put you through this program."

Madeleine had finished a few minutes before. She was giving Marjorie one of her disapproving looks, corners of the lips stretched toward her chin. "I think I must have missed something," she said, wiping her mouth on her napkin. "I thought you were studying to be a teacher. Where does law come in all this?"

Denise was smiling as if at her own private joke. "There's nothing surprising about this. Teaching sucks. Marjorie has found something more entertaining to do. A toast! To the four of us! May we always follow our hearts and inclinations, regardless of what anyone else thinks. And Marjorie," she added, "to ever greater conquests!"

She raised her glass again. Jennifer and Marjorie hesitated. Marjorie wasn't pleased at the innuendo.

"I'm sorry," said Madeleine, "but I'm going to have to leave. I've got to finish packing and catch a bus back home before five."

"Couldn't you at least wait until the rest of us are finished?" said Marjorie, crossly. It seemed typical of Madeleine to break up their party.

"You spend so much time talking and drinking that you don't get on with eating," Madeleine said.

"Why don't you have a dessert?" said Denise. "Just to keep us company."

"You know I don't eat sweets. They rot the teeth and undermine self-discipline."

"Well, it's reassuring to know you haven't changed," said Denise. "You probably won't have to make any great dietary changes while you're in Africa."

"It really is time for me to go," said Madeleine, this time standing up awkwardly in the booth. Denise's considerable bulk blocked her from getting out.

"Madeleine," said Jennifer, "Wait a minute." She took a little address book out of her purse. "Write your home address here." She offered her a pen. "I will write to you, I promise. I don't want to lose touch."

Marjorie could hardly believe what she was seeing. Jennifer had complained repeatedly about Madeleine even before the business with Hank. It seemed unthinkable that she would want to write to her. Madeleine must have had the same feeling. She laughed a short, barking laugh. "Surely you're joking," she said. But she wrote an address in the little book.

"Good-bye, everyone," she said, giving Denise a little push. Denise made way for her. She slid out from her place in the booth and stood for a moment, then slowly moved toward the door.

That movement and Jennifer's little gesture made Marjorie aware that this was the end, not only of their lunch together, but possibly of their relationship. The four of them, together for a brief moment in their lives, were now splitting up. She wanted to reach out and hold Madeleine back.

"Don't go just yet," she said. "We all have to make a promise. It's very important." She paused. "Let's promise to meet here in a year's time."

Madeleine stopped and glanced briefly at her watch. "I don't see how I can promise that. In a year's time, I'll probably be in Africa."

"But let's try to arrange something. Let's not lose touch. Agreed?"

Denise, quite drunk, raised her glass again. "Yes, even if you can't come to my opening, I'll invite you, to my new apartment, wherever it is. Good-bye, Madeleine!"

Madeleine, standing by the exit, turned and raised her hand as if to wave. Jennifer's face crumpled into tears.

"Marjorie," she said, "I will always keep in touch. Always." She wiped her face with a tissue. "But I don't know how you can be doing this—throwing away everything you've worked for over the past year."

"Dear Jennifer," said Marjorie, also struggling with her sadness. "Dear, dear friend. I'm not throwing away anything. I'm spreading my wings! I'm learning to fly!"

PART II

Jennifer's Story
Fragments of a Friendship

Chicago suburbs, 1987

It was early September and the dry summer's end had left the trees lining the street where I lived parched and yellowed. I was sitting in the twilit living room, looking out at the quiet street, not bothering to turn on a light. Forty-two years old and I felt gutted. I felt closer to a hundred. Marjorie dead, Marjorie, my closest friend and alter ego, my mirror opposite, bright and beautiful. I had always envied Marjorie her fearlessness, her openness to risk. She often got herself in awful messes, but her life was never dull. She soared while I plodded along, my nose to the grindstone.

But no, I had to be honest with myself. Lately, in fact since she joined me in the Chicago area, she hadn't been the same. There was a desperate quality about her, as though she was looking for something that always eluded her grasp. I remember her face that day she married Guiliano. That day in the registry office, where I was the only witness. It was early spring and she was wearing a broad-brimmed hat that partly veiled her face. She looked pinched, over made-up, a beautiful woman prematurely faded. She should have been ecstatic, but she seemed withdrawn, frightened, more like me than like herself.

I had been thrilled that she and Howard were coming to Chicago. Since I had entered the adult world of getting and spending, I had never had another friend like Marjorie. There were colleagues at work who were friendly enough, but they were essentially competitors, vying for better student evaluations, promotions, more highly acclaimed publications. With Marjorie, it was simple companionship, conversation, gossip, meals taken together, confidences shared. But that, too, had changed. Since she came to Chicago, our friendship was less important to her than it was to me. I could always sense an underground stream that carried her along, away from me, toward that torrent of her crazy relationships.

Even before her illness, Marjorie had changed. And, I suppose, I had changed in ways that made the old intimacy impossible. During her illness, which seemed to last an empty lifetime, it was tending and hoping and despairing, and trying to get information from doctors, who said, "I'm afraid that's something I can't tell you.

I need to speak to a next-of-kin." Where were the next of kin? God knows. Probably Mrs. Dunnock was shopping for her summer wardrobe at Saks Fifth Avenue.

Mrs. Dunnock, the next-of-kin. She hadn't come to the buffet. The guests were local people, friends of Marjorie and her loathsome ex-husband Howard. No sign of Howard, who appeared at the funeral but didn't bother to speak to me. The party guests were people I had only met briefly at those dinner parties I always dreaded so much. I was relieved to see them go; now I no longer had to put on a social face and say the required clichés. "To prepare a face to meet the faces that you meet." Now I could indulge my grief, weep, bang my head against the wall, pound my fists against the table.

Except that what I felt was mostly nothingness, mostly weariness. Gutted. The fish on the table ready for frying. The arrangements for the funeral and the little buffet had given me a purpose, but now all that was over.

I had had the party catered and most of the food I had ordered was untouched. What could I possibly do with forty assorted canapés, a load of vegetable and clam dip, a hollowed-out pineapple filled with pineapple chunks? The idea of eating was not so much repulsive as an extraordinary effort. I could no more lift a fork to my lips than I could clean up the mess in the kitchen.

Marjorie never cleaned up her messes. It was as if she had been born entitled to servants who would follow her, gathering up dirty underwear and half-empty coffee cups to dispose of properly. I admired this aloofness in her, this detachment from life's petty chores. I could never be that way, of course; I obeyed old maternal orders to clean up after myself. But I wished I could be more like Marjorie, more like a born princess.

Her mother had that air about her too, that sense that she was too good for the baser things of life. But in her, indifference bordered on lack of feeling. She couldn't bear to deal with Marjorie's illness and only came to see her a couple of times. Once near the beginning, possibly two or two and a half years ago, and once not long before Marjorie's death.

"Oh my dear," Mrs. Dunnock said to me in her finishing school voice, "you surely understand. I cannot bear hospitals and sick beds. You are so much better at dealing with these things." And she floated off, still beautiful and elegant at seventy, untouched by the tragedy that was unfolding. In the end, I was the one who had to deal with the messy details of death, the death certificate, the funeral arrangements, the cremation.

I should have screamed, "This is your daughter! Your daughter is dying!" But Mrs. Dunnock was already slipping away to something more suitable than hospitals and sick beds. And anyway, my tongue had frozen in my mouth.

But at least she came to the funeral. She greeted me, tall and slender in her fashionable coat. She took my hands in hers, briefly touched her cheek to mine. And then was gone. Didn't come to the house for the buffet. It didn't matter to me; she could offer no consolation. As far as Marjorie's father was concerned, there was no trace of him. I didn't know if he was dead or divorced or simply hadn't bothered to come. I understood why Marjorie seldom spoke of her parents.

The street lights had come on outside and the natural light had faded a tone or two into darkness. This was my street, my neighborhood, my shelter, where I had lived nearly twelve years. I had been happy here, felt safe, until Marjorie's illness, which had drawn me in like water rushing down a drain and consumed more and more of meager energy for over two years.

But now was the time to rouse myself, to think of practical realities, the house to tidy up, the cat to feed, course notes to look over for Monday, the details of Marjorie's trust. Marjorie's trust, the biggest monster of all monsters to confront. And still no sign of the two others.

How could I find the will to do all this? I barely had the will to carry a tray to the kitchen.

I heard an angry meow and looked down to see George, clawing the sofa leg. I hadn't fed him, and he wasn't one to make allowances for my moods. I tucked him under my arm, a small, struggling mass of orange fur, and took him into the kitchen. He jumped onto the work surface and watched my movements resentfully. I pulled the tab to open a can of tuna for cats. The smell made me recoil. But I spooned it out dutifully and set it on the floor for him. The purring, like the noise of a mechanical toy, began instantly.

George the cat. Inherited from my next-door neighbor when she moved last spring. Not a loving cat, not a pleasant cat. Sometimes he took a swipe at my hand when I was stroking him. A bit like life itself, like the nasty business of chance and unexpected events. Still, George was a living, sentient being, dependent on me. My responsibility. Something to live for.

The doorbell rang, jangling me from my thoughts. Visits were no longer welcome. Visitors were the bearers of bad news.

I went back into the living room and peered out the front window. In the gathering darkness, I could just make out a solid figure on the porch. The doorbell rang again, this time twice, sounding louder. I opened the door.

"Hello?" I heard the strange quavering of my own voice.

"Jennifer? It's Denise. Denise Spaulding."

"Oh, of course. Please come in."

Denise, a figure from the distant past. I remember her as a hyper-active presence, paint spurting from the tubes as she splashed it around Miss Mayberry's sedate living room, leaving splatters everywhere. Denise, a person too boisterous to disturb this place of refuge, this sanctuary for my grief, for my utter weariness.

I escorted Denise into the living room and turned on the light. At first I thought she hadn't changed much from Baltimore days, her broad face unlined, her hair still dark, without traces of gray. But as she took off her coat, I saw from her movements and from the way she was dressed that, yes, she had changed. She was more centered, more tranquil, more inward-looking. She wore no jewelry, no make-up. She was quite satisfied with herself as she was, without adornment.

She said something like, "I'm so sorry, Jennifer," and took my hand. Her hand was warmer than mine even though she'd just come in from the cool evening. She looked around, surprised to see that the guests had left. "Sorry to be late. I rented a car at the airport, and you know how the highways around airports can be. I got caught in traffic. So . . . I'm obviously too late for the—uh—party?"

"Never mind. Would you like a drink? Or something to eat? As you see, there's plenty of food left over."

"No, nothing, Jennifer," said Denise. "Unless maybe a whiskey, if you have any."

"Is cognac okay? I'll get some from the kitchen."

"Cognac's fine. Hey, maybe I could help you clean up some of this mess."

"No, that's . . ." I started but stopped myself. "Yes, thanks, Denise." It might be a good idea to do something. Then we wouldn't have to make conversation. Back and forth, living room to kitchen, the gradual clearing away of the mess, helping to steady me, to clear my head. Then we did the dishes together, pretty much in silence.

I found the bottle of cognac in the cupboard and poured two glasses. It was quite a good bottle that I had bought myself for a special occasion. It no longer mattered. I couldn't imagine any more special occasions. We passed into the space by the kitchen that I used as a dining room, and sat at the little table.

Denise raised her glass. "To departed friends!" she said.

"Departed." As if Marjorie had gone on a little trip and could return. Marjorie was now incinerated and reduced to the contents of a small urn.

And then, inevitably, although I had dreaded it and had tried to put it off, we talked. First about Denise, whom I had hardly been in contact with for years—I had had to hire a lawyer to find her. She explained that she was about to hold an opening on Long Island, was selling paintings now and again—"Usually to a fellow artist"— was making a reasonable living, earlier as a salesperson in various shops, more recently as a real estate agent.

"Am I making it?" she said. "You could say so, but only by compromising my principles. Real estate wasn't the route I meant to take." She sat filling my armchair comfortably, steadily downing my cognac.

And then, inevitably, we started talking about Marjorie.

"These past few months must have been awfully hard," Denise said. "Were you with her a lot?"

"Toward the end, every day. It's horrible to say this, Denise, but nobody, neither her family, her friends, nor her two ex-husbands bothered with her much. For me, it was easy at first, helping with the shopping and driving her to the hospital. After surgery, you see, she couldn't lift things, couldn't drive. That was when I still had some hope for her."

"It's been going on for a long time, then?"

"Not as long as most breast cancers. She should have survived longer. But at a certain point, she just seemed to give up." Marjorie had given up on herself early on. When I met her at the hospital to take her home after surgery, she turned on me and said, "I am maimed for life." She said it with piercing bitterness.

Denise was elsewhere. "Well," she said. "It must in a way be a release for you. Being able to get on with your own life."

Did I have a life of my own? I must have said it, whispered it, because Denise said, "What? I didn't hear you."

"Yes, yes, a release," I murmured. "Of course it is." Denise couldn't have been more wrong, but that's the kind of thing you say when someone dies.

I couldn't think of anything to say and Denise, too, was silent for a few minutes. Then she started speaking slowly. Quietly. "You know, Jennifer," she said, "I haven't been very good about keeping in touch. I'm sorry about that. There's so much I don't know. What was Marjorie doing before she got sick?"

I stuck to the facts at first. "She was working in a lawyer's office. Doing reasonably well. Financially, I mean. Married twice. I didn't actually catch up with her until she moved to the Chicago area about seven years ago. I only met her first husband a couple of times. The second was . . ." I couldn't think of any brief way of describing Giuliano.

Denise had picked up on my tone. "She had trouble finding the right man?"

I nodded.

"You know, Jennifer, that doesn't really surprise me, considering the guys she hooked up with in Baltimore. Remember Leroy?" Denise laughed quietly to herself. "You know what she told me? That she planned to get married four times. Four times! What an ambition!"

"I thought she never planned to marry at all."

"What were they like, these husbands of hers? Bad, of course, but more specifically?"

I took a deep breath. "Marjorie's first husband was a law professor. She met him in the Baltimore area. He was the kind of person who would disagree with you for saying 'it's a nice day,' demonstrate five faults in your reasoning, and put you down for your stupidity."

I could still see the figure of Howard Greenhouse, floating up in my mind like the washings on a beach after a storm. His great beetling eyebrows, his nasal hair, his expensive embroidered waistcoats over a nascent belly. I could hear him telling a group of people at a party about Marjorie's ill-informed opinions, her bad reading habits, her foolish extravagances. "But he's a horrible man," I remember saying. "Whatever possessed you to marry him?" And her reply, uttered with total conviction, "He's brilliant, Jennifer, absolutely brilliant. I thought you of all people would appreciate that."

Denise's voice brought me back to the present. "I know the type you mean. Do you remember Rufus? In Baltimore?"

I shook my head.

"No, I don't think you came to that horrible dinner party Marjorie and I gave. Rufus was someone I went with that year. My first boyfriend there, I think." Denise mused for a moment. "So, two bad marriages, one to a phony academic, the other to . . . ?"

"Giuliano. He was fifteen years younger than Marjorie, and . . ."

"Very good looking?"

"Gorgeous. And, to be frank, a Don Juan. He even flirted with me, and I would have loved to have a fling with him if he hadn't been Marjorie's property." That rang hollow. I would never have risked anything so foolish. But I remembered Giuliano's dark, sultry look, his black curly hair, his lithe body. "He could charm the fish out of the sea."

"Not the sort to settle down. They got a divorce?"

"A separation. Marjorie was still passionately in love with him, but I don't know why he even married her. He wanted a divorce, she wanted to stay married. So they separated."

"How long ago was this?"

"A couple of years ago. Just before Marjorie got sick. I sometimes wonder—well, I know that cancer isn't psychological—but I wonder if the break—up with Giuliano had anything to do with her illness."

"And you and Marjorie were . . . very close?"

"I loved her, Denise." I stood up and turned away, knowing that if I made eye contact, I would cry. My throat ached with the effort to keep back the tears.

Denise suddenly stood up. "I'd better be on my way. I don't seem to be doing very well here. First I arrive too late for the buffet. Then I upset you with intrusive questions. It's time for me to go."

And suddenly I realized that I didn't want Denise to go. I put my hand on her arm. "No, no. You mustn't leave now. You could even sleep here if you want. I have a spare bedroom."

"No. Actually I have hotel reservations. In Chicago. If you want I could come back tomorrow instead. Take you out to lunch. I'm spending a couple of days in the area."

But there was Marjorie's trust, Marjorie's legacy. I hadn't even broached the subject in the time—it must have been almost a half hour—since Denise's arrival. I said, "Well, Madeleine should be arriving later this evening. There's something the three of us have to sort out."

Denise looked at me with raised eyebrows. "No shit. I thought Madeleine was in Africa, spreading the gospel among the natives."

"Normally she is. But at the moment she's back in the U.S. on leave, and I was able to get in touch with her. I can't understand why she hasn't arrived."

Denise shook her head. "Well, I'll be . . . Madeleine. I hadn't thought of her in years. Hateful person." She gathered up her things and started putting her coat on. "That settles it! I'm off!"

"Oh, Denise," I realized that I should have approached the issue differently. "You can't mean you're leaving now?"

"Only kidding," said Denise lightly. "I'll actually find it interesting to see her." She hadn't finished her second drink, but now she swallowed it in a single gulp.

We looked at each other for a minute, both uncomfortable at the thought of Madeleine's arrival. Then Denise picked up a photo on the end table beside her. "Who's this?"

It was a picture of Neil. I had taken it on a picnic when we started going together.

"That was a partner of mine, actually just a summer affair. He's gone now."

"He looks sweet."

I hated the word sweet, but it did apply to Neil. I took the photo from her and looked at it. It had been there on the table so long that I no longer noticed it. "That was a couple of years ago."

"But no one since?"

I went to the front window, the one that looked out on the street. I didn't answer Denise's question and Denise didn't say anything for a long time. Then she said. "Relationships aren't all they're cracked up to be. When I break up with my latest partner, it's always . . . rejuvenating. Like rain after a long heat wave."

Denise had a knack for misreading my moods. "My point of view is different . . . I'm a species that mates for life. You probably couldn't understand that."

"Probably not. I've always thrived on variety."

"But what about that guy you were going with in Baltimore?"

"What guy?"

"Don't you remember? That good-looking black guy you brought to the sculpting party."

Denise's forehead rumpled in a frown. "A black guy? In Baltimore? Oh, yes Moses Lamb." She smiled as if enjoying a private joke. "No, Moses and I were never an item. We were just friends. I've had lots of relationships, but I . . . I never did marry." She poured herself a third shot of cognac. Leaning toward me, she said, "Do you really think that Madeleine will turn up?"

"Probably, though not out of love for Marjorie. I suggested on the phone that we had some business to attend to. She said she had a meeting in Chicago."

"Not a meeting of the Brothers of Light?"

"You remember! Yes, in fact the Brothers of Light are gaining in numbers and in power."

"The world gone mad. Or half the world gone mad. So Madeleine continues her mission."

"Apparently. It even seems she's done extraordinary things." I remembered the brief notes she had written on Christmas cards, faded post cards that had taken months to arrive. "She started up a mission school, brought doctors in, managed deliveries of food and medicine to the most remote areas."

Denise shook her head, smiling. "The marvels of faith," she murmured. Then she took my glass, which I had barely touched, and filled it to the brim. "Have some if this," she said. "It'll help to numb the pain."

"But Denise," I said, feeling all the distance between us, "I'm already numb. I've lost the person who mattered the most in the world to me, and I can't feel a thing."

Denise came over and sat beside me on the couch. She put her hand on my shoulder. "It's a natural defense, Jen. You do have feelings, but you're pushing them away because they're so painful." She took my hand. Hers was very warm and extraordinarily meaty for a woman's. "Take a few deep breaths. That sometimes helps."

I didn't believe it would, but I did as she said, feeling the warmth of her body close to mine. We sat this way for some time, but I began to feel uncomfortable, needing space for myself. I moved away slightly, and Denise went back to the chair opposite me.

After a few minutes, Denise broke the silence again. "But what about you, Jen? Did you do the Ph.D. and all that?"

"Yes, I actually did." This was a subject I didn't want to get into with Denise. Realizing I was hungry, I found an excuse to break off the conversation. "Denise, do you want to stay for dinner? It must be getting late, and I'm absolutely starving! There's not much to eat in the house, but we could pick up Chinese take-away. There's a restaurant not far from here."

"Are you sure, Jennifer? Can you put up with me a little longer?"

So Denise had self-doubts, too. Super-confident Denise. As an answer, I went to her and gave her an awkward hug. "It's helped to have you here, Denise. I don't want you to go just yet."

*   *   *

We had just come back from the restaurant with the hot, fragrant cartons of food. It was far too much for two people, but Denise had gotten carried away and kept ordering dishes that tempted her. I took the food to the kitchen and was about to dish it up when there was a loud knock on the door. Madeleine! I hesitated: The food could be an excuse for not confronting her right away.

"Could you get that, Denise?" I said, continuing to dish up.

I heard Denise greeting Madeleine and stood in the entrance to the living room to observe them without being seen. Madeleine! Her very presence intimidated me, and of all the people in the world, she was the one I least wanted to see. I didn't feel strong enough to stand up to Madeleine.

There she was, taller than average, straight-backed, heavy in the jaw. A commanding presence, as she had always been. She had cropped her thick dull brownish hair so it formed a kind of helmet around her face. Her face was long and thin with prominent cheek-bones; her eyes were glassy and almost colorless. She had aged considerably; her face was deeply lined and toughened from the African sun. She was wearing a mannish tweed suit and sensible lace-up shoes. She looked capable of mustering an army, or perhaps ordering the massacre of a thousand non-believers. If she was formidable at twenty, at forty she was a terror.

I took refuge in polite formulas to mask my fear. "Hello, Madeleine," I said. "It's Jennifer. I guess I don't have to introduce Denise."

Madeleine looked directly at me. Her expression was neither friendly nor hostile, merely observant. "Jennifer," she said. "No, Denise is quite . . . recognizable."

"Hello, Madeleine," said Denise. "Amazing to see you after all these years." She stepped forward and shook Madeleine's hand.

"Madeleine," I said. "We've brought home some Chinese take-away. Won't you join us for a meal?"

"I smelled it," she said in that mocking way of hers, her nostrils flared. "No, I don't eat that sort of food. Anyway, I've only stopped at your request. I've got to take the rental car back to Chicago pretty soon. I've got a meeting early tomorrow morning."

"Well, you can stay for a little while, Madeleine. Sit down and make yourself comfortable," I said. "You'll excuse us if we go ahead and eat." I headed back to the kitchen and returned with a tray containing the food and my chipped plates. The odors of almond chicken, moo-shoo pork, shrimp chow mein and Cantonese rice were making my mouth water. I hadn't eaten since early that morning.

I found the two women facing each other, staring at each other. Denise had filled her glass with cognac for the fourth time and gulped it down.

Madeleine took this in for a long moment. "I see you're using this tragedy as an excuse to get drunk," she said, stepping back.

"Madeleine," said Denise, "I've never needed an excuse to get drunk. And I was genuinely fond of Marjorie, as I assume you were."

Afraid this might develop into a full-blown fight, I changed the subject. "Are you sure you won't stay and have some tea at least, Madeleine?" I said. "I'll make some jasmine, if you like."

Madeleine simply shook her head, still eyeing Denise. I started serving the food. It had smelled so good a few minutes ago, but now I had lost my appetite. Denise sat down beside me on the sofa, and we ate in silence for a little while.

"Madeleine, for heaven's sake, sit down," said Denise, finally. "You're giving me the willies, standing there, staring at us."

Madeleine didn't move. Instead she asked, so suddenly that it made me start, "Did she make a good end?"

I put down my plate. "What?"

"Marjorie," said Madeleine. "When she passed away, was her soul at rest?"

Denise almost choked on a mouthful of rice. "Oh, for Christ's sake, Madeleine . . ."

"No." Madeleine shook her head like a school teacher trying to get a point over to slow-witted kids. "It's very important, how we make our end in this world."

This wasn't a topic I wanted to discuss. "Marjorie was very weak at the end. She was on heavy doses of morphine and just slipped away." I could see Marjorie's shaven head down, no longer propped up against the pillows. I could hear the very light sound of her breath.

"That would be typical of Marjorie." Madeleine's mocking voice brought me back to the room. "No will power."

Denise heaved her massive body up, almost upsetting the coffee table with all the dishes on it.

"Madeleine," she said, loudly and firmly. "You're talking a load of crap. Crap, crap, crap. Besides, you're upsetting Jennifer. She's been through hell these past few months." She moved to the middle of the room so the two were standing face to face, two strong beings, like two angry bulls, snorting and pounding the ground with their hoofs.

"It's quite unnecessary to use that filthy language with me, Denise," Madeleine said, keeping her voice low with an obvious effort. "And don't think Jennifer is the first person ever to confront death. In Africa I see it around me every day."

"Yeah, yeah," said Denise. "I'm sure the suffering of the natives affects you deeply. A lot more than an old friend's suffering. You don't seem to care much if Marjorie lived or died. And quite frankly, I don't see why you even bothered to come."

"I'm beginning to wonder myself. I've disrupted my schedule at some cost to come to this out-of-the-way suburb. And I find you wallowing in drink and self pity."

I didn't need Denise's presence, I didn't need Madeleine's presence, and I certainly didn't need a fight on my hands. I felt as though their anger was suffocating me. I suddenly found myself shouting, "Shut up, both of you! Can't you even be in the same room without abusing each other?"

They turned to me, surprised at my outburst. Madeleine was reaching for her purse. "Well, Jennifer," she said, "having paid my respects to the dead, I'd best be leaving. I'm obviously not welcome here. I have a long drive back to the city."

This was not the moment to break the news, but I no longer had a choice.

"Madeleine, stop!"

Madeleine was by the door. She hesitated a moment, looking at me questioningly. Gathering my courage I stood up. "I have a piece of news that concerns all of us. It has to do with Marjorie's house." I paused and took a deep breath. "Marjorie had a house in the suburbs, not far from here. She had no children, her two marriages both broke up, she had no heirs. To make a long story short, she left it to us."

"To the three of us?" said Denise.

I nodded, relieved to have gotten the message out.

Madeleine stared at me, wide-eyed. "A house? In the Chicago area? But why we weren't we informed? This is important."

"That's one of the reasons I wanted you to come. I thought it would be better if I told you. So we could discuss the matter."

Madeleine moved back into the room. "I'd have to see this house, of course, before I thought of accepting the bequest. But that's interesting. Very interesting."

I was astonished. Her reaction was not at all what I had expected. I had thought she would reject the Marjorie's bequest without a thought. If she really wanted her part of the house . . . it boggled the mind. Sharing a house with Madeleine! It had been difficult enough when the four of us were in Baltimore, when she was younger and less terrifying.

Denise gave me a blank look as if she'd been stunned by a falling object. She thought a moment. Then she said, "Well, I'm going to give up my share, Jen. It would make no sense for me to move out here at this point in my career. I'm well established in the New York area."

"I understand." Turning to Madeleine, I said. "But Madeleine, you have your work in Africa. Surely you don't want the burden of a house in Chicago. I'm inclined to agree with Denise. We should sell the house and each claim her share. I myself am not happy about living in that house. Too many unhappy memories. Too many ghosts. I haven't even been back to the place since Marjorie's death."

"Anyway," said Denise, "we don't have to make a decision right away. It will take some time before the property goes through probate and is available for us."

"It won't go through probate, Denise," I said. "Marjorie placed it in a trust, which means that it will be weeks or months, not years, before it's ours."

"Well, then, so much the better," said Denise. "We could sell out right away. And split the profit. Or even rent the place. You know that we don't get on. We certainly couldn't live together."

"Available soon?" said Madeleine, eagerly "I want to see this house. Jennifer, is it possible for us to have a look inside? I'll be free after my meeting, tomorrow afternoon."

"If I contact the successor trustee, I'm sure he'd let me borrow a key," I said, "and I suppose it might be a good idea for you to see it, too, Denise," I said, unhappily. I didn't even want to go back to that house.

Denise sighed from the bottom of her ample chest. "I don't know, Jennifer. I had plans for tomorrow." She thought for a minute. "Okay, I'll come and see the house out of curiosity. But there's not the slightest chance of my keeping my share."

"It's agreed, then," said Madeleine. "We'll come by tomorrow at about four o'clock. Good-bye, Jennifer, Denise." And with a curt nod, she left.

"Marjorie must have been mad to think that the three of us could live under one roof!" said Denise when she had gone. "And why would Madeleine want a house in the U.S. when she has a mission in Africa?"

"I suspect there's something Madeleine's not telling us. And I don't know what to think about Marjorie. I don't know whether this legacy was a whim or a serious dying wish. I sometimes even think it was a sick joke, a kind of revenge against the cruelty of life."

"If Marjorie went to the trouble of setting up a trust, she must have thought it out. But it is strange that she should want to bring the three of us together. She must have known that it couldn't possibly work. We didn't get along that well in Baltimore. And now that we're older, it will be even worse." Denise paused for a minute, reflecting. "But okay, Jennifer, I'll come by and see the house. To satisfy my curiosity if for no other reason."

Denise picked up her purse and looked around for her coat.

"Won't you stay a bit longer, Denise?" I said, more and more reluctant to be alone. "We never finished our Chinese meal. I could re-heat it."

"No, I'll be going too. I'll be here at about four tomorrow."

I got up and hugged her again, feeling her pleasant warm bulk. "Good bye, Denise. And thank you for coming. It has helped."

And then Denise disappeared into the darkness. I was left with the lingering smell of Chinese food and the meows of George. He had been hiding upstairs until the two visitors left and now came down to check out the situation. I picked him up, needing another creature to hold, but he raised a paw in warning. When I set him down, he jumped onto the coffee table to check out the food. He backed away in disgust, jumped down, and meowed to go out. Left alone at last, I turned off the standard lamp and sat by the window in the darkness, looking out on the dimly lit street.

*   *   *

I am running. Running as fast as I can for the floors are polished, slippery and I am afraid I might fall. The corridors branch out to the left and the right, and I must pay attention to the signs. But the signs are in various languages and alphabets and not very helpful. Running fast, for I might be too late. Time is running out. There is no one to ask directions for the people I see in the corridors are all masked with beak-like masks. My breath is coming short; I wheeze and gasp for breath. Time is running out.

And now, as if someone had waved a magic wand, I am in her room. Things will be all right, after all. I will hold her hand and she will speak to me. I cry out, "Marjorie!" But the bed, freshly made, is empty.

*   *   *

The situation was even worse than I had anticipated. I had expected an unpleasant confrontation but one that would blow over, leaving me to deal with the practical matter of selling the house, Marjorie's house, whatever that would involve. Instead, I' had entered a gladiatorial arena where three opposing wills were about to clash. Madeleine actually wanted the house, Denise and I were rejecting it for different reasons, and none of us felt we could live together. Knowing Madeleine and her will power, I would put money on her winning.

And all I wanted was to put the matter to rest and withdraw into what was left of my little world. What I dreaded even more than the discussions, the negotiations, the distinct possibility of losing to Madeleine, was the prospect of going back to Marjorie's house, with its memories and the great unsettled ghost of Marjorie looming over it, lurking in the hallways and the closets.

The following afternoon I was trying to prepare myself for Denise and Madeleine's arrival. That morning, I had busied myself cleaning my own house, doing a wash, getting some food in. Doing ordinary tasks, my mind empty and half attentive to the gestures I was making, helped to pass the time harmlessly, painlessly.

I fiddled around in the kitchen until the little clock on the table showed four o'clock. At that precise moment I heard a car pull up and seconds later the doorbell rang. I ran to the front door and let Madeleine in. To my astonishment, she had a pleasant expression on her face; she was almost smiling. As we were exchanging pleasantries, Denise arrived.

"Hi Jennifer, hi Madeleine," she said. "Shall we get going right away? Let's see this house that we've inherited." To my relief, her manner was neutral, without hostility.

The house was further out, in a desirable suburb, a couple of miles to the north of mine. We drove there in my shabby old Toyota with its hard plastic seats and grimy exterior. The two women lowered themselves into the back seat with some difficulty, giving me the position of chauffeur. I was thinking about Marjorie, remembering the conference I had with her successor trustee when he first told me I was one of the beneficiaries. I tried once more to understand why she had wanted to bring us together under one roof. For lack of an heir, she could have left the house to me. Or to her parents. The idea that Marjorie had done it deliberately, to spite us, kept coming to mind. But Marjorie wasn't a vindictive person, and she had no grudge against any of us. And the strange thing was that even after the failure of her two marriages, Marjorie still loved the house. She had once said to me, when everything seemed to be going wrong in her life, "This house is the only thing that keeps me going. I love living here."

Could that have been why she willed it to the three of us? Could she have wanted to give us the thing she loved most?

We were approaching the neighborhood. If the two women in back spoke at all, I was too preoccupied with my own thoughts to take it in.

We were driving down Ridgeway Road, where Marjorie's house was located; front lawns were becoming wider, houses bigger and more ostentatious. I lurched into the present, jump-started, my nerves tingling, almost trembling. I turned down the familiar road with the cluster of bushes where I had once skidded off into the ditch on a patch of ice. We were almost there. The big brick house next door loomed up on the right, its fluorescent green lawn an offense to the eye.

"Here we are," I said, pulling into the driveway.

The house remained unchanged except that it had an abandoned, unoccupied look, or so it seemed to me. Its soul was gone. The windows were blank, the front yard a tangle of weeds, even more than when Marjorie lived there.

I took a deep breath, got out of the car and walked the few steps up the path to the house. This house. I never wanted to see this house again, never open the front door and walk into the living room, never wanted to touch the fabrics of the upholstery or feel the carpets under my feet.

My hand was trembling as I turned the spare key Marjorie had given me in the lock. We entered the living room, which was just to the right of the front hall. The physical aspect of the house hadn't changed. The furniture was in place, there was no more dust than when Marjorie lived there. There wasn't even a smell of mildewed old house.

I sat down on the living room couch, shivering, despite the warmth of the day. The chill was emanating from somewhere inside me.

"I'll let you look around," I said to the two others. "There's nothing unusual. The dining room's just there"—I motioned toward the back—"the kitchen's behind the dining room, upstairs, three bedrooms, two baths. And, oh, a little room off the kitchen. Marjorie called it the breakfast nook."

The two nodded. I couldn't tell what impression the house had made on them. They went their separate ways, exploring.

I stayed planted on the couch, my coat wrapped tightly around me. It seemed safer downstairs. The master bedroom was the center of the horror, although waves of it emanated through the house. But the living room was bad enough. It was here that Marjorie had told me. She had a glass of wine in her hand though I thought it was too early to be drinking. She was sitting on the living room couch, looking a bit sallow, a bit pinched. She said, suddenly, "Jennifer, I've got a lump on my breast."

"How long have you had it?"

"I don't know. Quite a while."

A chill went down my back. "Have you been to see a doctor?"

"I'm afraid, Jennifer. I'm afraid I might have to have a breast removed. I can't bear the idea. I'd be disfigured for life." She put down her glass and buried her face in her hands.

"You don't even know what it is, Marjorie. It might be something perfectly harmless. See a doctor, if just to know."

"No! I can't! I'm too afraid."

At that moment though I knew nothing I had an intuition. It was all over for Marjorie.

Was it possible that I had given up on her, in a way willing her death?

If I had been a stronger, more persuasive person, would she have listened to me?

I looked out the front window onto the street. The leaves on the maple tree in front of the house had turned yellow with the dry autumn heat. There would be no display of color this year. There was so much to do in the yard. The lawn hadn't been mowed, weeds were invading everywhere, the bushes needed pruning. Even when Marjorie was living here, it was a mess. She wasn't one to care much about gardening. If she couldn't get someone to do it for her, it wouldn't get done.

I heard a creaking on the stairs and Denise came back into the room.

"It's a nice little house," she said. "How big is the lot?"

"Probably about a quarter of an acre."

"Great. We should be able to get $200,000 or even $250,000 for it, seeing that it's a good neighborhood. If we get a real estate agent who knows her stuff." She got up. "I'll have a look around the back," she said, putting on the jacket she had thrown on one of the chairs and going down the hall toward the kitchen.

A few minutes later Madeleine reappeared, her glassy eyes shining with a strange light.

"Denise is out in back, looking around," I said. "You might want to join her."

"No, I had a look from the upstairs windows. It's given me an idea of the extent of the lot." She sat in a chair opposite me and seemed to go inward, the fingers of her hands pressed against her forehead, her eyes unfocussed. Madeleine had always given me a creepy feeling, but never more than for those few minutes when

161

we waited for Denise to come back. She seemed to be deep in meditation. I didn't want to penetrate any further into the house where various demons were waiting for me. But I didn't want to stay put with Madeleine in a zombie-like state. I wandered back into the dining room just as Denise came up through the back porch to the back door. The noise—just by moving her large bulk, Denise made the floorboards groan—broke the silence and the spell of Madeleine's weird trance.

"Ah, Jennifer," she said in a voice that could certainly be heard in the living room and probably up to the attic where Marjorie's spirit was probably lurking, "Ah, Jennifer, I think we'll get a good price for this house."

"Let's sit down and talk this over," said a voice over my shoulder. I turned and there was Madeleine, fully awake, standing in the entrance to the living room.

I didn't want to stay in the house any longer than was necessary. "Please," I said, aware that my voice had turned to a whine, "let's go back to my house. We can use the phone there if we need to contact a real estate agent."

The two agreed, and soon we were sitting at my kitchen table and I was making coffee. Denise had the yellow pages open to "real estate agents," and Madeleine was watching her, the corners of her lips turned down.

As I put the cups on the table, she said, "I'm perfectly happy with the house. You can't bring in a real estate agent. I'm not selling my share."

"Oh, come on, Madeleine," said Denise. "You're just making things difficult for Jennifer and me."

"I see the hand of the Lord in this," said Madeleine, ignoring Denise. She paused, evidently reflecting. "Jennifer," she said abruptly, "you know I don't consume stimulants. Get me a glass of water."

I went to the sink and poured the water for her. She downed it in one gulp. "The Brothers of Light have a mission in Chicago," she said. "They have offered me the stewardship of this mission. I have accepted. The Lord is offering me this house so I may live comfortably as I pursue my career. I will not give up my share."

Denise gave me an "oh, no" look, the smile gone from her face. I was sure she had been elated by the prospect of so much money. It seemed crass to me to toss away a gift that must have had meaning for Marjorie. But the idea of living in that house—no, it wasn't possible.

"Madeleine," I said, "this is going to make everything so much more difficult. If we all shared the house, or all gave it up, it would be relatively straightforward. If we all go in different ways, I can see a legal mess."

"Not really," said Denise, warming her hand on her coffee mug. "All we have to do is have the house assessed. You and I can give up our shares, and Madeleine can buy us out."

"I'm sorry," said Madeleine, "I can't afford to pay two thirds of the value of this house. Besides, the utilities and the property taxes will make it unaffordable for one person. We'll have to share. It was Marjorie's dying wish."

Denise was incensed. "You're trying to railroad us into a situation we don't want, simply because it's convenient for you! I don't think Marjorie's last wish has anything to do with this. I'm not going to accommodate you, Madeleine. And what about you, Jennifer? You don't want the house either, do you?"

"I couldn't live in a house so full of ghosts."

Madeleine was unmoved. "Well, we'll have to see if the Brothers of Light could take it on. They might be able to move some of their mission projects out to the suburbs."

I felt sick at the thought of the Brothers of Light moving into Marjorie's house. Denise had other concerns. "And they'd pay us what, to cover our shares? I don't want them involved in the transaction. I don't trust them."

Now it was Madeleine's turn to be enraged. "You don't trust them! Upright, God fearing Christians! You with your drink and your self-indulgence and your foul language!"

I could see another fight looming. "Madeleine," I said, as calmly as possible, "This is getting out of hand. It's not a question of morality. We simply don't want the Brothers of Light in here. And I don't think Marjorie would have wanted them either. We have to respect her wishes too."

"Now you're the one who's being hypocritical, Jennifer. When you said you were going to sell out, you didn't seem overly concerned about her wishes. Now you're bringing her into the picture. If this is a purely mercenary transaction, as Denise insists, why do you care who buys your shares?"

"I don't know," I said. "But it seems a completely different issue. If we're working it out between the three of us, that's one thing. But I don't like your bringing in an institution to buy us out."

"Well, those are my terms and I'm sticking to them," said Madeleine. Turning to Denise, she said, "Go ahead and have the house assessed. You may find it's not worth as much as you thought. See what a real estate agent has to say before you begin planning to satisfy your greed!"

Denise lurched up as though ready to attack, but Madeleine had picked up her coat and was about to leave. I followed her to the front door. "You'd better get some reliable information about the value of the house and sort this out between you. And I'm keeping my share whether you sell out our not. There may be other like-minded buyers, Christian people I could happily share with. You have my number. Call me at the hotel when you've got the information." With that she barreled out the door.

I turned to go back to the kitchen, but Denise was already behind me, a look of thunder on her face. "That witch! I wouldn't share the Taj Mahal with her if I could have it for free! Count on her to spoil anything you try to do!"

"So what do we do now, Denise?"

"You know, Jennifer, the Brothers of Light might just not be so interested in a property in the suburbs. It doesn't sound like their bag, converting white bourgeois drug addicts, or whatever. Let's go ahead and have the place assessed. Odds on that Madeleine will be forced to sell out. Let's be firm on this, Jennifer. A lot of money could be at stake."

A lot of money! I cared very little about the money, and all I wanted, in the end, was to put the entire matter in someone else's hands. "I'll leave it to you, then, Denise. Bring in a real estate agent and see what she says. Then perhaps we'll be able to reach an agreement."

*　　*　　*

Denise called me the next day. "Jennifer, I'm not sure how to tell you this. Well, I've consulted a realtor, and apparently the house isn't worth as much as I thought. They say $150,000 at the most. And . . . even worse, they say that the house would be hard to sell. It's too modest for that area. People looking in that part of the suburbs want something much grander."

Denise paused.

"You're not saying you want to keep your share of the house!" I said. Denise had been so adamant about selling out.

"Something else has happened, Jennifer. I've been in touch with an artist friend in the city. She moved here a few years ago. She says the art scene here is stimulating. That I'd get new sources of inspiration."

"You're telling me that you want to share the house after all."

"Yes. Well, you wanted to respect Marjorie's last wishes."

"But you never consulted me!"

"I'm sorry, Jennifer. You yourself said you wanted to avoid a legal mess. Really, it's not as bad as you seem to think. We're three professional women. We each have our life, each of us will go our own way."

"You're going to have to give me some time to think this over, Denise. Call me back tomorrow."

Through the night and the next morning my mind worried the problem like a ball that kept bouncing in unexpected directions. I tried to think clearly of alternatives. There was the possibility of selling my share. I couldn't think through the repercussions; I would have had to contact a lawyer for advice. And all I wanted was simplicity in my life, a chance to heal. It felt as though Marjorie had sewed the three of us together like Siamese triplets, bound together, writhing to free ourselves. That was what I felt.

But, after all, Denise had a point. We could each go our way, not disturbing one another, minding our own business. This was what we had done in Baltimore. As for my fears about going back, surely this was sheer childishness, surely I could get over them. So back and forth until dawn, when, exhausted, I decided to give in. Marjorie's house, I reasoned, had many advantages, a better neighborhood, a bigger yard, more space to move around in. I could make the most of the move. It might, in fact, help me to get over this tremendous sadness at Marjorie's death. I called Denise, who had given me the number of the hotel where she was staying, and told her. "Yes, let's go ahead and occupy the house. But on one condition. That you and Madeleine see that it's redecorated. From top to bottom."

It took several weeks to sort the legal problems out and during that time Madeleine and Denise made arrangements to move. Not that either of them had many worldly possessions. They both had chosen to live simply, Madeleine through her choice of vocation, Denise through her choice of lifestyle. Then, as promised, they got the painters in and replaced some of the furniture. It wasn't long, about six weeks, before the house was ours and redecorated. It was about mid-October when the two women came to take me to the Ridgeway Road house.

I sat, surrounded by partly packed boxes, a mini-chaos that reflected my mood. Waiting for them to arrive. My reasoning voice told me that Denise was still my ally, but something within me no longer trusted her. Something was whispering that Denise was now in the enemy camp.

I was worried that my neurotic fears would take over again, that actually living in Marjorie's house would be too much for me to cope with.

And, in the meantime, George had disappeared. He had fled, frightened by the disorder, and possibly sensing my mood. I expected that would please Madeleine. When I told her that I had a cat, the corners of her mouth turned down in disapproval.

"I loathe cats," she said, condemning all those who chose to own one. "Just keep it out of my way."

Poor George, if he ever returned, would face a move and the close proximity of people he didn't know and probably wouldn't like. And where was he? There was no time to go and look for him; the two were about to arrive. I would have to wait until I got back, praying he hadn't left for good. George: not an agreeable cat, not an affectionate cat, but mine, my best, faithful companion. Another loss—the thought pierced me like an arrow.

But I heard the sound of a car engine outside; it was probably the car one of them had rented. Their heavy tread on the front steps, the sound of a knock on the door, the two heavy presences in my living room. Denise was smiling, obviously pleased with herself. Madeleine was guarded, neutral.

"Are you ready for this?" asked Denise.

I nodded, wondering if they had noticed. I was feeling worse then than when they first arrived, more than six weeks ago. It wasn't because I was mourning Marjorie, seeing her wasted face. It was more that the joy had gone out of everything. I had a constant ache in my chest, as if in fact I had some form of heart disease. I didn't want anyone to know; I didn't want to be consoled. I just wanted to be alone.

With an effort, I smiled and looked Denise straight in the eye. "Let's go," I said, my voice reasonably steady.

We got into the Toyota and I put the key into the transmission. My hand was trembling. Why was I so scared? Marjorie had died about two months earlier. I should have been better now, putting things in perspective and getting on with my life.

"I think you'll like what we've done to the house," said Denise, now sitting beside me in the passenger seat. Her large body overlapped the seat, encroaching on the gear box and my personal space. "We've kept the colors fairly neutral throughout, except in the kitchen and bathrooms, which we've splashed with color." I had thought it would be a good idea to redecorate, but now I wondered. A layer of paint could hardly free the house of Marjorie's presence.

I was still trembling as I pulled the car into the drive. But nothing terrible had happened. I followed the old route without getting lost or driving into a ditch somewhere. It took a minute for me to pull myself together, to get out of the car, to look the house in the face. The house, with its blank, staring windows.

"Are you all right, Jennifer? You seem a bit shaky. Can I give you a hand?" Denise said, as I leaned against the car door. One on each side of me, the two women led me toward the house, like the heroine of some Victorian novel, being led by two male relatives to be locked up in a madhouse.

But it's okay, Denise was telling me, and I knew it was okay. We were in the twentieth century and I was a free agent. I had made this decision of my own free will.

We went through the front door, and the smell of paint was overpowering. I imagined it overlaid a more sinister secret smell. The walls in the living room were now a uniform shade of pale yellow, instead of Marjorie's burgundies and beiges. They had replaced some of the furniture, notably the saggy old burgundy couch. The brand new one was sea green and looked too hard to sit on. They had replaced the lace curtains with heavy drapes in pale grey. I knew Marjorie would have hated every detail of the new décor.

"What do you think?" said Madeleine, speaking for the first time. "They've done a good job, haven't they?" I nodded.

"I'm going to look around," I said. I was still afraid, but I knew I had to confront my fears on my own. Their presence would have made it worse. I drifted into the dining room. The walls here were yellow, too, but nothing else had changed. This room evoked nothing for me. It was as though almost all my memories of happier times had been blotted out.

I heard Denise's voice from the living room. "Are you okay, Jen? Want to go upstairs? I'll go with you if you like."

"No, thanks, I'd rather go alone." I pushed myself up the stairs, clutching the banister. Turned right along the corridor leading to Marjorie's bedroom. Stood in the doorway looking in. The room was tidy. No unwashed pantyhose strewn on the floor, no lipstick-ringed coffee cups or half-full glasses on the bed table. She was gone, all traces gone. I couldn't linger. I peeked into the two other bedrooms. Both pale yellow, clean, tidy. One, the one on the end overlooking the back yard, was only partly furnished. I'd forgotten that. I could use my own furniture in it.

I went back downstairs, slowly. I could just make out scraps of conversation from the living room. Or did I imagine them? "Much worse than she . . ." "Maybe this was a bad idea . . ." "You don't think she's . . ." The voices fell silent as the stair creaked. I entered the living room. Composed a voice that sounded false even to me. "It's very nice. So neat and clean." I couldn't think of anything else to say. Denise and Madeleine were sitting opposite one another—Denise in the armchair, Madeleine on the horrible sea-green couch.

"We thought you might like the bedroom at the end of the hall," said Denise.

"Yes, that's all right." But every time I went downstairs, every morning when I left for work, I would pass Marjorie's room, the master bedroom, where she had lain, fading away. That memory would be refreshed every day of my life. "Why have you done this to me, Marjorie," I kept asking myself. "Why?"

I stared at my two future housemates. "For the moment," I added, "I think I'll stay put. I'll move in later on." I looked down at the floor, not wanting to look either of them in the eye. I had decided. I'd go home and unpack. I needed the shelter of my little nest. For now. That was normal, wasn't it? Maybe a couple of days, maybe a couple of weeks. I'd move when I was feeling better.

*   *   *

I am standing in front of a class. It's much bigger than any of the classes I normally teach. Some of the faces at the front are familiar, but in the rows further back, the faces are blurred into a watery substance. A sea of faces. I have an immense burden. I must explain something very important to all these people. But this important thing, this urgent thing, is something I myself don't understand. The burden of responsibility is crushing. I realize I must explain Marjorie's death. But is it her death or my death that I must explain? I am sucked into a golden light and disappear.

*   *   *

I moved in some time in November. Already I was feeling less panicked, more resigned. I had gone back to simply feeling numb. I moved into the smallish room at the end of the upstairs corridor. To my enormous relief, George reappeared the night after I went back to my old home. I moved him with a few of my belongings to Marjorie's house. He adapted better than I expected. He spent most of his time outside, but learned to climb the side of the house and meow at my window for food and company. He often slept at the foot of the bed, guarding me, consoling me. He had nothing to do with Madeleine or Denise.

My life at that point followed a stifling pattern. I went to school, worked in the library, preparing lectures and correcting homework, came back to Marjorie's house late afternoon, cooked a light dinner and had an early night. The little television I set up opposite the bed acted as a soporific.

Marjorie's ghost was still flitting around the house. I knew it was in the master bedroom, hovering over the bed. But as I never went there—that was the room that Madeleine had taken over—I only heard it in the attic, where it rattled around on windy nights. I had learned by an act of will to push memories of Marjorie's illness back into their boxes. I kept the lids tightly shut.

I saw little of the other two. At first Madeleine and I crossed paths in the kitchen, cooking dinner or sometimes breakfast. We would engage in polite small talk, the meaningless chirping of sparrows, and go about our business. After one encounter, though, I stopped lingering in the kitchen.

It was probably two or three weeks after I moved in. I had cooked a simple meal—probably a chop and some vegetables—and put my plate on the table in the breakfast nook. For some reason I got up and to look out the window where the dark leafless trees were silhouetted by next door's lights. I was thinking of an evening I had spent at Marjorie's house when she was still married to Howard. How I had encouraged her to divorce him. I wondered if that had been a mistake. Was Howard a better choice than Giuliano?

I suddenly turned to go into the kitchen and almost collided with Madeleine, who was carrying a plate of fried sardines and cabbage.

"What's the matter with you?" she asked. "Can't you even watch where you're going? You walk around like a zombie all day."

Madeleine righted her plate, from which a couple of sardines had slid off onto the floor, sat down at the little table in the breakfast nook and began spearing pieces of fish with her fork. I took my place opposite her.

How could I have been unaware that she was there? I smelled the food cooking and found the combined odor of fish and cabbage quite nauseating.

I looked at the meat on my plate. It no longer appealed to me, but I started cutting it up into little pieces. We ate for a few minutes in silence, our eyes on our plates.

When Madeleine had almost finished, she looked up and stared at me with her expressionless glassy eyes. "I don't understand how you manage to keep it up," she said finally.

"Keep what up?"

"This zombie-like state, going around with your eyes half-closed, not paying attention." She pushed a final piece of fish into her mouth and dabbed her lips with a napkin. "I understand that you're supposed to be teaching. How can you possibly do any kind of job in that state?"

"I don't know what you're talking about."

"That's exactly what I mean. You're not with it, Jennifer. You're elsewhere. You have responsibilities, to your students and your institution. Instead of doing your job, you're wallowing in self pity."

Instead of rage, which I should have felt, I felt enormous weariness. I didn't want this confrontation with Madeleine, who was sitting upright, like a totem pole, proud, immobile, and completely convinced of her righteousness. "I didn't ask for your advice, Madeleine," I said.

"You'd do well to heed it, so you don't go around bumping into people and tossing their food on the floor. Well. Aren't you going to eat your food? You should at least look after yourself, even if you can't take responsibility for anyone else." She leaned forward to look me in the eye. "And let me just say one other thing. You seem to think that Marjorie's death is an excuse. In fact, you leaned on her so much that you never learned to stand on your own two feet. For you, Marjorie's death is a blessing. It's God's will. You should rejoice that finally you can be a whole person."

Madeleine wiped her mouth with an air of finality. Then she rose from the table and went back into the kitchen to wash her dishes. I was left to stare at my food, feeling as if I'd just been beaten with a heavy stick. At least part of what she said was true and there was no response, or at least I could find no response.

Was Madeleine so harsh? That's the way I remember the scene. But it's possible, just possible, that I'm adding my own criticism to

Madeleine's. In any case, I started taking my dinners up to my room after that encounter. I preferred George's company.

*   *   *

Denise had a less regular schedule. But she kept up contact with me, occasionally coming to see me in my little bedroom. Her heavy presence took up considerable space. She always smelled of paint, paint thinner and alcohol.

I was astonished at how her painting absorbed her, how passionate she could be when a new image burst to life in her mind.

I especially remember her saying, "There's this great glowing yellow ball in the middle, crossed by stark black figures, which break through the surface." Her face was illuminated by the vision. "The ball is the sun, the creative-destructive force of the universe. The figures, like insects, are destroying it."

This sounded insane to me and I couldn't visualize what she meant. I said something like, "That sounds very dramatic," which seemed useless, wishy-washy. I envied her dynamism, her creativity.

One evening she came in slightly drunk, holding a bottle of Scotch in one hand, two dumpy glasses in the other.

"Have a drink with me," she said. "I've had a breakthrough." She sat on the little chair by the dressing table. I wondered nervously if it could take her weight.

"A new inspiration?" I asked.

"Better than that. I've always got inspiration. I've found an agent who will handle my work."

She set the glasses on the dressing table and poured out two drinks.

"Will that mean more sales?"

Denise handed me one of the glasses. "Cheers," she said, tossing back her drink. "Incredible sales. This woman has fantastic ideas about getting my paintings to the public. Terrific contacts. Gallery owners. The press. Rich benefactors. Maybe, for once in my life, I'll make some money from what I should be doing. You know, just to keep the money coming in, I've thought of getting a teacher's certificate. I hate the idea! What a relief if I didn't have to do that!"

I took a sip of my drink and felt it chewing up the lining of my stomach.

"Well, that's really good news, Denise, about the agent," I said, lamely. "I hope it will work well for you."

"You know, Jennifer," she said, pouring herself another drink, "When Madeleine and I first discussed taking our shares in the house, we both had the same thing in mind: Making a 180 degree turn in our lives. Madeleine was sick of life in Africa, the heat, the filth, the diseases. The lack of appreciation for what she was doing. I was fed up with selling real estate to make a living, never having the time or energy to paint, feeling all my creative energy used just to pay the bills. We both wanted a new start in life. That's why we came here." She leaned forward, giving me a drink-glazed look. "You know, Jennifer, that's what you should do. You should try something new. You're in a rut."

I knew that Denise was right; in fact to say my situation was a rut was a gross understatement. I was living in what felt like my own grave. But I didn't want anyone to know that. And I didn't want anyone to help me. I wanted to stay where I was.

"Well, it's hard to change when you're feeling low," I said. "I did manage to move here. That was step one. Now I'm giving myself some time to recover."

"You've been living here for almost a month and you seem in a worse state than ever. You never go out, you never entertain here, you never see anyone. You just seem to go to work and come home. Don't you think you should be making some changes in your life?"

"It's hard for you to understand, Denise. You seem to be able to break off relationship and start another with no pain. I'm different. With me, it's always been friends for life."

"Apart from the fact that that's quite untrue," said Denise, unperturbed, pouring herself another Scotch, "You need to make new friends, and the best way to do that is to take a giant leap, pick someone up on the street, go to a singles group—I don't know— even change jobs . . . Anything."

"There's comfort in the repetition of old habits."

"That comfort is being scared shitless of change. That comfort will end up by smothering you." Denise suddenly turned in her chair and looked at herself in the mirror. Then she turned back to me. "Jennifer," she said, gravely, "have you ever thought of getting help?" She reached into the pocket of her smock and pulled out a business card. "A friend of mine has been seeing this guy," she said. "She says he's terrific." She thrust the card into my hand. "Think about it."

She went slowly toward the door, leaving me with the card and an almost untouched glass of Scotch. I stared at the card:

> Norton Klein, M.S.
> Clinical Social Worker
> Consultations by appointment, 769-4242

Denise was gone. I felt exposed, stripped naked. Denise had found me out. Knew that I was clinically depressed. Unable to do anything about it. Destined for the scrap heap. Did my students, my colleagues, my supervisor, suspect?

I hated Denise for knowing. I hated Denise and Madeleine for starting their new lives. For excluding me. I hated myself for not having a new life. Not even the slightest inkling of one.

*   *   *

Norton Klein had an office in the middle of our little suburban town. It was in a hideous yellow building set back from the road, surrounded by black dead-looking shrubs. My appointment was at four o'clock on a Friday in November with classes finished for the week. I was feeling both apprehensive and hopeful. I was afraid of being exposed to hostile eyes. But at the same time, I held out unrealistic hopes: that this man had supernatural powers and would be able to cure me, that I would emerge from therapy a different, much improved person. Would therapy have helped Marjorie, if she had chosen that option? What would she think of my doing this?

I went up the stairs and pressed the bell under his nameplate briefly, lightly.

"Miss Hill?"

Norton Klein proved to be a small fair-haired man with sideburns, about my age, possibly younger. The look he gave me reminded me of the expression on the face of Tommy Smythers before he pushed me down the cellar hole when I was about four years old. It was the expression of a little bully who at last has found someone smaller and weaker than he is. It was already clear that we wouldn't get on.

Luckily there was no couch in his office. I think if I had had to lie down in his presence, I would simply have run away. Instead we sat in armchairs at opposite ends of the room, face to face.

I said nothing for what seemed like a very long time. There was a large clock just above Klein's head, with a second hand that ticked loudly. I watched the seconds pass, wondering where to begin.

Mr. Klein broke the silence. "What brings you here today, Miss Hill?"

"A couple of months ago, a close friend died. I haven't been able to get over her death."

Mr. Klein looked at me expectantly. The clock ticked on.

"When you say you haven't been able to get over his death, what do you mean? Are you functioning?"

"Functioning?" I had picked up "his death" but didn't correct him.

"You go to work, I assume? Look after your personal needs? Do the shopping, entertain friends, cook meals?"

"Well, yes, I suppose you'd say I'm functioning. I do have a job. But I have no taste for life. I just go through the motions. And I have insomnia. I wake up at four or five in the morning and can't go back to sleep. I'm plagued by thoughts."

Mr. Klein leaned back in his chair, the tips of his fingers touching under his chin. He drawled a little, relishing the sound of his own voice. "What sorts of thoughts?"

"Sometimes I think about her, see her face before she died. Sometimes I think about my own failures and inadequacies."

"So your deceased friend was a woman. How would you describe your relationship with her?"

"Very close. We were friends in college and housemates in graduate school. After that we drifted apart for a while. About seven years ago she moved to this area and we resumed our friendship."

Mr. Klein made no response to this but looked at me as though expecting more. He looked dissatisfied, as though he had ordered a large steak and had been served a sliver of meat.

"You're holding back, Miss Hill." He got up from his chair and walked to the window. Then he turned and looked me up and down. "What do you think your posture is telling me?"

I hadn't been aware of the way I was sitting. I looked down at my lap and my legs. My hands were clenched together and my legs were tightly crossed. He was smiling triumphantly, knowing he was one up on me. "As long as you hold back, I will never be able to make any headway with you. Do you understand?"

I nodded, hating him the way I had hated Tommy Smythers. I resolved that I would not continue therapy, that I would never come back to his office.

"Now," he continued, "we're going to play a little game to get you to loosen up. I'll say a word, and you'll say, without pausing, whatever comes into your head. Remember, don't pause to think. Just say whatever comes into your head. Let's start: Love."

"Death."
"Unhappy."
"House."
"Man."
"Father."
"Woman."
"Unhappy."
"Jennifer Hill."
"Bereft."

Mr. Klein stopped suddenly. He took out a notebook and started writing, his ballpoint pen gliding soundlessly over the paper. But what could he be writing? What could I have revealed about myself? I realized that I didn't want him to know anything about me, about what was going on. I don't want this to work, I thought. Why am I here?

Mr. Klein looked up from his notebook with a half-smile. "Let's talk about your family."

"What do you want to know?"

"Anything you want to tell me."

"My father's a workaholic. My mother's sweet and scatterbrained. She's a stay-at-home mother who collects things."

"What sorts of things?"

"Little fussy decorative items. Brass figurines. Miniature spoons. Smelly candles." I stopped, remembering the living room in the old house on Carleton Drive.

"And why is this important to you?"

"I didn't say it was important. I was only trying to describe what Mother collects."

"Well, if it's the way you characterize your mother, it's important. Apart from her collections, what sort of person is your mother?"

"As I said, scatter-brained. Fixated on unimportant things. The relative prices of a carton of orange juice in the A & P and in Kroger's."

"That doesn't sound scatter-brained to me. You don't have much respect for your mother, do you?"

I fidgeted, chewing a strand of hair. I was becoming impatient. "I don't see the relevance of this to my depression."

Mr. Klein leaned back, putting the pen between his teeth and looking pleased with himself. Then he took the pen and scrutinized it as if it were an exquisite artifact. "Everything is relevant, Miss Hill. Tell me about your father."

"We didn't see much of him, as he worked long hours. He loved to clown around when we were little, to make us laugh. I was his favorite. I suppose it was because I did well in school."

"His favorite? You had other siblings?"

Siblings. "I have a younger sister. Two years younger. Very pretty. Very sociable. Very popular."

"You were jealous of her?"

"Envious. I suppose in a way, at a certain time. We were such different people. After we got to a certain age, it didn't matter."

"What about high school? You had boyfriends, I suppose."

"Only one. Barney Howland." I could see Barney's perfectly round, perfectly expressionless face. "It wasn't very serious. We used to do our homework together."

"And later?"

"I went out with a couple of guys in college. But I didn't fall in love until I was in graduate school. And he went off trekking in the Himalayas. In search of ultimate truth."

"You never married?"

"No."

"You feel you are unfulfilled sexually?"

I didn't want to get into the business about Neil. "I'm sorry. I don't see how this relates to Marjorie's death."

"You want to talk about Marjorie's death? Talk about Marjorie's death."

In fact I didn't want to talk about Marjorie's death. We had been avoiding it since the beginning of the session. I felt as if it were an unspoken agreement between us. I sighed.

"She died at the age of forty-two. Of breast cancer. She might have survived if she had gone to a doctor sooner. But she was afraid."

That was the moment that I kept remembering. Over and over again. That moment in the living room when she told me, when she wouldn't listen to me, wouldn't let me help her.

But all I said to Mr. Klein was, "I couldn't persuade her to see a doctor." I started crying.

"And so you feel responsible for her death?"

"I suppose I do."

Mr. Klein leaned forward again, looking me straight in the eye. "Miss Hill, Jennifer. You must free yourself from that guilt."

"But how?"

He glanced at his watch. "Our time's up. I'll see you next week. But in the interim I want you to think about your guilt. What it means and where it comes from."

I left the session feeling dissatisfied and angry. I disliked Mr. Klein and felt we were going nowhere. I had serious doubts about going back.

I didn't follow Mr. Klein's instructions, to meditate on the nature and source of my guilt. It seemed perfectly clear: I felt guilty because I knew I could have been more persuasive. If I had been a stronger person, Marjorie might have listened to me and seen a doctor sooner. It was unavoidable; I was indirectly responsible for her death.

*   *   *

I am standing in an empty street. It is dark, about midnight. There are no cars; the houses on either side of the street are in darkness. I know I have an important appointment. I wait, feeling cold, and notice I'm wearing a light cotton nightgown. Suddenly Mr. Klein appears. He is wearing pajamas and looks harried. He takes my hand. "Come along," he says. "We must not be late." And then we're in an observation booth, overlooking an operating room in a hospital. My father is there too, but he looks much younger, the way he looked when Martha and I were in high school. We are witnessing an operation that is already in progress. It is not easy to see because the operating table is surrounded by surgeons whose faces are turned toward the body stretched out. I look and look and don't want to see. The surgeons are extracting something from the patient's body. It is a round piece of bleeding flesh. I scream, "I don't want to see! I don't want to see!"

I wake up, rigid with terror.

*　　*　　*

I thought of canceling my next appointment with Mr. Klein but ended up by going anyway. I knocked on the door of his office, tapped lightly, and instead of coming to the door to greet me, he called out, "Come!"

He was sitting back in his chair, twiddling his ballpoint pen. He was wearing a striped shirt and an alarmingly fluorescent pink tie. I sat down, careful not to clasp my hands or fold my legs.

"So, how have you been feeling?"

"Been feeling when?"

"Since our last session."

"I don't know. Pretty much the same."

"Jennifer," he said, sitting up to his full height, "Jennifer, if we are to proceed, we must deal with this issue of displaced hostility."

"Displaced hostility?"

"Toward me. Talk about your anger. I want you to talk about your anger."

"I'm angry that Marjorie has died."

"Your anger toward me."

This made me uncomfortable. He could sense my dislike. "I don't even know you. You said 'displaced anger.' I'm very much aware that I'm angry about Marjorie's death."

Mr. Klein sighed as if for some small but annoying loss, say the loss of his ballpoint pen. "All right, Jennifer, let's go with that. Let's go with your anger over Marjorie's death."

It was true that he was annoying me more and more by using my first name too often and by repeating parts of his sentences. "I'm angry that Marjorie had to die young. And never be happy. And always be searching for something she couldn't find."

"And that something was . . . ?"

"Love, I suppose. A special sort of love. A love that was based on—I don't know—appreciation, respect."

"And you weren't able to give that love?"

"Me?" I was astonished. "I'm not talking about friendship. I'm talking about love between a man and a woman."

Mr. Klein smiled as if he had made an important point. He tapped his pen lightly on the table. "And?"

"She was always falling in love with the wrong man. She seemed fatally attracted to bastards, men who would put her down or use her."

"And what was your role in all this?"

"Well, at various times I tried to advise her, but she never listened to me."

"So you felt excluded."

That seemed wrong. "Excluded? Not really. Just frustrated to see her in so many awful relationships."

"And—I know I've asked this before—how would you describe your relationship to her?"

"Well, I think I said we had known each other for . . ."

"You've already told me that. I don't want facts and figures. I want feelings. Describe a memory you have of Marjorie."

"I can see Marjorie sitting beside me. It's a cool May morning and we're still at school. We're cutting Miss Harriman's Medieval History class. We are sitting by a stream that runs through the campus and talking. Marjorie loves English literature, especially the Romantic poets, and she wants to impart her enthusiasm to young minds. I remember her saying, 'When I read Keats and Shelley to them, they will fall under the spell of that poetry; their hearts will be opened.' Or something like that. The idea of influencing young people that way once enthralled me."

"And?"

"Marjorie never became a teacher. She gave it up."

"It's not unusual for young people to lose their ideals. It's not altogether a bad thing. We all have to make our compromises with life. But why is this memory so important to you?"

"I'm not sure I agree about giving up one's ideals being a good thing. Marjorie had a magnetic personality. She would have been a wonderful teacher. This moment by the stream—it represents an idyllic moment for both of us." Tears came into my eyes as I thought of Marjorie as a young woman, full of hope and enthusiasm.

Mr. Klein was looking at me dubiously. "This was Marjorie's moment, not yours. Did you always let her dominate you?"

"Well, it was the natural thing. She had the stronger personality." I didn't tell Mr. Klein that for a long time I lived in Marjorie's shadow.

"The stronger personality. Who in the family did she remind you of?"

"No one. My father dominates my mother, but he isn't at all like Marjorie. He's cool, detached, intellectual. Marjorie was incapable of detachment."

"Yet she didn't give you what you wanted, emotionally."

"I don't know what you mean."

"You wanted an exclusive relationship, but she was always after men."

I was angry now. My face was hot and I knew I was blushing. "What are you implying, Mr. Klein? That there was something unnatural about my relationship with Marjorie?"

"Well, unnatural is perhaps not the right word. Nowadays homosexuality is becoming more and more widely accepted. And then, how can you explain this obsession over a friend's death? We mourn a friend's death but it doesn't plunge us into depression."

My feelings were so strong and so mixed that I couldn't explain them to myself, let alone to this horrid little man. But I knew with absolute certainty that I wasn't homosexual. I would have laughed but I was too angry. Trying to keep my voice at a normal pitch, I said, "Marjorie was a . . . vibrant person. I witnessed her slow, painful wasting away by cancer. I don't think it's so difficult to understand why Marjorie's tragedy haunts me."

I looked at Mr. Klein. He was looking half-amused, skeptical. I wanted to wipe that expression off his face. "And you have to understand, Mr. Klein," I said, "that the only true, passionate love of my life was a man."

"And where is that man now? I hear you use 'was,' not 'is.'" He looked at me with a triumphant smirk.

"The feelings I had for that man were . . ." I broke off, realizing that anything I said would be twisted in the sense Mr. Klein was aiming for.

"Were what?"

"Never mind." I closed my mouth and hardly spoke for the rest of the session.

Mr. Klein closed his little notepad. "You're not helping me by clamming up," he said, "and you're certainly not helping yourself. I want you to think before the next session why you're coming here and what you expect to accomplish."

I couldn't think of any response to this, but I did think over the week that followed—I thought of quitting therapy altogether. I'm not sure why I went back. It was partly out of curiosity, the need to know what Mr. Klein would dish up next. But more than that, it was the need to have someone to listen to me, even if that person misconstrued everything I said.

*   *   *

That night, as if the session had pushed a button in my brain, memories of Marjorie kept flooding back. Not memories of Marjorie ill and fading away, not Marjorie in her fights with Harold and Giuliano, not even the Baltimore Marjorie, but a younger Marjorie, the Marjorie I knew in college at a time when all things were still possible.

The first time I remember seeing her was in the Survey of French Literature course our sophomore year, on a sultry afternoon in September. The professor, young Dr. Roulin, was talking with some passion about the concept of honor in seventeenth century French theater. Suddenly the class's attention shifted to the back of the room. A dark-haired girl with drooping hazel eyes had put her hand up. I remember noticing how pretty she was, even though her face was strikingly pale, contrasting with her dark hair.

"I don't think those values have any meaning for us in the twentieth century," she said. Her voice was nasal and marked by a snooty Eastern seaboard accent. "I can't identify with the heroine. Or the hero, for that matter."

"But the conflict between duty and honor is universal, Miss Dunnock." Professor Roulin leaned forward, looking questioningly at Marjorie. "Have you never felt torn between your parents' expectations and your personal desires?"

"Not really," said Marjorie, "and in any case, it's not the same thing. The seventeenth century code of honor seems highly artificial, a set of rules imposed on people."

I was surprised that this girl was challenging the teacher and that he even paid attention to her point of view. He replied, "Ah, Miss Dunnock. You must see the study of literature in part as a journey into the past, an insight into concepts of heroism that throws light on the meaning of humanity."

The dark haired, soft-eyed girl shook her head. "If that's the case, I'm afraid I'm still in the dark," she said. An embarrassed titter rippled through the classroom.

From that point on, I watched Marjorie, admiring her from a distance. I was in awe of her for saying what I partly felt to be true. I admired her for her looks and her style, which set her apart from the other female students. Instead of sweater sets and pleated skirts, she wore suits with softly detailed blouses and two-inch heels rather than loafers. I thought of her as a sophisticated Eastern type while I, like the majority of the other girls, was a crass Midwesterner. I never thought we'd become friends.

I'm not sure when we actually first spoke. But I think it must have been a month or so later in one of the dormitory study rooms. We students used these rooms to avoid disturbing our roommates when we had to study far into the night. That night I was studying for an exam in biology, which was my nemesis sophomore year. I got a "C" on the first exam and I was afraid my second would be even worse. It was after eleven when I went into the room, course notes and text under my arm. Marjorie was at one of the tables, her head bent over a pile of papers.

Hearing me come in, she raised her head. "Hello, fellow sufferer," she said. She looked at me for a minute with heavily lidded eyes. "Aren't you in my French lit class?"

"Yes, I'm Jennifer Hill. You're Marjorie Dunnock. Your comments are famous. Well, I have a biology exam tomorrow and I'm scared out of my mind."

"Ah, the sciences. How I hate them! What is the possible use of taking two years of science, spending two hours a week in a smelly lab, cramming in facts that have no relevance to life?"

"I couldn't agree more." I sat at a table on the other side of the room from Marjorie and opened my notebook. We worked in silence for some time. In spite of my fear of the exam, I found myself becoming sleepier and sleepier. I must have been fast asleep when I felt a tap on my shoulder. I raised my head and looked up groggily. Marjorie was standing beside me.

"Look, Jennifer," she said. "I'm bored out of my mind. And you're not getting much done unless you expect to learn from osmosis with your head on that book. Want to go for a cup of somewhere in town?"

Jolted into semi-wakefulness, I stared at her. "But we're not supposed to leave the dorms after ten fifteen. It must be well after midnight by now."

Marjorie crossed the room and turned an old fashioned alarm clock she had brought with her in my direction. "One fifteen. Who cares about the silly rules? I know an easy way of getting out through the tunnel that connects the dorms." She had obviously used this escape route before. "Don't worry. We won't get caught. Who's going to do a late-night bed check?"

And so it began. We used to go to an all-night greasy spoon in the little town where the college was located. With booze and drugs unavailable, we would drink coffee until we were virtually electrified with caffeine, trembling, our teeth on edge, our hair practically standing on end. We cut classes, too, and compulsory convocation. We smoked in Marjorie's dorm room, with her roommate Faye, who was destined to flunk out at the end of the year. But Marjorie and I got away with our little misdeeds because we were relatively bright and because Marjorie knew where to stop. We got good grades. I began to imitate Marjorie's style of dressing and began to ask questions in class. College life began to be a lot more fun.

As far as men were concerned, we didn't do a lot of dating. Marjorie had her admirers, of course, but few dared to ask her out. And with rare exceptions, she turned them down heartlessly. The few exceptions were always a surprise and a disappointment to me. For a while she dated Harvey, the campus poet. Harvey was articulate and bright enough with a magnificent shock of blonde hair, but he had a terrific overbite which I found revolting. And then there was Phil, the brooding philosophy major, who spoke in riddles. He was relatively good-looking but moody and temperamental. He never was on time. There were others, too, I suppose, but none were worthy of Marjorie. She knew that. She dreamed of passionate romance. She also schemed about seducing the more attractive professors. This shocked me. I had had similar fantasies of course, but I never put them into words.

I dated half-heartedly during the four years of college. The guys who asked me out tended to be considerate, mildly attractive and easily forgettable. I, too, longed for something more exciting. There would be time after we graduated and went out into the great world.

We weren't as exceptional as we thought. The great world would prove a test for both of us, and we would emerge from our year in graduate school a bit battered, a bit less innocent and far less hopeful. Realizing how life diminished us both, I felt sad and partly resigned. It might have been better that Marjorie died young. She was less willing to make compromises than I was. I might have been the one better equipped to deal with disappointments.

*   *   *

And now we were coming into the lowest time of year, when night seems to overtake day. One evening Denise came to tap on my bedroom door. It was a Saturday evening, I think, and I was trying to decide whether to go to the library for a supply of books, or settle on the bed with a cup of cocoa and turn on the television to numb my mind.

Denise opened the door a crack. "Can I come in, Jennifer?"

The light from the hallway flooded my dim room. "Of course." I hadn't seen much of Denise lately. She looked thinner, somehow, and was wearing jeans and a clingy sweater. I was used to seeing her in clothes that hid her ample figure.

"How are you doing?" she asked.

"I'm okay. Why don't you sit down?"

"Well, I really wanted to show you something. I've moved some old paintings I've finished from the studio downtown to the house. I thought you might like to see what I've done in the past few years."

"You know I'm no expert on art." I surprised she'd come to ask my opinion. I hadn't seen anything Denise had painted since we moved in.

"No, no. That's okay. I just want a gut reaction. Come down with me. The paintings are in the basement."

The basement. I had hardly ever been there, even when Marjorie was alive. The basement held no secrets for me, but I felt a premonitory tingle. I didn't like to leave my room. I followed Denise down the stairs to the ground floor, to the back kitchen and through the door leading to the basement steps. I hesitated at top of the staircase, taking a deep breath. I didn't know what to expect. She went down first; I followed her.

The basement was divided into two rooms, the back room where the furnace was located, and the front room, more fully finished, with a linoleum floor and light oak paneling. It was in this room that Denise had hung her pictures. She had installed a number of small bright lights that shone directly on the paintings. The one at the end of the room was the most powerfully lit and the most striking. It showed the sun, a pale yellow ball, depicted with swirling brushstrokes moving toward the center where the color deepened to a yellowish-orange. The sun in this painting filled the entire canvas, which had no frame. It hung alone.

"It's magnificent," I said. "But what does it mean?"

"Whatever you like. My paintings have no special meaning. They suggest. This painting could mean creativity or creation. It could mean hope. It could be summer as opposed to winter. It's whatever light means."

"Where are the insects?"

"What?"

"You spoke of this painting a number of weeks ago. I think that was the last time we had a conversation. You said there were little black figures, like insects, destroying it."

"Did I? I must have decided not to include the little black figures. I don't remember."

"Maybe you're more positive than you were when you first got the idea."

I turned to look at the other paintings, a couple of portraits and a large canvas, which had been hung on the back wall. The portraits were highly detailed studies of women's faces. Surrounding the large canvas were a number of smaller pictures, some sketches, some paintings, which had been done as studies for the master painting. This was a panoramic view of a circus, a Bosch-like creation, with all the traditional circus figures—clowns, trapeze artists, elephants, acrobats—spread across the canvas. Above all, and larger than life, was the lion tamer, with great muscular arms and shoulders and strongly lined face, wielding a whip. There was something grotesque, something disturbing about the picture, something that seemed out of character for Denise.

"Why did you choose to do a circus painting?" I asked, leaning forward to see the detail. "Is there some kind of symbolism is this?"

Denise shrugged. "I've always loved the circus," she said. "The performers . . . seem to have a kind of freedom that most people lack."

"But the figure of the lion tamer," I said. "He looks so menacing. And he's so big. Is there a reason for that?"

"The lion tamer dominates the whole. You can see symbolism in that if you like. Anyway," she turned toward me, "these are old paintings, paintings that I did in Brooklyn. I'm starting a new series now."

"Different subject matter?"

"Some studies of people. In a more abstract style. You can come down to the studio and have a look, if you're interested."

My eyes went back to the painting at the end, obviously a more mature and more original painting. "Are the new paintings similar to that one?"

Denise's eyes lit up. "Do you like that one? I did it in a kind of frenzy, in the course of an afternoon. I've been preoccupied with light, the workings of light, since I moved here."

"That's a powerful painting, Denise. I hope you do more like it. How long has it been since I've seen any of your paintings? Are you planning an exhibit?"

Denise sighed. "Yes, but there's still a lot of work to be done. As I said, my current pictures are a series of studies of people in bars and cafes. And when I finish those, well, I'm not sure."

"And what about showing your work?"

"Well, I'll see if I can exhibit solo, which isn't easy. Then a new idea will come to me. I may do some sculpture. To adorn and complete the show."

"Sculpture? Of what?"

"I'll figure that out when I get to it. I never plan ahead."

I stood for a few minutes admiring the paintings. My eyes kept traveling back to the one of the sun. It was as though it simultaneously drew in and threw out light. "It's amazing," I said. "It reminds me of that Van Gogh painting of the night sky—what's it called?"

"'Starry Night.' It's because of the brush strokes. The composition and the intent couldn't be more different."

"Oh," I said, embarrassed again by my ignorance. "Shall we go upstairs again? There's something about this basement that gives me the creeps. Not your paintings, Denise. It feels as if there are unquiet spirits down here."

Denise laughed outright. "You have an over-active imagination, Jennifer. There are no ghosts down here. I've been here in the middle of the night up till the early morning."

We went back up to the kitchen. Denise made me a cup of tea and poured herself a Scotch. We took our drinks out to the back porch. It wasn't heated, and I shivered, pulling my cardigan tightly around me. You could see nothing of the garden or the old oak trees through the enveloping darkness.

"Denise, the last time we spoke, you mentioned getting an agent. How has that worked out for you?"

"Oh, that woman." Denise took a sip of her drink. "It didn't. That woman. She was on the biggest ego trip you could imagine. But apart from that, I'm pretty happy here. I'm beginning to make connections. Knowing Ellen Bagtree has helped."

"Ellen Bagtree?"

"That woman I knew in New York who moved out here. She's into the feminist stuff. And conceptual art. I can't follow any movement, you know. I just paint."

"I thought that circus painting had a message. Something about power and oppression." Denise shook her head, not bothering to answer. We sat for a few minutes looking out at the darkness.

Then Denise said, "How's it going with you?"

"A little bit better. I just keep going to work and coming home. I still feel numb and unconnected."

"What about the therapy?"

"I don't know. That therapist . . . I guess I basically don't trust him. He's a bit of a prick."

"That's too bad. It's Norton Klein, you're seeing, isn't it? I was told he was pretty good."

"Maybe his approach isn't right for me."

Denise finished her drink. "Tell you what. Have you ever thought of taking up some form of art? To get some of those feelings out?"

"I have absolutely no talent."

"Don't put yourself down. Anyway, it's not a question of talent. It's—I don't know, but when I paint, it's like my whole being is involved. I come to life. You need something like that, Jennifer."

I looked at her dubiously. It seemed unlikely that I would ever come to life. Partly to change the subject, I said, "How is Madeleine these days? I hardly ever see her."

Denise leaned back and stretched. "Yah. Madeleine's fine. She's changed since Baltimore days. Softened. I see her from time to time. She's much easier to talk to now."

"I didn't have that impression when she first came here. If I remember correctly, you two didn't get on well. You hated each other."

"She was defensive then. She was going through a kind of mid-life crisis and didn't want anyone to know. Her attitude toward religion has changed. She's much more open-minded."

"Really." I couldn't imagine Madeleine open-minded. "How's her new job?"

"Great. She's doing a lot of work with troubled adolescents. Dope addicts, especially."

"She must have changed!" I couldn't imagine Madeleine working with troubled adolescents either. She was—or at least used to be—far too rigid. Since that confrontation in the breakfast nook, I had avoided Madeleine altogether. She certainly hadn't been approachable then.

"You should talk to her some time. When she's not being an ass-hole, she's quite an inspiration." Denise finished her drink and got up. I had sensed for a few minutes that she was no longer with me, that she wanted to get back to work. "I'm going back downstairs," she said. "I have a new idea about the lighting." Before passing into the kitchen, she turned to me. "And don't forget about painting. I'd set you up, if you wanted to try it."

I nodded and watched her cross the kitchen toward the basement stairs. I sat for a few minutes on the back porch, feeling the stillness. I had no aspirations beyond getting through the next few months, beyond the great gulf of Christmas and the sparse lights of January, then into blackest February. With lesson plans and corrections, meetings and classroom lectures. Young faces of students ever-changing; the old ones of colleagues always the same. My face more drawn and wrinkled. Denise and Madeleine moving on to conquer new worlds, me stuck in the slowly moving vortex of the seasons, slowly borne down to the abyss of winter, slowly borne back up to the blazing heat of summer. I thought of Denise's painting. To achieve something like that, that would be enough. And all I can hope for is up-dating stale old class notes.

*   *   *

It was suddenly Christmas, a time I had been dreading since Marjorie's funeral. Christmas had always been a difficult time for me, a time of unfulfilled expectations. And now it was a time of reckoning, a time when the report card came in, listing my deficiencies. No husband, no children, no strong career, no accomplishments. Now added to that was the sense of loss. No Marjorie.

The advantage of Christmas over New Year's, the other black hole of the year, was that there was always a lot to do. With classes over for the holiday, I was rushing around, buying presents for family and colleagues. There were decisions to be made: which book to buy for Daddy, which style of nightgown for Mother, which perfume for Martha. I had to struggle through the crowded shops, have my senses hammered by the decorations and constantly repeated music. All this kept me feeling alive.

After a great deal of soul-searching, I had decided not to go back to see my family in Michigan. I didn't want to be reminded of my feelings and fretted over by my mother.

On the afternoon of the twenty-second, I went out to buy last-minute presents for Madeleine and Denise. I had no idea what to get for either of them, so I simply bought Madeleine a pair of rather expensive lined gloves and Denise a good bottle of Scotch.

I lingered in the streets, looking in department store windows and the tempting merchandise. There was a mauve silk dressing gown in the window of Seeman Gates that I loved in an abstract sort of way; I couldn't imagine possessing it or, even less, wearing it. Then the handbags! The extravagantly wrapped boxes of chocolate! The high, laced boots! I hesitated a moment, thinking about buying myself a present. Marjorie wouldn't have hesitated to buy a present for herself. But for me . . . no, that would be pathetic. No one would know, but it was just something I couldn't do.

I took a bus to our neighborhood and walked the six blocks to the house. People had put lights up in their windows; Santa Clauses perched on the roofs of some houses. There was a glimmer of snow on the ground, a hint that winter had just begun. By the time I got to the house, I was numb with cold and it was just getting dark. From the street, I could see that there was a Christmas tree lit up in the living room, casting its light on the snowy lawn. I hadn't noticed a tree when I left to go shopping and was surprised it had gone up so quickly.

Denise met me at the front door. "Merry Christmas!" she called out, exuding her customary smell of alcohol. "Come have a look at the tree! Hilda and I have been making decorations all week!"

She took my arm and guided me into the living room. The Christmas tree was bright and comical. The decorations were mostly colored birds, but there were a few more traditional figures, lopsided angels and tipsy-looking Santas.

"It's fun," I said. "How did you make all that?"

"Most of the figures are cloth, as you can see, painted and stuffed. Some are dough, some are papier mache. Fantastic, isn't it? Come and meet my friend Hilda Manning."

She led me back to the kitchen, where Hilda was mixing a great bowl of cookie dough. She was an older woman, in her late fifties or early sixties, with long, wispy grey hair pulled back in a pony tail and an unfocused look. I wondered if she had also been drinking.

"I like your tree," I said. "What are you making?"

"Pecan bars," she said with a broad smile. "They have a pastry base and a gooey nut topping. Devastating!"

"Hilda is an art therapist," said Denise. "I thought you might want to talk to her, you know, about how art might help you."

I felt as though a spotlight had been shone on me. "I'm afraid I don't have artistic tendencies, Hilda," I said.

Hilda put down her mixing bowl and looked at me closely, near-sightedly. "Denise might be a step ahead of both of us. But if you'd like to get acquainted, we could meet for a cup of coffee some time. When the Christmas business is over."

"That would be nice," I said, lying, though Hilda seemed harmless enough. "But right now, I'd better go. I have Christmas presents to wrap."

"Why don't you come down later and sample Hilda's pecan bars?" said Denise.

I left, knowing I wouldn't go back, despite the tempting smell of baking that wafted up to my room. I was angry with Denise for discussing my problems with someone I didn't know, and I was dubious about art therapy, which sounded phony to me. I took refuge in my room and only came back to the kitchen to cook dinner at around eight. By that time, Hilda had left. But Denise was in the living room, tacking up evergreen branches.

"I love Christmas," she said. "Even the hokey commercial part of it. It's supposed to be for kids, and I guess I'm a kid at heart."

"I like your decorations."

"It's too bad we don't decorate every day. Or at least every month. I'd like to put lots of color and stuff all over the room— balloons and crepe paper and stuffed animals, you know, like for a kid's party."

I just smiled, wondering if Denise had been hitting the bottle a bit more than usual. "Well, I'd better get something to eat." I was actually very hungry.

"Say, Jen. I'm giving a little party on Christmas Eve. Would you like to come? Madeleine will be there."

As if that were an incentive! But I couldn't refuse. There would be no escaping the noise anyway. "Yes, I'd like that," I lied again. "Could I bring something?"

"Umm . . . I'm not sure. I'll let you know." Denise thought for a minute. "Why not? Could you bring an appetizer? That's all we're serving. Appetizers and mulled wine and Christmas cake."

"Sounds delicious. I'll make chicken liver pate." I went back to the kitchen and opened a can of soup. I was already dreading Denise's Christmas party.

*   *   *

The next evening Madeleine came into the kitchen as I was cooking dinner. I always dreaded these encounters because Madeleine had a way of prodding me in my weakest parts so it really hurt. I emptied the contents of my stir fry onto a plate and was about to go upstairs with it, when I looked up and saw her watching me with her glassy stare.

"Hullo, Madeleine."

"Jennifer. What are you doing on Christmas Eve?"

"Well, as you know, Denise is giving a party. She's invited me. I thought she had invited you too."

"Huh. Yes, She did invite me. But I'm not going to a drug fest on the night before the birth of Our Lord. I will be as far away from this house as possible, in body as well as in spirit."

"Well, I'm not too keen myself, but I'm not sure how to avoid it." I wanted to end the conversation and get out of the kitchen as soon as possible; my dinner was cooling.

"There are many good ways of spending Christmas Eve, Jennifer. Have you ever thought of doing something useful?"

"Umm." Madeleine's idea of something useful wasn't promising.

"The Brothers hold a soup kitchen every night, and Christmas Eve is very special. We're expecting record numbers. You could help serve."

"I don't think so."

"Well, think it over. I could give you a ride downtown. It might do you good to help people less fortunate than you. Lift your spirits."

I took my stir-fry and went upstairs with it. To spend Christmas Eve in a soup kitchen serving to those less fortunate than myself wasn't highly tempting. But on the other hand, the idea of a raucous party, rowdy people enjoying themselves and getting drunk, was even less appealing. On reflection, I decided to join Madeleine. I would throw my lot in with the rejects of society rather than the joyful party makers. I would feel more affinity with the downtrodden.

On Christmas Eve Madeleine came back from work in the city and picked me up in her battered jeep. We were both silent as she drove me to a benighted neighborhood downtown—all boarded-up shops and derelict buildings. You could imagine drugs being sold and consumed at every street corner. In this area the Brothers owned an ancient building they had modernized to make into a kitchen and dining halls to feed the needy.

It was almost dark when we got there, and I was feeling withdrawn and sleepy. We entered the kitchen by the back alley. After the grayness of the street, the brilliant light of the kitchen shocked me to painful wakefulness. The scale of the enterprise was surprising. The meals were being prepared factory style, with huge vats of stew, canned beans and mashed potatoes burbling on a large stovetop. Cheerful, efficient individuals in white uniforms bustled around, stirring the vats, adjusting the flames under them, and adding ingredients. The kitchen was very hot and smelled of a combination of disinfectant and commercial gravy mix. There was a hum of fluorescent light and gentle chatter, as the staff encouraged one another with positive comments. It was impossible to tell if these people were men or women; they were all round in face and body, smiling, and perspiring.

Just above the door leading into the dining rooms was a painting of Jesus, looking martyred. I shared his feeling. I wanted to escape, but Madeleine was holding my arm with a firm grip and wouldn't let go. She gestured to the workers.

"This is Jennifer Hill, one of the women who live in my house," she said. "She has volunteered to serve with us tonight. Jennifer, this is Petunia, Holly, and Hildebrand."

The three beamed at me. "Bless you," said the shortest, roundest one, who I took to be Petunia.

We went into the dining room, which was as brightly lit as the kitchen. Madeleine showed me the cafeteria line and handed me an apron and hairnet. "You'll be serving potatoes and vegetables," she said. "It shouldn't be too difficult for you." She guided me into position behind the food area and stuck a ladle into my hand. "Just be sure not to overdo with the portions. Make each ladleful flat. We have almost five hundred to serve tonight."

Two of the kitchen workers brought in the vats of food. To my relief, it was one of them, not Madeleine, who was to serve beside me. Madeleine, it seemed, was directing proceedings.

The doors opened and a great mass of people plodded in. They took their places in line quietly. They were gray, all the more gray for the harsh light, gray in their dress, gray in their withered skins, gray in their expressionless faces. Once in a while one of them, usually a man, protested the small portions, but most of them passively took their plates and went to settle somewhere in the endless room, under the dazzling light, stooping over their plates, shoveling food in. With the hairnet exposing my face, I could feel the light stripping all my disguises away, showing the circles under my eyes and the lines around them, revealing my sad, circumscribed life. Behind the vats of food, I was being useful, for once, but it gave me no joy. I could only feel the heaviness in my legs and pain in my feet as the endless procession of hungry people came on.

It was almost ten o'clock when the last portion was served. I went heavily back to the kitchen to see what cleaning up was left to be done.

"We've got it under control, dearie," said one of the round-faced workers. "You look a little peaky, so we won't ask you to work. Help yourself to whatever's left of the food."

I shook my head and looked around. Madeleine was nowhere to be seen and there were no chairs in the kitchen. I went back into the dining hall and slumped down at one of the empty tables. It hadn't been cleared yet; the sad remains of the stew—bits of gristle too tough to chew—lingered on some of the plates. In the center of the table a candle in the shape of a potbellied Santa was burning, the wax spilled over like spent lava. The Brothers' concession to the worldly aspects of Christmas. I was looking around to see who was still eating when Madeleine appeared.

"Come on, let's get these tables cleared," she said briskly.

I wondered briefly where she had been, but was too tired to think. "Only a short time more, and I can go home," I told myself. Madeleine was stacking dishes on trays and taking them into the kitchen. I found a table where the trays were stacked and helped her, feeling awkward in my exhaustion and worried that I might drop a plate. Madeleine was going from table to table where some of the latecomers were finishing off their dinners. She was greeting them, and they were thanking her profusely; these were probably the habitués, those that came frequently. At the last table, she sat down and said a prayer; all the diners bent their heads and mumbled the words after her.

At last it was time to leave. Madeleine smiled her most radiant smile at me. "You feel better now, don't you?" she said as we got into the car. I said nothing. I was so tired that I fell into a deep sleep on the way home.

*   *   *

I was still half-asleep when Madeleine dropped me off at Ridgeway Drive. She was going back to the city to spend the night at the shelter. I stood outside, chilled and exhausted. I could hear the music even before I reached the front door; the entire house seemed to be rocking. As I went in, all my senses fell under attack, by the noise, the smoke, the crowds of people. The noise, of thumping music, voices competing to make themselves heard, piercing shrieks of laughter—it all seemed too great for the house to contain. It was as if all that seething life was causing the structures, the roof and the walls, to swell and expand. I entered an enormous cloud of smoke—marijuana smoke, I was pretty sure. Clawing my way through the living room, I made it as far as the back porch, where I took in deep breaths of cold night air. I wondered whether the neighbors had complained, but who in the party would even know unless the police suddenly arrived.

I would have liked to stay on the porch, but it was too cold, so I went back into the kitchen. A couple was locked in embrace, leaning over the kitchen sink. Another couple was exploring the liquor cabinet, taking out bottles, unscrewing the lids and drinking straight from them. There was a woman sitting on the floor, propped up against the stove, weeping. No one noticed me.

I went into the dining room, where the noise was louder. It was crowded with people, many swaying to the rhythm of the music, some smoking or drinking. The snacks had gone long ago. I looked for a sign of Denise or Hilda, but could find neither of them. There was no point in staying on, so I went upstairs, closed myself in my room, and put the TV on full blast. It didn't drown the noise, so I turned it down, took a Sominex, and watched the figures on the screen until I fell into a drugged sleep. I woke up after a couple of hours. The noise had lessened. I could hear car doors banging as people got in to make their way home. By about five, it was over, and I went to sleep until just about nine.

It was useless to try to sleep any longer, so I went downstairs to see if I could make myself a cup of coffee. I surveyed the living room, wondering how people could make so much mess in the space of a few hours. It was as though the spirit of the house, and with it, Marjorie's spirit, had been violated. With the noise, the mess, the carousing. How could Denise have done it? And how could she know so many people?

I went into the kitchen to make coffee and survey the damage. Even though I hadn't had a drink, my head ached from the smoke and the lack of sleep. Setting aside a couple of dirty pots—someone had probably made an early morning meal of oatmeal or gruel—I put the kettle on the stove and boiled water. I needed a battle plan to deal with the mess. The first thing I did was to open a couple of windows to get in some fresh air. Then I emptied ashtrays and half-full glasses, got rid of the remnants of food, and took a huge bag of garbage to the bin in back. I vacuumed, I put glasses in the dishwasher, I scrubbed the kitchen. As I worked, I began to feel better. The house was freezing cold with the windows open, but at least it was fresh air coming in.

After about half an hour, I got myself a bowl of granola and sat down in the breakfast nook. The milk was just on the turn, with little solids floating to the surface, but not to the point where it tasted revolting.

This is my Christmas, I thought. Christmas eve in the soup kitchen, Christmas morning with piles of filthy mess to clean up, sour milk on a bowl of stale granola and no friends or family.

I thought of Christmas in Michigan. It wasn't a whole lot better. Once I had tried to explain my feelings about Christmas to Marjorie. It was after the Christmas break that year we had shared the house in Baltimore. I had come back early. I was sitting up in bed in my little room under the roof, listening to the wind and half drowsing. Then, unexpectedly, Marjorie burst in, flushed from the cold and exuberant.

We talked about Christmas. She imagined a Midwestern Christmas to be full of frigid walks and fireside warmth and family feeling. Marjorie couldn't imagine a Midwestern family as stress-filled and conflicted as mine.

How young she was then, how full of life! She was excited about the clothes she had bought in New York, the semester about to begin, her teaching. I was cozy, sleepy, unresponsive. As usual, I only served as ballast to Marjorie's balloon.

The sound of voices on the staircase brought me back to the present. In a few minutes Denise and Hilda appeared. They came to the doorway between the kitchen and the breakfast nook. They looked perfectly refreshed in spite of the night's orgy.

"Hey, Jennifer," said Denise. "Thanks for cleaning up. I owe you one."

"Me too," said Hilda. "You're an angel." She came over, leaned down, and gave me a big hug. "Hope we didn't keep you awake all night."

"Well, it was pretty noisy. I did join the fray at one point, but the food was gone and I didn't see either of you."

Denise giggled. "We actually found it a bit much at one point. We escaped. Went for a little drive."

Hilda and Denise were an item then. I was surprised. I knew that Denise was bisexual—she had told me as much—but Hilda was so much older and not especially attractive.

"We're going to make breakfast," said Denise. "Will you join us?"

"Well, I don't want to intrude."

"Don't be silly." Denise had her head in the refrigerator. "What do you say, Hild? Will you make one of your killer omelets with all the veggies?"

"Whatever's there. But what about . . . ?" She nodded in my direction.

"Oh, we have a couple of small presents for you, Jen. They're under the tree."

I was touched and childishly pleased. "Just a minute," I said. I ran upstairs to get Denise's present and was down in a flash. "Sorry I didn't get anything for you, Hilda."

"Don't worry." Hilda was smiling broadly. She handed me a beautifully wrapped package. The paper, which had a pattern of exotic birds, was hand-painted. "It's not much," she said.

Denise handed me another small package and opened the one I gave her.

"It's a bottle of malt whiskey! That's really special. Thanks, Jennifer."

"But Denise," said Hilda. "Didn't we say . . ."

"Yes, I am going on the wagon. But after New Year's."

I realized I had probably made a serious mistake. I didn't know that Denise was trying to deal with her drinking problem. An expensive bottle of booze was not the thing. And it seemed so crass, somehow, in its commercial wrapping.

Hilda had given me a couple of packets of seeds, of foxgloves and cosmos. I didn't want to admit it, but I didn't even know what cosmos looked like. But I said, "For the coming spring! How wonderful!"

"I don't want to disappoint you, honey," said Hilda, "but you won't even be able to plant the seeds until late May . . . or even later. A question of much-delayed gratification, I'm afraid."

Denise's package contained a set of water colors.

"This comes with a lesson on how to use them," Denise said.

"You're really pushing me into art! Well, I'm very pleased. Thank you both so much. And as far as breakfast is concerned, I've already had my granola."

"All right," said Hilda. She was already breaking eggs into a bowl. She stopped and turned to me. "Jennifer," she said, "I . . . uh. I do art therapy. I am licensed. Why don't you come, just once, to see what it's like. It might help. No commitment."

"Well, I'm not sure. Am I supposed to bring my new water colors?"

"You don't have to bring anything, honey. Just come."

$$* \quad * \quad *$$

"Draw me your house," said Hilda. We were sitting in her brightly lit studio in the countryside not far from our town. There were crude drawings, probably done by her clients, all over the walls and strewn on the table in front of us. The place smelled of fresh baking and stale cigarettes.

"You mean the house I'm living in now."

"You were thinking of the house you used to live in? No, not today, honey. I want to see the house Marjorie left to you." She gave me a very large piece of shiny paper. "You can use anything you want—pencil, crayons, watercolors."

I looked at her doubtfully. She had a kind, weather beaten, wrinkled face and wispy hair, pulled back into a pony tail that didn't suit her age or her personality.

I decided on the crayons and proceeded to draw. The paper was far too big. My house, my picture of the house, came out in the lower right-hand corner. It came out viewed straight on, too square, with a sharply pitched roof. I scribbled green bushes in front of the house on both sides. All it needed to look like a child's drawing was a sun with beams projecting.

"I'm afraid I can't draw."

"That doesn't matter." She looked at the drawing. "It seems very closed. Draw me one of the rooms inside. You can use the same piece of paper."

I began to draw the living room. But I couldn't get the perspective. I couldn't figure out where I would be standing to see most of the room.

"Draw the part or even the piece of furniture that has meaning for you," said Hilda, seeing me flounder.

I drew the couch and spent a lot of time coloring it burgundy. Then I drew a coffee table that partly obscured it. And a lamp beside it.

Hilda came around the table and looked over my shoulder. "I thought the sofa was green."

"Oh, I'm sorry," I said, foolishly. "You're right. But burgundy is the color it used to be . . ."

"Before Marjorie died."

"Yes," I said and found myself crying.

Hilda moved to the chair beside me and pressed a piece of kleenix in my hand. "Just have your feelings, Jennie," she said. "You don't need to say anything."

After a while she said, "Did anything happen in that room that has a special meaning in terms of Marjorie's illness?"

The same image, the same memory came back.

"It was there that she told me she had a lump on her breast. I told her she should see a doctor right away, but she didn't want to. She was afraid." I stopped myself.

"That was the first you knew about it?"

"Yes."

"Tell me your feelings about that."

"I think now . . . that I put too much pressure on her. That if I hadn't been so scared myself, she might have listened to me."

"You don't know that, Jennie. We often feel guilty about the death of loved ones, but it's not our fault. If you're going to get over this trauma in your life, that's one thing you're going to have to accept: You're not responsible for Marjorie's death." She looked at me with her kind, vague eyes. I felt this was too pat. And I hated being called Jennie.

"Let's draw the bedroom," she said. "I mean Marjorie's former bedroom."

"I can talk about it without drawing it."

"I know you can, but I want you to draw it."

I knew Hilda wanted me to draw the bed, possibly with Marjorie in it, so I didn't. I drew Marjorie's dressing table with cosmetic tubes and bottles on it and a mirror behind it.

"So why have you drawn this?"

"I don't know. I suppose that Marjorie was very concerned about her appearance. She was beautiful before she got sick."

"Why is that important?"

"Because . . . I don't know. It seems all the more cruel that she died relatively young."

"Draw Marjorie's face in the mirror."

"I can't draw people at all."

"It doesn't matter. Just give an impression."

The face I drew bore no resemblance to Marjorie. It was just a circle with the features barely indicated, surrounded by a tangle of black hair.

"I'd like you to enlarge that face. Draw it on its own, trying to make it as big as possible."

For some reason, I felt angry. I drew a haggard face with exaggerated cheek bones and deep pouches under the eyes.

"This is Marjorie sick?"

"It's not really Marjorie at all. I don't know why it came out that way."

"You felt angry drawing it. And it represents your fears, of physical decay, of death."

"It's just my effort to draw Marjorie. It's hard for me to make a drawing look like anyone in particular."

"When you draw something, anything, and the process of drawing awakens strong feelings, that drawing represents a struggle inside you. We're going to have to stop now, Jennifer. Do you feel that you've come any closer to understanding your grief?"

I didn't want to say no. I didn't dislike Hilda; she seemed kind and innocuous. I didn't want to hurt her feelings by saying she had wasted my time. "I'll have to think about it." I hesitated. "Hilda, the therapist I'm seeing, Mr. Klein, thinks that it's all—I mean my depression is all to do with repressed homosexual feelings for Marjorie. Do you think that's true?"

"Jennie, I can't comment on another professional's opinions. But I would take a different approach."

I left the sunny workroom feeling calmer but relieved I had only agreed on one session. That night, on the edge of sleep, I saw that haunted face again. I saw the cheeks and the eyeballs fall in as if eaten by worms from within. And I knew that face was my own.

*   *   *

I canceled my next two sessions with Mr. Klein. I was still angry with him, but more than anything our meetings seemed irrelevant. He was a large cat chasing a mouse that didn't exist. The prospect of watching him try to catch me out was no longer threatening.

After two weeks I did go back, reluctantly. His first comment when I settled in my armchair was, "You've canceled our last two appointments. You know what that means, don't you?"

I smiled, knowing my expression was insincere. "I know what it means to me. And I'm pretty sure I know what it means to you."

"Let's start, then, with you." I watched him to see if his expression, usually cunning or neutral, had changed. It hadn't.

"These meetings have become largely irrelevant to me because you're on the wrong track."

The pen came out again, tapping on the pad. "I see. And what do your cancelations mean to me?"

"That we're on the brink of some kind of break-through. And that I'm resisting because I'm scared."

"Why would you be scared?"

"I'm scared of any change. I suppose you'd say I'm scared of losing my defenses."

"And what would I have to do to reassure you, to make you give up your defenses willingly?"

"But Mr. Klein, I don't believe we're on the brink of anything. You keep riding this hobbyhorse of homosexuality, but that has

nothing to do with my depression. You've got it wrong, Mr. Klein."
My heart was beating fast, but Mr. Klein looked unperturbed.

"So why are you so emotional about this?"

"Because I'm challenging authority. I seldom stand up for my rights."

Mr. Klein sat for a few minutes, reflecting. "When patients are feeling challenged by their therapist, they often rebel. You mentioned resistance. Yes, I think this is the case with you. I think you may have been right in breaking off our sessions for the time being. I think you should go home and let some time go by. But don't lie to yourself, Jennifer. We are making headway and we could possibly have a breakthrough. If you let it happen. So I'll leave it up to you. When you're ready to work with me, come back. But you're going to have to be willing to face reality."

He spoke those last words with emphasis, standing up so he would appear to dominate me. I stood up as well. I shook hands with him. I wished that I had worn heels.

I left, feeling dissatisfied. What should have been a major confrontation with fireworks had fizzled out. I was disappointed and at the same time relieved.

I saw Mr. Klein once after that, in the supermarket some months later. He was struggling to control his little boy, a monster of six or seven, who was pulling cans and boxes off the shelves and throwing them on the floor. I smiled a greeting. I felt vindicated.

*   *   *

It was in mid-February, that month that has nothing to recommend it except for the slight lengthening of the days. I had taken up drawing. Most likely it was the session with Hilda that got me started. It had triggered in me a desperate need to re-capture Marjorie's face. I could no longer picture it. I could describe it in words—the winged eyebrows, the drooping hazel eyes, the strong mouth and chin—but the image was gone. Strange to say, I didn't have a photo of her. There was one in the college yearbook, which I spent some time studying, but it was posed and lacked life.

First, for practice, I drew my mother and sister, using old photos to copy. I drew them over and over again. Eventually I was able to achieve a kind of caricatural likeness, but it was never quite close enough. Then I tried to draw Marjorie's face, but it escaped me even more completely. I worked and worked on it, as though, by drawing Marjorie, I could conquer her death. And even as I failed, my drawing sessions became an obsession, occupying most afternoons after school. I would go into the dining room, taking a sheaf of paper, some number two pencils and various photographs, including Marjorie's from the yearbook. Then I would settle at the dining room table, choose a picture, and try to copy it.

I used the dining room table because the bedroom seemed too cramped. I no longer had that fear that haunted me when I first moved in; the dining room seemed safe. And neither Madeleine nor Denise came there in the afternoons.

And then, one day I tried drawing Neil. Why I wanted to recapture his image at that point, I don't know. Perhaps it was a fear, as with Marjorie, of losing him completely from my memory. I took the framed photograph from the living room and propped it up on the dining room table. After many attempts, I made a reasonable if simplified likeness. But it wasn't Neil, just as my drawings of Marjorie weren't Marjorie. The quality that made him Neil was missing. I tried to capture it, as I had tried to capture Marjorie, but that quality, that essence, wasn't there.

*   *   *

It was strange, that enormous effort to bring back Neil's image. I hadn't even thought about him for some time; I had deliberately pushed him out of my mind for a couple of years. From the time I gave up on hearing from him again. But the evening after attempting to draw him, I recalled his face, exactly as it had been. And with it the story of our short romance.

We were enrolled at a writer's workshop in the Finger Lake area of New York State. I had been working summers for a number of years, but that particular summer I decided to give myself some time off and do something different. The Lake G. Workshop was a small one, probably run on a shoe-string, and its organizers were unable to hire well-known authors as instructors. But by that token it was easy to get into and put relatively few demands on participants. I sent away for the brochures, and studying them, decided it was just what I wanted: an unspoiled rural landscape, a picturesque little town nearby, pleasant accommodations. And I had always wanted to write. I wondered if I had an unexploited talent.

I met Neil across a conference table. It was Dr. Harvey Rosenburg's Poetic Vistas class. Dr. Rosenburg at first struck me as handsome, with the striking lock of white hair emerging from his black pelt, rather like a skunk's back. And his great hooked nose. But the moment he opened his mouth the illusion was shattered. Dr. Rosenburg was a gas bag. He was more interested in listening to the sound of his own voice than is fostering young poets.

One day toward the beginning of the session, Dr. Rosenburg was singing the praises of the heroic couplet. I looked up from the sketch I was working on to meet the glance of the young man opposite me. We shared a conspiratorial smile. Neither of us could take Dr. Rosenburg seriously.

I fell in love with Neil before we spoke. His naughty glance, his iceberg blue eyes, his unruly brown hair. His loping gait. His self deprecating responses in class ("this probably doesn't make any sense but," "I'm no expert, but," "this may sound crazy, but,"). I knew he was too young for me. I was very much aware of being "older," thirty-nine, so close to the dreaded forty!

I don't remember the first time we spoke. It may have been in the canteen where I often went for coffee. I don't know. I only remember vividly his falling on one knee as I was coming out of some other class and saying, "Jennifer, Jennifer, will you be mine?"

A couple of students leaving class turned around to stare, compounding my embarrassment. I pulled him to his feet and muttered something like, "Of course, you silly goose."

He offered me a bouquet of wilted daisies that he had probably picked on the campus lawn.

We took lots of walks near the lake. Had picnics from prepackaged sandwiches we bought at the local grocery store. Drank a lot of cheap bubbly wine. Took a canoe out on the lake and capsized it. As I hit the water, it was like an electric shock. I felt paralyzed; I was sure I would drown. Then Neil pulled me out and I was lying by his side on the shore, wrapped in his jacket, feeling happier than I ever thought I could be.

And waking up in the single bed in his dormitory room, where we clung to one another all night to keep from falling out. I would see the sun stream though the window and hear him breathe softly by my side. I would tiptoe down to my own room and find Fran, my crotchety roommate, writing at the desk.

"Out all night again?" she would ask crossly. I smiled, knowing she envied me. Knowing how it felt.

And that last night, when we had to write our poems for Dr. Rosenburg's class. We wrote two collaborative efforts, spurring each other on to greater and greater silliness with the stimulus of a couple of bottles of wine. We stayed up all night and eventually produced a parody of Alexander Pope and a parody of Wordsworth. We got a C and a C+ for our efforts. A real disgrace for someone who has been through graduate school. I don't even know what happened to the two poems.

Neil was an English teacher at a high school in New Jersey. He seriously wanted to become a writer, or at least that's what he told me.

The summer evaporated. We promised to correspond and we did. At first. I hoped he would come to the Chicago area for Christmas, but by Hallowe'en the letters had stopped. I kept hoping. I lived the days of that summer over and over again. I finally wrote him a letter saying that if he hadn't wanted to see me again, he should at least have been honest about it. But there was no answer to that either. Just a wall of silence.

I knew what Marjorie would have told me, if I had ever confided in her: that for Neil, it was just a summer romance, just a bit of fun. What did I expect anyway? Certainly not a life-long commitment. That wasn't what I was after. I just didn't want the love-making, the marvelous sense of aliveness, ever to stop.

*   *   *

After the session drawing Neil, I stopped drawing people. There didn't seem to be any point to it, as I was unable to get any face quite right. But I didn't want to give up drawing altogether, so I decided to find an easier subject.

One afternoon I went to the little communal bookcase in the living room. Most of the books in it were Madeleine's religious books; if Denise had art books, she kept them elsewhere. But on the bottom shelf, lying on its side, I found an Audubon guide to eastern wildflowers. I picked it up and began paging through it. The illustrations were photographs, not drawings, but the little flowers appealed to me, their subtle colors, their intricate form. They would be my new inspiration. I bought a sketch book and quickly filled it up with drawings of trilliums, lady's slippers, and violets. When I had real difficulty, I cheated; I traced the outlines and filled them in.

One afternoon I was busy drawing Virginia bluebells when I felt a presence near me. An odd feeling of being watched, the odder because I was used to having the dining room to myself in the afternoon. I looked up. There, standing in the opening that led to the living room was a small child, not more than five or six. It was a little girl, with short, curly hair, wearing overalls. She was gazing at me solemnly.

It was as if a fairy had waved a magic wand to make her materialize.

"Where did you come from?" I asked.

The child didn't answer but came straight to the table where I was sitting and looked at my drawing. Her head barely reached to the level of the dining table. "Can I draw too?" she asked.

I lifted her to the chair beside me. She was surprisingly heavy for one so small. I tore a page out of my sketch book, and handed her a pencil. Within minutes, she had drawn the outline of a cat, very expressive. She began decorating the edges of the picture with flowers.

"Let's see. That's very good." It had taken me a half an hour to replicate a flower; she could give the impression of one in minutes. "Do you like to draw?"

She nodded, looking at me wordlessly. Her eyes were an extraordinary, deep blue and expressed a liveliness you seldom see in adults.

"Are you my aunt Jennie?" she asked, finally.

I was surprised, annoyed that she called me "aunt." "My name is Jennifer," I said. "What's yours?"

"Sally. I'm staying with Aunt Denise. Her room is upstairs."

"Oh." I didn't remember Denise mentioning a niece or a visit from one. But now I understood why the little girl was there. "Do you know how long you'll be staying?"

Sally simply shook her head, eyeing me steadily. I was beginning to feel uncomfortable when I heard Denise's step on the staircase. A moment later she came into the room.

She lifted Sally up and set her on the floor. "Has this little monster been bugging you?"

"No, really, she hasn't. She's just drawn a picture of a very nice cat."

"That must be George! Sally has an instinct for finding pets. And putting them under her spell."

"George didn't run away from you?" Sally shook her head. "You must be a very nice girl. George is afraid of people who aren't nice."

"Okay, Sally, you've bothered Jennifer enough. Let's go. Jennifer, you wouldn't like to go with us, would you? I'm taking Sally to the zoo."

I said, to my own astonishment, "I'd love to go. I haven't been to a zoo for ages. And I want some time to get to know my new friend."

*   *   *

It turned out that Sally was only up for the weekend, but we had a good time those two days. We went to the zoo on Friday afternoon; on Saturday morning Hilda came over and we baked cookies—or rather, Hilda baked cookies and Sally and I watched and sampled the dough; and on Saturday afternoon Denise and I took Sally to the public pool, where she had a good go on the slides. I was surprised at how much I enjoyed myself, for the first time, I think, since Marjorie's illness. I had had little to do with children since I grew up. My sister was only eighteen months younger than I was, so she was my playmate, not my charge. And now that childhood was a faraway place, children intimidated me. I never understood what they were thinking or knew what to say to them. But with Sally, everything came easily. I simply liked her and wanted to be with her, to watch her, to make sure she was safe.

The following Sunday I was correcting papers from school at the dining room table. Sally hadn't come that weekend and the house was strangely quiet. I looked up to see Denise standing across the table from me.

"I need to explain about Sally," she said, sitting opposite me.

I looked up from my drawing of a purple trillium. Denise had an odd look on her face, as if she didn't really want to talk to me. "What about Sally?" I said. I had no reason to suspect there was anything about her that needed explaining.

"She's a sort of lost child. An after-thought. She's the youngest of four kids. Her parents are very busy. Both in hotel management. So she gets left alone a lot."

"She is very quiet."

"She's not very verbal and she's not very sociable. Sometimes I wonder if Ralph—that's my brother—and his wife Rita, have given up on her. Well, maybe that's too strong a way to put it. They just don't seem to take much interest in her. That's why I want to have her up her on weekends from time to time."

I looked at Denise closely. I was shocked that parents could give up on a child like Sally. "I like Sally a lot," I said. "I think she's a beautiful child. And she has a lot of artistic talent. Whenever we do something, Sally has to draw it. And she draws so easily, just putting a pencil or crayons to paper and filling a page."

Denise raised her eyebrows. "Artistic talent? Naw. All kids like to draw. Anyway, I hope you'll be around when Sally comes next week. I think she liked you too."

*　　*　　*

A week later I was at the dining room table, this time trying out watercolors, when Sally appeared. This time she was carrying, or rather dragging, a very beat-up stuffed animal, eyeless and missing one paw. It could have been a dog or a squirrel or a rabbit, any small mammal. Sally was eyeing me with the same neutral expression that she had had the first time.

"Sally," I said. "Who have you got with you?"

"That's Otto," she said, pulling herself up with some difficulty onto the chair beside me. "I want to draw again."

"Would you like to paint, Sally?" She nodded. "Have you ever painted before?"

"Nooo."

The paints and the glass of water were already in place. I got up from the table to get some extra brushes from the case I kept them in, in the sideboard. As soon as I turned my back, I hear a sharp cry. I looked around to see pieces of glass strewn over the floor and paint-stained water dripping down the side of the table. Sally had upset the glass I was using to clean my brushes.

"Sally!" I said, less angry than concerned. In the short time it took me to turn around and assess the situation, the little girl had disappeared. I knew she had gone toward the back door and I ran out after her to the yard. She was sitting on the step leading to the little garden space, facing away from me, holding Otto. When she heard my footsteps, she got up and began to run.

"Sally!" I shouted. "Sally, it's okay. I only wanted to know if you were hurt."

Sally stopped and turned slowly, still clutching Otto in her arms.

"I broke your glass," she said. "I broke it."

"I know, Sally," I said. "It's okay. It's only a glass. Did you get cut?"

Sally turned away from me. I could see her shoulders shaking with sobs. I went up to her and turned her toward me and held her gently.

"Come back in, Sally. We'll do some painting together."

I led her back to the house, put her on the living room sofa, and brought her a glass of juice. She wouldn't talk or play, she just sat there for a long time, not crying, just holding Otto.

Not knowing what to do, I went in search of Denise. I knew she had to be in the house somewhere; I didn't think she'd go off and leave Sally. I found her, not in her room but in the basement, re-arranging paintings.

"We've had a little accident," I said. "Sally broke a glass and she seems terribly upset."

Denise sighed heavily. "That kid is the bane of my existence. I wish I'd never offered to take her in on weekends." She put down the painting she'd been moving and went upstairs.

"What's the matter, kiddo?" she said, sitting down beside Sally.

Sally said nothing, merely clutching her stuffed toy more tightly.

"So you broke a glass," said Denise. "It's not the end of the world. Look," she picked up the glass of juice I had set down on the coffee table. "Have some juice."

Sally turned away and pushed her face into the sofa cushion.

Denise got up and turned to me, shrugging. "I don't think there's much we can do, Jennifer. Sally doesn't want us around. We'll just have to leave her alone and wait for her to come out of it. I'm going back downstairs to finish some work."

Sally fell asleep on the sofa, and I went back into the dining room to clean up the mess on the floor and finish my little painting.

At around supper time, I went to seek out Denise in the basement. "Denise," I said, "Do you think we should prepare something for Sally to eat?"

"Yeah, that might be a good idea. Jennifer, I don't know what's the matter with the kid. She can be very quiet, but I've never seen her sulk that way."

"Maybe she gets severely punished for small misdemeanors."

Denise frowned. "I doubt it. Ralph and Rita are pretty laid-back parents. I don't think they're into harsh punishment."

We put together a little meal of mashed potatoes, corn, and hot dogs. Sally seemed less cowed than sleepy, but she was hungry and came to herself quickly. She ate every bit of the food on her plate.

"Do you want seconds, Sally?" asked Denise.

Sally shook her head. "I want to go to bed now, Aunt Denise," she said.

The next morning I was sitting at the dining room table doing corrections when Denise came down with Sally in tow. Sally, smiling contentedly, came up to me and put her little round hand on my arm.

"Aunt Jennifer," she said. "Aunt Denise is making pancakes. Could you have breakfast with us?"

"I've already had breakfast," I said. "But I'll come and sit with you in the breakfast nook. Maybe you and I can help Aunt Denise."

We made the little meal together and ate at the table in the breakfast nook.

"What are you doing today, Denise?" I asked.

"I have to work, Jennifer," said Denise. "I'm going to take Sally downtown to see the studio. Maybe she'll try her hand at painting again."

"Would you like that, Sally? I asked. Sally, her mouth full of pancakes nodded, happily. I breathed an internal sigh of relief. At least no permanent damage had been done. I would get on with my corrections and see the two later that afternoon.

*   *   *

It was mid-March by now and a semblance of spring had come to the Chicago area. There were no longer traces of slush in the streets, the trees had an expectant tinge of green, the air felt softer.

With the hint of spring, I felt a surge of energy. I wanted to do something. I had come to the end of my efforts at drawing and was unsure what to do next. I had a sudden idea: I could create a garden behind the house. What was there at that time could hardly be called a garden; it was a dried-up patch of grass and a few scraggly rosebushes. At the far end was a stand of evergreen trees that stretched down to the road that ran parallel to Ridgeway.

Looking out from the back porch down to the little semi-circular space, I realized that I could plant the seeds Denise gave me at Christmas here, the cosmos and foxglove! I knew that the seeds wouldn't grow and bloom for months. If I wanted to see something growing and blooming right away, I would need advice. I looked up "Garden Centers" in the yellow pages and found that there was one nearby. I went there on a Saturday morning.

"I'm sorry, ma'am," said the tall, weather-beaten sales assistant. "You won't see much growing around here for another eight weeks! Tell you what, though. If you're willing to sport out a bit of cash, we've got some hothouse grown bulbs that bloom early. Your best bet is snowdrops. And crocus will come out a little later. How sheltered is your garden?"

I came home with the snowdrop and crocus bulbs. I spent the rest of the morning preparing the soil, turning it over and removed rocks and tree roots. It wasn't such bad soil, really; I actually liked the smell of it and the feeling of it in my hands. And the hard exercise of digging felt good. "Sorry, Marjorie," I told my friend in my head, remembering how she had loathed getting her hands dirty. "This is my project. It has nothing to do with you!"

I had started planting my bulbs when I saw Denise and Sally coming down the steps from the back porch. It had been a couple of weeks since our little fiasco with the watercolors.

"Jennifer, could you play with Sally for a few minutes?" Denise said. She was tense and unsmiling, her shoulders pulled up. I knew there was something wrong.

"Is there a problem, Denise?"

"Not really. I just need to discuss something with Madeleine."

"Go ahead. I need a little helper. Do you want to help me plant these flowers, Sally?" I looked at Sally closely to see if she was still upset, but could fathom nothing from her expression. She nodded and without saying anything, but her eyes were on Denise as she headed back to the house. I gave Sally a small spade and showed her where to dig. She was happy at first but after a while, I sensed she was getting bored, so I took her for a little tour of the garden, explaining about the rosebushes.

Sally looked at the miserable little bushes skeptically. "Will they really have flowers, Aunt Jen?"

"Of course, but they need a lot of care. Just like a puppy or a kitten. You have to feed and water them and chase away their enemies."

"Roses have enemies?"

"Yes, unfortunately, lots. Bugs and infections called fungus." I showed her the back of one leaf, which was riddled with black spot. "It's not supposed to look like this. It's supposed to be smooth and green."

At the back of the garden was an old plank suspended from one of the oak trees by two ropes. It must once have been used as a swing. Discovering it, Sally sat down. "Do you want me to push you, Sally?"

"No, I'll just watch you." I planted two more crocuses.

"Aunt Jen," said Sally suddenly, "Why was Aunt Denise angry with that other lady?"

"What other lady?"

"I don't know her name. She wears ugly clothes. Like a man."

"Oh, that must be Madeleine. She actually lives here, but her job keeps her very busy, so we don't see much of her."

I waited for Sally to give a further explanation, but she just shook her head. "I don't understand why grown-ups are always fighting," she said.

I finished planting the crocus and wiped my hands on my blue jeans. "Shall we go back to the house? I think I smell something baking. Could it be cookies? Aunt Denise will let us have some."

"Yes, it's Mrs. Manning," said Sally, knowingly. "She's making chocolate chip cookies."

"Well, we'd better go back before someone else gets them!"

I took Sally's little hand and led her back to the house. As we went through the kitchen door, the smell of baking got even stronger. Hilda was there, in her stained apron, taking trays out of the oven.

"Hello, you two," she said. "Have you been busy gardening? Sally, sit down in the breakfast nook. I'll get you some juice and cookies, as soon as they cool." Sally and I sat down at the breakfast nook table.

"I went to Sunday school this morning," said Sally suddenly. "That other lady took me. I think that's why Aunt Denise was angry."

I was surprised. I wondered how Madeleine had contrived to get Sally to Sunday school. Denise certainly wouldn't have approved. "Did you like Sunday school?" I asked. "Was it good?"

Sally looked at me for a little while, not sure what to say.

"Sally," I said, "you can tell me how you really felt. It's okay if you liked it. It's also okay if you didn't."

"It was all right."

"And would you like to go back there?"

Sally looked at the table. "Well, no." She said finally. "I didn't like the teacher. Very much. She asked me about what church I go to." Sally studied the table. "I don't go to church."

Hilda brought a tray with two glasses of juice and a plate of cookies. "Have a cookie and forget about it," I said. "Shall we have another try at water colors?"

Sally took a cookie and bit into it. "Maybe," she said

*　　*　　*

Several weeks later as I was getting ready to leave to go to the garden center, the doorbell rang. Annoyed at the disturbance, I hurried into the hall and opened the door. A squat, blowsy woman was standing on the doorstep. Her hair was a fluffy mess dyed blonde and her complexion had that off-color look that comes when you drink too much or stay up too late, night after night. She had Sally by the shoulder, Sally, looking red-eyed and woebegone.

"I'm Rita, Sally's mom," said the woman. "I know she's only supposed to come every other week, but . . . I'm in a bit of a bind this weekend, and I wondered if you could just . . . take her."

"I think Denise has gone out for the day," I said, wondering how I could possibly entertain Sally. She looked as though she had been brought against her will, and I wasn't happy about losing my Saturday and possibly my Sunday to a petulant child.

"Look, said Rita. "I've got an appointment in Chicago today, and I can't really take her along. Couldn't you just this once?" She pushed Sally forward.

Realizing that the little girl must feel unwanted, I kneeled down and gave her a little hug.

"Okay," I said. "We'll go to the nursery together." I looked up to ask Rita when she'd come by to pick Sally up, but she was halfway down the path to the car.

She waved, and before I could even say goodbye, she had started up the car and was headed toward the city.

I took Sally by the hand and led her back into the kitchen. "Have you had lunch? I could make you some tuna fish sandwiches."

Sally shook her head. "Are you going to take me to see the babies?" she asked.

"Babies? Oh, the nursery. No, Sally, it's for baby plants. I'm going to buy some flowers for the garden. Don't you want to come?"

To my horror, Sally began to cry. "I want to see the babies! I don't want to look at plants." She threw herself down on the floor and sobbed.

"Oh, Sally. I know you'll like the plant nursery. Come on. It'll be fun."

"Where's Aunt Denise? Why isn't she here?"

I sighed. This was going to be difficult. I was furious with Rita for dumping the kid on me, furious with Denise for going out. "She'll be back later, and maybe we'll see a video together. Would you like that?"

Sally continued sobbing, and not knowing what else to do, I picked her up and carried her out to the car, hoping the movement would shake her out of the mood she was in. After we had driven a little way, I looked over at her. She had stopped crying and was looking out the window. By the time we arrived at Freddie's Plant Center, she seemed a lot calmer. I took out a tissue, wiped her face, and gave her a hug. This might work. I was hopeful.

"Now we're going to find some beautiful flowers for Aunt Jennifer's garden." The crocus and snowdrops had finished blooming, and I was looking for something showier.

I took her by the hand and led her across the parking lot into the store. I had first come to Freddie's when I started the garden, about six weeks before. I loved the place. It was huge and you could lose yourself among the stands of plants in bloom. In the center was an extravagant fountain, with flowers in pots, mainly tulips and daffodils, spiraling up from the base. As we entered, the atmosphere became damp and earthy. It was too early for a spring planting, but the bulbs were out in bright display.

"Hold on tight," I said. "I don't want to lose you!" I was looking for conventional spring bulbs and special something to put in between them, something that would survive in partial shade. I had picked up several daffodils and was wondering if I should buy the bright red tulip bulbs or the more subdued pink ones, when I felt a tugging at my hand. I looked down at Sally.

"I want to go home!" she said, not loudly enough to attract attention, but in a voice that seemed to be suppressing terrible pain. I bent down to look at her face. How stupid I had been! A garden center was hardly the place to take a little girl who had just been dumped by her mother.

"Look, Sally," I said. "I'll just pick up a few things and then we'll go right home. Okay?"

Sally nodded, her lips pressed together.

I had to get her involved, but I had no idea how. "What I want you to do, Sally," I said, "is to find a special flower for my garden."

"I don't know how," she said, sniffing.

"All you have to do is to choose a flower you like. Choose the one you think is prettiest. Come on, let's see if we can find something different. Something that will make the garden look bright."

Sally walked over to a display of primulas, and chose a very dark purple one.

"That's beautiful, Sally," I said. "That's really colorful." I looked dubiously at the squat, low-growing plants with their intense colors. Absorbed in my thoughts, I had stopped paying attention to Sally. I suddenly realized she wasn't by my side.

To my horror, she was standing by an adjacent display of pansies, had picked up a pot, and was tearing the petals off the flower.

"Sally!" I cried out, more harshly than I had intended. "Stop that!" I stooped down to take the plant from her.

A voice said, "Can I help?"

Feeling shamefaced, I stood up to face my accuser. I found myself face to face with Ben, the man who had advised me on bulbs. I was relieved. He was a very nice man and unlikely to make a fuss about the pansy.

"I'm afraid Sally has destroyed one of your pansies," I said. "I'll be glad to pay for it."

"I wouldn't worry about that. We've had worse losses with a heavy wind." He stooped down and took Sally's hand. To my surprise, she didn't move but looked at Ben unflinchingly.

"Your name is Sally, is it?" She nodded and continued to watch him. "Well, you mustn't hurt the plants. They're our friends, you know. You're tired, aren't you? I might just have something to perk you up." He reached into his pocket and pulled out a somewhat crushed lollipop. Sally took it without unwrapping it and continued to gaze at Ben. He got up and turned to me. "Now, is there anything I could help you with?"

"Say thank you to the nice man," I said, taking the lollipop and unwrapping it. As I gave the candy back to Sally, she made a noise in her throat that could have been a "thank you."

I turned back to Ben. "Yes, as a matter of fact, I'm buying hothouse grown bulbs again. I've got some daffodils and tulips, but I need something colorful to mix in. My roommate's niece has chosen this primula for me. Should I get some more? Will they also survive in early spring?"

"As a matter of fact, primulas are a good bet. They're hardy and they're actually in bloom now, at the moment. You said your garden was sheltered. You should be able to keep them going for some time."

I hesitated, trying to picture the primulas next to my delicate pink tulips. I could plant them elsewhere, of course.

Ben was evidently quite taken with Sally. "Did you say the little girl was your niece?" he asked. It hardly seemed worth correcting his error. "Well, she has beautiful eyes. She'll break a few hearts when she gets older." He gave me a swift, almost imperceptible wink. "What do you think of the primulas? Will you take a half dozen?"

I still wasn't convinced, but I felt I had to buy them to keep in Ben's good graces. "Yes, why not?" I suddenly liked the idea of the bright colors. "Give me twelve, in all different colors."

"I remember those snowdrops and crocuses," he said with a grin. "You bought them a couple of weeks ago. Did you get them up?"

"Well, they were lovely, but they've finished blooming. Now I need something showier to brighten the garden. These primulas should really do the trick!" We loaded the flowers into onto the cart. Ben wheeled it to the check-out point. "Good-bye," he said. "Good luck with your planting. If you have any problems, don't hesitate to come back."

I had Sally help me put the plants in the trunk of the car. By now she had consumed most of the lollipop and seemed a lot happier. "Where are we going now, Aunt Jennifer?"

"Back home to the garden, to drop these off. And after that we're going to look for Aunt Denise." It occurred to me that Denise was probably at her studio downtown. Sally might enjoy the trip.

"Aunt Jennifer," Sally said, as we got into the car. "Is that your boyfriend?"

"Who? The man in the store?" To my surprise, I felt myself blushing. "No, Sally, he just works there."

"I think he liked you, Aunt Jen. Do you like him?"

"Well, he's not my boyfriend, Sally," I said, hoping to close the subject. "Let's hurry back and, maybe we'll have time to drive downtown and see Denise's studio. Would you like that?"

Sally was smiling now. She knew she had made a conquest in Ben and was quite pleased with herself. A few minutes later, as we were driving along, I looked over at her and saw that she had fallen asleep. Her head was propped up against the window, the lollipop stick in her hand. She looked angelic, as children do when asleep. Whatever had happened before she came, the trip from home, a possible fight with her mother—all that must have been quite exhausting. She slept all the way home. When we got there, I wasn't sure what to do. I didn't want to wake her, so I picked her up, astonished that one so small could be so heavy. I managed to get her hot limp body up the path to the house. There I could go no farther. My arms were aching and my lungs felt as though they would burst. I set her down at the front door.

"Can you walk as far as your Aunt Denise's room?"

Sally looked at me, heavy-eyed and resentful, but nodded her head. I took her hot little hand in mine, wondering if she could have a fever, and pulled her upstairs. As I opened the door to Denise's room, I was surprised to find Denise there stretched out on the bed, asleep. Hearing us come in, Denise stirred and sat up. When she saw Sally she almost did a double-take.

"What's the kid doing here?" she asked.

"It's a long story." I helped Sally onto the bed, where she stretched out and almost immediately went back to sleep. I sat down in the armchair by the bed, panting. "How did such a small child come to weigh so much?"

"Where have you two been?"

"I took her to the garden center. I had to buy some plants. It was a terrible mistake, I'm afraid. But I didn't know what else to do."

"Don't worry. You shouldn't have to take responsibility for Sally anyway. But what happened? Did Rita just come and dump the kid on you, did she?" Denise was sitting upright now, scowling.

"Well, more or less. She said she had business in Chicago and couldn't take Sally."

"Bullshit. I think she just wanted a little freedom. But this won't do, you know. She can't just bring her here at the drop of a hat because it's convenient." She shook her head. "I told you, Jennifer. That child is an afterthought. Her parents simply don't care about her."

*   *   *

That night I kept thinking over what had happened, wondering what I should have done with Sally, wondering why she tore that pansy to pieces. Was she angry because she felt the adult world ignored her? I had to admit that I was ignoring her, doing what I had planned to do that afternoon rather than thinking about her. Or was she curious about what was inside the flower? Or was this a cruel streak in her nature? I wondered what her mother had said to her before she brought her to us. I wondered if Denise was right, that the child was neglected or whether Rita had a legitimate reason for leaving her with me. I had my suspicions, but I would never really know.

I thought about Ben, his warm smile, his kindness. Sally had picked up on an attraction between us, but Ben wasn't really my type. I was amazed to be thinking about a man that way. I thought again of Neil and wondered if a relationship like that was still possible for me.

*   *   *

I didn't see Sally the following week or two weeks later, and there was no opportunity to ask Denise, now setting up a joint show, why she hadn't come. Instead, I busied myself in the garden. I planted all the bulbs and spent hours there weeding and watering. It was an early spring, unusually warm for April and on weekdays after work, I would often sit in one of the little seats I had bought to put there, reading or watching the changes in my planting. George loved the garden as much as I did and kept me company there, often sitting at my feet or prowling around among the plants.

As April mellowed into May, I continued to enjoy the garden. The early bulbs had stopped blooming, but the primulas were still in bloom and I was beginning to fantasize about planting annuals, the colors I would choose, how I would arrange them. Even the grass, which I had begun watering weeks before, was beginning to poke up. Neither Denise nor Madeleine had ever come to see my little garden. I didn't need or want them there. But I would invite them after I'd put in the annuals, the pansies and the impatiens.

But one Saturday morning when I had come out to have a look around, I felt an alien presence. I turned to see Madeleine coming toward me. She had a tray of plants in one hand, a trowel in the other, and an unpleasantly determined look on her face. Seeing her, I felt my stomach twist.

"Hello, Madeleine," I said, as soon as she was within earshot. "What's up?"

She came through the little rose arbor and set down the tray. "I'm going to plant some vegetables, Brussels sprouts and corn. It's high time we made use of this waste space."

"Waste space!" I shouted. "This is my garden. Can't you see?"

Madeleine cast a quick look around. "Well, there's not much here. There's plenty of room for a few vegetables. Besides, I have as much right to this space as you do."

"Madeleine," I said, "It's too early by about a month for those vegetables. Don't you know you can't plant them before Memorial Day?"

"A warm spring like this one? Surely there won't be another frost at this point."

"Well, you're probably wasting your effort, but if you insist, there's also space in front of the house and along both sides. I don't see why you have to spoil the effect of my flowers with some scraggly vegetables."

"Spoil the effect of your flowers?" Madeleine gave a short, strangled laugh. "What flowers? I have a much better plan. I'm going to bring some of the shelter people here. Get them involved in growing things. That would be a better use of this space than . . . whatever this"—she made a broad gesture—"is supposed to be."

For a minute I was too choked with rage to speak. Then I went right up to Madeleine and stood face to face with her. "Madeleine, this house and its garden are not an extension of your job with the Brothers of Light. If you want your delinquent kids to grow vegetables, you'd better find a place in the inner city. This is my space. I've made it mine."

Madeleine backed away slightly. "I repeat, I have just as much right to this space as you do." She went over to one of the borders where nothing had been planted. "I don't know why I can't plant a row of corn here."

"Because, first, corn is ugly. And second, we can't work in the same space. That's why I try avoiding the kitchen when you're cooking. And third . . . and third because I need some personal space to myself."

Madeleine stared at me in disbelief. "I don't know what you mean. There's more than enough space in the house for three people. Even if we were all there all the time."

"Well, I don't feel at home in the house. I feel as if I have no right to the kitchen, no right to any of the downstairs. I take my meals up to my tiny bedroom. To be in my own private space!" Calming slightly, I added, "I don't see how your plan to bring out inner city children can go forward until you consult with Denise and me. You can't suddenly bring those kids out here."

"Possibly," said Madeleine, coldly, "But I can still plant vegetables here for my own consumption."

"Plant them in front, Madeleine." I seized the tray and marched up the hill past the house. Just in front of the bushes that grew up against the house, I laid down the tray, took the trowel out of Madeleine's hand, and began to dig.

"What are you doing? What are you doing?" Madeleine was now shouting, a thing I'd never heard her do before.

"I'm making place for your vegetables. Come get a shovel and help me. We'll have it done by noon!"

And so I divided the space outside the house as we had divided the space within. But as I predicted, Madeleine's garden never thrived. It was too early to plant vegetables, and she didn't spend enough time nurturing them. And though it went against the grain,

223

though I would have liked to care for the little plants myself, I determinedly let them die.

*   *   *

I woke up one morning—it was still before dawn when the light is just beginning to pearl—with the sense of a strong presence near me. I hadn't thought of Marjorie for some time; and yet she was there, always there, like an indivisible part of me. I don't mean to say that I actually believed she was with me or ever saw her. It was rather that she was my observer, sometimes approving, usually disapproving of what I was doing. She disliked my choice of clothes, and I could hear her comments. "Can't you be a little more stylish? You're dressing like a middle-aged frump!" She criticized me when I was insincere or when I waffled. She even criticized me for doing housework. "Leave it! Let someone else do it! You're stifling your own spirit!"

But that spring morning in the pre-dawn grayness, she finally appeared, in a dream or in one of those visions that come when you're between sleep and wakefulness. I hadn't been able to picture her for a very long time, not as a young girl in college or when she was ill and near death. Now I saw her form at the window opposite the bed. She looked very young, younger than she was when we first met. Her hair fell to her shoulders and she was wearing a gauzy dress the color of dawn, between gray and very pale purple. Strangest of all were her wings, not white, like an angel's wings, but dark grey and far too large for her body. I wasn't afraid. I merely watched her, wondering what she had to tell me.

I felt rather than heard her speak. "Jennifer," she said. "It's time for you to let me go. You've held on to me for too long."

I thought, rather than said, "But you're the one who's holding onto me!"

Then I heard the sound of powerful wings moving against the wind. And she was gone.

*   *   *

I woke up from that dream or that vision feeling an emptiness in the house. I got up, went downstairs, and made myself a cup of coffee. It was still early, just twelve minutes past seven, and no one was around. I sat in the breakfast nook, looking out toward the garden, which was barely visible from that angle. Sally hadn't come for over a month now, and on the rare occasions I saw Denise, neither of us had mentioned her name. For my part, I was afraid to know. I didn't even think about reasons why Sally hadn't come, fearing, I suppose, that something terrible had happened. Not even entertaining the more probable explanation that Denise was fed up with looking after the little girl.

But now, feeling this strange emptiness, this emptiness that seemed a sign Sally was gone, I had to know. It was too early to wake Denise, so I waited, feeling cold down the back of my spine and trying to focus on plans for the garden or for my classes. I had time. I didn't need to be at the college until ten that morning. But was the minutes crept past, I felt more and more nervous, fearing Denise wouldn't wake before I left, fearing I would have to go through another day without knowing.

Finally I went to Denise's bedroom and pressed my ear against the door. By then it was just before eight. I couldn't wake her up to ask her why Sally hadn't come, but I couldn't wait for her to stir. She might be having a morning in bed, she might even have a lover with her, for all I knew. I searched for an excuse to knock on her door, but my mind was paralyzed. Finally at eight, I heard the soft purring of her alarm clock. She would be down soon.

I went back to the kitchen and put a couple of slices of toast in the toaster. Not that I had the slightest appetite, but I needed to keep myself busy. About ten minutes later, I heard Denise come clattering down the stairs. I moved quickly to the hallway.

"Denise! Can I have a word with you?"

"Not now, Jen, I'm supposed to meet a fellow artist in the city." Denise was getting her jacket from the rack in the hallway.

I realized Denise was in a hurry. I realized how strange my sense of urgency must seem.

"Just a quick question. I'm making plans for the weekend and I was wondering whether Sally would be coming."

"Sally? I thought I told you. No, Sally won't be coming anymore."

Denise was putting on her jacket, searching for her car keys in the pockets.

"But why?" My voice sounded childishly pleading.

"Roger and Rita have a new job. The family's moving to Indiana."

I drew in my breath and it seemed to stab my heart. "Okay, that's fine. I just wondered."

Luckily Denise was in too great a hurry to notice how upset I was. I waited until she was out the door and then ran up to my room. I was crying blindly, crying till my throat was about to split. I threw myself on the bed where George was sleeping. He stretched out one paw. I stroked and stroked him, thinking, "You're the only baby I'll ever have."

All the boxes had been opened, all the demons let out. And now, what was left?

* * *

A week later I still felt battered. I felt as though I had been in a storm at sea, clinging on to the sides of the boat, with the wind tearing at my body. But with Marjorie's final disappearance, with Sally gone, something had changed inside me. Or I became aware of a change that had been coming for a long time.

I knew I had act, to scramble up the side of the pit where I had been buried for so long. I stood in front of the full-length mirror opposite the staircase, looking at myself critically. It was the first time in ages that I had taken stock of my appearance. I needed to consult Marjorie, that expert on appearances. Strangely, it was now difficult for me to conjure up Marjorie's voice; I had to imagine what she would say. I thought, "She would probably say that that I look okay, that I was right to buy the smaller size when I bought the blue jeans I'm wearing." Marjorie used to tell me that I had a nice figure and should show it off. But now the bulges of middle age were beginning to show. Around the belly, on the upper arms, which were becoming a bit wobbly. I was going to take a little hip-length jacket, quite stylish, to hide the bulges.

I looked straight in the mirror. The lines around my eyes and mouth had deepened, but it no longer seemed very important. I was middle-aged, in my forties; I had to accept my shortcomings. My hair, which I had cut short after Marjorie's death, had grown out now to almost shoulder length. I'd had it blown dry for the occasion, which was probably foolish, as the wind was likely to whip the style away. I knew Marjorie would approve anyway. "Not foolish!" she would say. "Your hair is gorgeous. You have to show it off." I had even put on a little make-up for the occasion, around the eyes, on the lips. The overall effect, a middle-aged woman in a tailored jacket and tight-fitting jeans, natural blonde hair casually styled, wasn't so bad. "Not half bad," Marjorie would say.

I heard footsteps and saw Denise coming downstairs. She was in her painting attire and smelled, again, of whiskey. "Hey, Jennifer. I haven't seen you standing in front of this mirror very often. Got a special date?"

"No, don't I wish! Madeleine told me about this group that goes walking on Saturday morning and I've decided to join them. I think their leader is a botanist from the university. He doesn't lecture or anything, but points out any rare birds or butterflies or wildflowers the group runs across."

"Madeleine put you on to this!"

I nodded. "You know, Denise, she's been quite decent since that argument about the garden. I thought it would go the other way, but it didn't." I had mentioned the set-to with Madeleine to Denise, and she had been amused.

"That actually doesn't surprise me. Madeleine would have more respect for you because you stood up for yourself. Jennifer," she added. "I've heard so much about this garden of yours. Why don't you show me around?"

"I'm afraid there's not much to see there at the moment." There was little in bloom, and I was sure Denise would be disappointed. "But I can show you what I'm planning to do. I don't have to leave for the walk for about another half hour."

We went to the back of the house and down the steps to the garden. It was a morning in late May, warm but windy, with the clouds chasing each other across the sky.

I had put a rambler rose at the base of the little archway that marked the entrance to the garden. It was the wrong time of year, but I had seen it in a catalogue, and the blooms, yellow edged with red, were so unusual that I couldn't resist ordering it. Despite the early planting, the foliage looked green and healthy. Denise followed me through the arch into the garden.

I hadn't been in the garden for since the day before. I now went there every day, twice a day on weekends. I had dug up plots for some annuals I had bought at Freddie's—pansies, petunias, marigolds—and they were ready for me to do the planting. Though there was little color now, the garden was looking organized and cared for. The odor of fresh earth was in the air, and I could imagine the flowers in bud, waiting for rain and sun to coax out the blooms.

"You see," I said, pointing to the plot I had dug in the middle. "This is where I'm going to plant my summer garden. It's going to be mostly pansies of all colors, with some marigolds mixed in. If you had come earlier, you would have seen the spring blooms. Remember the cosmos seeds Hilda gave me? I'll plant them here—" I showed Denise the borders where the spring flowers had died out. "And they'll bloom in the fall. I want to keep the garden blooming all summer and into the fall." I mentally promised myself to come back after the walk, to water and weed.

Denise turned around and took a deep breath. "I didn't know you had done all this, Jennifer. I'm impressed." She looked around the garden. In one of the border beds, she spotted a purple primula, still in bloom.

"What a wonderful flower!" she said. "I don't think I've ever seen this before. What's it called?"

"It's a primula. Funny it should still be blooming. Sally chose that," I said.

Denise shook her head in surprise.

"I told you, that girl's an artist. Well, what do you think?"

"It's a magical place," said Denise, "It's so full of promise."

A magical place, full of promise! I hugged myself, a self congratulatory hug, feeling proud of my creation. My creation! The mild damp breath of spring touched my face. I found a bud on one of the small rose bushes and held it in my hand for a second, knowing that before long it would bloom. The future was full of possibilities. For the garden. For my life.

And soon it would be time to leave for the walk. I would go out into the world again.

PART III

Denise's story
A Life in Painting

Chicago suburbs, September, 2006

Denise woke to the play of light on her bedroom wall, little dancing pompons. They probably came from sunlight filtered through the leaves on the oak tree outside her window. She knew from their size and shape that it must be a little after ten in the morning. Later, they would disperse; their forms would be less precise, more spread out. She imagined how she would capture the image in paint, how to make the little round forms appear to dance. She quickly dismissed the plan; no painting today. Practical considerations. She pushed that thought away too; she was too comfortable, too deeply sunk into the coolness of the bed. She couldn't deal with the nitty-gritty. Not yet.

She drowsed. The dream that came to her was of an endless line of men in suits, men without faces, men leaning toward her to shake her hand. These men's faces were in no way horrible or deformed; they were simply not there, blanks without eyes, noses or mouths, It was in some ways a frightening dream, but Denise wasn't frightened; she was annoyed. In her dream she was trying to get to an important place, but there was this row of faceless men in suits. In her way. This dream was getting her nowhere.

"Might as well get up."

She swung her legs over the side of the bed and put her feet on the little rug on the floor. It took an effort. Sometimes she thought that movement, of swinging her legs up and over the side of the bed, was the biggest effort she had to make all day. She gazed down at her feet. "Nice little feet," she thought with some affection. Her feet were, in fact, small and perfectly formed, the little toes like schoolchildren lined up in order of height for some picture-taking or sporting event. "Nice little feet," she repeated to herself, shifting her weight onto them to stand up. As for the rest of her body, best not to dwell on it too much. "I'm too fat," she said, "too old and too fat. How'd I ever get to be so old and so fat?"

She waddled to the bathroom and turned on the shower, stripping the big, baggy tee-shirt she slept in up over her head. She stepped in. "The Foundation," she thought, sighing. "I'll have to deal with those people today. And no more pompons dancing on the wall."

She soaped herself and felt the stinging of the hot water up and down her body. "Practical considerations," she repeated, thinking of the paintings hung in her studio downtown. She had already dealt with most of the practical matters. She had had Sally's friends transform her studio into a gallery, hanging the pictures according to her instructions, bringing in a couple of tables and seats for the guests, returning the unwanted pictures to the house where they could be stored in the basement. She had left the arrangements for the food and drink to a catering company. Food wasn't something she paid a great deal of attention to, and drink? Well, drink, that was over. She remembered what some guy who had given up smoking or drinking had once said, "It's like a mistress you once loved and had to separate from. The desire always remains, a tantalizing memory." Or something like that.

So, was there anything else, anything she had forgotten?

She leaned against the bar at the side of the shower to guide herself the area of dry land on the other side of the tub. Another huge effort to lift one foot out, then the other, taking care not to slip and fall.

"Too old and too fat," she repeated to herself, taking a towel from the rack opposite and rubbing herself down vigorously. "What can I wear that's not too tight?" She moved in front of the bathroom mirror and stood there, towelling her thick, dark hair. It fell into place automatically, into the short, mannish cut she had favored for years. There were little flecks of silver here and there, but by and large, her hair was still dark. "Not bad, at sixty-three," she thought. "Not that I can claim much credit for it. It's hereditary."

She put on the faded bathrobe that hung on the inside of the bathroom door and padded, bare-footed, back to her bedroom. She wouldn't make the bed or tidy up the room. It was a luxury that she had treasured from the moment she moved into this house, a bedroom of her own, her private nest that was like a second skin to her, messy, cluttered and filled with her favorite art works. This passion for privacy dated from her childhood and also her years of relative poverty, when she had shared a one-bedroom apartment with the odd people who answered her ad in the paper. She remembered the smell and confusion of other people's belongings. But all that had changed. She had been in this house, in this room, for twenty years, and there were some boxes lurking in the corners that she still hadn't unpacked. She and her possessions were permanent residents now.

She opened the closet door and looked in. Clothes had become a problem with her slowly, inexorably expanding girth. She used to wear loose tunics over blue jeans, but her once slender legs were now too plump for tight pants, especially in the thigh area. She chose a long, loose navy-blue dress. She would liven it up with a little jewelry, possibly a silver pendant, worked in scroll-like patterns. Or would she choose a sparkly necklace? "Not appropriate, Denise," she told herself. "We're meeting serious people today!"

But not all so serious. There would be friends and enemies from the art world, including lovely Mary Ellen and Bobbie. And those people who were family to her now that Hilda was gone. Jennifer and Graham and Madeleine and Sally. Gorgeous, golden Sally, her talented niece, who might be receiving a grant from the Foundation. Might be. Sally was too independent, too much her own person. And a young woman. Denise could already see the grant going to some fast-talking young man.

The Foundation. It was strange that both she and her niece were both having dealings with that organization, such a bastion of the Establishment. She had been offered a job doing outreach and organizing exhibits. Sally had applied for a grant for young artists. It was so improbable. Both of them involved with the Establishment.

Thinking of Sally, she cast aside the navy blue dress and chose one with more shape, an A-line dress, with a scooped neck, bright red. She slipped it on. She put on little ballerina shoes. Overall, the effect wasn't too bad. "I am big. There's no point in trying to hide it," she thought.

She went downstairs, leaning heavily on the banister. No fragrance of coffee wafted up to her. Jennifer always used to get up early and make coffee, but Jennifer was long gone, living with that good-looking Graham, her new man. It was a relief to see Jennifer happily settled, but Denise did miss the coffee. Madeleine, probably already at work, was politically opposed to coffee anyway. So Denise would have to settle for instant.

She headed to the kitchen, at the back of the house, and put on the kettle. While waiting for the water to boil, she went into the little adjoining room, the breakfast nook, and looked out the window. It was a beautiful autumn day; the sunshine had almost burnt off the morning mist. It was a day so quiet, so shimmeringly glorious that it filled her with nostalgia.

Nostalgia for what? Just because she was having a retrospective exhibit was no reason to feel regret for the past. The past was the past, well and for the most part happily lived. There was enough negativity in the world. You didn't need to wallow in it.

She thought again of the pompons on the bedroom wall, fascinated by the movement of light. From the breakfast nook window she could see the light dancing again among the oak leaves, dappling lightly on their green surface. She loved rendering the play of light in her paintings.

But no painting, today. She thought again of the Foundation. It worried her that Sally might not get the grant. Sally was young and sensitive; she was likely to think that a rejection of her application would mark her as a failure. As far as Denise herself was concerned, she took all this—this recognition from the establishment—with a grain of salt.

Four days before the opening of her retrospective, she had received a formal offer on very expensive paper: "The Kelsey Foundation, supporting the arts in the Chicago area since 1952, has the honor to offer you . . ."

She didn't feel especially honored. Prior to the notice, she had gone for an interview at the Foundation headquarters. She found herself sitting across from a Miss Gibble, a woman with a pinched nose and very thick glasses. "It is a serious commitment, you understand. There should be six exhibits per year which you will be completely responsible for—organization, contacting artists, choosing and assembling art works, publicity, etc. And, of course, a complete write-up after each one."

"I see," Denise had said, noncommittal. She had almost turned it down on the spot. It was the idea of doing a write-up that stuck in her throat. She hated writing.

But Mary Ellen, a good friend and colleague from adult ed., was in favor. They discussed the offer over an order of fatty spareribs at a neighborhood Chinese restaurant.

Mary Ellen looked at her with her sharp round eyes. "So now that you're finished at the adult ed program, you'll have something useful to do."

Denise bristled. "What do you mean, 'something useful to do?'"

"Well, you've spent the summer holed up in your studio, doing nothing but painting. The job with the Foundation will give you a purpose."

"You don't think painting is a purpose?"

"Denise, you've been painting for forty years. Surely by now you're painted out anyway, aren't you?"

"No, Mary Ellen, I am not painted out." Denise had been painting for over fifty years, but she didn't call that to Mary Ellen's attention. "I may be old, fat, and more often tired, but I'm most certainly not painted out. I have plenty of ideas."

"Well, don't you think it would be a good idea to make some changes in your life? Get out into the community and give something back. Mingle with the public, be active. Too much solitude isn't good for you."

Denise thought for a moment. "You know, Mary Ellen, I've been waiting all my life for an opportunity to devote all my time to painting. And now that I have that time, I'm being lured away by an institution. An institution that probably is going to be more demanding that the Greater Chicago Teachers of Continuing Education for older Learners."

Mary Ellen shook her head, as though Denise had been giving a lecture on quantum physics. She had never been able to understand how important painting was to Denise. But she did have a point. Since her retirement from part-time teaching, Denise had spent more and more time on her own, in her studio. It might be a good idea to get out into the community. Mix a bit more with other artists.

In any case, Miss Gibble said the Foundation wouldn't expect a response until the end of the week. That left her Friday morning to mull it over. Today she would be focused on other things.

Denise suddenly realized that the kettle had been screeching for some time.

She reluctantly left the breakfast nook for the kitchen, poured boiling water over the little pile of brown powder, and stirred it. She took it back into the breakfast nook and squeezed herself onto the bench beside the table. It was too tight a fit, really. The table took up too much room. It could easily have been replaced by a smaller table, allowing for more comfortable chairs and a bit more breathing room. But no one had thought of that. The breakfast nook remained as it was in Marjorie's time, cramped and uncomfortable. At least for Denise. Madeleine and Jennifer were so skinny that they'd fit in anywhere.

Denise sipped her coffee, which was tasteless, even though she'd put in a huge amount of powder. No food, yet. She loved breakfast as a meal, all that nice grease, bacon, fried eggs, sausages, toast dripping butter. But not in the morning. Her stomach wasn't ready. Certainly not at ten thirty in the morning. She gulped down the rest of the brown liquid, left her mug in the sink, and went back toward the front of the house.

There was a full-length mirror at the foot of the staircase. Denise contemplated her bulky form. She looked like a great dark-haired Santa Claus in her red dress. "Too old and too fat," she repeated once again. "Should I put on make-up? Line my eyes for emphasis? Paint my lips?" She shook her head. "This is Denise, as God made her," she said. "They will just have to accept me as I am."

*   *   *

Denise drove her aging Ford into the suburban town in relatively light traffic. It was a Wednesday morning, well after the rush hour. Her studio was in an old building not far from the town center, on the second floor. The place was full of memories for her. It had been the scene of wild parties in her bad old drinking days. It had also been the scene of frantic creativity. Sometimes Denise, possessed with an idea, had painted until the first rays of dawn peeped through the arrow-slits of windows. Sometimes Sally would come to see what Denise was up to and paint or sculpt herself, her golden fleece of hair sticking up all over her head like a projection of her inspiration. Tomas, unbelievable Tomas, that great bear of a man, had come to see her work. He had looked at her "Paintings of Painters" series and growled, "You're painting with your fingertips, Denise! You need to paint with your gut!"

Yes, this studio had certainly worked its magic for Denise. She had first seen it about twenty years ago when she moved to the Chicago area. At the time, it was dark and not especially clean, with mildew on the ceiling and foul-smelling rags balled up on the floor. But it was what she wanted. A studio of her own. The landlord had rented it to her at a good price and had kept the rent low over the years. She cleaned it up, painted it, and made it her own. Vertical blinds at the little windows, track lighting, a music system, even a kitchenette in one corner. She used to come here not just to work, but to get away from the house she shared with Jennifer and Madeleine. To get into her world, her world of art.

And now she was thinking of giving it up when the lease ran out in April. She was thinking that possibly she wouldn't need it anymore. With the demands of the Foundation, she could probably do what little painting she had time for at home.

She parked the car along the street near the building, went in and labored up the steps. No elevator. She reached the second-floor hallway out of breath, partly from the effort of climbing, partly from excitement. She had had Sally's friends, Toby and Alex, arrange the exhibit according to her instructions. But she hadn't been back for several days. Now it was time to give it a good hard look. It was a little after eleven, so there was plenty of time before the opening at five o'clock that afternoon. She could make adjustments, take down some of the work, re-arrange some of it. Nothing was written in stone.

She unlocked the door, went in and switched on the light. Looking around, she breathed a sigh of satisfaction. It was very mixed. Except for a brief period in college and graduate school, she had always painted what moved her or inspired her and that varied considerably.

She had had Alex and Toby hang the pictures more or less chronologically, where wall space allowed. As she looked at the pictures on each wall, she could see how her painting had grown and changed, from heavy lines and strong colors to technical mastery, to greater abstraction. She always painted with strong feeling, but as she grew older, she changed her subject matter and technique.

In the middle of the wall facing her was a canvas covered by a curtain. "That should arouse some people's curiosity," she said to herself. "But it's for Jennifer. Only Jennifer will see it."

As she stood there, her eyes moving from one painting to the next, she had an eerie feeling. They were staring back at her. Real presences that she had created. Were they watching her as she watched them?

And slowly she made the round of the exhibit, starting with the childhood drawings and sketches. There was a bundle that she had found among the papers in her parents' basement when she cleared out their possessions after her mother's death. In that bundle were images that caught her fancy when she still lived at home—flowers, grass, moving in the wind, her brother's hands, her own hands, clusters of clouds over an open landscape, animals: horses, dogs, cats, giraffes. It was a childhood impulse to capture the images she saw or held in her mind, to give them form.

But it was the two that she had chosen to hang here, in her retrospective, that moved her, that made her remember.

The two works were a sketch and a watercolor. The watercolor was a happy circus scene, a clown in the foreground playing to the crowd, in the background acrobats riding a line of elephants that crossed the stage. She must have drawn it when she was twelve or thirteen, doing the outlines in pencil and filling in with watercolor. "Not a technique approved by art teachers," Denise thought, smiling.

The other was the one that brought back frightening memories. Done in harsh black pencil, it showed two children clinging to each other under a table. Looming over them is a giant figure, its face in a leering grin, a knife in its hand.

She stared at the picture of the children under the table. She remembered how she imagined it.

The first picture: The Children under the Table.

Unable to sleep, Denise watched the big blocks of light cross the ceiling of her room. Left to right, sometimes right to left, briefly illuminating the patches of mildew on the ceiling. She knew it was the lights of cars passing on the street below, but when she was younger, she imagined it was bull-like monsters with great searchlights on their nostrils.

Roger stirred and whimpered in the little cot across the room. As she was two years older, her parents allowed her the bed, and Roger knew his place well enough not to question the arrangement. Now he was murmuring, "Daddy, Daddy."

Denise got out of bed and went to Roger's cot. "What's the matter?"

"Where's Daddy?" he whimpered. "Why didn't he come home for dinner?"

Denise bent down and gave her brother, now sitting, a little hug. "It's okay, Rog. Don't you remember what Mom said? He's working late. He must have come in a while ago."

"But he didn't come to kiss us good night." Roger's lips were trembling.

"He probably didn't want to wake us up. Now go back to sleep, Rog." Denise pulled the covers up to Roger's neck and patted them down. She didn't say so, but she was worried too. Dad was staying out late more and more often, and she knew with the certainty of childhood that it wasn't because he was working. She knew it was some dark, unmentionable secret that her mother would never tell her. She lay back down and listened. Tonight she heard nothing, but other nights there were the muffled sounds of angry voices. There was something terribly wrong, and she could only suspect what it was. She watched the lights cross the ceiling again, listened to the wind, which seemed to catch in the eaves of the old house, battering away. A few minutes she floated toward sleep. Then one of her fantasies grew in her mind, so sharp that she felt as though she were acting a part in it.

It began with reality, the reality of a late afternoon on a Friday night, probably in November. The light was just fading and the two children were sitting at the little kitchen table, listening to the radio. Friday night they listened to "I love a mystery" and "The Shadow," and they liked to keep the light off for greater scariness. The scariness was very important.

Then Denise's fantasy began. There was a noise, over the theme song of "I love a Mystery," the terrible sound of furniture being overturned, the higher pitched sound of glass smashing, and their mother's voice screaming, "Stop, Rick. Please stop!"

In her fantasy, Denise had to protect Roger. He was younger and smaller. She thought quickly. They could have rushed out the back door into the tiny back yard, but it was too late. "It's Dad, Roger," she whispered. "He's drunk. We've got to hide."

They dived under the kitchen table just as he entered the room. Denise put her arm around Roger and held him tight. "Don't move," she hissed. "Don't even breathe." They could hear his boots heavy on the floor; they could hear his labored breathing.

"I know you're there, you little bastards. Little bastard brats!"

Denise could imagine Roger clinging to her. In the background, the sobbing sounds of the theme music for "I love a Mystery." Denise clenched her teeth. "I am not scared. I will not let myself be scared," she said to herself, feeling something hard inside her, something that was steady and would not let her give in. She kept stroking Roger's back. She could feel him trembling.

"There you are, you little bitch!" Her father reached under the table and pulled her out by the arm. She stood up immediately and looked up into his face. He was a monster. Nothing about him resembled the real Mr. Spaulding, nothing except his gentle blue eyes, and they were hideously splotched with red. His mouth was like a huge red cave. He had a knife, or sometimes a baseball bat, in one hand, poised, ready to strike.

It was then that she showed her greatest courage. She tried to speak, to say something defiant, but her tongue wouldn't move. But she just stood there as straight and firm as she could and stared him in the face. After what seemed an interminable space of time, he slowly put his weapon down, turned and crashed out the back door into the garden toward the railroad. Denise took a sharp breath. She hadn't breathed from the moment her father grabbed her and pulled her out from under the table.

And then she would stretch her hand out to Roger and help him out from under the table.

The images faded and Denise was wakeful again, listening for the sound of the front door opening, for the muted sound of her parents' voices. That night she never heard her father return, and she slept only fitfully until the next morning, always half listening.

In her fantasy, her father was half man, half monster, a figure created out of her uncertainty, her fear about his absence. But she never saw Mr. Spaulding brandishing a knife and in fact she never saw him drunk until much later.

The next afternoon Mr. Spaulding, the real Mr. Spaulding, came back early from work. The kids were playing in the tiny space they called a back yard. They suddenly heard his voice, like melted gold pouring out. "Where's my darlings?" He came bursting out the back door, a short, shambling man with lively blue eyes and bristly brown hair.

"It's Dad!" Denise shouted. And they ran to meet him, to be swept up in his arms. First Denise and then Roger, twirled around till they were dizzy. He had brought a treat, as usual, two paper cones of chocolate candy wrapped in gold foil.

Rick Spaulding was often simply not there for his kids. But when he was with them, he was gentle, loving, and fun. Denise's happiest childhood memories all revolved around him—trips to the zoo, ice cream sundaes in the local drugstore, double-feature binges at the drive-in movies, best of all, the circus—he was always the planner and the leader of Denise and Roger's outings. Mrs. Spaulding seldom joined them. She was usually in a tearful heap in bed. Denise called her "the dish rag."

When Denise needed support and help, she turned to her father—if he was around. He was the first to look at her drawings. She kept them hidden away and was reluctant to show them to anyone. But one day she screwed up her courage and took a pile in to him as he was sitting in the living room, reading the newspaper.

She took his arm to get his attention and put the pile of papers in his lap. He picked them up, one by one, slowly, and looked at them. Then he turned to her with a brilliant smile.

"These are wonderful, Denise," he said. "You have a talent, my girl. And don't you ever, ever forget it."

She never did forget those words, through the disappointments and rejections she received as an artist. Her father had told her she had a talent.

And so Denise grew up having two fathers, one the terrible Drunk Dad of her fantasy and the real one, Happy Dad. She liked to pretend that Happy Dad and Drunk Dad would some day have an enormous fight. And Happy Dad would win. And be with them every night.

But in fact, Drunk Dad proved to be more than a fantasy. And Drunk Dad won. Rick Spaulding died at forty-two of liver cancer.

*   *   *

Denise stood in front of this childhood drawing, admiring the power of the dark strokes she had used to create the image of the monster attacking the children. It was a shame that this was the only image she had drawn of her father. It wasn't him; it was a depiction of childish fear. Denise's real father—she had loved him very much and a sense of lightness and buoyancy had gone from her life when he died. But that was a grief that would always be with her, and she couldn't indulge it now.

She moved to the series of paintings nearby, a little further to the right on the same wall. These were her early experiments, her expressions of freedom. They were crude, colorful, and, above all, full of energy. She had painted all the images, real and imaged, that struck her fancy—angels, and unicorns and wizards and mythical beasts, as well as real people and animals. She had tried and mixed acrylics, watercolors and oils, and come up with some disastrous, muddy-looking canvases. Of course, she had only chosen the more successful experiments to show in this exhibit. Even so, it was a motley display. She smiled, admiring her own youthful imagination. Knowing nothing, she had tried everything. And it had been joyful and liberating.

She marvelled that she had been able to paint so much in so little time. She had left home when she was sixteen and rented a place in a rooming house, simple but clean and decent. She was working as a waitress in a diner, week days after school, all day on weekends. One day a week she cleaned for one of her mother's friends. At the same time, she was going to school, determined not to drop out, determined to make something of her life. She would come back after finishing work in the diner, do the minimum of homework, and paint until the early hours of the morning. Looking back, she was astonished that she didn't drop from sheer exhaustion. But she couldn't remember even being tired.

She looked at the paintings in this section. There were a couple of lurid landscapes, a couple of heavily outlined portraits, one of a friend and one of an older woman, possibly a teacher, and in the center of all of them, the most violent, entitled "Nudes on the Beach." It showed four or five nude women, painted in green, lolloping on a pink beach. The ocean, in the background, was vermillion red with white scrolls to represent the waves. It was an awful picture in every way, and Denise loved it.

The Second Picture, Nudes on the Beach

She did it on a dare, a dare to herself. She had met Jeff Tozer when she was working at Mack's diner. It was breakfast time on a Saturday morning. He was with a group of young people, mostly young men, who had been drinking all night and came in for breakfast. College students, Denise guessed.

Jeff was the quiet one. She noticed him, saw he was looking at her in a certain way. And then he started coming regularly, at the beginning of her weekday shift, about four o'clock. He would sit alone at one end of the counter, his eyes on his plate. He usually wore a bright red Ohio State sweatshirt and tight-fitting blue jeans. There was something about him that was different. Jeff looked like someone, Denise thought, who would always behave like a gentleman, who would speak without using obscenities, who would take a girl to nice restaurants. And, unlike the boyfriends she had had, Jeff would always be able to take up the tab.

Jeff was also good-looking. He had light-brown hair, longer than was fashionable, which flopped attractively over one eye. His eyes were a sort of muddy pale brown, the color of coffee with just a little cream. They didn't go with his fair complexion, the complexion of a sweet little fair-haired boy pulling a toy truck by a string.

He always ordered lemon meringue pie and coffee and lingered longer than necessary.

Denise was instantly attracted to him. When he came near her, it was as though her body was lighting up like a Christmas tree. She was afraid he could tell. She had to take special care not to spill his coffee because her hands were shaking when she served him, just a little bit.

After a couple of weeks he introduced himself, "I'm Jeff Tozer," he said. "And I love your pie."

"It's not my pie, Mr. Tozer," she said innocently. "It's probably not even baked on the premises."

Jeff looked at her with an odd expression on his face, the corners of his mouth pulled down as if he were suppressing a laugh. After a moment he said, "I don't care where you bake it, Miss," he said. "It's delicious. And call me Jeff."

The management of Mack's didn't encourage friendly conversation between waitresses and customers. Sensing she was being watched, Denise leaned forward and whispered, "My name's Denise."

From that moment on, they had a discreet little flirtation, talking briefly when it was quiet at Mack's, and always exchanging smiles and glances. He would come in at his usual time, sit at the end of the counter and order pie and coffee, ask her how she was and if possible add a casual question. She told him she was a native of Cincinnati, was still in high school, and loved to paint. She learned that he was a history major at the University of Cincinnati, was less than an enthusiastic student, and loved softball. He was surprised that she was still in high school. "You look like a grown-up woman," he said. "I was afraid you might be married."

Denise began to look forward to their flirtation. She wasn't dating at all at the moment, she didn't have time. And Jeff was a heady diversion.

At Thanksgiving, she had a break. No school on Thursday and Friday and Mack's, which only did short-order cooking, closed too for the weekend. When Jeff came in on Wednesday afternoon, she whispered, "I'm off tomorrow, off for the Thanksgiving weekend!"

He looked up at her with a lopsided grin. "Hey, Denise," he said. "Wanna come to Florida with me? Just for the hell of it? See some nice scenery and swim in the deep blue sea? Where do you live? I'll pick you up tomorrow at seven o'clock so we can get an early start."

And so she said yes, on a dare to herself. "I dare you to go to Florida with Jeff Tozer," she said early the next morning. She was speaking to her reflection in the bathroom mirror down the corridor from her little room. She put together a plastic bag—she didn't have a suitcase—of things to take with her. A change of underwear, a toothbrush, a bathing suit. "Off to Florida with Jeff Tozer!" The idea was hugely exciting: to go off with an older man to see the ocean! Denise had never seen the ocean, which had a kind of mythic aura about it. The vast, shimmering ocean. Denise, who had never been further than just over the Kentucky border to visit her grandmother, Denise would see the ocean.

She knew she was taking a risk, and that was part of the excitement.

She put on the skirt and sweater she usually wore for school and went down to meet Jeff outside her apartment. To her relief, she found him there already, leaning up against a baby blue car parked along the curb. He was whistling between his teeth, his hands in his pockets.

She looked him straight in the eye. "You're serious about this?"

He nodded.

"Let's see that deep blue sea," she said. "I'll paint it!"

Jeff looked at her, squinting slightly. "Is that what you're going to wear?"

"This won't do?" she said with a broad gesture that took in her entire figure. She wasn't fat at seventeen but stocky and large-breasted.

Jeff shrugged, but he had a big smile on his face. "I guess. Well, this is my car." He pointed at the car he had been leaning against. It was a 1957 Pontiac WITH FINS. Denise was impressed. She had a few classmates who had cars, but none as stylish as this. At seventeen she didn't even drive.

So they drove out of town, southward. At first Denise was elated. An adventure! She kept looking at Jeff's profile, his floppy brown hair, his delicate little ears, his hands on the wheel, smooth and white. He was a competent driver, not racing, not taking risks.

But they drove and drove and didn't seem to be getting anywhere as the sun came up and tilted over them in its winter course, as the afternoon faded and dusk began to set in. They drove on state highways—the Interstate was only partly completed—through leafy towns and stinky industrial areas and by ploughed up fields, the harvest long since taken in.

Jeff had the car radio on too loud blasting Buddy Holly and the Platters over intermittent static. Neither of them spoke. Denise became drowsy, wondering sleepily when and where they would ever stop. As darkness fell, Jeff leaned over put his hand on Denise's knee, and gave it a squeeze. Denise pulled away. Jeff put his hand up her skirt. "Get out of there!" she said loudly, and seizing the intruding hand, thrust it away.

In the dark, Denise could just make out Jeff's profile, the jaw clenched. She knew he was angry, she knew what he expected. He was just an ordinary horny guy, no different from the guys at school. She wondered whether he might act violently. But he just drove on. Denise felt a kind of sinking in her chest as she realized she was no longer attracted to him.

"Do you wanna get something to eat?" he said eventually. Denise hadn't eaten since she grabbed a slice of toast that morning. Her stomach was rumbling and she felt edgy from hunger. They stopped in a small town and parked the car on the main street. Not many lights were on, but they found a little cafe that was still serving. Jeff had a hamburger, Denise, meatloaf, potatoes and gravy. They stared at each other across the table, a young couple with nothing to say.

She said, "The meatloaf's good."

He nodded, taking another bite out of his hamburger.

She asked him, "What are you planning to do when you graduate?"

"Go into business. I guess."

"What kind of business?"

"Oh, who cares? Just business." And he went on eating.

When they were about to get into the car, he handed her the keys. "Will you drive for a while? I'm beat."

"I don't know how to drive."

"You really are a useless commodity," he said getting back in on the driver's side.

A useless commodity. She took her place, almost ready to cry. As Jeff started the car, she leaned against the passenger window, feeling its coolness on her cheek. "What did you expect?" she asked herself. She had always prided herself on her common sense and competence; she had had to take care of herself and Roger for as long as she could remember. And here she was riding off God knows where with a man she didn't even know. She was no more sensible than those girls in her high school class who got themselves pregnant by the first guy they went out with.

What had she expected? Respect? Consideration? A little romance?

"I am a fool," she told herself. "Here I am in a stranger's car, racing off to Florida, behaving like a pie-eyed idiot."

Now all she could see were the occasional lights of the houses, more and more widespread as they travelled the quiet roads through Kentucky. She comforted herself by the idea that she was at least going to see the ocean.

This was going to be her own personal adventure, not a shared adventure.

Dawn was almost breaking that they reached the north Florida coast. Denise was asleep when she felt the car bumping and jerking over uneven ground.

"Hey, Denise, we're here," Jeff said shaking her shoulder. He threw open the driver side door and sprang out of the car. "That, what you see there, is the At-lantic Ocean, kid!"

Denise stretched sleepily. It was dark and it was cold and it certainly wasn't Miami. The water was there, for sure, a great grey sleeping whale. Denise got out of the car and ran toward the water, feeling the sand suck hard at her feet.

She suddenly felt jubilant. It wasn't what she had expected or hoped, but there it was, the ocean. As she reached the edge of the sand and smelled the rancid salt smell and heard the murmur of the waves, she shouted out, gleefully, "Hallelujah!"

It was her adventure! It had nothing to do with running off with a strange man or traveling to a place she had never seen before. It wasn't even the thrill of seeing the ocean that was important. With a great rush of excitement, she took in this experience. She was free, she had triumphed over her background, untold possibilities were opening up before her. "I'm Denise," she said to the immensity of the ocean, "I'm seventeen years old and I'm making it on my own! I am going to be great painter!"

But Jeff was suddenly at her side. He had a bottle of whiskey in hand. She had no idea where he got it; he hadn't had a single drink in the time—it must have been almost twenty-four hours—they had been traveling together. She had assumed that, like her, he simply didn't drink.

"C'mon, kid, have a drink with me. Let's drink to the ocean! Let's drink to us!" Jeff crouched down, opened the bottle and took a big swig.

"I don't drink Jeff. Ever." For someone who had grown up finding Jack Daniels bottles stashed away behind the couch, in the watering can on the porch, in the winter boots in the closet, who knew from a certain moment in childhood the smell of whiskey spilled on the carpet—for someone like her, the only answer was never to touch a drop of the stuff.

She turned away and was walking back toward the car. He grabbed her by the arm, swung her around, and tried to kiss her. She gave him one resounding wallop to the jaw.

Jeff staggered back, letting go of her arm. "You bitch! You filthy little whore!" He shouted after her. "Who do you think you are, you stuck-up little slut! You're nothing but a two-bit waitress! You aren't even pretty!"

He doubtless said some other things as well, but Denise was too far away to hear. She was doing the only thing she knew how to do; she was walking back toward the highway. She had $2.78 in her purse, from her last day's tips. She would walk until dawn, then hitchhike her way back to Cincinnati.

The highway was empty for at least an hour before the top edge of the sun peeped over the horizon. Denise was cold and a blister was forming on her left heel. She bent down to take off her shoe for a minute and saw the flash of headlights coming toward her. It was a big container truck. She stood up and put up her thumb. The truck pulled over and stopped.

"Hop in, little lady! Where're you heading?"

Denise saw the driver's glance, sizing her up in the faint light. It would be a long trip home.

$*$ $*$ $*$

She managed to get back to Cincinnati by Sunday night and kept her job at Mack's. But Jeff Tozer never came back to order lemon meringue pie and coffee. She never saw him again.

Thinking back on that trip, she had sympathy, even affection for Jeff Tozer. He must have been sorely disappointed. He had picked up this friendly waitress who seemed grown-up and earthy, and when he got her into the car, she wouldn't even let him touch her. She thought of Jeff's vulnerable good looks, wondering why she was ever attracted to him. Not her type at all. Too smooth, too sweet. She preferred a stronger, hairier animal. Anyway, she wasn't ready for sex then. She was too afraid of early pregnancy and the bondage it could bring.

As for the trip itself, it gave her a taste of freedom. She had wanted to go and she had gone, without asking anyone's permission. She had gone on a dare to herself. And when she got back, she painted "Nudes on the Beach." She painted it fast and furiously in the free time she had after work. It was her boldest painting of that period, with heavy brush strokes and psychedelic colors. Looking at it, she smiled again, knowing it had more to do with her confused sexual feelings than it did with the sea or the beach. She had barely seen the sea.

She moved on. There was just one painting on its own beyond her adolescent works. She stopped in front of it, and admired it. It was the portrait of a young girl, more professionally done than those early adolescent paintings. Here she wasn't simply expressing raw feeling; she was observing and making her observations come to life. She had brought out the highlights in the girl's hair, the pouting mouth, the line on her eyelids, the texture of the scarf around her neck. It was accurate, it was realistic; looking at it, you were curious about this girl, wanted to know more about her.

Denise did this painting while she was in college outside class, not as an assignment, but for herself. The portrait of a dark-haired girl in her early twenties. Denise stared into the girl's face, remembering. The girl stared back, through heavily-lidded eyes. She looked sleepy, but at the same time defiant, as though her mother had woken her to do a chore she didn't want to do. Her thick hair was braided and looped over her ears, like that of a Pre-Raphaelite maiden.

251

The girl was Harriet Birch, who had been a sort of friend during their sophomore year in college. Their friendship had lasted just long enough for them to paint each other's portrait. Denise remembered the portrait Harriet had painted of her. It was beautifully executed but too flattering; Harriet had softened her features, had given shape to her plump cheeks.

Harriet must have destroyed that portrait. There was no doubt in Denise's mind that that had happened. She could see Harriet taking a sharp kitchen knife to the canvas and systematically shredding it.

The Third Picture: Harriet Birch

High school was one thing. In high school you made book reports, memorized facts and charts, solved problems. But when Denise entered college, she entered a world of make-believe. Everyone was pretending to be someone they weren't; professors were droning experts about subjects no one in the outside world cared about. Students were mini-experts or loyal followers of the professors, fawning at their feet. Professors and students alike talked, quite seriously, about when the Middle Ages ended or how many stressed syllables were in a line of poetry, or what was the nature of reality. Denise observed, baffled, unable to enter into the spirit of things.

At that time she was trying to figure out whether her salary and tips from waiting table would cover her rent. She had managed to get a scholarship to the university, but it didn't cover her living expenses. So she had taken out a loan and was worried about paying it back. All this made her wonder about the university. Was it worth the effort?

It was during her freshman year, at the peak of unreality, that she saw Harriet Birch for the first time. It was a performance of A Midsummer's Night's Dream, and Harriet was playing the part of Titania. The whole production seemed like an exaggerated form of the make-believe Denise saw every day in the classroom. Harriet over-acted; even Denise, who had little experience of the theatre, could see that. But she was so beautiful, with her enormous dark eyes and her wild mass of dark hair and she moved with such grace that it didn't really matter.

All Denise could think of was how she would paint this woman's portrait. She thought about her constantly, imagined her in different situations, digging in a garden, diving into a swimming pool, eating a messy sandwich. It wasn't a physical attraction like the one she had felt for Jeff. It was rather the kind of fascination some people feel for celebrities. In the weeks and months that followed she saw Harriet once or twice in the school cafeteria, always flamboyant, always strikingly dressed. She heard a lot about her from the other students, who spoke of her with the kind of envy celebrities attract. She was having an affair with Dr. X. She was getting straight A's. She was about to flunk out. She was going to spend a semester in Paris. She was having a nervous breakdown. Denise didn't know what to believe, but she savored the rumors like a kitten lapping up its cream. She never expected to get to know her.

But she actually met Harriet at the beginning of her sophomore year. Denise was at the first meeting of her life drawing class. She noticed when she arrived that there was a strange atmosphere in the classroom. There were ten or twelve students, mostly women, and they were chattering nervously to one another. Denise thought at first that it must be in anticipation of drawing a nude model. But when the young man appeared, the students took little notice of him, continuing their buzz of talk. Then there was a sudden silence and everyone looked toward the door.

It was Harriet Birch. She swept in, wearing scarlet pantaloons and a skin-tight top. She was no less made-up, no less theatrical, than when she had played Titania. She looked around the classroom, her heavy eyebrows drawn together, like a hawk, scanning the sky for prey. Then, briefly, she looked straight at Denise, and to her astonishment, took the place next to her.

There was a sort of collective sigh as the instructor entered the room. Denise, who had been trying not to stare at Harriet, glanced up at the person standing by the lectern. He was no less extraordinary; Denise didn't know where to stare—at the girl or at the young teaching assistant. He had flaming shoulder-length red hair and a pointed beard. He looked like an enormous randy fox. He introduced himself as Floyd and gave a few instructions to the class.

"Detail isn't important," he was saying. "Try to capture the movement, the general lines of the body. Make it fluid, make it live. You have ninety minutes to work. I'll answer individual questions."

Denise cast a glance at the nude model, a well-muscled, tanned young man, and made a decision. Very quickly she would do a sketch of Harriet to be finished later. Then she would work on the sketch of the model. Ninety minutes would be enough time to do both. She drew in her breath and observed her neighbor's extraordinary profile—the deep forehead, the prominent nose and chin, the hooded eyes, the beautiful, wild hair.

The teaching assistant was making the rounds of the class. Denise sketched frantically, hoping to sketch a likeness of Harriet before he got to her place. But something about the way she was turning her head gave her away. Suddenly the red fox was standing behind Denise. He picked up Denise's sketch book and looked at the portrait she had started. He laughed.

"You're right," he said in a low voice. "She's a lot prettier than the model."

Harriet looked up from her sketch book. "Who? Who are you talking about?" she asked, looking at the instructor with disdain.

"You," said Floyd. "It looks as if this young lady finds you more interesting than the model."

Harriet left her easel and stepped behind Denise. "My profile!" she said. "But my profile is hideous!" She tore the page from Denise's sketchbook and ripped it in two with one decisive movement.

There was a sudden silence. Heads, until then occupied with the paper in front of then, suddenly bobbed up and stared in Harriet's direction. Some students left their stations to observe the little drama at close range. Work stopped.

"Go back to your drawing," Floyd shouted and after a few minutes, the class settled down. He turned back to Denise. "I think you'd better stick to the subject," he said. He put his hand gently on her head and turned it toward the model. "If you want to draw another person, draw her out of class." He spoke evenly, as if reading from a script. But there was a twinkle in his eyes that made Denise suspect he wasn't entirely serious. In any case, she turned to a new page of her sketch book and started sketching the model. She was too embarrassed to explain what she had meant to do. She was aware that Harriet kept casting glances in her direction.

At the end of the period, Harriet stood beside Denise's station, evaluating her drawing.

"That's not bad," she said, lightly. "If you're still interested, why don't you come to my studio. We'll do each other's portraits. Full face. Next week after class. Is that a date?"

*   *   *

The following Thursday, Harriet appeared in a less flamboyant get-up. She was wearing skin-tight black jeans, a silky black top, and black tennis shoes with gold laces. Her hair was curling in untamed splendor around her face. Denise was more entranced than ever. She sensed without knowing precisely why that these clothes cost more than her own entire wardrobe.

Soon the class was over and they were walking along the city pavement toward Harriet's studio. Harriet was talking nonstop.

"That teaching assistant knows absolutely nothing. You ask him a question and he has no idea how to answer. It's an insult to the students that the University lets incompetents like him teach a class." She paused, still walking briskly, and took a breath. Then, turning toward Denise, she said, "Do you know that he's a lecher? He sleeps with any student he can get into his bed. Can you believe that, Denise? I can't stand the sight of his disgusting orange beard." She shuddered.

Denise was following along, in a sort of trance of excitement, hardly listening to Harriet's prattle. It was a dream! She was going to Harriet Birch's studio! She was going to paint this fabulous woman's portrait!

She was keeping in step with Harriet, watching their feet move in tandem. Harriet's were long and pointed, Denise's little and plump. Suddenly she began to make sense of what Harriet was saying. She looked up at Harriet's face, the curve of her nostrils as she poured out her wrath against the instructor.

Now Harriet was talking about her studio. "Daddy and Mama are renting it for me. Daddy thinks my talents are literary, but he's letting me try out painting. The studio isn't as inspiring as I hoped.

It's . . . well, you'll see. It's just sort of like a big warehouse. Actually it would make a good dance hall. Or even a theatre, if I decide to put on my own plays."

Denise, watching Harriet's lovely face, felt the distance between them like a crack in the earth between her feet and Harriet's. It slowly deepened and widened She realized they would never be friends. "I'm probably making a mistake even going with her," she thought. "She tore up my drawing and didn't even apologize."

They arrived at the building where Harriet's studio was located. It was on a pleasant, tree-lined street across from a little city park. The building itself was plain. It could have been a lock-up garage or an abandoned warehouse. As Harriet took out a key and opened the door, Denise felt suddenly cold. They entered the building. Harriet ran up the stairs to the second floor, and with a dramatic gesture, threw open the door of the studio. It was a single, dark, vast room, over twice the size of Denise's apartment, probably bigger than the house she had grown up in.

"I'm going to change," Harriet announced and disappeared into a walk-in closet at one end of the room.

While she was in the closet, Denise looked around. In the middle of the room a work table and an easel without a canvas on it. A couple of upholstered easy chairs by the work table. Aside from these few items, the room was surprisingly empty. Denise expected dozens of paintings, some hung on the walls, some stacked along the walls. That is how her studio would be. But there was only a little pile of sketches and paintings on the work table. Denise spread it out and thumbed through the sketches. Some were dreamlike landscapes and others were idealized female faces.

Denise picked up one of the landscapes and was examining it, when Harriet reappeared. She had put on a navy blue robe with a pattern of silvery moons and stars. She had done her hair in a complicated series of braids and poofs, decorated with a great silver comb so that her bangs stuck up like a horse's forelock. She was elaborately made up, with violet eye shadow and heavily-lined lips.

"What do you think?" she asked striking a pose, lunging forward like a fencer, the robe dropping provocatively off one shoulder.

Denise felt like laughing. But she still wanted to paint Harriet, so she had to be polite. "Well, I just wanted to paint your face," she said, "so what you're wearing, really, isn't especially important. And, to be honest, I'd rather paint you without so much make-up."

Harriet disappeared again and this time came back in full riding gear with boots and a crop in one hand.

Denise was quickly losing patience. "Didn't you hear me, Harriet? No costume! Little or no make-up!"

"How dreary!" said Harriet. "Without a costume, without make-up, no interest whatsoever."

"I think your face is fascinating, without make-up. Or, if you like, just a little. A little eyeliner, a little lipstick."

"Come show me what you mean." Harriet ushered Denise into the closet, which was like a backstage dressing room, with reams of costumes, a three-way mirror at one end and a dressing table with a lighted mirror at the other. Denise stared in astonishment. "So many costumes! Where did they all come from?"

"My dresses? Some are Mama's, some came from a second-hand shop. Let me show you!" Harriet was pulling some of the costumes from their hangers.

"No, Harriet." A lot of Denise's awe of Harriet had evaporated. "I'm here to paint, not to play at dress-up."

Harriet cast a resentful glance at Denise and sat down at the dressing table. Denise stood beside her as she took a sponge and removed most of the make-up from her face.

"Now show me what you mean," she commanded.

"Well, I'm not very good at this since I don't use much make-up myself. But if you just . . ." Taking the eyeliner, Denise drew a soft, somewhat wavering line along Harriet's eyelid. She found a lighter shade of lipstick and filled in her lips.

"Well, what do you think?" she asked, stepping back to get the general effect.

"I look like nothing. I look like a ghost," said Harriet, pouting.

"Well, that's the way I want to paint you. It will be a gorgeous painting. You'll see."

Harriet took the eyeliner and made a more expert-looking line. She looked up at Denise almost pathetically. "You're sure I'm all right this way? *Au naturel?*

"You're beautiful. I don't know why you have so little confidence in yourself."

"When I paint you, I'll want to make you up. You're just like a man as you are."

To Denise's surprise, Harriet stood up and, pulling her head toward her, kissed her on the lips. It was a light kiss, like the touch of a butterfly's wings. Harriet turned away quickly and went back into the studio area, leaving Denise stunned, unable to move. She took a few seconds to collect herself and then followed Harriet. She found Harriet posed on the one easy chair opposite the easel. Denise went over to her and adjusted the angle of her face.

"Let's get started, shall we?" she said, taking up the brushes and the paints on the work table.

*　　*　　*

So the two girls began their relationship, which consisted of Thursday afternoon painting sessions at Harriet's studio. They took turns; first Denise painted Harriet, then Harriet painted Denise. Denise took great pains with her portrait, getting each detail perfect—the contours of the face, the slope of the chin, the eyebrows like a bird's wings. But most of all she labored on the expression, the pouting lips, the passionate eyes.

When Harriet came to paint Denise, she wanted her to choose a costume from the vast hoard in the closet. Denise refused. "Paint me as I am, as you see me," she said. To Denise's surprise, Harriet did as she was told. When she showed it to Denise, Denise was surprised to see a workmanlike portrait, but one that was too flattering, one that resembled Harriet more than it did her.

A week after the portrait painting session began, Floyd invited Denise to come to his apartment for a drink. "That sounds like a proposition," said Denise. "I'm not sure I want to get involved with a teacher."

In fact, she wasn't especially attracted to Floyd. She didn't like red-haired men. But with the birth control pill available, she no longer had to worry about the consequences of having sex. Floyd's invitation was tempting. It was as if he had offered her an exotic drink or a strange dish. She wanted to try just it to see what it was like.

So she accepted the second invitation and on a chilly fall day walked the six blocks to Floyd's apartment. Floyd was waiting outside, a drink in his hand. He ushered her into a tiny, windowless living room. It was not much bigger than Denise's.

"Do you mind if I have a look around?" she asked as he took her coat.

"That's okay by me, if you don't mind mess." He eyed her up and down as if seeing her for the first time, as if assessing her.

He made a gesture toward the back corner of the room. "I've got a kitchenette here," he said. The kitchenette consisted of two burners and a small sink with a cupboard above it. There was no sign that it had ever been used.

He opened a door at the back to reveal a very messy bedroom, with an unmade bed, various unfinished sketches on the walls, a sculpted head on one of the little tables.

"That's, excuse the mess, the bedroom. There's a little bathroom down the hall. That's it. Not much, is it?"

"It's fine," said Denise. "In fact, it's a little bigger than mine." She sat tentatively on the couch. Floyd moved to the kitchen area and extracted a bottle of wine and two glasses from the cupboard. He came back, sat beside her, poured her a glass of wine and lit the candles that were on the little coffee table.

"Here's to you," he said, raising his glass.

Denise still wasn't used to drinking, but she felt again that it was something she needed to try. A small glass could do her no harm. She took a small sip. It was syrupy sweet and vile. It burned her throat. She set down the glass and cleared her throat. Floyd was moving closer. He put his hand up her tee shirt, released the catch on her bra and had a good feel of her breasts.

"You don't waste much time," Denise said, pulling his hand out of her top.

Floyd was undeterred. "You're so big!" he said, finishing his wine in one gulp. "God, how I love big women!"

The love-making, which followed very quickly, was disappointing. It was swift and energetic and didn't allow Denise to feel much. "Is that all there is to sex?" Denise wondered afterwards.

But again out of curiosity, she went back the next week and the following week and began to enjoy it. And look forward to it. Floyd was a third year graduate student, writing a thesis on Cezanne, which, by his own admission, he would probably never finish. He was funny and irreverent about the university. He loved nothing better than getting stoned and laughing hysterically about the antics he saw at committee meetings.

Denise was aware that Floyd was seeing other women—doubtless plenty of other women. It was strange, but Denise didn't really care. Lovemaking with Floyd, painting with Harriet simply became part of her college life.

*   *   *

Someone was pounding on the front door. The noise was so loud and so intrusive that it reminded Denise of those SS men in World War Two movies seeking out Jews in hiding. She and Floyd were sitting at the little table in Floyd's bedroom, smoking weed and drinking Gallo wine.

The pounding grew louder. "I'd better answer that," said Floyd. "Denise, put some clothes on, quickly!" Floyd threw on a bathroom and went through the bedroom to the living room. Denise followed him, alarmed and wondering who could be on the other side of the door. She wondered if Floyd, who drank more than he needed, was in some kind of trouble with the law. Or if a jealous husband of one of his lady loves wanted revenge.

"Harriet!"

Harriet came barrelling through the front door, her face flaming red, her hair a terrific mess. "So you two are together! I knew it! And I know what you've been up to!"

Harriet brushed past them into the bedroom, where the smell of marijuana still hovered sweetly. There was a scented candle burning on the table between two half full glasses of cheap wine. The bed linens were scrambled as if put through a mixer. It was quite obvious what had been going on.

Denise and Floyd followed Harriet, feeling intimidated by her rage, but more than anything, like fools.

THE SEEKERS

Harriet, who had been staring at the disarray wheeled around to face Floyd. She was dark, not flushed, with rage. "You filthy old lecher! You rutting baboon! How many innocent young women have you corrupted?" She shuddered visibly. "You have no right to her. Come with me, Denise!"

Denise, who was staring at Harriet in astonishment, didn't move. "This is . . . is . . . a private matter, between Floyd and me. It's none of your business, Harriet."

"Shame on you! Shame on you, you great fat whore!" And with that, Harriet seized one of the burning candles and hurled it in Denise's direction. It hit the floor, and Floyd had the presence of mind to pick it up and put it out before it did any damage.

Denise and Floyd watched Harriet, speechless.

Denise went into the living room, wondering if it would defuse the situation if she left. Harriet followed her. She was still shouting, "Great fat whore!"

"Harriet!" said Denise, "Calm down, for Christ's sake! I have the right to choose who I go with. It's no concern of yours."

Harriet's voice was now hoarse and menacing. "How can you do it! How can you be attracted to that lecher! I can't understand how you'd let him touch you, much less sleep with him."

"It's just a bit of fun, Harriet," Denise said, feeling the huge discrepancy between Harriet's rage and her own mild pleasure in Floyd's company.

Harriet swallowed hard. "I don't want anything to do with you, you filthy piece of shit," she shouted, or tried to shout, her voice breaking.

"Don't you want to paint me anymore?" Denise said weakly.

"Paint you!" Harriet swept her arm across the top of an available bookcase, knocking a bunch of decorative objects on the floor. "That is what I think of your painting."

And with that, she stomped out.

Denise and Floyd stared at one another, stunned.

"Are you two . . . ?" Floyd put his hand together.

"Floyd, we aren't even . . ." Denise stopped because Floyd seemed to be having some sort of odd fit. At first she thought he was furious with her for being friends with Harriet and inadvertently causing this upheaval. Then she realized he was

261

laughing hysterically. He was having a drug and alcohol-induced fit of the giggles.

"You and Harriet," he gasped. "You and Harriet . . ." He was unable to finish whatever he wanted to say. At first Denise was indignant. What was so funny? Why was he laughing at her? But suddenly the laughing bug hit her. And pretty soon they were both laughing raucously, rocking back and forth, holding their sides. And then they were on the floor, rolling over and over in glee.

*   *   *

Denise stared at the Harriet's portrait. Her idol for a brief period when she started college. Looking at it, Denise was impressed by the technical skill. She had actually made Harriet's eyes so real, so lifelike, that they seemed to be staring back at her.

After the scene in Floyd's apartment, Denise went to Harriet's studio once, to retrieve her portrait, that is, the portrait she had painted of Harriet. The two never spoke again, and Harriet moved her work station in life drawing class away from Denise's. When Denise heard scraps of gossip about Harriet, she just smiled to herself.

After the relationship with Floyd was finally finished, Denise started dating a man called Charlie Banks. He was majoring in Political Science. He was tall and loose-limbed and ordinary and for some reason permanently apologetic. At the same time, she made a couple of women friends who were also arts majors. When Denise started her junior year and took mostly studio classes, she felt at last that she was in the real world.

Looking at Harriet's portrait, Denise acknowledged that she was attracted to her. What if she had had an affair with Harriet and a friendship with Floyd? It would have been exciting but messy and in the long run, disappointing. Her one regret was that she never painted Floyd.

She moved to a group of studies hanging on the back wall. In the middle was a very large canvas, the largest on display. It was a panoramic view of the circus, full of color and movement. The little pictures that surrounded it were studies she had done of the various figures developed in the larger canvas: the bearded lady, the ring master, the tightrope walker, a lion, a group of elephants. There were also sketches for a gypsy scene, a caravan decorated in vivid colors. Denise had done both series in the early seventies when she was living in Brooklyn, shortly after taking her Master's degree.

The big circus scene had taken a lot of effort and had been very important to her at one time. Now she looked at it critically, musing.

The Fourth Picture: A Circus Panorama

"I'm going to conquer the art world!" This is what she was thinking when she rented her little apartment on a quiet street in Brooklyn. Sprung from graduate school and the Victorian house she had rented with Jennifer, Marjorie, and Madeleine, she wanted first of all to live in New York. But any safe part of Manhattan turned out to be too expensive for an aspiring artist with no job and no special skills. So Denise widened her search and found an apartment in Brooklyn. It was furnished and just adequate for one person, with one small bedroom and a tiny kitchen. What it did have was a spacious living room, north facing, with plenty of indirect light. This is where she would paint.

Even the relatively low rent was too much for her, so by advertising she found a roommate, another artist called Libby Rosen. Libby was a pretty girl in her early twenties who favored lots of colorful scarves and vests and jackets, unbuttoned and worn in layers so that her clothes were always flapping around like the wings of some exotic bird. She had large blue eyes and an expression of permanent surprise as though caught in some act of naughtiness. She called herself an artist, but she spent more time in bed with a succession of boyfriends than she did painting.

Libby's sexual antics occurred at all hours of the day and night. Denise soon let her use her bedroom and moved her bed into the living room. She herself had more privacy that way. She hated going into the living room to paint and only to discover a dishevelled young man peeping out from Libby's many shawls and blankets on the couch.

Denise was unsuccessful at finding a job in the art industry and worked as a saleswoman in several local shops. She didn't strictly mind selling, but it took too much time and too much energy from her painting. And when she got her first pay check, she was disheartened by the amounts taken out for tax and social security. Some weeks she spent almost nothing on food so that she could buy good quality art supplies. She was thinner then than she had ever been, before or after. She and Libby often dined on cheese and soda crackers.

It was during these years in Brooklyn that she acquired the habit of waking with an image in her mind. She would turn it over and over, refining it as though she were actually painting it, and then she would fall asleep again. Sometimes the image came to her in an early dream, more sharply defined and more brilliant than in reality.

It was in one of those early morning images that she first saw the circus scene. She remembered the time that her father, in one of his happy, sober spells, had taken her and Roger to the Big Top. She fell in love with it immediately. She loved the excitement and the color and the air of chaos. More than anything, the unsavory element attracted her; the sense that these were people on the fringes of society, not quite the types you would see sitting behind a desk in a well-ordered office, people who earned a poor living by enjoying themselves. This is the impression Denise had as a little girl. She loved the idea of running away to join the circus, but that was only one of her fantasies.

The image of the circus wasn't altogether clear in her mind. She saw the elephants, the ringmaster in his smart uniform, the acrobats, the fierce lion tamer. But she wasn't sure how to put it all together. She began working on different elements, the attitude of the ringmaster and the face of one of the clowns, making studies for the final picture.

At about the same time, she became preoccupied with another image: the fortune teller. She saw her as a vague form, draped in filmy scarves, bent over an outstretched hand whose palm she was reading. When she finally came to capture this image, Denise asked Libby to pose for her. Her coloring was wrong of course, but the bird-in-flight impression she created suited the character.

Then she realized that the fortune teller had nothing to do with the circus—though to her the gypsy's way of life was similar to the circus people's—and she felt she had to situate the gypsy in a caravan. But the caravan idea didn't work. She couldn't get the details right; she couldn't make an interesting scene. So Denise did only a few sketches of the caravan scene and concentrated on the various elements of the circus. The fortune teller would have to stand on her own.

For a long time she had no idea how she would put the circus scene together or what the angle of view would be. Then she decided to include all the parts without concern for perspective; she would make the lion tamer, with his cruelty and power, the biggest figure even though he was furthest from view. She couldn't fit the lions in, so it was as if the lion tamer was directing the entire show. With his whip. Beneath him at ground level, was the parade of circus animals, clowns, acrobats, freaks. The tightrope, the swings and the acrobats would be at midlevel. And the lion tamer, seen from the waist up, flourishing his whip, would occupy the top. The entire painting would be in the shape of a pyramid and done with a maximum of color and movement. It was a tremendously difficult and absorbing project.

At that time Denise had a job in bookstore downtown. She was working long hours to make as much money as possible and had less time for painting. She also had less energy. The details of the various figures—the expressions on their faces, the textures of their costumes, the angles of their bodies—all needed to be meticulously worked out. She spent several months on the face of the lion tamer alone, making it hard and heavily lined. It was four years before the painting was finished. She was immensely proud of it. It was her masterpiece.

Not long afterwards, one of the local galleries was showing an exhibit of artists under thirty. Denise decided to enter her circus picture.

"What the hell," she said to Libby. "It might be a way of getting my art out there."

Libby stared dubiously at the huge canvas. "There's no harm in trying," she said.

A week after she had submitted the canvas, Denise got a note from the gallery owner. "Your painting has been rejected. Please come and pick it up. We have no room to store rejected paintings."

Denise swallowed her disappointment. She couldn't understand how such a monumental, brilliantly conceived painting could have been rejected.

"Well, if I go to pick it up, at least it will be an opportunity to discuss my painting with the gallery owner," Denise said to Libby. "I'll find out why it's been rejected."

Libby was applying makeup to go out with her latest boyfriend. "I wouldn't do that if I were you."

Denise gave Libby one of her hard stares. She hated it when people insinuated that something was wrong without explaining why. "Why not?"

"Look," said Libby, "I know you've worked hard on that painting. But sometimes our best efforts don't work out."

"Go to hell, Libby," said Denise and put on her coat.

It was late afternoon on a blustery November day. Denise took a bus downtown and walked along the main street. The lights in the shops were on, blurred by a spittle of rain. Gallery Clovis was open until nine o'clock. Denise could just discern a light toward the back of the room looking out on the street. She rang the buzzer. She was actually quite scared, knowing that the gallery owner's assessment was likely to be negative. It could even be devastating. She took a breath and balanced herself firmly on her two feet.

A tall thin woman came to the door and threw it open with a broad gesture. "Come in, young woman," she said in a deep, hoarse voice. "Don't let all the cold air in!"

As Denise came in, the woman, smartly dressed in a wide collared white blouse and tailored skirt, looked her up and down. "Are you the exterminator?" she asked.

"Exterminator?" Denise imagined little insects chewing at the canvasses. She blinked in the light. The woman towered over her. She would have done so even if she hadn't been wearing three-inch heels. Her face was angular and she wore her shiny black hair drawn back from her face in a chignon. Denise, usually confident, felt intimidated.

"Uh, no," she said. "I need to ask about one of the paintings," she said.

"Sorry, young woman," the woman took a cigarette from a pack on a table at the back of the room. She put it between her lips, lit it, and inhaled sharply, as though her life depended on it. "The paintings don't go on sale until after the opening. The sixteenth."

Denise looked nervously around. The exhibit had already been set up and the paintings were all contemporary in style, Minimalist and Conceptualist. All slick and polished without a brushstroke out of place. She had a strange, queasy feeling; she was observing a club to which she had no access. Observing from the outside. She felt very small. She turned to the tall woman, "Well, are you the gallery owner?" she asked hesitantly.

"Yes, yes," said the woman, impatiently, "I'm Clovis, Clovis Steinhalz. What is your business with us?"

"Well," said Denise, blurting it out, "I've come to find out why you rejected my painting."

Clovis took another deep drag on her cigarette, her nostrils flaring dangerously as she inhaled. "You do have a nerve, you know. A rejected painting is rejected. I have my standards, you know."

"Well, I'm sorry," said Denise, feeling the last vestiges of her self confidence slipping away. "But I need to know. It's not that I'm questioning your authority. But I'm a fledgling painter. I need to know."

Clovis laughed shortly. "All right, then. Miss . . . ?"

"Spaulding. Denise Spaulding."

"Miss Spaulding, you may regret this, but if you're so determined to know, which painting is it?"

"The circus painting," said Denise, keeping her voice loud and clear with some effort.

"Huh!" Clovis drew her breath in as if she had known all along. "The circus painting. Miss Spaulding, this is an adult's gallery. We don't show paintings for little people." And to Denise's amazement, Clovis got up, went straight to one of the piles of paintings in the corner of the room and pulled out "A Circus Panorama." Of course it wasn't hard to find, being about twice the size of the other canvasses.

Denise felt she had gained some ground. The gallery owner had completely misinterpreted her painting. "Little people! I wouldn't want to show this painting to any child I know," she said. "Look at the lion tamer."

"Well, Miss Spaulding. I'm afraid you may have missed the boat. By about a hundred years. We show contemporary, professional work here. Not the work of fumbling amateurs."

Denise felt as though she had been reduced to a small pile of ashes. But she wouldn't give in. She still had to defend herself. "I thought this was an exhibit for young painters," she said. "Young artists starting out. To promote whatever art . . . I mean . . ." she broke off, not knowing how to continue.

Clovis threw her cigarette butt on the floor and crushed it with her stiletto heel. "Anyway," she said, "Regardless of the quality of the painting, to hang it would be unfair to my other painters. It would take up far too much room." She went toward the door, put her hand on the doorknob and was about to usher Denise out.

But Denise stood still, refusing to leave until she had salvaged something from this ill-advised meeting. "You wouldn't consider showing a smaller canvas?" she asked.

"That depends on quality, of course. But it's possible I could find a space for one. Possible."

Denise sighed and turned toward the door. Looking back over her shoulder, she said, "I'll have my roommate's boyfriend stop by to pick up the circus painting. And he'll bring the smaller paintings. You might just have a look at them."

"I will do that, Miss Spaulding. I will just have a look at them." And with that Clovis opened the door and gestured for Denise to leave.

She went out into the gathering darkness, wishing she had directed a couple of well-aimed blows to Colvis's pointed chin. Sometimes violence, however futile, could be a big relief. She thought uncomfortably of Libby, who hadn't liked her painting and had warned her not to come. What could she possibly say when Libby asked her how the meeting had gone? Denise shivered in the damp evening, pulling her jacket more tightly around her. She had never even had the chance to take it off. She hadn't stayed in the gallery long enough.

"I still love that painting," she told herself, firmly.

The next day, she sent Libby's boyfriend Tommy to the gallery with a number of studies for the circus scene as well as "The Fortune Teller." She had little hope that Clovis would show any of them. But to her surprise, the gallery owner sent back a note saying she would have "The Fortune Teller" hung.

The opening was on a Friday at five o'clock. That happened to be the day that the bookshop where Denise was working stayed open late. She didn't have to—there were other employees available—but Denise volunteered to work that evening. She knew it was a cop-out, it was an excuse not to go to the opening. She couldn't bring herself to face Clovis and the other artists, so contemporary, so professional.

But she did go back to Gallery Clovis the following week to see how her fortune teller had been displayed and to view the other paintings. It was early in the day; the gallery was almost empty. She let herself in and looked around for Clovis. She wasn't there. In her place, presiding over the table at the rear of the room, was a young girl, probably in her early twenties. She was wearing a turquoise tunic over tight-fitting jeans. A thick auburn braid fell down her back.

"Hello," she said, smiling to show over-sized, perfect teeth. "I don't remember seeing you before. Is this your first visit to Gallery Clovis?"

Denise wasn't sure what to say. "Well," she said slowly, "yes and no. I came once when Ms. Steinhalz was here. I've come back to see the exhibit."

"Oh, yes. Well, I'm standing in for Ms. Steinhalz. Please have a look around."

Denise took her time looking at the paintings. Most, as she had observed before, were Minimalist or Conceptualist. "Is it possible for a contemporary painter not to like contemporary art?" she asked herself. On one of the side walls, she saw, to her relief, a couple of nicely executed impressionistic landscapes. She looked for some time before finding "The Fortune Teller," hanging inconspicuously down a little corridor leading to the back entrance. Her heart sank. It wasn't well-lit; it wasn't in a place that showed it to advantage.

"It could have been worse," she thought. "Clovis could have put a curtain over it."

She took a couple of steps back to assess the painting at a moderate distance. "It's still good," she thought, "not as good as the circus painting, but not bad at all."

The girl in the turquoise tunic came and stood beside her.

"This is well done, I think," she said. "Look at the movement of the woman's veil. And the way the artist has captured the hand, stretched out in the darkness."

"I'm pleased you like it."

"My word! You're the artist!"

"My name is Denise Spaulding."

"D.S. Yes, I can just make out the initials in the corner of the painting. I'm Emily. Emily Golding. I work here from time to time. When Clovis is out of town."

Denise imagined Clovis making an appearance at exhibits of famous painters in Los Angeles, in Chicago.

"I paint, too, a bit," Emily was saying. "You saw my landscapes."

"I liked your landscapes."

"Well, I like your fortune teller. I'll buy her, if you'll accept less than the list price."

Denise opened her eyes wide. "You're kidding."

"Don't get excited. I can't afford to pay you much. It's listed at thirty-five dollars. Would twenty-five be an insult?"

A few minutes later Denise was floating along in the apple-sharp November sunshine, dazed. "I've sold a painting! Sold a painting to a fellow artist! Maybe the club isn't as exclusive as I thought. Maybe I will make it after all!" It wasn't her masterpiece, "A Circus Panorama." Perhaps if Emily rather than Clovis had seen it, she might have pushed to have it shown. But never mind, she had sold! She had sold her "Fortune Teller!" All the work, the mundane jobs, lack of privacy, the penny pinching—all now seemed worthwhile.

Even so, she painted very little in the years that followed, but not because of her failure with Gallery Clovis. It was largely because of circumstance. Shortly after the exhibit, Libby moved back to Iowa to take care of her ailing mother. Denise then had a series of roommates that didn't work out. The last one was Leslie Perk, a garrulous woman who worked for the city bureaucracy and would follow her into the bathroom to complain about her snotty supervisor.

This drove Denise to the point of madness. She realized that she couldn't live in such close quarters with another person. But she couldn't live alone; her salary from the bookshop wouldn't cover the constantly rising rent. She would simply have to earn more money. So she made an important decision: she enrolled in a forty-hour program to qualify as a real-estate agent.

At first the money wasn't that good, and to cover expenses she kept her job in the bookstore for a year. But soon she began to earn very well. She moved to a two-bedroom apartment in a more stylish part of the city. She continued to have a series of roommates as a sort of insurance, worrying that the money would dry up. But a roommate in a two-bedroom apartment is less intrusive than one in a one-bedroom apartment, and Denise was able to keep a modicum of privacy.

But she couldn't paint. She kept up her contacts with a few artist friends, but she couldn't paint. It was something about the energy involved in selling real estate, as well as the stress and the irregular hours. She would have an idea for a painting, get out materials to start it and even put a few strokes on the canvas, but then something would happen, usually a frantic phone call from the office or from a customer, and she would abandon the unfinished work.

Too bad that she lost all those years, just selling real estate. Denise took one last look at the circus painting. She wondered where "The Fortune Teller" had ended up. She knew now why Emily had wanted to buy it, why it was a better painting than "Circus." "The Fortune Teller" suggested more than it detailed, the barely sketched hand appearing from the darkness and the shadowy face. It was a gesture, a moment in time, not a drama, as the circus was. It signaled a direction she would aim toward in the future.

She moved to the area where the next group of paintings were hung. These were her bar scenes. In them, she was able to suggest character and mood without heavy detail but in a few simple strokes. There was one of the bartender standing behind the bar, arms outstretched in a welcoming gesture, face florid and smiling. Several of the paintings showed customers sitting together, clinking glasses, conversing. One person sitting alone had his head bent down over his drink. But the painting that held her attention was one of a woman at the bar.

The woman was half-perched on a barstool, leaning over the counter, her face turned aside so that only the contour of the right cheek was visible. Her pale hair tumbled in an untidy mass of curls to just below her collar line. An expensive fur coat was draped around her shoulders and a silver sandal dangled precariously from her right foot. The woman's hair, the pale flesh of the foot, the sandal, and the glass on the counter beside her were the only light spots in an otherwise dark painting.

Denise stood in front of the painting, reflecting. She knew that woman, had seen her many times before.

The Fifth Painting: The Woman at the Bar.

It was a special day for her, the day she going to get a prize from the real estate company she was working for. It was for the best earnings of the year. The year was 1982. It was a splendid day at the beginning of the summer, and the tables, ringed by colleagues from her little company, were set up with china and crystal, ready for one of those creamed chicken and frozen peas luncheons. She had taken special care in dressing: she chose her best real estate selling outfit, a navy blue linen suit, expensive silk blouse and two-inch heels. Uncomfortable, but as she told herself in putting them on, necessary to give her the extra height needed to impress people. Even more uncomfortable were the panty hose that squeezed her belly and her plump thighs. Sacrifices she made to give the right impression, the impression of control, of professionalism.

The director of their little company, a gregarious man with a shiny bald head and a big red nose presented her with a plaque. It had her name inscribed on it! "Denise Spaulding, best sales 1982." And she was actually pleased. Delighted with herself. The director asked her if she wanted to say a few words. She stood up to take the plaque and looked at the faces around her table, smiling and expectant. All she could think of to say was, "Thank you, my colleagues, thank you, Jim and Harry, for your support. Without you I couldn't have done it." That, of course, was a barefaced lie. She had done it all on her own.

She sat down and took a sip of her drink. It was white wine. White wine, and on this day of her glorious success, she was thinking, "Too bad it's not something stronger." She relished the congratulations and the looks of admiration from her colleagues. But all the time she smiled and chatted and nibbled her creamed chicken, she was somewhere else. She was anticipating the moment she got home so she could start on the bottle of Jack Daniels she had picked up on the way to the ceremony. The glistening, tempting bottle that was hiding in the bottom of her enormous purse. And as she clinked glasses with the woman sitting next to her, she thought, "This isn't right." She remembered a line from one of Woody Allen's sketches, "My whole life passed before my eyes. But it wasn't my life! It was someone else's life!"

She thought, "I'm leading a fake life. My tailored suit, my expensive, leased car, the clients whose requirements I sit up nights trying to meet—none of this is my life."

When she got home, she opened the bottle of Jack Daniels and drank the first glass in one gulp. Then she got out her paints and began painting. What she was painting had nothing to do with real estate. She painted her real life, the life she lived for through the boring working hours, the life of the bottle and the bar culture that went with it. The woman with the fur coat and the dangling sandal—that woman was her, more than the smiling woman in the tailored suit who accepted the plaque.

But as she laid down her paint brush having almost completed the painting, she thought uncomfortably of the awards ceremony and the falseness of the life she was leading. "Has it gotten out of hand?" She thought sadly of her father, of his ravaged face, of how she had vowed she would never follow his path. "But it's in control," she told herself. "I enjoy it, but I can stop when I like."

Then she drank most of the bottle of Jack Daniels and collapsed, unconscious, on the living room couch. But she had also finished the first painting in her series of bar scenes, the woman in the fur coat. She went on to do a dozen more, which she exhibited the following year in a group show on Long Island.

If she had had the time and the will to paint more, possibly her life would have changed. But the bottle is a stern task master. She had always thought of the lion tamer in her circus painting as the scourge of poverty. But by mid-life she had exchanged the scourge of poverty for the scourge of drink. The lion tamer had a double face.

Her pictures at the Long Island exhibit had a moderate success, in that some critics had even noticed them. "Denise Spaulding shows technical skill and compassion in her small studies of people drinking." "A revival of social realism? Do we need this?" "A spotlight shone on the darker aspects of humanity."

But life went on as before, inauthentic and drink-sodden. It wasn't a bad life in many ways. She earned enough money to support her habit, maintained an outward appearance of respectability, and enjoyed her drunken nights and weekends. She even had a degree of comradeship with some of the other bar regulars. The bartender would greet her in a loud voice, "Hey, Denise, what'll it be tonight? The regular?" She never got drunk enough to lose control in public. No one knew that she went home to enough more rounds to make her collapse.

After the awards ceremony, she did have recurring doubts. She wanted to go back to what she was before, to regain her creativity, to be in control. But the lion tamer flourished his whip, and Denise had another drink.

*   *   *

The Woman at the Bar, Part 2.

Then the letter came.

Denise sat on the living room couch, scanning the handwriting on the envelope, wondering who possibly could have written it. The handwriting was small, neat and cramped. The return address was a town in Illinois. Illinois? At that time she knew no one in Illinois.

She opened the letter and read it. Then read it again. It said,

"Dear Denise,

"I know I haven't been in touch for ages, and you are probably surprised to hear from me. My name is Jennifer Hill, and I roomed with you in Baltimore back in the 60's when we were in graduate school.

"I have some terrible news. Marjorie Dunnock, one of our other roommates, has just died.

"Could you possibly come to the memorial service? It will take place on September 7th.

"I also have some important news concerning Marjorie's will. I need to discuss this with you, preferably in person.

"Please call me when you receive this and I'll give you directions to get to my house. From there, perhaps we can go to the chapel together.

"Sincerely, Jennifer"

Denise sat for a long time with the letter on her lap, stunned. She was shocked to hear that Marjorie had died so young. "Younger than I am, in her early forties."

Marjorie had never been a close friend. At first Denise saw her as privileged and snobbish, with her nasal Eastern Seaboard accent, her expensive clothes, love of high culture, of opera and French literature. But when she got to know Marjorie, she liked her better. She found that she was spirited, fun-loving, adventurous. She had a kind of irregular beauty—off-center nose, eyes too large, lips too wide, complexion too pale for her dark hair—that appealed to Denise. They had often gone drinking together at Nick's, a bar near the campus.

Yes, of course she would go to the memorial service. She didn't realize then that she would only come back to Brooklyn to pack. It was Jennifer's letter that got her to Chicago, but it was Madeleine's insight that persuaded her to stay.

*   *   *

The Woman at the Bar, Part 3.

Denise was sitting in an easy chair in the hotel lobby. It was an old fashioned hotel lobby, dark and cave-like, with massive leather easy chairs distributed over an Oriental carpet. The September sunlight was streaming in through one window to her right, dancing on a fine shower of dust.

She felt sleepy and comfortable, sunken into the worn leather cushion. It was Madeleine who called this meeting. Madeleine O'Connor. The fourth of a quartet that shared a house in Baltimore. Not her favorite person. She was not looking forward to this meeting.

But when Denise saw Madeleine a couple of days earlier at Jennifer's house, she had changed. The years she had spent in Africa as a missionary had prematurely aged her; she was now quite wrinkled. But there was also a softness in her face that hadn't been there before.

She had called Denise the night before. "There's something we need to discuss. Be in the lobby of your hotel at ten o'clock. It's the Majestic, isn't it?"

Denise knew that Madeleine wanted to discuss the house with her. Marjorie had left the three women her house in the suburbs, a strange legacy that neither Denise nor Jennifer had welcomed. But Madeleine, possibly tired of the hardships of life in Africa, wanted to move back to the United States. She in fact welcomed the inheritance. That was probably why she wanted to meet with Denise. She hoped to bring Denise around to her point of view.

Denise wanted no part of the deal and was sure no one could change her mind. She couldn't imagine living with Madeleine. And Jennifer? Well, she did feel sorry for Jennifer, huddled like a small furry animal, like a mole, in her little den, her eyes extinguished from weeping. But she couldn't live with her either. The idea was grotesque! And anyway, Jennifer had agreed: the three would sell the house and take the profits. No, moving to Chicago and living with Madeleine and Jennifer was quite out of the question.

Denise's stomach grumbled. After taking care of this problem, after getting rid of Madeleine, she would go to the little hotel grill and get some breakfast. And afterwards, a whiskey at the bar.

But suddenly Madeleine was looming over her. She felt unprepared, defensive. Madeleine was the last person she wanted to catch her off guard.

"You seem deep in thought," Madeleine said, looking at her probingly. "I hope I'm not disturbing you."

"Not at all," said Denise, watching her suspiciously as she settled in the chair beside her.

"I'll come to the point right away," Madeleine said, running her hand along the leather fabric of the armrest. "I want you on my side. You see, I'm making a change in my life. A very big change. I think you might want to make a change in yours."

"You don't want to go on with your missionary work in Africa? Jennifer told me you were doing wonderful things out there."

"Wonderful things," said Madeleine, her voice ironic, as it frequently used to be. "What I have done in almost twenty years is a drop of water in the sea. But I've done what I can. I'm coming home."

Denise looked at Madeleine in surprise. It was unlike her to admit any degree of defeat. "What about the hospital you founded? The food distribution? The medicines?"

"As I say, I've done what I can. But without being there, you cannot imagine the hopelessness the people. I may have helped a small number of people to better health. I don't think I saved a single soul." She leaned back in her chair, her eyes half-closed. "I'm tired, Denise, tired. Tired of the heat, the disease, the filth. I need to direct my energy before I'm too old to serve."

Madeleine had mentioned that her religious organization had offered her a job in Chicago working with disturbed young people. "And the Brothers of Light have offered you a job here?"

"It's providential. I can see it in no other way. God wants me to serve in the inner city. It's a call I cannot refuse."

Denise squirmed involuntarily. Madeleine hadn't changed much after all. Still convinced she was one of God's chosen. "And you see this inheritance of a house as part of God's plan?" she said. "Well, unfortunately, this plan doesn't include me. I have no intention of leaving Brooklyn."

"That's why I arranged to see you." Madeleine paused, her alarmingly pale eyes fixed on Denise's face. "You see, I know you're ready for a change too."

"And what makes you think that?"

"Denise, you have a Master's degree in Fine Arts. Surely you didn't intend to spend your life selling real estate."

"I don't see how moving here is going to get me back to painting again."

"Well, it might not. But at least you wouldn't have the worry of paying the rent. You'd have a nice place to live, expenses paid."

"You're just saying this to win me over."

Madeleine smiled. "Of course I am. I never denied that. But listen, we're both half-way through our working lives. At forty, there's still the possibility of changing. Later, it becomes more difficult. It's to my advantage to accept this offer of a house and a job in a new location. I think it's also an opportunity for you."

"What about Jennifer? She doesn't want to live in a house that reminds her of her best friend's illness and death."

Madeleine stroked the arm of the chair thoughtfully. "She may not want to live there. But in the end, it will be better for her. She has to confront her fears of illness and death." She lowered her voice. "Just as you have to confront your problem."

"What problem?" Denise was suddenly alert.

"You have a drinking problem."

Denise was too startled to answer immediately. "Oh, don't think I don't know, Denise," Madeleine continued. "I've seen it so many times, in Africa, among the expatriates who lose hope, especially. Sometimes among the natives."

Denise was shocked. No one had ever confronted her this way before. "You think I have a drinking problem?" she said, stupidly.

"I know you have a drinking problem. Right now, for example, you're thinking that as soon as this conversation is over, as soon as I leave, you'll go straight to the bar and get a drink."

Denise squirmed. Madeleine had read her mind. Or almost read her mind. "You know, you're wrong," She said slowly, determined not to show her discomfort. "I don't have a drinking problem. Sure, I like my liquor, but that's not the same as being an alcoholic. And even supposing I was? How could moving here help me?"

"It might or it might not. But making a total break from your past, starting over in a different place with people you don't know—that's the easiest way to change."

"You want to save my soul, Madeleine?"

"Only you can save your soul, Denise. That's one of the great lessons I've learned from working in Africa. No person can lead another to God's way. Salvation has to come from within." She paused clasping her thin, age-spotted hands. "And I think, quite apart from the question of your spiritual salvation, you should be concerned about your health. Look at you. How much weight have you put on in the last twenty years? And that's only the tip of the iceberg. Over time, there will be much more serious effects, to your liver, your heart, and most alarming, to your mind."

Denise stared at Madeleine. Where had Madeleine possibly gotten the idea that she drank? She thought back to that first night at Jennifer's when Madeleine had finally joined them. Surely not!

But yes, Jennifer had opened a bottle of good cognac early on. How much had she drunk that evening?

"Well," Madeleine interrupted her thoughts. "You may not be aware of what alcohol can do to you. But think about what I said. Above all think of the positive aspects of moving. A good place to live. An opportunity to get back to painting." Madeleine reached out and took Denise's hand. Surprised by the gesture, Denise drew away involuntarily. "Denise. Call me tomorrow. Early."

Madeleine got up and walked toward the lobby entrance. As she reached it, she turned back and looked at Denise once more. She smiled, a surprisingly attractive smile that Denise had seldom seen. Then she was gone.

Denise took a deep breath. She was stunned to realize her secret was obvious to other people. To Madeleine! She felt a sudden rage. How could Madeleine of all people know that she drank? How could she call Denise an alcoholic?

Her idea of getting breakfast and then a drink no longer appealed to her. Instead she lurched out of her chair and went out into the chilly sunshine. Her anger, her outrage propelled her through the streets. For the first time since drinking took over her life, she tried to imagine what it would be like to quit: to live without looking forward to that first evening glass of whiskey, to live without that buzz, that feeling of sinking into a relaxed state where there was comradeship and meaning.

She couldn't live without alcohol. She had to admit that to herself. It enraged her to think that Madeleine could gloat over her weakness. Madeleine the bigot. Madeleine, who, she thought, had as much insight as an earthworm.

She walked for a long time, breathing more and more heavily, not even thinking of the future. As time passed and her energy flagged, she realized that she was lost. She had to hail a cab and take it back to the hotel. By that time her anger was more or less spent. She was sorely tempted to go to the bar and drink away the humiliation. But she knew she had to think clearly, to decide what on earth she was going to do. She went to her room and lay on the bed, exhausted from her anger and the long walk along city streets.

What should she do? She knew that Madeleine had a point, that her life in Brooklyn had become a lie. She saw herself in her expensive suit and heels, accepting a reward. For service to a real estate agency!

And if she moved? Madeleine was probably right. If she moved, there was a better chance of getting back to painting, and possibly of stopping her habit before it destroyed her. She hated Madeleine for being right; she didn't want to give in to her, knowing that she had her own best interests, her mission, at heart. But the image of the lion tamer came back, the lion tamer who cracked his whip and held her in the power of drink. She thought of her father, late in life, a sick, broken man. She thrashed out these thoughts over a sleepless night. In the morning she called Madeleine.

"I've reconsidered," she said. "I want to share the house."

She returned to Brooklyn, gave in her notice, and packed up her things. She was settled in Marjorie's house by late October.

*　　*　　*

Denise stood in front of "The Woman at the Bar," deep in thought. She hadn't left that woman behind when she moved to Chicago. That woman came with her and kept her company for the next three years. Denise took a deep breath and left the "Woman at the Bar" to come around to the wall on the left, where her most recent paintings hung.

There was a series of taps at the door, three short taps followed by a long one.

Sally.

It was Sally's knock, she recognised it immediately.

Sally! She came the light years back to the present and felt a sense of dread. Had she had news from the Foundation about her fellowship? Possibly bad news? But the decision wasn't due until Friday. Maybe Sally was just coming for an early viewing of the exhibit.

She opened the door. Sally stood there, a miserable heap. Glorious Sally, who could light a room up just by entering it, was wiped out. Her face was crumpled with tears and her eyes had lost their luster. Even her brilliant golden mane of hair looked limp and tired. She was wearing an old, paint-splattered pair of jeans and a loose-fitting men's shirt.

"Come in, come in." Denise folded the girl in her arms. Sally was a half-foot taller than Denise yet Denise felt her arms could go around her twice.

"I didn't get it," she said in a hoarse voice.

"Oh, baby, I'm so sorry. So, so sorry." Denise led Sally to one of the benches and sat her down. "But how did you find out? I thought the fellowships were being given out on Friday."

Sally drooped against the back of the bench. "Jody Pierce told me. She has a couple of friends on the Foundation's fellowship committee."

"Are you sure? Are you sure it's not just vicious gossip?"

"I don't think Jody would tell me if she wasn't sure."

"Who did get it? Do you know?" Denise kept stroking her niece's hair in an effort to soothe her. Sally had enormous talent, but she lacked the toughness that had gotten Denise through times like this.

"A guy called Harold Melton. He did—I don't know—some form of computer simulation. A bunch of lines. Crisscrossing. Something like that."

"Oh, it's so unfair! Your "Wood Nymph" was an exceptional piece of work." Denise had admired Sally's sculpture, done in wood, which showed the figure of a young girl emerging from the crotch of a tree. The bark was carefully textured, and Sally had spent a great deal of time perfecting it.

"Not exceptional enough. Or not whatever the committee was looking for. I obviously am not making it." Sally put her face in her hands and sobbed.

"Sally, Sally." Denise held Sally for a moment. "The judgments these committees make are always political. They don't always mean much in terms of the value of the sculpture, painting or whatever. You have to realize that. If you take every rejection to heart, you'll be dead as an artist before you begin."

"Well, I think I am dead as an artist." Sally took a crumpled piece of Kleenex from her pocket and blew her nose loudly. "I haven't even passed the first test."

"Sometimes you have to have faith in yourself and not rely on what other people think." Denise released Sally and stood up. "Hey, would you like a cup of tea? I have that Red Zinger that you like so much."

"No, no." Sally was getting up too. "I just came to give you the bad news. I'd better go."

"No," said Denise firmly. "You're not going until you feel happier." She went to the little kitchenette and put the kettle on. She turned to look at Sally.

"Tell you what. I think your sculpture is a marvel. I bet I can find someone who'll buy it from you."

"It's not even that, Aunt Denise. I love my sculptures. I love doing them, and in a way, that's enough reward. But I was counting on the fellowship money to live off for a year. So I could spend all my time sculpting and not have to go to work."

Denise came toward her niece with two steaming cups of tea. She sighed. "I know, baby. It's the perennial artist's problem. How to pay the bills. I wish you could find some rich man to sponsor you."

"What a horrible idea!" Sally was indignant at the thought. Perhaps a bit of her spirit was coming back. She took the tea from Denise and sat back down to sip it.

"Sally, are you hungry?" Denise suddenly realized she herself was famished. She hadn't eaten at all that day and it was well past noon. "I think I've got some chocolate chip cookies in the cupboard." Sally shook her head, but Denise went back to the kitchenette found an old a box of cookies on one of the shelves. She offered them to her niece, who gently pushed the box away.

"When did you last eat, Sally?"

"I don't know. It doesn't matter, does it? I mean, Aunt Denise, I've just found out that my most important work so far has been rejected by a committee of experts, that I'm going to live in poverty for the next—for the rest of my life, and you're offering me chocolate chip cookies!"

Denise had already eaten one and was putting her hand in the box for another. "Eating helps, Sally. I'm serious. How can you face your critics on an empty stomach?"

Sally let out an odd sound that could have been a giggle. "I'm not facing my critics. I'm going back to my hovel and lying face down on the bed and crying my eyes out."

"Okay," said Denise. "If you think that will help. But remember what I said. This isn't a final judgment on your work. And, I hate to say this, it's probably not the last rejection you'll have. I've had more rejections than I can count. And I'm still alive. And painting."

Sally took a cookie and bit into it. "I know, Aunt Denise. It's not like it's my first rejection either. Not quite. But I worked so hard on "Wood Nymph". And I was counting on that money." Sally began crying again, softly keening.

"There's one other thing you should know, Sally. When you accept a fellowship from that type of foundation, there may be strings attached. By that I mean that you may monitored by people telling you what to do. You want to be independent, Sally, not beholden to an institution."

Sally shook her head. Denise wasn't sure she was hearing her.

"And just one more thing, Sally," she continued. "The values those people, the committee people, have aren't the same as yours. Think back on your interview. You may have said something radical—or something that seemed radical to them. Maybe the final judgment had very little to do with your sculpture."

"All I know is that my sculpture has been rejected. That's final. That's finished." Sally was still crying, but almost soundlessly. She stood up and wiped her face on her sleeve. "I'm going back now, Aunt Denise. I just wanted to be the one to tell you. I didn't want you to hear it from anyone else."

"All right, but instead of throwing yourself on the bed and crying your eyes out, I want you to wash your face, change into something pretty and come back to enjoy the retrospective."

Sally threw her hands up in front of her face. "Oh, Aunt Denise, I've been here for hours and I haven't even looked at your paintings."

"Probably just as well. In the mood you were in you would have hated them all. Come back in a couple of hours with a good mood and an open mind. And think about what I told you."

Sally got her purse and turned toward the door.

"Give me a hug," said Denise and put her arms around her niece. It was like hugging a rag doll.

Sally went through the door, turned and gave Denise a crooked little smile. After she had left, Denise sank back down on the bench, shaken. She hated being old, knowing in advance what horrible things can happen. She had sensed that the fellowship committee would reject Sally's sculpture. Now she was worried that Sally would lose confidence and abandon her art. It hurt inside, it positively ached, to see her lovely, sparkling, talented girl so beaten. She wanted to nurture her, protect her from all the nasty tricks life plays. No, she told herself. You have to let go. Give her some credit for inner strength. After all, she is your niece!

She was still hungry. She finished Sally's tea and investigated the bottom of the bag of cookies. All gone. She thought of the Foundation. Those bastards! What was the word, philistines? They only looked for commercial appeal, cared little for true creativity. These were the people who were luring her away from painting by offering her a job in community outreach. Could she really work for an organization that had rejected her niece's work? She knew she couldn't change these people's attitudes. Of course she couldn't. But she could, possibly, help a few artists like Sally by getting their work out there.

She sat there, feeling very hungry, very tired. She realized that she had lost the desire to meet her guests, personal friends, art friends, critics, members of the Foundation. It was too much! She had experienced an entire life, or a large part of a life, in one morning. Too many emotions in one morning. She looked at her watch. It wasn't morning! It was two thirty in the afternoon!

She had to collect herself. Only a couple of hours and Sally's friends would arrive to set up the table and put out the food. She hadn't visited her most recent paintings. She needed to look at them again, to see how they had evolved, to remember. She got up and went to the wall on the left, where the last two groups of paintings hung.

The Sixth Painting: Sophonisba Anguisola

She paused for a minute in front of the small paintings Thomas had disliked, "Women Painters Painting." The eight formed a group, each showing a woman artist from an earlier era painting the portrait of a modern woman artist. It was a clever idea, perhaps too clever, one that Hilda had inspired. Hilda, Denise mused, the days with Hilda had been full of light and happiness, the smell of spices, of garlic and cumin, as Hilda loved to cook, and the smell of paint. Looking back at that time, she realized she had never been so contented, so pleased with herself, so physically sated, as during the early days of her relationship with Hilda.

They met at the dentist's office not long after her arrival in the Chicago area. Denise, who never had problems with her teeth and never saw a dentist, suddenly developed a tooth ache. At first she tried to ignore it, but it filled her head like a loud incessant drumming and it made it impossible for her to work. And so, on a clear November day, she found herself sitting in Dr. Finkelstein's comfortable office, staring into a fish tank, waiting for the dentist to call her in for whatever torture he had in store for her. Sitting two seats over was a woman in later middle age, wearing paint-stained blue jeans and a lumberjack's shirt. More as a distraction than an effort to make contact with this woman, who struck her as washed-out and unattractive, she spoke to her.

"You're not by any chance a painter, are you?" she asked. "I couldn't help noticing the paint on your jeans." As soon as she said this, she realized that had possibly been rude. That she probably shouldn't have commented on the women's paint-stained jeans.

Instead the woman smiled, her face crinkling into a thousand little lines. "I do paint," she said, "But by profession I'm an art therapist." She came over, and to Denise's surprise, took her hand and shook it. The woman's hand felt warm and dry, like fallen leaves in the sun. "Hilda Manning."

"Oh, I'm Denise Spaulding. I moved here from Brooklyn a couple of weeks ago, and I'm just getting back to painting."

"Fantastic!" said Hilda crinkling again. "I know quite a few artists here. Maybe I could introduce you to some of them. It's hard making connections in a new place. You've got a place to live, I assume."

Denise smiled. It would take too long to tell the tale of her unlikely inheritance. "Oh, yeah," she said. "Quite a nice place, actually."

The dentist appeared at the waiting room door, terrifying in his immaculate white coat. "Ms. Manning," he intoned.

Hilda took a scrap of paper and wrote something on it hastily. "Here's my name and telephone number. Give me a call. We'll get together for a drink."

Denise smiled, remembering. The early days with Hilda, days of tea and honey and enormous vegetarian meals and big parties. And shared bubble baths. They kept their separate houses, but Hilda came to see her frequently. She would come to Denise's studio to see what see what she was painting. Or she would come to the house to cook a meal that turned out to be far too big and invite anyone in the vicinity. Madeleine always refused if she was around, complaining of the cooking smells, but Jennifer sometimes joined them, picking at her food delicately like a spoiled cat. And sometimes the neighbors came over.

Sometime during that period Sally, then a silent little girl, spent weekends at the house. Her parents, Denise's brother Roger and Rita, were going through a painful divorce. They couldn't deal with a needy little girl. It could be a nuisance having the kid around, but both Jennifer and Hilda were fond of her. Hilda loved making a huge batch of cookies for her to sample. Sally would look at the gigantic plate with big eyes and take one or two cookies. Hilda and Denise would finish the rest, Denise ballooning out like a sail in the wind.

Hilda was a great friend and a considerate, gentle lover. With her, Denise was happier than she had been with anyone. She thought their relationship would last forever.

But Hilda had her own agenda, which unfolded slowly over the years. It started early on with Denise's painting. One day when Hilda came to the studio, Denise was re-touching her most ambitious study of light, "Sunburst." It was a painting she had started before coming to Chicago but kept going back to.

"Hey, Hilda," Denise called out, looking over her canvas. "Come and have a look at this." She was happy with the direction she was going in, full of images that she wanted to capture.

Hilda came around the back of the canvas. There was an ominous silence.

"What's the matter? Don't you like it?"

"Denise, it's awful. You might as well be painting the male reproductive organs."

"What? I don't know what you're talking about." Denise was shocked. "I'm looking into the source of light. I'm re-creating its power."

"Exactly," Hilda sounded as if she had scored a point. "The sun. The male principle of creation-destruction."

Denise laughed shortly. "This isn't about sex, Hilda. This is the blinding, exhilarating experience of light."

"Well, I know what it means to me," Hilda said as though she had won the argument. "Come, take a break. I'll make you a cup of tea."

Denise, deflated, put down her paint brush. She had lost the urge to paint. She unfolded two metal chairs and sat down in one, waiting for her tea, like an obedient child.

Hilda filled the two crude mugs with boiling water, set them down on the floor and sat opposite Denise. Hilda, usually so mild and dry and straw-like, had become menacing, like someone's nightmare high school teacher about to keep bad students in after school.

The two sat in silence for a few minutes, waiting for the tea to steep. Denise sensed that Hilda was about to make some global criticism of her painting. Up until that point, she had always been supportive and positive. But maybe she hadn't meant that. Maybe she really didn't like Denise's paintings at all. Denise waited tensely for the axe to fall.

Eventually, Hilda picked up her mug and took a sip of the scalding tea.

"What are you getting at when you paint, Denise, really?" she asked.

Denise stirred uncomfortably on the hard metal seat. She suddenly realized that she was very cold. "I'm not getting at anything. I just paint the images that" she wanted to say "obsess me" but that sounded like craziness. "I just paint the images that I have in my mind."

"Did it ever occur to you that your painting could have a serious purpose?" The high school teacher was standing to declaim. "That you could, for example, teach people about the forgotten women artists?"

"You want me to be socially conscious, Hilda. Well, you know that's not my style."

"So why do you paint, Denise? What's the point of it?"

That was a question Denise had never asked herself. She painted because she loved painting, because her father had told her she was talented, because she liked the results of what she did. It had never occurred to her that she had to justify her painting.

But after this conversation, she began to have some doubts. She realized that her friend had a point. She was messing about, playing, when she could be doing something useful. Hilda gave her a friend's dissertation to read, "Forgotten Women Artists, 1500-1700." She was shocked to learn that there were so many talented women artists, some well-known in their own time, who had virtually disappeared from the eyes of the modern world. She had been to college, to graduate school even, and had never heard of Sophonsiba Anguisola, Rosalba Carriera, Artemesia Gentilsechi, Judith Leyster. And yet they had all been prolific and talented, had painted as well as their male contemporaries. They and many others.

This ignited Denise's sense of injustice. Forgotten! And just because they were women! There must be some way of memorializing them. Then she conceived the idea of painting the portraits of women painters. As in classical painting, she represented them in the process of painting. Each one would be shown, as in her own self-portrait, with brushes in hand, painting. And the picture she was in the process of painting would represent the style of a modern woman painter, either in a typical work or in a portrait. Women of the past anticipating the present. It was a challenging subject, and for the next four years it absorbed her to the exclusion of anything else.

Denise looked at the picture of Sophonisba Anguisola painting Kaethe Kollwitz's anguished face and wondered. She wondered if this series ever got any kind of message out to anyone, if, in fact, it meant anything to anyone but her. And possibly Hilda. In the end it was a strange sort of exercise, which ended up more as a memorial to her relationship with Hilda than as a memorial to women painters.

That relationship ended a couple of years later, before Denise had finished her "Women Painters." It was Denise's fault, of course. About two years after she and Hilda linked up, she had gone back to drinking at a local bar called the Blue Moon. She had never stopped drinking, but her relationship with Hilda, in its happy phase, put a brake on it. When she began to feel a rift between them, Denise went back to her old habits. She went to the Blue Moon, especially on weekday evenings after teaching, evenings when Hilda often had a client. She also began picking up men there. Picking up men without much discrimination.

She managed to keep up a respectable facade, as she always had. She never missed class and she never arrived to class drunk. But she was beginning to feel more and more stressed and frustrated. It was like the bad old real estate years all over again. She was living according to someone's rules that weren't her own. But cheating, always cheating, on the sly.

She didn't have the courage to break off the relationship with Hilda. In fact, she never told Hilda about her various affairs. But things resolved themselves in another way.

One Friday evening in July she had followed a man home after meeting him at the Blue Moon. They were already pretty drunk by then, but they split a bottle of Scotch and passed out on the couch, too drunk for sex. Denise went back to the house the next morning, feeling as if her head was a ball of yarn and her mouth was full of cat piss. As she came in the door she saw Hilda at the top of the stairs. She came down slowly, as if exhausted, to meet Denise. She looked as if she hadn't slept all night. Her face was a bomb site, her eyes deep craters.

"Where the hell have you been?" Hilda croaked. "You've been out all night!"

Denise had no excuse. All she could think of to say was, "I fell asleep in the studio."

Hilda laughed shortly. "And is that an excuse? Is that an excuse for breaking your promise?"

"What promise? I didn't promise you anything."

"You don't even remember. You don't remember, do you? That you were going to bring ice cream for Joyce's party. You disappointed that poor little girl to go out and wallow in drink."

"Joyce?" Denise had no memory of a girl called Joyce.

"Joyce Peters. Helen's little girl."

"Oh, for Christ's sake, Hilda! Anyone could have brought the ice cream. I just happened to forget, that's all."

"Well, recently you've just been forgetting too many things. It amount to a pack of lies, Denise. You promise and promise to stop drinking, you promise to be there for me and none of it means a goddamn thing. Your drinking is killing your brain, Denise. I think you're partially brain-dead already." Hilda's voice was hoarse, almost spent.

"You're right, Hilda. You're one hundred per cent right. And I'm sorry I don't fit your concept of rightness because I'm fallible and because I'm weak. But I can tell you one thing, Madame Right. I'm sick of your rightness and I'm not going to be your project to correct anymore!"

Denise lumbered upstairs, feeling enraged but also nauseous. She went into her room, slammed the door and hurled herself on the bed. She half expected Hilda to follow her, but she didn't. Denise lay there, exhausted but unable to sleep, still furious with Hilda, for confronting her, for being right. Then it occurred to her that something Hilda had said struck a chord: it was about Denise's forgetting. She had completely forgotten about the ice cream, but that wasn't the only thing she had forgotten recently. She had forgotten a meeting with her supervisor, which was quite serious, she had forgotten to bring a book about Morisot to one of her students, she had forgotten to bring supplies into her class. "Am I losing brain function?" she asked herself, and she was frightened. Frightened enough to think for the first time of joining A.A.

And Hilda was gone. After she recovered from her initial rage, Denise tried to contact her, but she didn't answer her phone and was never there when she stopped by her house. Gradually the realization of her loss sank in. For a long time this feeling was with her, an ache that she tried to ignore but that wouldn't go away.

And even now, years later, she felt all the sadness of a relationship that had failed. What had happened to Hilda? For a long time she got news of Hilda from mutual friends, but gradually the connections died out. Hilda could be dead for all she knew. Was she even living in Chicago? Denise longed for her to come, to see that she had conquered the drink and finally achieved something. Could she possibly come?

Denise was old now, had learned long ago that longing for something you couldn't bring about was a terrible waste of energy. If Hilda comes, she comes.

She went back to the bench and sat down again. What a terrible weight of memories! Why did each group of paintings evoke such sadness?

She had had a wonderful life! She knew that. There was so much that had been glorious! So many glorious days! She had created, she had loved, she had laughed. Looking back, she had no regrets.

But she still felt so tired. She stretched out. "Just a short doze," she told herself.

As she dozed off, she remembered a time, early on in their relationship, when she and Hilda had gone for a drive in Hilda's beaten-up VW convertible with the top down. They were driving through the countryside in late September. Denise leaned back, smelling the autumn leaves, seeing the play of light on canopy overhead. Hilda stretched out her hand and Denise held it. They exchanged a look, the look of complicity between lovers. She leaned back again and looked up at the leaves above her head.

The play of light on the canopy! Denise remembered the pompoms of light that had caught her attention that morning before she got up. She held the image in her mind for several seconds, then drifted into sleep.

She woke to a knock at the door and feeling guilty, checked her watch. Four seventeen. Still too early for the guests to be arriving. She got up, smoothed her dress, patted her hair into place and opened the door. Her mind was partly in a cloud of images from some distant dream, pompons of light, dancing on a bedroom wall. She shook her head, ridding herself of the dream.

The couple burst in. "Hello, hello! Hope we're not bothering you."

It was Mary Ellen and her latest companion, Bob. Mary Ellen was carrying a tray of hors d'oeuvres. She was a short, twitchy woman with curly brown hair. She was in perpetual motion as if she had too much energy for her small body to contain. Bob was short, shiny-faced, and obliging.

"I know you're having it catered, but I just had to bring something." She put the food down on one of the tables and turned to face Denise. "Don't you look gorgeous!" Denise felt crumpled and disheveled. "I always thought red suited you best." Mary Ellen turned to her partner. "This is Bob. I don't know if you've met Bob."

Denise had in fact met Bob.

"Hey, Denise," he said, stretching out a plump hand, "I hear congratulations are in order. That's great news about the job with the Foundation."

"Thanks, Bob," said Denise, taking his hand and trying to remember what she knew about him.

"Isn't it wonderful," Mary Ellen was saying, "finally to have some recognition? I can't think of anyone more deserving." Mary Ellen couldn't stop; she was touching her hair, smoothing her jacket, putting down her purse and picking it up again, pivoting on her high-heeled shoes.

"Hope you don't mind us coming early. We've got a party at six and lots of preparations to make. Hey, Bob, have a look at Denise's paintings. Aren't they marvelous!" Mary Ellen took Bob's arm and was about to lead him around the room

Bob stood still for a moment, taking in the exhibit. He whistled softly. "Gee, look at all those paintings, all those paintings." He was standing in front of the paintings she had done as a child, the two children under the table and the early circus painting.

Denise suddenly felt embarrassed. What had she been thinking of, including those childhood works in the exhibit? "I did those as a child," she said. She was apologising for the childhood paintings without intending to. "The paintings are more or less in chronological order, starting on this wall. My later works are over here."

"I like this one," said Bob. He had moved to one of the bar scenes. "I like something I can relate to." He laughed nervously, jiggling the change in his pocket.

"Denise," said Mary Ellen. She was now standing between the women painters painting and the studies of light, looking at the curtained painting. "What's this? Why have you covered it up?"

"Oh, that's a surprise. It's a present for Jennifer."

"Can't we just have a peep?"

"I'm afraid not, Mary Ellen. I'm going to unveil it at the opening."

"Oh, then we probably won't see it, if you're giving it to Jennifer. Well, what is it? You can at least tell us that."

"No, Mary Ellen. If you're that curious, you can ask Jennifer. After the opening." She knew it made no real difference whether Mary Ellen and Bob saw the painting. But it was a matter of pride. If they couldn't even come to the opening, she wouldn't oblige them.

Unfazed, Mary Ellen was studying Denise's most recent paintings. "Look at these studies of light," she said, turning to Bob. "Aren't they marvelous? I'm sure that's what the Foundation was honoring Denise for."

"Yeah, very interesting, Denise." Without moving, Bob turned his head in Mary Ellen's direction. Well," he said, looking at Mary Ellen. "We'd better be pushing off. You understand, Denise. Lots of preparations for the party. Nice to see you again. And again, congratulations. That's a real flower in your cap, that thing from the Foundation."

"Feather," said Denise. "Feather in my cap."

"Oh, yeah, feather. Of course."

"Can't you stay for a few minutes, just to chat? The party won't begin for a little while."

"No, thanks, but we really are pressed for time. Bye-bye, Denise," Mary Ellen kissed her lightly on the cheek. Whispering in her ear, she said, "Wonderful exhibit. And don't you even think of turning down that job!"

They were gone. Denise had a sour taste in her mouth. "They couldn't even bother to spend some time with me, let alone my paintings. If everyone rushes through that way, the retrospective will be over pretty quickly." But Mary Ellen was a nice person; she had been supportive when they taught in adult ed, had supported her through that awful time in A.A. And she and Bob had made the effort of coming to see something they didn't much like, just to please her. They were both impressed that the Foundation had offered her a job. Well, whatever else you might think, the Foundation did have enormous status in the community.

Denise turned back to her paintings, but for the moment her mind was elsewhere. She kept thinking of the job with the

Foundation, wondering whether, in spite of Sally's rejection, she should accept it. She had done community outreach a few years ago and she had enjoyed it. Would it be a better way to go, to make connections with other artists, with the art-loving public? Instinct said no. But . . . She would have to postpone the final decision.

She turned to look at her most recent paintings, which had always been her favorites.

The Seventh Painting: Sunburst.

The one that hung in the middle, "Sunburst," was the most daring painting Denise had ever done. The dynamic principle of light, a series of heavy brush strokes in yellow swirls toward a deep golden center. All around were more recent studies, "Flaming Torches," "Sunshine on Waves," "Streetlamps at Twilight," "Lamplight through an open window," "Reflections on a Puddle." All this—and she no longer wanted to remember. Because it concerned Tomas, and because everything about Tomas was darkness and shadows.

She first saw Tomas at the end of one of the meetings of Alcoholics Anonymous. She hated to go to A.A.; to pick herself up and get there every night took a lot more effort than resisting that next drink. It was the people that got her down. She felt sorry for them, but the stories of their broken lives were so depressing. And she hated to talk about her own problems, revising the failures and disappointments.

And it rained. It rained and rained that fall. It seemed to rain every night as a sodden accompaniment to the defeats and confessions of failure. That evening, the evening she first noticed him, it was getting on toward ten o'clock and Denise was gathering up her coat and purse to begin the wet trip home. She saw him, saw a man sitting at the back of the room. He had avoided joining the circle of AA members, observing from the outside. At first he reminded her of her father, why, she later was to wonder. But then, at that first moment, she noticed resemblance, the same unkempt appearance, hair a little too long, noticeable stubble on the chin, shabby raincoat. He was smoking.

She stopped to talk to him. "You should put that out," she said, trying to keep her tone light, "That will kill you just as surely as drinking."

"And why does this worry you, young lady?" he growled. His words were polite; his voice was unpleasant, repelling even.

Denise smiled to herself. It would be a challenge to charm this man. "Whether something is my business or not has never stopped me from speaking my mind." She held out her hand. "I'm Denise Spaulding," she said, "and I guess you'd call me a recovering alcoholic."

He introduced himself as Tomas (accent on the second syllable) Schneider. He had an odd accent, possibly Russian. He made no comment on his condition as an alcoholic.

They went out for coffee together, splashing through the puddles to an ill-lit corner cafe that wasn't licensed to serve liquor. He wanted a drink. She could sense it. She hung up her dripping coat and took a seat at a booth. She ordered coffee; he ordered tea.

"American tea is hot water, but American coffee is unspeakable," he said, giving the waitress an angry look.

Denise sat opposite him, wondering what to say. He remained silent, unapproachable. "Why do you sit on the sidelines instead of joining the group?" she asked finally. "Why come at all if you're not going to join?"

"I am not a person who joins anything," he said. She noticed again his faint east-European accent. Or was his speech a little bit slurred from drink? "The sidelines are a good place for me to observe humanity."

"That sounds like the point of view of a writer. Are you a writer?" She smiled, hoping to get a smile back or at least a change of expression. He continued to scowl.

"I was, once, an editor. I ran a small publishing house."

"You don't do that anymore?"

"It's finished. Shut down. Bankrupt." He took the mass of his unruly hair in one hand and pulled it. Ferociously. Denise was afraid it would come out.

The waitress arrived with the drinks. Tomas put four sachets of sugar in his. "To mask the taste of chlorinated water," he explained.

"And you, young lady? You're in one of the so-called helping professions? A nurse, perhaps? Or a teacher?"

Denise stirred her coffee, the color of the water in the gutters. "I'm far from being a lady," she said. "And I'm certainly not young."

"It's only a manner of speaking. I fear I've offended you."

"Not really. It's just strange to be called something I'm obviously not. And I'm afraid I'm not a useful member of society, either. I'm a painter."

"A painter!" The expression on Thomas's face changed. His eyebrows relaxed and the hint of a smile played around his lips. "A painter! But I must see your work."

"Well, if you're really interested, my studio is about ten blocks from here."

He looked at her directly, almost flirtatiously. "Of course I'm interested. I love painting. Or at least some painting." He was reaching into his pocket to find his wallet.

"Aren't you going to finish your tea?"

"No, let's get out of here. The rainy streets would be a vast improvement over this misery of a cafe."

Denise looked at Tomas probingly. She half wondered if she should let him come into her studio. Would he want a drink when they got there? She had no idea how he might behave. But he seemed determined, and she was attracted to this strange ruin of a man.

By the time they covered the distance to the studio, Denise was totally soaked. They went in; she switched on the little lights and turned up the thermostat. She took Tomas's coat and her own and hung them on the radiators. Tomas looked around. "Quite spacious, your studio." He did appear a smaller, less overpowering presence in the relatively empty space.

Denise had a few unfinished paintings from the Painters Painting series hung; one that she was working on at the moment was on an easel in the center of the room. Tomas approached it. He looked at it closely; he backed away. There was an un—comfortable silence.

"This is not art," he said finally. "You paint with the tips of your fingers. To create art, you must paint with your gut. With your soul, if you like." He touched the surface of the painting.

Denise flinched. "You mustn't touch that. The paint is still wet."

"It's too bad," he continued, leaving the easel and looking at the paintings on the walls. "You are skilful. But all of these paintings lack something. Do you have any others, on different themes?"

Denise went into the storage room and brought out her "Sunburst" painting.

"Incredible!" Tomas said, backing away. His face, for the first time since they entered the studio, had lightened. Again, a semblance of a smile played about his lips. "You are capable of this, this brilliance, and you paint crap like that?"

"You like my Sunburst?"

"But it is fantastic! This is the way for you to go! This is your future in art!"

Tomas had no more credentials as an art critic than Hilda or any of Denise's other artist friends—probably fewer. But she felt instinctively that he was right. And when he left, he took her hand, held it briefly looking into her eyes and kissed it. Denise was totally vanquished.

The next morning when Denise came to work at her studio, she found Tomas waiting for her, sitting on the steps outside the building. He had a bunch of brilliant yellow roses in one hand.

He followed her up to her studio. "You were right," he said. "I judged you wrongly. You are more artist than any woman I have met."

He wanted to move into her studio, to help her by criticizing her paintings. To lead her in the right direction. He wanted to take her out, to wine her and dine her. They went out a couple of times, to restaurants too fine for Denise to appreciate. He would appear in a slightly threadbare suit and tie, courtly and full of suggestions about her painting. But after a couple of elegant meals during which she counted the glasses of wine that he drank, she had to cut off the relationship. She couldn't do it.

There was no possibility of a relationship. They were pulling in opposite directions, he toward drink and self-destruction and she away from it. Denise knew how easy it would be for her to lapse. She had to say good-bye to him after one of those beautiful meals when he drank too much and talked rhapsodically about art and poetry. She said good-bye when he led her to the front porch of the house and kissed her lingeringly. It took a greater act of will to say good-bye to Tomas than it had to smash that whiskey bottle after her last drink.

He was a beautiful man. She knew she could have loved him more than she had loved anyone, ever. But she couldn't endure the torment. There was no way she could have helped him. She knew that from her own experience with Hilda. A relationship with him would have damaged them both.

She wondered if he was still alive. If he came to the exhibit, he would have cutting remarks to make about her paintings. Almost all of them. It would be hard to bear, being torn to pieces like that. But better his scorn than most people's admiration. She called up his image in her mind, the bristly hair, the brooding eyes, the bitter mouth that would sometimes stretch into the semblance of a smile.

Denise heard footsteps and a clattering in the hallway. She put her hand to her cheek and wiped away the tears. Then she took a deep breath and opened the door.

The Opening.

There were Toby and Alex, young and energetic and cheerful. They were carrying great boxes containing the food.

"Oh good!" Denise was happy for the distraction. "You're here in plenty of time."

"Well, I'm afraid not," said Toby. Toby, Denise remembered, was the one with the tattoo of a dragon on his arm, with "Mom" inscribed above it. She wanted to ask him why but had never quite dared to. "It's already almost five, Ms. Spaulding," he continued. "People could be coming any minute."

Denise glanced at her watch and was surprised. How could the time have gone so quickly? "Let me give you a hand then," she said, and together, the three of them unpacked and arranged the sandwiches. It looked like enough food to feed an army. Before they finished, there was another knock on the door and in came Jennifer and Graham.

Jennifer embraced Denise enthusiastically. "Denise, it's been too long! Wonderful to see you again." Jennifer was wearing a faded print dress, unfashionable and feminine. Her face was more pinched and wrinkled than ever, but she was smiling.

Graham approached Denise rather cautiously and shook her hand. "It's a great moment, Denise, and we're delighted to be a part of it." He nodded at Toby and Alex, his slick hair gleaming. He always seemed to Denise too sleek, too slippery, like a baby mammal licked clean by its mother. Too much the perfect lawyer, impossible to pin down. But Jennifer was happy with him, and that was what mattered.

"Denise," Graham said. "I hear you've retired from teaching. What are you going to do with all your free time now?"

"I'm not sure, but the Foundation has offered me a job doing outreach."

"Splendid," said Graham, showing his brilliant teeth. "Giving back to the community. I can't think of a better way to spend one's golden years. What do you think, Jennifer?"

Jennifer was standing in front of Denise's studies of light. She turned her head to look toward Graham. "I think she should dedicate this time to her painting," she said. "She's never been able to do that. She's always had to work. Look, Graham." Jennifer gestured toward the painting in front of her. "This is my favorite, 'Sunburst.' Isn't it magnificent? And look at these other studies of light."

"You see, Graham," Denise was trying to say, "That's my predicament. I'd like to work for the Foundation, but . . ."

"Denise," said Jennifer. "What's this painting in the middle? The one that's covered up?"

Before Denise had a chance to answer, Alex had turned on the overhead lights and the spotlights for the paintings. He flung open the door and propped it open. And now people began to come in. First there was a group of colleagues from adult ed, Jerome and Susie, and Eleanor and Bobbie. Then came some friends of Sally's, mainly young men, whose names Denise didn't know. And then a group from the Foundation. People kept coming and coming. It was like one of those films where it changes from black and white to Technicolor. With the women's dresses and make-up and the artists' odd get-ups. And the glasses tinkling as Toby poured out wine. And all the pictures coming to life under their spotlights.

Suddenly Sally was by Denise's side, a young man in tow. Sally transformed, her fleece of hair in tight shining curls, her face perfectly made up. She was wearing a vest in woven tapestry over a poet's blouse with a ruff and huge sleeves. And blue jeans, paint-stained and worn. All eyes followed her movements, women's in envy, men's in admiration or lust.

"Aunt Denise!" she said, hugging her. "This is wonderful! I love it!" Denise wasn't sure whether she meant the exhibit or the party. "Meet Freddie," she said, indicating the young man on her arm. He was too scrubbed and too pink, his ears sticking out.

"Hello, Freddie," said Denise, taking his plump hand. "He won't last long," she thought. And the pair drifted off, arm in arm, to look at the paintings.

Denise went to one of the tables and helped herself to a canapé and a glass of diet coke. She wondered at the resilience of youth, how a new boyfriend or a pair of shoes or some special materials could make Sally bounce back from the deepest depression. Had she been like that? She didn't think so, but then she never grieved as Sally did. She thought of how Clovis had rejected the circus painting. Something hard always prevented her from giving way, through rejections, bad reviews, broken relationships.

She sipped her diet coke and contemplated the scene with satisfaction. So many people milling around, eating and drinking and making noise. The paintings were secondary, almost irrelevant. But Miss Gibble from the Foundation was upon her. Miss Gibble in a stern skirted suit with her thick, bottom of bottles glasses.

"Miss Spaulding," she was saying, "I'd like you to meet my colleague, Mr. Snark. Mr. Snark, this is our new outreach coordinator, Miss Spaulding."

"Pleased to meet you, Miss Spaulding," he was saying. But the noise from the crowd blotted out the rest. Denise wondered if, looking at the paintings, he had withdrawn the offer. But no, Miss Gibble had introduced her as the new outreach coordinator.

She mouthed some words, not much caring what she said. It all seemed too much, all of a sudden. Looking toward the light shining in from the corridor, she again remembered her morning vision. The pompons! They seemed to be escaping her now in the chaos of the party. She moved through the room, clutching her unfinished diet coke, shaking hands, smiling, but feeling terribly impatient. She glanced at her watch: only ten past six. It felt like the middle of the night. She wished these people away, but they stayed on and on drinking and talking. She made her way to the door and stood in the corridor, breathing the cooler air. She looked at the window at the end of the corridor to see how much light was left in the fading sky.

And there, making her way slowly up the staircase was Madeleine. Reaching the top, she stood towering over Denise, taller than ever. Madeleine was in black for the loss of some higher-up in her organization, black, which made her seem large and menacing.

"Oh, hello, Madeleine," she said. "I didn't think you'd be able to make it."

Madeleine merely nodded by way of greeting. "Well, I'm here to see what you've been up to. Are you going back into the studio?"

"Go on, I'll join you in a minute." Denise watched Madeleine disappear into the studio and went to the window at the end of the hallway. She took a couple of breaths of air to clear her head. "My God!" she suddenly thought. "The curtained painting! I still have to deal with that before I'm free of these people!"

She went back into the exhibit and stood at the far end of the room, by her childhood pictures. She looked at the hidden canvas. No one had pulled back the curtain.

People were beginning to drift out, emptying the room. Denise wasn't sure if it had been a long time or a short time since they had come. Food had been eaten and wine had been drunk; there were half-empty glasses and paper plates on the tables and benches. It was time now. Or almost time.

Miss Gibble and Mr. Snark were making their way over. "Congratulations, Miss Spaulding," said Mr. Snark, his eyes focused on a spot just above Denise's head. "Impressive exhibit. But I don't know who persuaded you to include those childish works. A terrible mistake, if you ask me."

Miss Gibble leaned forward, looking Denise straight in the eye. "We'll see you, I presume, on Friday?"

Denise shook their hands, forcing a smile. And they were gone. And the people from adult ed. Sally and company were off to another party. Only a handful of people were left. The temperature of the room went down several degrees. And the lights and colors had dimmed.

One of the artists Denise had met in A.A. approached her.

"Don't ever stop painting, Denise," she said. "I love your work."

She grasped the woman's hand, feeling moved for the first time since the party began. "Thanks, Audrey," she said. "That means a lot to me."

And now it was just Jennifer and Graham and Madeleine. Jennifer approached. "Denise," she said. "Thanks so much for inviting us. It was wonderful. A special occasion."

"Don't leave just yet," said Denise. There was one last task to perform and then she would be free. "I have something I want to show you."

Madeleine, who had been standing in front of Denise's bar scenes, suddenly turned. "Yes, you have one painting on the far wall that's covered by a curtain. That's what you were going to show us, isn't it, Denise?"

"That's exactly what I had in mind," said Denise.

"I know what that painting is, by the way," Madeleine said.

"How could you possibly know that?" asked Denise.

"Well, there are just three of us, if you'll forgive me for excluding you, Graham. We're missing one. And it's obvious who that is."

She went to the back wall and drew back the little curtain. And there she was! A dark-eyed woman in her early twenties was looking down at them from her frame.

Jennifer gasped. "It's Marjorie!"

Madeleine drew back to view the painting. "Well," she said. "Congratulations, Denise. You've made an extraordinary likeness."

The face in the painting stared back at them with great luminous eyes. Denise hadn't taken the time to look at it closely when she unpacked it, and it had been Toby or possibly Alex who had hung it there and put up the little concealing curtain. She took in the painting for the first time in years. It brought back Marjorie: her impatience with sitting for the painting, her preoccupations with school and tutoring some kid. It was a painting that Denise had had to do hastily, as it wasn't part of her assigned work. But it was successful: a fifth presence in the room.

"The reason I covered it up was to surprise you, Jennifer," she said. "I thought you might want it."

"Oh, Denise," said Jennifer. "I couldn't. I couldn't take it." Her jaw was clenched in an effort to keep back the tears.

"I'm offering it to you. As a present. I know how much Marjorie's friendship meant to you."

"It's not that. It's that . . . I couldn't live with the image of Marjorie as a young woman. I couldn't bear it."

Denise felt a kind of sinking in her chest. She had been so sure that Jennifer would want the painting.

Madeleine was staring at it, motionless, transfixed. "I knew it," she said. "I knew she found redemption for her sins."

"As far as I know," said Denise impatiently, "Marjorie never even looked for redemption. She enjoyed her sins and probably would have kept on sinning if she had lived."

"Look at the tilt of her chin, the light in her eyes," said Madeleine. "It's Saint Mary Magdalene, Saint Mary Magdalene seeking the Lord's forgiveness."

There was an embarrassed silence. Suddenly Graham said, "She does look a little like one of El Greco's paintings of the Saint. As Madeleine says, it's in the eyes and the position of the head."

Denise felt unreasonably annoyed. "Well, I wasn't imitating El Greco, and I never have. And I certainly wasn't painting Mary Magdalene."

"I don't think you're in a position to say," said Madeleine. "God sometimes guides our hands." Turning to Jennifer, she said, "If you really don't want it, Jennifer, I'll take it. In fact I'll buy it."

This wasn't at all what Denise had intended. "That won't be necessary, Madeleine," she said. "If you want it, we'll keep it in the house, possibly hang it in the living room. I wouldn't mind looking at it from time to time. After all, it's because of Marjorie that we're all together, here and now. She brought us together."

"You're right," said Jennifer. "I hope you're not offended that I don't want the painting. It's not because it isn't good. It's too good. I couldn't have Marjorie staring down at me every time I took a cup of tea into the living room. Or sat down on the couch to read a book. But if she was hanging in your living room, well, I think I could deal with that."

"Well," said Graham, "that sounds like a good solution to the problem. Denise, it's been a great party, a great exhibit. But now, if you'll excuse us, we'd better go back to the house. You'll be joining us, won't you Denise? The party? You're invited, too, of course, Madeleine."

"Thanks, Graham, I might drop in later," said Madeleine. "I have some work to do at the mission. Good-bye, Denise. You will remember to hang the painting in the living room?" And she was gone.

"You can come with us now, Denise," said Jennifer. "Have a drink while we prepare dinner?"

Denise laughed shortly. "Jennifer, you know I don't drink anymore. But I will join you later. I promise. I have something important I must do right now. Something I urgently need to do."

As Graham and Jennifer left, a strange quiet invaded the studio. Denise sat down on one of the benches, looking at the portrait of Marjorie. She could feel her presence, almost hear her voice, high-pitched and nasal, saying, "Is it almost finished, Denise? When will it be finished?"

Then she closed her eyes and slowly, slowly, the image of the pompoms dancing on the wall came back to her, not in perfect clarity but slightly blurred as they moved in the force of the morning breeze. She went to the cupboard, where she had hung her smock and put it on. She took out the paints and the brushes.

Then she set up her easel and began to paint.